The Better Half

Sarah Harte studied law and French at University College Cork. She worked as a corporate lawyer before she switched to writing. From Cork she moved to Dublin, where she now lives with her husband Jay, their son Conn and Lucy the dog. *The Better Half* is her first novel.

The Better Half

SARAH HARTE

PENGUIN
IRELAND

PENGUIN IRELAND

Published by the Penguin Group
Penguin Ireland, 25 St Stephen's Green, Dublin 2, Ireland (a division of Penguin Books Ltd)
Penguin Books Ltd, 80 Strand, London WC2R ORL, England
Penguin Group (USA) Inc., 375 Hudson Street, New York, New York 10014, USA
Penguin Group (Australia), 250 Camberwell Road, Camberwell, Victoria 3124, Australia
(a division of Pearson Australia Group Pty Ltd)
Penguin Group (Canada), 90 Eglinton Avenue East, Suite 700, Toronto, Ontario, Canada M4P 2Y3
(a division of Pearson Penguin Canada Inc.)
Penguin Books India Pvt Ltd, 11 Community Centre, Panchsheel Park, New Delhi – 110 017, India
Penguin Group (NZ), 67 Apollo Drive, Rosedale, Auckland 0632, New Zealand
(a division of Pearson New Zealand Ltd)
Penguin Books (South Africa) (Pty) Ltd, 24 Sturdee Avenue,
Rosebank, Johannesburg 2196, South Africa

Penguin Books Ltd, Registered Offices: 80 Strand, London WC2R ORL, England

www.penguin.com

First published 2011
2

Copyright © Sarah Harte, 2011

Set in Garamond MT Std 13.5/16 pt
Typeset by Palimpsest Book Production Limited, Falkirk, Stirlingshire
Printed in Great Britain by Clays Ltd, St Ives plc

A CIP catalogue record for this book is available from the British Library

ISBN: 978–1–844–88265–6

www.greenpenguin.co.uk

Penguin Books is committed to a sustainable
future for our business, our readers and our
planet. This book is made from paper certified
by the Forest Stewardship Council.

To Niall and Kay Harte, to whom no
thanks could ever be enough, and to Jay Bourke,
for his steadfast encouragement

Seize the day, for the world is fleeting,
In the eyes of the wise the moment is better than the whole
  world,
Alexander, who ruled a whole world,
At the very moment when he died left the world.

Qazvin or Isfahan, about 1600

Part I

I

Days that change your life start out like any other. There is no big sign written across the sky saying, 'Hello, your world is about to be ripped apart.'

This day was windy. A great gale was blowing down our road. Shrewsbury Road was the dog's in terms of addresses. The imposing, detached Edwardian houses were set well behind wrought-iron railings and mature greenery, with wide lawns and gravelled drives – you couldn't beat it for snob value, which was why we lived there.

The door of my SUV swung open and I climbed into its cream leather interior, my hair whipping round my cheeks. The angry clouds were so low they were practically touching the Rangy's roof. The branches of the trees swayed violently. The shrubs lining our drive had been flattened by the wind. I'd prayed to St Francis for good weather – even though, come to think of it, he might not be the patron saint of meteorology. I had an inkling that he was lost causes or maybe animals. I was never that well up on that stuff.

I checked myself in the mirror. I'd spent the morning being plucked and polished and buffed. I had a new facialist who was keen as mustard. She'd spent two hours with me, discussing my diet, lifestyle and mental health. 'It's all part of teaching customers,' she'd said, 'to care for their skin in a holistic way.'

I didn't like to rain on her parade by telling her about the amount of stuff I had shipped into my face. Like, I was all about eating organic food and that, but when it came to cosmetic interventions, it was bombs away.

The facial injections had been done in good time so the bruising and bumps had died down. I thought they'd made a positive difference. Frank didn't agree. 'Anita,' he'd said, the other day, 'if you don't stop filling your face with that crap you're going to look like a fucking stroke victim.'

True, I had a little trouble eating soup – but only straight after the procedures. All my friends had had work done, even those who didn't admit it. It was the norm now and you had to keep up. Nobody wanted a forehead like a ploughed field when her friends were line free. And, in fact, you *had* to make your face swell like a puffer fish with fillers because being stick thin gave you lines. Bigger girls with generous bottoms had lovely smooth skin and plump cheeks.

It was like social death in the world I moved in to look your age or to be fat. It wasn't allowed. There were rules. To be fat was like having some incurable disease. It was fine to pump yourself with poison, cut yourself open, starve and stretch yourself. You were expected to do what it took to battle time and the evil forces of gravity.

I'd got some more movement back since the injections, anyway. Maybe a little too much, I thought, fingering my forehead. Despite all the time and cash I'd spent, the mirror wasn't lying. I had won some minor battles, courtesy of my dermatologist, facialist, colourist and personal trainer, but there was no doubt that time was winning the war. I could fight all I liked but in the end, like the little Dutch boy with his finger stuck in the dike, I would lose.

I hated my ageing body and face. I had a boyish bum that had gone all flat like an old person's. My stomach was thin but slightly wrinkled, like fruit. There was no escaping the pouches under the eyes or the crêpy skin on my boobs. There were rings on my neck and my hands were going the way of gnarled tree roots. I was turning into a tree.

4

In my bleaker moments I thought my face looked like a balloon that the air had been let out of. I could give you an exhaustive list of my flaws at the drop of a hat. And I could give you a fairly comprehensive list of my pals' defects too. Carrying those around in your head was the adult equivalent of a comfort blanket. I might have a flat, droopy bum but Shannon's boobs were like punctured tennis balls on the end of long, droopy socks.

It was hard not to mind the way men had stopped noticing me. Once heads had twisted and hungry horny looks had come at me when I walked down the road, or I'd heard piercing whistles when I sashayed past a construction site, hips swinging. Now there was just a loud silence. I was almost past my sell-by date. I went to dinner parties and men looked at me vaguely. Once they'd have been falling over to listen to me – if I'd recited the alphabet backwards in Urdu they would have been spellbound. When my boobs had started to sag and my arse began to go flat, they'd started to look over my head. I felt as if I had once been in colour and now was only black-and-white. I had become the invisible woman.

I had highlights done, a creamier blonde than usual. Would Frank notice? I darted a look into the mirror. He probably wouldn't notice if I got a Mohawk. I zapped the electric gates and pulled out of our drive. Sometimes, looking at Frank, I wondered what he thought about, what he dreamt about at night. Did I ever pop into his mind or was his head full of planning permissions, cranes and cement?

Whoosh, down our road I went. I looked in the mirror again. My hair was a bit bouffant but it would fall, hopefully. All in all, I didn't look that bad. I'd stayed away from the *vino collapso* the night before in preparation for the party. Not including five – or six, maybe – small glasses of wine that you'd barely count. It wasn't civilized to refuse wine with your food.

Of course, the truth was that the party planner had done the work. I'd have liked to plan it myself, to be able to say it was all me, but I just didn't have the nerve. Like, I might have made some awful mistake and not even known it until I saw it bounced back at me in somebody's eyes or bitchy remark. I hated entertaining. I hadn't grown up around it, which made it that much harder.

The idea of my ma and da throwing a dinner party in our small kitchen was about as likely as the Queen of England rocking up for tea. All those things you had to know – like which cheese to serve, which wine to offer, which bread went with what. In our house, posh would have been Laughing Cow, Blue Nun and Pat the Baker bread.

As days went, I was busy. Normally I had bags of time looming ahead of me, just waiting to be filled – there was an irony there: when you had little enough to do, time expanded. That day I was a woman on a mission – a woman on the trail of a perfect party. That makes me sound like an empty-headed bimbo with screwed-up priorities. The sort of spoilt silly cow who people said was a complete waste of space. And, lookit, I knew I wasn't organizing world peace. But I wanted to impress my husband. To have him say to me, 'Anita, you did a good job.' I wanted him to notice me.

I turned onto the Merrion Road, indicating too late so that the taxi man overtaking me shook his fist at me, his mouth open in a big angry cave shape. My heart nearly stopped – for a second I thought it was Darren, my sister Karen's hubby. Guilt shot through me and I felt my face burn. I would roast in hell. I hadn't invited my sister to the party. 'No way, Anita,' Frank had said, waving his hands. 'She's not coming here in her fake Juicy Couture tracksuit, like feckin'

6

Pocahontas, with her belly hanging out, chewing gum, a fag pokin' out of the corner of her mouth.'

Calling her Pocahontas was low. I'll admit Karen was a bit heavy on the old spray tan but she scrubbed up well. She'd be chewing gum, all right, but she'd make the effort. She was a bit revealing in her style of dress for a woman of her age – she had a thing about getting her chest out – but she was my sister.

'She'll let the side down and that's it. End of story.' Then Frank had played his trump card. 'I mean none of my crowd are coming, not even Mam.'

Not even his beloved mam – second only to the Virgin Mary in importance. But that was because 'Mam' was sick with a chest infection and the rest of his family were too scared to come to Dublin and leave her in case she cut them out of her will. Not that there was that much to leave but she had an iron grip over her kids like nobody I'd ever met. Not that I could say so – say anything about Frank's family and you'd live to regret it. But it was open season on mine.

Anyway, there was a difference. Karen lived twenty minutes down the road and would have loved to come in her yer-all-a-load-of-stuck-up-shites-but-I-did-yez-a-favour-and-came kind of way. And Karen, who could be a scary bitch, might find out about the party, I thought, my heart rate ratcheting up.

I'd say to her that, with the growing uncertainty with the economy, we were keeping things low key – 'Just a quiet dinner for the two of us.' That, of course, was the exact opposite of what we were doing. Frank had his arse hanging out the window on the biggest property deal of his career and we were throwing the party to show people that, contrary to the talk going around – and there was plenty of that in a town like Dublin – we weren't about to go bust.

7

My breathing slowed and I began to enjoy cruising through the early-afternoon traffic. I loved driving. That nice safe feeling it gave you. The sense of purpose you got when you knew you were going from A to B. Coasting around, head cocked up behind the wheel of my Range Rover, the radio on, driving around the leafy streets of Dublin 4, a woman in control of her own destiny. Destiny's Child, minus the big arse. Sometimes I didn't want to stop. I just wanted to keep on driving to the soothing thrum of the traffic. I didn't want to be confronted by the present, never mind the future.

Very often, like now, I started to juggle figures in my head. I loved numbers, always had done. And not just the ones on my credit card, as Frank tried to claim. When I was little the teacher would give me extra sums to do because I whizzed through what the rest of the class was doing. When I was eight I was doing what the twelve-year-olds were doing. I even got put up a year at school on account of it. Mental maths was fun. Like multiplying by nine was really multiplying by ten minus one. So, 9×9 was $9 \times (10 - 1)$, which was $9 \times 10 - 9$ which was $90 - 9$ or 81. That was a simple one. I was always doing mental maths in my head to amuse myself.

I was just having a lash at quite a complicated one when the guilt about Karen came lunging at me again. Okay, it wasn't my fault that Frank and Karen had never seen eye to eye. The first time I'd led Frank home like a prize pig to meet Ma and Da, Karen was in the corner eating a bag of Taytos, her eyes like laser beams taking it all in. I'd been blabbing about him non-stop. Frank the big business man, the Flash Harry who took me out to dinner – even though back then he barely had a seat in the arse of his trousers – with nothing but a van, a lad to help him and a couple of ladders.

Karen had taken a long, hard look at Frank, who was all trussed up in his good suit – in those days we didn't have the casual-clothes thing down – with everything but his face polished. 'So this is Del Boy,' she'd said.

Frank had never forgiven her. All the same it was a lousy thing not to invite your own sister to your party. And there was more to my guilt than that. A little voice in my head told me that part of me was relieved Karen wasn't coming. I wouldn't have to feel those beady coal-black eyes following me round the room and boring into my back as I schmoozed or 'talked posh', as she would put it. *Jaysus*, as she might have said – or as I might once have said, which Karen would be quick to point out.

Frank had been most specific about what he wanted for his fiftieth. I was to throw him a 'surprise party'. He wasn't joking. 'Something that'll make Will and Ciara's last bash look like a fucking tea party. I'm serious, Anita, I want something that'll have Will ragin' with jealousy.'

That was the other reason we were pumping money into the party: to best everyone we knew. Particularly Will. Frank was ultra-competitive. He hid it well with his I'm-just-a-country-man-of-the-people routine. Inside, though, he was always trying to get one over on someone. He was weighed down not by a chip but more like two concrete blocks, one for each shoulder. A matching set.

Will and Ciara had been our neighbours before Frank trained his sights on Shrewsbury Road. They were the king and queen of our social circle, a sort of alpha couple. Frank was obsessed by them. He hated Will because – although he hadn't figured this out – he wanted to be him. And it was obvious to me that he would have loved to marry Ciara and have her long, lithe, silky limbs wrapped around his short powerful ones. Fat chance. Apart from all the other reasons Ciara would never have gone for Frank, Will was very handsome. I loved Frank – he was the father of my children, the man I'd spent my life with since the age of nineteen – but, with his pink face and thick middle, Frank looked like a stuffed tomato beside Will.

I was pretty sure that it was Will's flowing Prince Valiant hair that really fried Frank's mind. (Frank's looked like a toilet brush.) That and the fact that Will was always talking about the jolly japes he'd got up to at college. Frank droned on about having gone to the University of Life but deep down it drove him mad that he hadn't made it to old Trinners or UCD.

Will was also my gynaecologist. 'The fanny doctor', Frank called him behind his back, if only at home – and Ella, our youngest, went completely mental when he did. Gave him that look of hers which would turn you to salt and of which I was secretly proud. No flies on our Ella. Generally speaking, when Frank was out and about he tried to sound posh and to can the bad language. A tall order, I always thought, when you were a hayseed who came from the arse-end of nowhere in County Offaly.

Through Donnybrook village, past Donnybrook Fair, where I could be almost certain one or other of my friends would be sitting over a skinny decaf latte. Maeve would be moaning about something – the difficulty in getting a reliable cleaner, a good facial or how her husband didn't appreciate her – or retailing gossip, which was her favourite sort of conversation. She was really only enlivened by scandal.

Ciara – of Ciara and Will – might be chewing the ear off someone about the right music school for her children: could the Dublin Institute of Technology *conservatoire* really be better when it was less expensive than the Leeson Park establishment? Was it better for your child to focus on one foreign language, and become really proficient in it, or study two – or maybe go off piste altogether and learn Mandarin, what with

China being an up-and-coming power? And which did 'a young gentleman' – her son Jack was six – really need: sailing, golf or both? Ciara really got off on that kind of chat. She was an *über*-mummy and her energy for such discussions was really something.

I drove down the Stillorgan dual carriageway past University College Dublin, crossing to the giant, sprawling Sandyford Industrial Estate. It was a slightly out-of-the-way place for a clinic but it was where Will had his medical suite. I was having a smear-test. My ma had died from cancer and, while I wasn't neurotic about my health, I was good at having myself checked out.

A nurse would do the test, which was just as well. I mean, there was no way around it. I'd had thoughts concerning Will that I wasn't proud of. It was just sometimes when I hadn't had sex with Frank for a while that I got to thinking about Will. Images of him and his firm behind crept into my mind. I was always the main protagonist, which struck me as kind of interesting. Will was really only a bit player. It was all about me being seized and wanted and desired. When I had guilty fantasies about Will and his stethoscope, they were always silent movies. They didn't involve him opening his mouth – for talking purposes at least.

I always felt disloyal afterwards, not just to Frank but to Ciara. You didn't have dreams like that about a friend's husband. It just wasn't cricket, as Will himself might have said. That was a 'Willish' thing to say: while he was easy on the eye he was definitely on the boring side. With Will, roses were red and violets were blue.

I swung my jeep into a space, got out and ran towards the space-age-style glass building with a jacket over my head. I was forced to narrow my eyes against the wind and now the rain: the skies had torn open like a soggy paper bag. It was freezing too. I had ordered heaters for the marquee. They would be up and running, I had been told, by tea-time. The party planner had smiled her lipsticked smile, drawn on like a perfect bow, and guaranteed that my guests would not freeze. They would not be wiping their noses with their napkins, their extremities gone blue.

Frank was coming home from London. His flight was delayed. He would make it in plenty of time but he was stuck in Heathrow due to some security alert. He was like a bull. He had rung me again and again to fire questions about the party. Would the band be good enough? Was I absolutely sure? He hadn't wanted the one that most of our friends used. Was I sure about the marquee? We had hired a vast speciality tent from England, complete with sofas, armchairs and a dance area. He was worried it might look like a circus Big Top. Were we having a girl swinging from a trapeze?

The answer to that was no. It wouldn't be in keeping with the *Great Gatsby* theme the party planner had persuaded me to go for.

Weather aside, most things were under control, I thought. But then I remembered my dress. Jesus. In the boutique, with the nice lighting and flattering mirrors that stretched you out a bit, I had thought it sexy and daring. 'You look amazing, you'll really stand out,' the youngest, most beautiful assistant had said, so that my aged, gullible, an-eejit-born-every-day face had pinked with pleasure. That morning in the privacy of my room I'd held it up to me and thought I looked like something that had been let out on day release. Frank hadn't thought to ask about the weather. Surely he couldn't blame me for that, I thought, as I took the lift to the third floor. The doors opened onto a long corridor. There was a sign on the door of Will's suite: *Please wipe your feet on the mat before entering.* That was classic Ciara. She had overseen the redecoration –

remodelling, she called it – of Will's suite and she was a total control freak. It was something she tried to hide with a modicum of success. 'Oh, this old thing? I just threw it on,' she'd say, of a dress she'd sourced from some young designer nobody had ever heard about up a back alley in Milan. And after serving up a gourmet meal she'd been preparing for a week, she would bat away your compliment saying it was just something she'd flung in the oven.

'You're so slim,' I heard a woman with a bum the size of a small African country say to her at a party. 'How do you do it?'

Ciara had shrugged. 'I don't know, a high metabolism maybe,' she had said, even though I knew full well that she did yoga, ran, lifted weights, starved herself and got pipes stuck up her arse for colonic irrigation. Fair enough, I was competitive, but Ciara was *chronically* competitive. She had a syndrome rather than a tendency.

A lot of the women we knew had it. If you 'worked in the home' – and, let's face it, in our circle you weren't exactly worn out with domestic duties, what with the army of foreign nationals ready to pick up the slack – you had to find something else to go head to head on. That left a couple of possibilities. Kids provided a rich vein of material whereby fascinating information was traded: 'Adam eats broccoli, carrots, all his vegetables and hates sweets' – which usually meant that if Adam came round to your place he was to be found face-down in your biscuit tin. Or 'Amanda is particularly gifted at gymnastics' when Amanda, a sweet little duckling with the co-ordination of a drunken sailor, was busy hurling her blocky form around the hall next to your graceful swan.

Women also competed about their husbands' jobs and how busy the men were, meaning how much dosh they were pulling in. I'd even heard people compete over their dogs. My friend Ciara liked to claim that her mutt Cleo was extremely clever: 'The dog psychologist said Cleo had anxiety issues. Once we got those resolved, there was no stopping her. Say what you like but Cleo is seriously intelligent.'

Cleo, a fat ball of fluff that liked to chew her paws, didn't seem particularly gifted to me, but that wasn't the point. The point, I think, was that the ball had officially gone out of court when you found yourself in competition over your dog.

But by far the most fertile ground for competition was weight and looks. Peers were scrutinized to see how well they were holding up as the years rolled by. You couldn't win. If you were fat you were looked down on – although everyone was thrilled to bits by your extra poundage and encouraged you to stay well padded so they could feel better about themselves – 'It suits you!' If you were super-thin people wanted to claw your eyes out and got their revenge by saying, 'She's gone very thin, God love her.' Translation: 'She looks as old as the prehistoric man hauled from the bog.'

Anyway, Will was obviously cleaning up: the waiting room was rammed with women flicking through magazines. No downturn in the economy biting at his bum, I thought, as my feet sank into the new cream carpet. Frank would be thrilled. Not.

'Fannies are recession proof,' Frank had said the other day, with a real envious look on his face when we saw Will roar past us in his new Porsche. 'Women need their bits seen to no matter what.' It was fair to say that Frank suffered from fairly severe attacks of the green-eyed monster.

The receptionist took my details. A small blondey one with a smile that didn't reach her eyes. Her voice was polite but detached. That was a skill: to be able to talk to people without getting involved. Frank was always giving out that I drew people down on us. 'Just don't give your life story every time you open your gob,' he'd said to me, a few weeks previously, on holiday in Miami when I'd got talking to a nice woman by the pool. 'Now we're going to have to nod at them and talk to them for the rest of the fucking holiday.'

He had a point, I suppose. But there was another way of looking at it.

'Do you not think, Frank,' I'd said, slathering oil on his broad, freckly back – Frank still had the Irish thing of being up for a tan even if it meant dying of skin cancer, 'that life would be a lot less enjoyable if you were always guarding what you said and you didn't take time to talk to your fellow man or woman?'

He'd grunted at me, his trademark sarcastic grunt. 'It's called having fucking verbal diarrhoea, Anita.'

'One moment – I'll just put you on hold.' The receptionist lifted her eyes from the computer screen so that they landed on the golf ball of a diamond I had on my finger. I won't lie. I loved that ring. Frank had carted it home after he closed his first big property deal. We had been like two complete eejits, drinking champagne, me waving my finger around and thinking we were the dog's. That was the start, really, of the boom in Ireland.

'You're here for a smear with Dr White's nurse.'

She said 'Dr White' possessively, as if she owned him. Ciara suspected Will's receptionist of having the hots for him. Big surprise there.

'Yes.'

'Just take a seat,' she said, her eyes once more on her screen.

Bet you didn't dance with Will last week at a ball fronted by a rock star's wife and your woman who ran the orphanage out in Calcutta, I thought, as I sat down. The ball of the year.

Le tout Dublin. The glitterati and clitorati in the Round Room of the Mansion House. A *Who's Who* of fake-tanned, big-titted Dublin – but one of the shindigs you didn't want to be left out of. And Will had swept me around the pink ballroom in full view of everyone. I won't lie: I was chuffed.

Half the women in the waiting room had rounded stom-achs belling out in front of them. I chose to sit beside one who wasn't visibly pregnant. It was funny but it made me sad to think I wouldn't be going again. Like, don't get me wrong: I don't miss the sleepless nights as you stagger out of bed to heat a bottle, bitterly eyeing your spouse who is pretending to be sound asleep. Or the desperation of being stuck for hours on end in the playground, pushing the kids on swings, twirling them on the roundy thing that makes you both dizzy, wondering if you'll ever get out from that behind those railings.

But when you know that the door is closing on all that because your body's past it, when you know you'll never get a whiff of that velvety smell at the back of their necks, or watch their chubby little legs kick up in the air when you take their nappy off, or hear the gurgling sound they make when you first jam a bottle into their mouth, it makes you feel a bit empty.

A woman I knew click-clacked across the waiting room, her hair cut in a razor-sharp super-shiny bob. Her son had been in Dylan's class. I automatically ducked my head. She was one of those who always left you feeling a bit crap about yourself after you talked to her. Super-Mum. She had some kick-arse job in a law firm, merging this with that or some-thing. 'Clever you,' she'd said to me once, at the kids' sports day, when I was handing out medals, as though she thought I was a bit slow.

Dylan wasn't the best at school. Not compared to her lad.

Dylan had arsed around for a couple of years after he'd left. His gap year had turned into a couple of gap years.

'If he'd get a feckin' job he'd get all the life experience he needed,' Frank had said.

He had just started being a stockbroker a couple of months back. I wondered if I could walk over to your one and drop into conversation how Dylan was doing. Update her a little. Enjoy a bit of parental conceit. The last time we'd spoken, her son had been going great guns studying medicine. Dylan had been working in a bar in Sydney, drinking more than he sold, I suspected, with corn-rows in his hair, which did nothing for his round face. Maybe I could ask how her son was keeping and then just sort of slide in that my son was a stockbroker now. That would be pathetic. I wondered if she'd had a bit of work done – she looked a lot perkier around the gills than I remembered.

Anyway, I had Ella, who was brilliant. Her English teacher had said to me around the time she was leaving school that my daughter was 'intellectually brilliant'. Words like 'exceptional' were regularly bandied about when Ella's teachers discussed her. Sometimes she lapsed into the American TV 'OMG' way of talking – when you ditch proper sentences in favour of teenage argot – but her conversation was peppered with big words like 'rhapsodizes' and 'Valhalla'. She learnt a new word a day and had done since she was tiny. I'd ask her what today's word was and try to memorize it. I didn't use them much out loud because I was afraid of using them in the wrong context or mispronouncing them, like a woman I heard at a dinner party going on about 'connojures' of wine. I hadn't a clue what she was talking about and felt a bit bad about myself until I got home and realized the poor dozy cow meant 'connoisseurs'.

Ella's first word was 'helicopter'. I was dead proud of that and told everybody I knew at the time. Half of them didn't believe me. Whatever. Frank and I knew the truth. Our girl was practically a genius. She had been able to read the paper at the age of three. Frank and I had treated her like a performing seal, getting her to read out loud for our families. It made a nice change from watching Dylan run around the place head-butting things.

Ella got one of the best Leaving Certificates in the country – straight As – and her gorgeous beaming face had been splashed all over the papers as she held up her results. Most people would have seen it, but there had been loads of mothers who'd schlepped past me, saying something general like 'It's great it's all over' so I knew they were jealous as hell. Ella had it all going for her. Brains and looks. Sometimes I thought it was the very fact of Ella that kept me sane. Not to be knocking Dylan, because in a way he's my pet, but Ella was what I had achieved in life.

I know it's sad but I loved to imagine her pushing her bike across the Trinity campus, like in a movie, with her knapsack on her back, the light fading and her Trinity scarf – I couldn't say that word 'Trinity' enough – wrapped round her beautiful swan-like neck. My daughter the law student and nobody, not even Ms Big Job in the Law Firm sitting a couple of seats away tapping at her phone, or anybody else could take that away from me.

The young one next to me had gorgeous skin. Plump and unlined and peachy. She was slightly on the heavy side although the weight kind of suited her – and for once I meant that sincerely. Anyway, the skin more than made up for it. Do not covet your neighbour's skin – that should have been in the Ten Commandments. Actually it was her bracelet I noticed first. A white-gold Bvlgari number with diamonds similar to the one Frank gave me for my last birthday.

She was well put together. Her suit was sharp and she had a snazzy leather briefcase on the floor. Half these young ones looked like they could run the nation. I could see that my Ella would turn out like that, just finishing first law so she was, and wouldn't take rubbish off God nor man.

Ciara had done a great job on the waiting room, especially considering there was no natural light. It was all subtle downlights, creams, beiges and fawns to give an illusion of space. A giant painting hung on one wall by an artist I knew Ciara was very keen on. It looked a bit like the ring from a wet glass repeated across the canvas but it had cost a small fortune. Ciara was very up on her art.

Frank had bought loads of paintings when things were good. 'I mightn't know a lot about art but I know what I like,' he said, whenever the subject came up.

I knew that when you said that you may as well have plastered a sign saying 'Oink' across your head. Certain types of people automatically pegged you as a savage who lived in a tree and filed your teeth when you said it. Frank knew that, too, but he said it, I think, to challenge people to take him on – and because there was nothing else he could say. It was his way of publicly marking it down that he did not intend to change himself for anyone, when in fact he had made huge private strides to do just that. Frank was big on self-betterment, but of the stealthy variety.

Frank could bullshit with the best of them about wine but the problem with art was that you could put what Frank and I knew about it on the head of a pin. We hadn't grown up being dragged around art galleries or being talked to about that kind of stuff. It was a language we hadn't spoken from birth. When I'd met Frank his idea of art was *The Boy with a Tear*. There were quite a few areas in the cultural arena where we'd had to learn on the hoof, and even though we'd made up a fair bit of ground in some areas, art was one of those where we'd always be playing catch-up. This drove Frank spare.

Will was definitely minting it, I decided, then went on to wonder if I'd be able to say a few words at the party – you know, welcoming people and talking a bit about Frank. I'd sort of mentioned to the kids that I was thinking of it and they hadn't been very encouraging. Ella hadn't said anything, just shot me a doubtful look, and Dylan – born tactful like his father – had laughed and asked me if I was joking. I'd never actually do it anyway. Even thinking about it practically gave me the trots. Which showed you how far I'd travelled the wrong way: when I was in school – and I find this hard to believe – I was on the debating team.

My stomach rumbled. 'Excuse me,' I said, patting it and going a bit pink.

The young one next to me caught my eye and smiled.

'I must be hungry,' I lied. It was an understatement. I was completely off carbs. I was so famished I'd have fallen on a plate of buttery spuds and wept for joy. I'd have sold my body for a slab of white sliced pan plastered with butter. I suffered badly to be thin. I spent my life ready to gnaw my hand off. But if it was a crime to be fat in the circles I moved in, it was an even bigger crime to like the kind of foods I craved. The sort of foods I'd grown up eating – fried sausages, chips and frozen potato waffles. So I bought organic this and free-range that, but I dreamt of suet puddings and Angel Delight and packet custard and the thick end slice of shop-bought Battenberg cake.

'Your perfume is lovely,' I said to the young one, for something to say. I was a bit embarrassed about the rumble. 'Is it Jo Malone, the orangey one?'

She smiled. 'You've a good nose.'

'I used to wear it,' I told her.

'My boyfriend bought it for me,' she said. 'He's mad about it.'

'It's nice all right,' I said, thinking I might go back to it.

She was smiling at me again. 'Is it very hot in here,' she asked, fanning her face with her hand, 'or is it just me?'

Her accent was one of those rootless transatlantic ones where you hadn't a clue if the person was from the bogs or Dublin, the United States of America or the Planet Zog. You could tell underneath, though, that she was country originally. 'I'm okay,' I said.

The girl removed her suit jacket and laid it on the seat next to her. She had great boobs, I thought. You needed boobs to wear my party dress. Mine, of course, were like a spaniel's ears so I'd have to haul them up with a boulder-holder bra. My friend Maeve had had hers done. They were two hard grapefruits now, stuck to her front.

'Maybe it's a sign,' the young one said, shaking her head, 'that I'm pregnant.'

I smiled at her. 'Is it your first?'

She nodded, giving a small bashful smile. It brought me back to when I was having Dylan. I was even younger than her. I'd been twenty-three. Young and thrilled and scared out of my mind. Frank had been over the moon, his chest stuck out like a bantam cock, that I'd got knocked up on our honeymoon.

'I'm a bit nervous,' she said. 'I'm just getting a check to make sure. I mean, I've done a test and I think I am. I just want to be sure. Is it as bad as they say?' she asked. 'I mean the labour.'

I lied: 'Not a bit of it. It's grand.' All women had a duty to lie about that and not to describe the bowel-wrenching pain. Anyway, it was worth it. Every bit of it. Including the piles and varicose veins and stitches.

She puffed her cheeks out.

'Honestly,' I said, 'the day you have your baby is the best day of your life.' I felt a pang then, thinking of the day I'd had Dylan, and my eyes misted. They had slapped him up on my tummy and Frank had shouted out something like 'Is he okay?' And then Dylan had looked right at me. I would never forget that as long as I lived. In a sort of a way – and this was no disrespect to Ella because that was a very special day too – it was the most perfect moment of my life.

'That's good,' she said, reaching towards her bag and plucking out a lip salve. She had lovely lips. Pink and full and pillowy. The type a couple of my cronies had tried to buy with their credit cards. She went silent for a second. Then she said, 'I hope my boyfriend's into the whole kids thing.'

'I bet you he'll be thrilled,' I said, touching her arm. I had no basis for coming to that conclusion. The guy, whoever he was, might not want children at all.

'He's in London today on business,' she said. 'He doesn't even know I'm here. The pregnancy wasn't exactly planned,' she confided.

'Lots of the best things in life aren't planned,' I said, thinking she was lucky to be starting out. People were interested in you when you were pregnant. You became public property, but in a nice way, with people touching your stomach and asking when you were due. You were the centre of attention. When you were pregnant you had a sense of purpose.

'He's married,' she said, 'separated – or almost.'

'Oh,' I said, a bit taken aback. In my day you'd no more have admitted that than said you were a child molester. Things had got a lot more tolerant.

'I hope you don't think I'm some sort of home-wrecker,' she said, swivelling to look me in the eye.

I did, actually. 'No,' I lied, 'not at all.' And it wasn't for me to judge. He who is without sin shall cast the first stone and all that.

'He and his wife have been finished for years,' she said. 'They got married when they were super-young and they've nothing left in common.'

'It happens, I guess.' I wondered if you could say that about Frank and me. We had the kids in common for one thing.

'It's their kids that have kept them together,' she said then, 'but they're grown-up now so there's no other reason for him to stay.'

My heart hurt a little for the other faceless woman. Going about her life, not knowing that her husband was on the brink of trading her in for Little Miss Big Knockers, that she was about to be discarded like an old shoe. Hopefully, she wouldn't mind. Maybe she was dying to be shot of him. Maybe it would be a whole new lease of life.

'My boyfriend's a lot older than me, so I think he's more conservative about stuff like divorce,' she said, shrugging her shoulders. 'It's a generational thing, I guess.'

The way she was talking sort of implied she and I were on a wavelength. Maybe she thought I was younger than I was, I thought, feeling pleased.

'Not that I'm saying anything against your generation.'

Right.

'I hope he wants the baby.'

She looked about ten suddenly and I thought of my Ella. I reached out and touched the young one on the arm again. Frank always complained that I was too tactile and over-familiar. 'I'm sure he will,' I said, not knowing what else to say.

She frowned, making an impatient sound. 'It drives me mad that he won't tell me anything about her. It sort of makes you obsessed, wondering what she's like. I haven't even seen a photo.'

I could imagine how something like that might get under your skin.

'Which is kind of weird because he's very high-profile,' she said, obviously proud but at the same time a bit slow to spill the beans, which I thought was a good sign. It was a shame, though, because I was itching to know.

She crossed her legs and sat back further in the chair, a small smile dancing around her mouth.

'Oh,' I said, wondering if I could flat out ask who he was. Her brow was furrowed. It was obvious that she was fairly itching to tell me.

'I won't say his name but he's a property developer.'

My snout began to twitch and I started to run through a list of possible suspects. Some of those property developers were out-and-out boyos.

'The wife sort of seems to keep below the radar.'

Like me, I thought. I did that too. Like, I was involved with a couple of charities and I went to a fair amount of balls and lunches but I rarely got my picture taken. Mostly because I hated the way I looked in photos. And because there had always been a small part of me that thought if you allowed the media to build you up, it would come back at some point to bite you in the backside. Say what you like about the Irish but we're especially talented at tearing each other down. We don't go in for people making out that they're the dog's. It's in our DNA.

Frank loved having his mug in the paper. It drove him spare that I wouldn't go along with it. 'For fuck's sake, Anita, it's only a feckin' picture.'

I wondered why the wife didn't get her photo taken. Maybe she and I would get on.

'She's blonde, I think.'

The young one had curly red hair, very shiny, a bit like an Irish dancer's.

'I got that much out of him. They have two kids. A boy and a girl. The boy is doing law and the girl is a stockbroker. No, it's the other way around. I shouldn't say any more – he'd kill me if he heard me.'

She waved her arm so that I was faced with the bracelet. The bottom of my stomach fell away. Her mouth was moving and words were coming at me, assaulting me. I stared at the bracelet.

'He's so proud of them, always banging on about them. I hope he'll be as proud of this baby,' she said, touching her stomach. 'He'll be an old father. He's fifty.'

Her face took on a set look. 'The wife is throwing him a big party tonight.'

There was a roaring in my ears, as if I was hearing from under water.

She wrinkled her nose. 'I'd say she's desperate to hang on to him. Of course, I can't go . . .'

Will White came to the door with a chart. 'Fiona Keane,' he called out, ducking his head into the waiting room and smiling. He raised his hand in a little wave.

I blinked at him.

The young one gathered her stuff and got up. 'Great to talk to you,' she said, giving me a perky little wave.

I stayed mute. As her back retreated, a wave of her perfume engulfed me. I might vomit, I thought. My muscles were frozen. Maybe I was paralysed.

'Are you all right?' somebody asked. Was it the receptionist, another woman? I didn't know. I had moaned, I think, the low, hurt moan of an animal.

Then I found myself outside. The wind jabbed at my cheeks and nipped at my fingers. The black sky spewed great thick raindrops onto my face, so that my makeup ran, and went down my back and front so that my top and bra were stuck to me. My blow-dried hair collapsed like a fallen soufflé and stuck to my face, strands poking into my eyes. Somebody ran past me with a coat over their head. I stood there like a statue, the sound of the traffic rumbling in the distance. I could hear my rasping, shallow breaths. I stared down at my dirty toes, at the water running through my jewelled flip-flops. I wanted to die.

2

I drove around in circles for I don't know how long. The Range Rover slid in and out of lanes, weaving through the caravan of cars crawling home in what was ironically called the 'evening rush'. I was barely aware of the cacophony of beeps and raised fingers that punctuated my dead-eyed, sloppy manoeuvres.

The man on the radio babbled in the background about the weather, saying something about 'record precipitation'. I had nowhere to go, I thought, clutching the wheel. The phone rang and rang. The party planner's number flashed up again and again. I could picture her mega-watt smile sliding from her face when the hostess never showed up. When the hostess was found floating in a canal her blonde bouffant floating around her head in knotty tangles.

In the end it was my need for drink and Valium that took me home.

'Where the hell were you?' Frank asked, bursting into our bedroom swaddled in a towel, trailing a cloud of aftershave behind him that would have felled a horse. Frank was a bit heavy on the old aftershave sometimes. His short springy hair was wet from the shower and plastered back on his skull. He didn't wait for an answer, just motored on. I wanted to scream at him but no sound came out of my throat.

I could hear the excitement in his voice. Frank loved the social swim. He loved razzmatazz. He liked nothing better than to think of himself as a player, not just in business but socially. Frank was never really off the stage.

I had always found hosting parties nerve-racking. Frank rose to the occasion, visibly inflating, sprinkling *bons mots* here and there. If there were ribbons to cut or babies to kiss he'd do it gladly.

Maybe he was excited at the prospect of becoming a father again. I flinched at the idea. He had spent most of Dylan and Ella's childhood out busting his balls. There was always some project 'kicking off', which meant he couldn't be with us. Maybe this was a second crack of the whip for him.

'We've had to abandon the marquee – the fucking thing practically blew down. We should sue those bastards.'

That was always Frank's first line of thought. Who to sue? Frank was macho: he spent his life suing people. He was one of the reasons the Four Courts – or Four Gold-mines, as they're known – were so fecking busy. If he wasn't suing neighbours over boundary disputes, he was suing ex-business partners and other developers. Plenty of the actions he initiated ended up being settled once he started giving evidence – often not in his favour because Frank had bullied his lawyers into taking the case when he hadn't a leg to stand on.

Frank looked in the mirror, sucking in his flabby stomach. Then he trained his gaze on me and whistled. 'I like your dress, missus.' He came over then and cupped my bottom with his hand. 'You're looking very well.'

That showed exactly how much attention he was paying me. I looked terrible.

'Fancy slipping into something more comfortable later?' he continued, kissing the side of my head and kneading my buttocks.

I wanted to howl at him. He had given her my bracelet. My perfume. *My smell.* He had stolen some of my identity, parcelled it up and given it to *her.*

'People are starting to arrive,' he said.

I looked as if somebody had told me I'd five minutes to live. He hadn't noticed.

'Shake a leg. It's showtime!' he said, and waltzed out of the room, leaving me on my own. After a while I picked up a lipstick and began to fill in my ever-thinning lips. He was discarding them for plump pillowy ones.

Eventually I made it to the top of the stairs. I could hear chatting and raucous laughter. Dazed, I sank to the floor. Frank hadn't even wanted to know why I'd been late. I leant my forehead against the banister. I'd driven the Jeep around the city for hours, catatonic, unsure what to do, where to go. Now an army of uniformed waiters, the women sporting little frilly hats on account of the *Great Gatsby* theme, charged back and forth ferrying trays of glasses. Through the banisters my eyes bored into Frank's treacherous back. He was holding court, surrounded by a constellation of associates. A woman with a red slash for a mouth shrieked with laughter at something he had said.

Frank's affair was pure cliché: he was a middle-aged man grappling with his mortality and the advancing years. 'You're only as young as the woman you squeeze,' Frank used to joke, because I'm five years younger than him. Well, the man was as good as his word. He'd found a girl young enough to be his daughter. When I thought of it I felt crazy. The two big achievements in my life, its twin pillars, were marriage and motherhood. Frank might be proposing to take the first away, and the second was crumbling because my children had grown up. That was a gut-wrenching thought.

I visualized myself moving to the top of the stairs and bellowing down at the red-faced husband I loved in spite of everything, 'Don't do this to me, Frank, you unfaithful pig. DO NOT DO THIS TO *MEEEEE*!'

In the run-up to the party – like a sad, deluded, carried-away sap – I had harboured fantasies of a grand entrance. I would sweep down the stairs *Gone With the Wind*-style – since I was little I'd had a thing for Scarlett O'Hara – so that my guests' eyes would be drawn to the red fabric of my dress, which would contrast with my blonde hair. I had always had a taste for melodrama. Oh, the woeful irony of that delusion. Instead I slunk down to the party, sedated – and there was every chance some of my guests were feeling dead sorry for me. Some of them might have seen Frank with Little Miss Big Knockers and admired her round, shapely bottom and boobs. Some of them may have seen the affair as evidence of Frank's legendary charisma.

Frank might not be classically good-looking but he had always had a certain raw magnetism, even back in the days when he wore black shoes with white socks, like a bogger garda. Sometimes I thought I'd got lost somewhere in the great sea of his personality, a pale, uninteresting person, in 2D compared to the 3D of his muscular persona.

My eyes panned the room. No sign of my children. Dylan had slipped off by now. He had a new girlfriend, an underwear model trying to break into television. She was called Biba. She hadn't wanted to come to the party – not her kind of thing, apparently – so Dylan had offered to come on his own. We'd never met her but Dylan was like a fool after her. His heart was too big and he didn't have his younger sister's smarts. Bright enough, though, to spot that the ice sculpture looked like a penis. He'd had that clocked in zip time: I got a text – *Ice sculpture lks like giant schlong Dx*.

He was right.

Ella had come with her boyfriend, Christopher. They kept themselves to themselves, lost in the intense bright burst of first love. They were both finishing first law in Trinity College.

30

Christopher looked like Rupert Bear with his skinny body and a scarf thrown back around his neck. He was very polite. A little bit in love with himself, maybe.

'What a geek, Mum,' had been Dylan's verdict.

'That fella is missing in action up his own arse,' Frank had said, after he had overheard Christopher – a poncy name, according to Frank – talking to Ella about the urgent need 'to de-Catholicize the Irish Constitution'. 'I don't know how she sticks listening to that shite.'

Frank was torn about him, though. Christopher's father was a judge, which was a big plus, something to be dropped casually into conversation on the golf course. On the other hand, the fact that Ella, his little girl, had a boyfriend at all was a big no-no.

According to Ella, Christopher was off-the-charts bright.

'Like you so, love,' I'd said to her, but she'd just shrugged, as if to ask what I would know about stuff like that.

'Just don't let Dad drink too much,' she'd said at breakfast, when she'd told me that Christopher would be honouring us with his presence. 'Please don't let him go on about how much the party cost. And, oh, my God,' she'd said, making a face, 'does he have to, like, tell everyone that he started his business from nothing?'

Ella wasn't overly keen on being reminded of her parents' origins. Dylan didn't give a rattling damn. 'Better *nouveau* than never,' was Dylan's mantra. 'I'd rather be a Johnny-come-lately than a Johnny-not-come-at-all.'

I tried to catch Ella's eye during Frank's speech when he kicked off with 'I started my business with a van and a ladder . . .' but she'd been looking the other way, her back stiff. Sometimes, I thought, she looked at her family as if she was viewing zoo animals through a glass screen.

Paul Hogan was encircled by a crowd of admirers. He was

a sort of celebrity banker – always in the news pontificating about this, that and the other. He was bankrolling Frank's big development just like he'd lent money hand over fist to half the developers in town. Several of the male guests licked every nook and cranny of Paul's posterior. And Frank was no exception. It used to be the other way round but the tide was turning and now the likes of Frank had to kowtow to the bankers and keep them sweet, 'getting them to keep faith and not pull the plug', being the deadly subtext. Frank had given Paul a special mention in his speech: 'And there's a fella here I'd like to thank . . . for the way he changed the culture of lending in this country, for his vision . . . for the vision that the older, snootier, more establishment bankers didn't have, one of the main reasons behind the kick-starting of the tiger economy . . . Please give it up for Paul Hogan – the man's a legend . . .'

To thunderous applause, catcalls and roars, Paul had pivoted around with his big flashy smile giving a mock-regal wave. He walked in the swinging-dick way that suggested his balls were so big he had to turn out his legs – and made you wonder if they were in fact the size of marrowfat peas.

My eyes drifted. Frank's accountant Dermot was talking to my friend Maeve. Dermot Thornley was a celebrity accountant, often described as 'a friend to the stars' and reputed to have the Midas touch with money. He and his wife hung around with a fast, ritzy set and were regularly photographed with its members in the pages of the society magazines. Their presence at the party would help Frank secure column inches in the social diaries. Frank Lawlor, his glittering friends and their glittering lives: that was the sort of bull that Frank wet himself for.

It was hard to tell from here but Maeve's eyes seemed to have widened. Dermot was leaning in and saying something into her ear in a way that suggested he was flirting with her. I had once heard him pontificating at a party that monogamy was just a blip, that we would all look back on it and see it as crazy. Maeve would be well able for him. Bold, brazen, sexy dark-haired Maeve, who had her hip cocked out now. Maeve had pizzazz.

I needed to dislodge myself from my perch, where I was marooned inside my floating brain. I moved down the stairs slowly into the main part of the house, which was ablaze with lights. I paused on the bottom step, a little disoriented. Frank was in full flight, parrying questions about his planning permission. 'I'll get my planning,' he was saying. 'No question.'

The reality was different. The newspapers were querying whether he would win his appeal to build his Dubai-style resort off the coast of Wexford, including two seven-star luxury hotels – the design had been described as like something out of a Buck Rogers cartoon: an enormous conference centre, a golf course and three swimming-pools built on different levels. Wexford County Council had refused permission. When he'd heard, Frank had turned the air blue.

'It's not like I didn't take effing tables at fundraisers, or do my time on the chicken-and-chips circuit, or buy enough fecking drinks in the tent at the Galway races.' He had appealed to An Bord Pleanála. There had been an unprecedented number of submissions made to the planning board about his development: local residents and public representatives had banded together and objected to it. It had been described as a 'gargantuan monstrosity' by the barrister representing one group of objectors, which had provoked a tirade from Frank.

'What the fuck does that smug, curly-haired, speccy-four-eyed, short-arsed gun for hire know about architecture? How many people does he employ?' Frank had bellowed. 'What sort of risks has he taken, except lining his own feckin' pocket?'

They were saying that Frank had bought his enormous site at too inflated a price, at the very top of a market that was now spiralling downwards, and that he was too heavily borrowed. They were saying that there was no market left for this sort of upscale development and that he'd missed the boat, timing-wise. Basically they were saying that even if he got his permission to build – and this was by no means certain – he was screwed.

To look at Frank now, puffing on his Cuban cigar, you'd have thought he didn't have a care in the world. But Frank was a good actor. I knew that now for sure. Old Frank with his secret life.

When I was a young one, myself and my mates used to spend hours lying on our beds, smoking fags in our Frankie Says Relax T-shirts and Bananarama hair, discussing fellas and love and going the whole way and what we'd do if they did the dirt on us. With our fresh skin and big hopes, we were clear: we'd sling them out the door if they even so much as looked at another young one. 'His fecking feet wouldn't touch the ground – I'll tell you that much for nothing.'

Now I had no clear plan. My mind was a blank. There were no concrete thoughts, just a giant hole where Frank and his girl had taken a sledgehammer to my existence. If I could just get through the party . . . I thought, gliding towards the kitchen.

The hired staff were buzzing about our giant kitchen like a swarm of bees, dwarfed by the giant proportions of the room. Frank had blasted off the back wall of the original kitchen and extended it. At this moment it seemed stupidly big. Like a football stadium. But Frank could never have enough room.

Our house had been over six thousand square feet when we'd bought it – it had had three reception rooms, seven bedrooms and three bathrooms – and Frank had thought we needed to extend it. He was raging when we were refused permission to bulldoze the whole place and build a thirty-thousand-square-feet-plus 'modern villa'. Frank had a lust for tearing old things down and replacing them with big bright shiny new ones. His idea for adding turrets to the house had also been vetoed. Frank wanted to live in a giant modern house tricked out like a castle. Ideally he would have liked to stick up an enormous coat of arms, like the ones that got sold to good-natured but dopey Americans.

In the end he got away with lobbing a couple of thousand square feet onto the house – hence the enormous kitchen – and converted the coach house out the back as a pad for Dylan, renovating it at vast expense. I figured that, with Dylan, it might be a case of till death did us part. My guess was that he would never want to leave behind the surround sound and mood lighting, the weights rooms and the under-floor heating.

Anyway, Frank saw space as something to be concreted over and colonized. He needed to own things, to possess them. He had sued several people over boundary disputes.

His family were like something out of John B. Keane's *The Field*. 'You'll never go hungry if you own a few acres,' was their basic motto. There was probably a degree of horse sense in this, but it also meant they'd push you over a cliff for a few square feet of ground.

I grew up in a tenement flat the size of a postage stamp. My ma kept it spotless. She had very high standards, but there were always other people's bodies, smells and noises in it. The bedroom I shared with my sister smelt of cooking. Sometimes our clothes smelt of lard. The telly was always on

35

in the corner of the sitting room, somebody fiddling with the rabbit-ears aerial to get a better reception. There was never silence and there was never space. I was happy to live in a big, beautiful house. Sometimes, though, recently, I'd caught myself wondering if there might be a limit to the amount of space four people needed. I'd said as much to Frank when his big plans to level the original house had been shot down.

'You sound like a fuckin' Communist, Anita,' he'd said.

Now the rain beat against the panes. The wind howled. Something blew past the window – a plastic bag being sucked up into the ether. I would happily have floated after it. My husband was having sexual relations with a girl – a plump girl. This fact should have been beside the point but it seemed very relevant to me. After all my years of sweating on the treadmill, killing myself to keep my thighs slim, he'd gone after a chubby girl. The revelation that Frank lusted after thighs and a soft belly and curves when I had tortured myself to look like an exclamation mark seemed a very big deal to me.

The head waiter approached me, looking worried. 'Is everything all right, Mrs Lawlor?'

For one split second I considered telling the truth: 'Things couldn't be worse. My husband, the one you hear laughing and joking without a care in the world, is boning a girl not much older than our son and she's possibly in the family way.' I closed my eyes briefly. When I opened them the waiter was staring at me.

'Are you okay, Mrs Lawlor? Would you like to sit down? Maybe I could get you a glass of water.'

I needed to speak: several pairs of eyes were trained on me – their mad hostess, let down from the attic for the night. 'I'm grand, thank you,' I said, in my best posh voice, into which I'd put a lot of work. 'The food looks delicious. Thank you all very much.' I dredged up a smile before backing away, glassy-eyed.

My movements were mechanical. I went back into the party and wandered about, pausing here and there to say hello and God knew what else. I could see Ciara and Will in the distance. Ciara's long, elegant black dress made her look even more willowy than usual; her pale smooth hair was twirled up in a bun and her red lips made her skin seem like porcelain. She had innate style. Always knew when to stop, that less was more. It was a skill I wished she could pass on. I had tried so hard to copy it but it was dawning on me that I would never nail it.

Will had an arm around her. He looked gorgeous in his tuxedo, as if he might have been born in one. Frank, by contrast, seemed awkward in his. Somehow he always managed to make it look rented. Will and Ciara resembled movie stars, but I knew without looking into Ciara's eyes that all was not as it seemed on the surface.

You see, I'd learned that you never knew what went on behind closed doors. Not even behind your own closed door, it turned out, I thought, seeing a group of women I knew. Some were friends, others acquaintances. They stood by a cluster of large potted plants that had been brought in for the party, exotic birds of paradise in their party frocks. A tight knot, their heads bent like daffodils as Maeve told an anecdote – whip-smart, sometimes funny, always razor-tongued Maeve.

She was always telling tales about her husband and the way he pissed her off. Ultan was chairman and principal of Mohally Murphy Equity. MM had been one of the huge successes of the boom, snapping up property, development land, hotels, companies all over Europe and beyond for consortia of well-heeled Irish investors. Ultan Mohally was a tall, thin, ascetic workaholic with a serious manner and the eyes of a shark. He was a virtual social recluse, without friends or hobbies, and was now reputed to be a multi-millionaire. He hit the news at regular intervals for the increasingly audacious deals he was putting together. Frank and many of our cronies had invested in a number of the syndicates he had masterminded.

Typically, Ultan had not come to the party, instead sending a case of ridiculously expensive wine as a present. Maeve, an accountant, had met him while she was on secondment to his firm. They had married three months after a whirlwind courtship. Eight months later she had produced a long, thin baby called Maximilian Sebastian Ultan Mohally, who looked like a miniature version of his father. A baby girl, Madison Portia, had followed two years later; she had turned into a small girl with glossy black curls and a ceaseless whine.

Maeve and Ultan lived in a twenty-thousand-square-feet Georgian home, which she redecorated on a yearly basis with the help of a retinue of staff. 'I'm like the girls in the Janis Ian song,' Maeve had said at her birthday party after a good few jars. 'You know – the clear-skinned girls who married young and then retired.'

Maeve had been having sex lately with Max's tennis coach, a Frenchman who slunk around the gym with his sallow limbs and dark come-hither eyes and silky hair, igniting flames in the chests of the mothers who brought their kids for tennis lessons and sometimes paid him to go to bed with them. There was a lot of maternal servicing disguised as dental treatment among the women at our gym.

But who was I to judge? My husband was swinging it about. Ultan lived to work. It was impossible to imagine being intimate with him. Maeve had once told me she had never come with Ultan. At least, I'm pretty sure that was what she'd said. We'd been pretty jarred at the time. We were booze buddies. My poison was a Cosmo, hers a Margarita without salt. There were bars and restaurants we could walk into and they'd start throwing together our drinks before we'd even ordered.

Maeve bitched about Ultan. Lots of women bitched about their husbands, even when they loved them. They let off steam about their fellas, gave out yards about them, but in a semi-indulgent way that let you know you couldn't join in and say, 'Yeah, I always figured Michael was tight as a duck's arse.' I did it myself. It was therapy for married women – or 'the girls', as our husbands called us.

But you wouldn't introduce any really bad stuff to that circle. You wouldn't confess that your husband beat you or that he gave you no money or that he came home so drunk he peed in the marital bed. You might drop hints that he was no Casanova or that he could do with being a little more generous or that he was fond of a drink, but there were understood limits. You wouldn't say that you thought he was shagging a twenty-something and possibly fathering her child. You wouldn't say that, although you were upright and seemingly functioning (apart from the drugs and booze coursing through your system), you felt dead.

Dead woman walking: that was me, I thought, as Maeve beckoned to me. Another woman was making a little fluttering gesture with her hand. I was trapped in the headlamp glare of their curiosity. There was no choice but to go over.

'Hi there, we were wondering where you'd got to,' Shannon said.

She was our American friend. A former corporate lawyer, she was smart. But as the youngest colleen of a large, solidly Catholic Irish-American family, she had grown up on lore of the Emerald Isle, where people were pious, good, simple folk from an agrarian land where values were wholesome and the maidens pure. Simply put, she was gobsmacked when she married an Irishman and was parachuted into the middle of us reprobates.

She leant forward and hugged me, pressing me so hard against her tanned breastbone that her dress rustled a little. I had to steel myself against the warmth of her greeting so that I didn't start to cry. 'Hello,' I chimed, inhaling her flowery scent.

Shannon went to the same gym as Maeve, Ciara and I. We met for coffee two or three times a week in some configuration, usually in Harvey Nichols in Dundrum, where we'd sit in the glass-cube café pushing our scones around our plates and sipping skinny decaf lattes. Shannon was mad for the exercise. She went at it like a lunatic on the cross-trainer, pounding away as if the survival of the human race depended on it. If tall, sinewy, rake-thin Shannon missed a day in the gym, you knew there had been a death in the family. In her immediate family, that was. We all exercised a lot but Shannon was like the Duracell bunny. She could have outrun Forrest Gump. 'Guys,' she'd say, 'I have to exercise like this because otherwise I'm gonna turn into a blimp.'

It was hard to believe. With every successive year Shannon seemed to shrink. She had once worked in a large firm where the bone-crushing hours had wrung her inside-out. She had spoken of meetings called by colleagues late at night, gruelling deadlines, and American clients working on American time, with their maniacal devotion to duty. 'I mean, obviously I gave up my job as an attorney when I moved to Ireland but I don't think I could have kept that kind of pace up once I'd had the kids. I was pretty much maxed out.'

She had told us of the kind of difficulties that women

encountered in her firm. 'I worked for this one woman. She was a really cool kick-ass chick, smart and hard-working, but her life was, like, total hell. She had a couple of kids, a daytime nanny and one for the night. Sometimes she even hired extra help at the weekends. You could totally see that the whole thing was eating away at her. Then one day she found this note lurking at the bottom of her son's school sack like a ticking bomb waiting to detonate. There was a costume party the next day. She was working on a takeover. She ended up hysterically begging the poor little guy to be something kind of inappropriate like a sheikh because she only had a dish-towel to put on his head.' Shannon laughed. 'That was like her wake-up call. She left, which was kind of sad but it took guts to walk away like that.'

Shannon was married to a stockbroker, a tubby man who looked a bit like a docker and zoomed around the city in a camel coat and an array of flash cars. Jimmy had an easy smile and an appetite for the finer things in life. A partner in one of the leading stockbroking firms around town, he had bought a private plane and a large yacht, although he couldn't sail, and he also kept horses. 'I love the gee-gees,' he'd say, in his broad Cavan accent.

Shannon was project-managing the construction of their new home in Sandymount, a state-of-the-art modern house. 'I need something to do,' she'd said. 'I get so restless.'

I had persuaded her to talk to Ella about her experience of a legal career. Ella had said it was way too soon, that I was jumping the gun. 'You need to take a chill pill, Mum.'

I didn't care. Young girls needed mentors to guide them and point out the pitfalls. I didn't want anything getting in Ella's way. Shannon had given her some very solid advice. She was obliging like that.

A flurry of attention was directed at me.

41

'Your dress is so cute,' said Shannon. Sometimes Maeve grumbled that Shannon was too effusive. 'Jesus, she'd get excited if two flies crawled up the wall.' But the thing about Shannon was that she meant it. She didn't have a bad bone in her body.

A chorus of compliments on my dress followed. I gazed at my friends. They must be joking. I looked underdressed, in that my outfit was the size of a sticking plaster, and beyond mutton dressed as lamb. I was ridiculous in scarlet and feathers, my feet, like little pigs' trotters, shoved into towering sparkly shoes that were slightly too small.

'Everything going well?' Maeve asked. She laid a bejewelled hand on my arm, her pendant diamond earrings swaying hypnotically. She was treacherous, that one, with an appetite for other people's weaknesses. In a flash you could have told her too much and there would be no taking it back. She could siphon information from you when you had no idea you were being prised open like a clam. Her conversation seemed random but was a series of probes that went far beyond what you might have called intrusive. Maeve and I were friends but you couldn't tell her everything. She'd trade it in a flash for other gossip.

I trawled inside my sedated brain for the right words, nailed a hostessy smile to my features and smiled brilliantly at her. I parted my lying lips to speak. 'Everything is great,' I said.

I knew then what my response to my discovery would be. My resolution had crystallized. I was dimly aware of a ball of rage deep inside me that I had pushed down. I would fight tooth and nail for my marriage and my place in life. I would paper over the cracks. From where I was standing I had no choice.

*

42

The largest of the three reception rooms twinkled with candles. We were using it as a ballroom. Frank and I – watched by the assembled crowd – twirled around the floor to the strains of the band the bank were paying for. Frank was drunk on the attention. Performing. The larger-than-life property developer, the man they said had 'the balls of an elephant'. We were a sham on more than one level, I thought, as he turned me round and round.

Past the large curved bay windows, beyond the marble fireplace, back towards the centre of the floor, Frank moved boldly, confidently, powering his stocky frame around the room with surprising elegance, verging on grace. He had taken ballroom-dancing lessons for the party, so he could show off. They had been a deathly secret. It was pure Frank, one-in-the-eye stuff – *I'll show them*. He hadn't asked me to come with him. I hadn't thought it strange. Maybe he had brought his Irish-dancing colleen with her shiny red curls.

A sea of faces. They were here for Frank, of course. He was the draw. For many I wasn't even the side salad to his main course. I was just the garnish. If I'd collapsed in a heap on the floor, there were people who would have stepped over my crumpled form to get to Frank.

Frank's eyes gleamed.

'Do you love me, Frank?' I asked, with a sort of tugging in my chest.

He looked at me in a stunned mullet sort of way, tipping back his head. 'Of course,' he said, yanking me around in another wide arc. It was significant, I thought, that he twirled me faster and faster – so that we couldn't talk any more.

The storm had passed. The guests had gone. All the Aston Martins, Jaguars, Bentleys and top-of-the-range Mercedes had purred away, ferrying our guests back to their plush homes. Ella and Frank had gone to bed. Dylan was still out.

I'd succumbed to the demon drink – the clear golden liquid that made everything that bit better. The morning light burst into the drawing room and edged up the walls, illuminating the ornate plasterwork, the cornices and the giant rose in the centre of the ceiling. We'd been told by the estate agent that it was very large by the standards of the time when the house was built, which meant that the original owners had been flash bastards like us. Frank hadn't liked it when I'd made that connection. And he'd gone mental when he'd heard me saying it to some friends. 'Stop talking through your arse, Anita.'

Right. Like they might have thought the pair of us were born with a silver spoon.

I sat on the floor in the middle of Frank's presents – his booty, his swag – a vat-sized glass of wine next to me. Bottles of vintage champagne, golf clubs, bulging envelopes containing God knew what. My legs were tucked under me. The too-small shoes were kicked off, the red feathered dress lying on the floor in a heap. I was in my bra and knickers.

Frank had neither thanked nor praised me for organizing the party. Nothing. He'd gone to bed humming to himself, a little unsteady on his feet, a half-drunk bottle of champagne in his hand, his bow-tie undone. 'That was some *party* – that'll show those cunts,' he'd called back over his shoulder. 'Frank Lawlor is going nowhere. That's what you've gotta do,' he went on. 'When the going gets rough, you mow the front lawn, paint the front door and put on a new suit.'

I liked that about Frank. He was a fighter. I respected his instinct to fight like hell for what he'd got. Like I was going to fight for my marriage. My life. I had put all my eggs in one basket. Little Miss Big Knockers couldn't just take everything

44

away from me. She had said that Frank and I had nothing in common. Was that true, I wondered, taking a long slow slug of wine. It was hard now to remember what we had talked about on our last holiday. I scrunched up my nose, trying to fight my way through the fog in my head.

The hot sun in Miami had beaten down. We had stayed in the Delano. It was an Ian Schrager-designed hotel. Schrager was part of the Studio 54 posse who had hung out with Andy Warhol. *Vogue* had once described the Delano as America's coolest hotel. A slew of celebrities had stayed there, including maybe Madonna. Of course, even though I practically stopped the milkman to tell him all this, I'd never heard of Schrager or the hotel until somebody had filled me in. Competitive holidaying was very big: Irish people who used to think that a week in Brittas by the beach in a caravan, or a weekend in some damp bungalow with slug trails in the rain in Kerry, was a brilliant getaway had got into the habit of parroting things like: 'I preferred Umbria to Tuscany. We stayed in a wonderful converted monastery at the top of a hill and the views were to die for.' Or: 'Lamu was divine. You don't know Lamu? It's a small Muslim island off Kenya. You fly Amsterdam, Nairobi, Lamu and then you take a boat to get to the island. It was so worth it, though.' Cue smug laughter, so you'd want to beat the head off them while you made a mental note to Google it.

I had said things like that myself at the beginning when people first started to make a few bob. I used to hear myself going on like that about a holiday and couldn't believe the bull I was coming out with. Not that I had much choice, because even if we were tragically bored on holiday and the weather was dire and we'd fought like two Jack Russells the whole way there and the whole way back, Frank would insist on talking it up. 'Oh, it was a-*mazing*,' he'd say, with a grin on his face.

45

Anyway, after a couple of years of trotting out that kind of thing, bragging became second nature. You felt compelled to outdo your friends – which was lovely behaviour when you thought about it.

In fairness, the Delano Hotel had been nice: an art-deco building on Collins Avenue in South Beach all tricked out in pastel colours. The sand had been white, the sea azure, the beach huts striped in peach and pistachio, the umbrellas cream, with white-clad staff offering guests free smoothies and popsicles. The bodies on the beach were buffed and flawless. Perfectly toned bottoms wore barely there thongs and string bikinis struggled to contain massive fake but pert boobs on stick-thin women, their faces shaded by massive designer sunglasses. There was not a spot of cellulite in sight.

A beautiful man with a huge Afro had cartwheeled along the beach in the latest designer gear before stooping to do press-ups. There were biplanes flying overhead, powerboats and jet-skis out at sea, palm trees. The loungers around the pool turned into flat beds at night so that the Delano guests could lean back and look at the stars as a DJ played by the pool.

Frank had paced up and down with his phone, muttering, issuing orders, raving. He didn't actually like holidays. He liked to be busy all the time. He loved working. He couldn't see the point of holidays. He took them so that he could boast about them afterwards.

We'd had dinner together, me dressed up to the nines in white to highlight my tan, my makeup looking a little hard, and Frank, in his freshly laundered short-sleeved shirt, the colour of a boiled lobster, rogue sweat stains spreading down his back although he had only just stepped from the shower. I had picked at some seafood ceviche and yucca chips, which was a way of eating but not taking in any calories. Oh, and I had drunk a lot of cocktails. Peach Blossom, the house special, was my favourite, an explosive mix of Absolut peach vodka, pineapple juice and a dash of peach schnapps. Frank had talked about business and the banks, and the planning system being run by muppets, and political parties he had no sway over otherwise he would have got his planning in a second. I stared at him, anaesthetized by alcohol, my buddies the Peach Blossoms.

We'd had a silent communion, I told myself now, drinking half my glass of wine in one swallow. Frank and I had history. There was lots of water under the bridge. *She* couldn't just write me out of the picture. I started to feel more confident. *I will take you down to Chinatown, bitch.*

There was the sound of someone stirring upstairs. The rattle of a door. I cut my eyes towards the stairs. I drained my glass as I watched Frank's short powerful bare legs come into view. He wanted me to come to bed, I thought, my leaden heart doing a little jig at the idea that my husband might actually want me.

He stopped and leant over the banisters, his hand gripping the rail.

I stared at him. His eyes were moist. I had never seen Frank cry. Not even when the kids were born.

'Anita,' he said, running his hand over his face. 'Mam . . .' He broke off and tried again, the tears running down his face unchecked. The colour was bleached from his face.

My heart did a back flip.

'Mam,' he said. He sat down heavily on the stairs. In a voice that was low, hoarse and beaten, he finally managed, 'Mam is after dying.'

3

My eyes were swollen and red. I had cried buckets in the church with the snot and tears running down my face so that even Frank had turned to look at me. I felt dead embarrassed to be hogging the whole scene but I just couldn't help myself. Frank's sister-in-law Mary had looked a bit put out by my performance. She'd been going great guns as chief mourner cocked up beside DJ, Frank's older brother – like a pet fox with her ferrety face – until I'd stolen her thunder. All she was missing was the Jackie Onassis mantilla. Why, I don't know, because Mam had been a total cow to her. But then maybe that's what people did at funerals – cried for their own reasons. Or maybe, God forgive me, poor Mary was so relieved at not having to live with Mam any more that she was crying from sheer gratitude.

'Jaysus, I never knew you and that old wagon were so close,' my sister Karen hissed in my ear afterwards.

I felt a sort of jangly hysterical laughter bubbling up inside me. My sister had come the whole way down to Offaly on the bus for Frank's mam. Darren, her hubby, was working and Karen didn't drive. I felt like a pure louse for not inviting her to the fiftieth. 'You're awful good to come, Karen,' I said, hugging her tightly. Sometimes around Karen I found my language reverting back to that of my youth, before I'd re-invented myself from top to bottom.

'Ah, it's nothing,' she said, loosening my grip and giving me that slanted ironic smile of hers. Then she shot back,

'You must be wrecked, what with this coming hot on the heels of the party and all.'

That was classic Karen. She never let you away with anything.

Frank seemed touched that Karen had made the effort. 'At least Pocahontas didn't come in a black tracksuit,' he'd said to me, before the Mass began, with a soft look in his eyes. That had been when I'd felt my eyes spring leaks.

The church was small and cute, set in the middle of grassy fields, near the village of Enniskane. The graveyard was behind it. Crows and jackdaws cawed and chattered in the high, rustling trees. There was a smell of wild garlic and flowers. The place looked like an illustration on the front of a chocolate box. The country did my head in. Once a Dub always a Dub. I missed the soothing sound of traffic, the Dublin buses trundling along. Nice clean gleaming footpaths. There were no decent shops either.

Along with a couple of castles and monasteries, the Grand Canal and the Bog of Allen were the two main attractions in Offaly. Big deal. We had the Grand Canal in Dublin too. Frank's family went on about the Bog of Allen as if it was the ninth wonder of the world. 'Being from a bog, Frank, isn't something to shout home about,' Karen had said once. Frank had reared up in the seat and looked like he wanted to give her a dig.

I let on that I thought the place was great. Frank's family got very thick with you if you didn't praise everything to the skies.

Ella had said a poem in the church. She had walked up to the pulpit and my heart had soared into the rafters. I'd felt so proud, the dark brown eyes looking into the middle of the congregation, the steady, clear voice. She had looked so sure

49

of herself beneath the stained-glass window, the embodiment of confidence, this person Frank and I had created together. Our daughter. I'd felt like howling.

Afterwards Dylan carried the coffin out of the church with Frank, looking as manly and neckless as his father. The Lawlors had no necks. Frank and Dylan and Frank's brothers had heads like bowling balls plonked on their broad shoulders. It was nice to see them together under the coffin. It was hard for Dylan sometimes: his relationship with Frank was rocky, and Ella overshadowed him.

Things came easier to her. She had walked first, talked first. Dylan had been more halting, requiring more coaching and care. Even in her high chair she had been self-possessed and in control, whereas Dylan had squirmed and waved his arms like windmills, throwing his food everywhere. On the rare trips down to see Mam, Ella had scaled the ancient barn wall, without a backward glance, just like Frank had done. Dylan had stood doubtfully at its base wanting to climb up and please Frank but unable to pluck up the courage to do so. Frank's attempts to coax him had turned into frustrated shouting: 'For fuck's sake, Dylan, what kind of a girl's blouse are ya?'

But Dylan had never been envious of his sister. He had been three when Ella was born and we had thought he might be jealous, but he had hung over her carrycot adoringly from the first day we'd brought her home from the hospital. He'd had to be stopped from smothering her with love.

We were at the graveside now, having walked the short distance from the church behind the hearse. Irish funerals were a big deal – not like in some other countries where they shoved you in the ground when you were still warm or drove up in a car to view your dead body through a window. Irish culchies, though, really threw the book at it. There had been the wake when Mam had been laid out in her own bedroom surrounded by candles, people coming to see her. She'd never been left alone. There'd always been a core contingent up with her, praying, right through the night. And there had been constant pots of tea on the go, and booze, and women moving tactfully about, speaking in hushed whispers, making sandwiches and bringing cakes, and people waiting outside, chatting. Then she'd been removed to the church, where mourners lined up to shake hands with the whole family, saying things like 'I'm sorry for your troubles.'

We'd had the Requiem Mass. The Lawlors had put on a good show, what with Frank putting his hand in his pocket and Father Willy – Mam's cousin – leading the charge in concelebrating the mass with five other priests. Mam would have been pleased. For all her Irish-mammy 'Don't mind me, I'll just sit here in the dark' carry-on, she would have expected to be sent off in style.

Mam had been mega-religious. The Lawlors had been head, neck and tail of the local church. They'd been altarboys, helped with collections, weeded in the grounds – although that wouldn't have stopped them burying you at the side of a bog if they thought you were encroaching on their land.

Mam had a big Technicolor picture of the last pope on her wall. Sacred Heart pictures were dotted in each Lawlor bedroom, complete with gleaming votive lights and creepy red eyes looking down on you. 'What Mass will you be getting?' she'd ask, when you went down there for a visit before you even had your coat off. They said the rosary after dinner. After Frank and I had become engaged I'd brought Karen down there. God knew why. She'd been at a loose end or something – between jobs. She'd gone through a phase of telling her bosses what she thought of them, which meant she changed jobs a lot. Things like sexual harassment were more commonplace in those days and 'girls' generally put up with it. But not our Karen. She would come bursting into Ma and Da's, spluttering, 'The perverted bastard put his hand on my arse so I told him to bleedin' fuck off.'

Anyway, we'd ended up in Frank's just before the bells of the Angelus had begun to toll. Mam had got down on her knees and outstretched her hands, instructing us all to follow suit. I'd closed my eyes and fallen to my knees clasping Karen's hand, afraid for my life that she'd burst her arse laughing and Mam would fillet us. Afterwards we'd run down the boreen towards the town for a drink, quaking with laughter once we were out of earshot. Karen had bellowed, 'Oh, Jaysus, I thought I'd die wanting to laugh. Frank's ma is a bleedin' holy roller.'

And when Frank went home he still pretended he went to Mass, hiding down the road in the hotel reading the papers rather than telling her the truth – Frank who'd take shit off nobody, Frank who said it like it was, 'like it or lump it'. But not with Mam. Dylan and Ella had been told to lie too. When they were small we'd more or less had to buy their silence with sweets, which was morally dubious, but Frank wouldn't hear of anything else.

Frank adored her. It was a real case of the Irish mammy and her adoring son. An image of Mam with her short heavy limbs, her Pioneer pin, the small gold cross hanging around her neck and the set lines of her mouth loomed large in my mind. Frank would never have confronted her with a lover and a child – which was why, of course, I was distraught: my insurance policy had expired. Mam and I might never have been bosom buddies but she'd have been in my corner on this one.

Now we were on the home straight: the burial. One cloud floated across the sky. The sun was blazing down. DJ was staring down into the grave, his mouth hanging open a little, the hair slicked back as usual, large dark sunglasses covering his eyes. DJ's personal motto was 'Bullshit beats brains any day.'

'Your man DJ is a dead ringer for Mr Ed the talking horse in those glasses,' Karen whispered, and I had to clench my stomach to stop myself laughing.

Mam always said that DJ was the bright one, which was a fairly major insult to Frank. DJ wasn't in danger of getting a call from Mensa. In fact, as Frank often said, 'That fella couldn't find his own arse with his two hands.' Anyway, Frank had set him up with a shop and a pub half a mile up the road from their farm, but DJ didn't exactly break his balls. He seemed to spend a lot of his time driving up and down roads in an SUV with a bull bar going to see a man about a dog. Mam had liked to make out – at least around Frank and me – that DJ was some big-shot tycoon. That was Mam through and through. She'd have wanted to cut Frank down to size.

Mam had set her kids up against each other. They spent their lives scrambling to impress her and win her love. That was why Frank was as he was. It all came back to Mam. Nothing was ever enough for her, no matter what Frank achieved. If he'd climbed the Matterhorn to bring her back a flower, it would have been the wrong flower. Everything that man did at some level was to impress his ma. All the Lawlors were the same.

Father Willy had gone on about Mam in his eulogy as if her ascension into heaven was a sure-fire bet.

'Is he talking about the woman we knew?' Karen had murmured to me. I'd had to stifle a laugh. Crying, laughing, I was all over the place.

There had been no mention of Frank's father. He'd been written out of the script. He hadn't been violent or a drinker.

He seemed to have been filed as a non-event. Mam had ruled the roost. Frank hadn't said much about his da. He had been a shy man, I gathered, who liked to eat lumps of butter, which might have gone some way towards explaining why he was claimed quite early by his angina. And Mam had been carted off by a heart attack. I worried about Frank, whose lips could often look blue.

The undertakers were letting the coffin down into the black hole now. That was always the hard part, closing the coffin for the last time and lowering it down into the grave. My heart had nearly broken when I had buried my own ma and da.

Frank's shoulders were hunched and his face was ashen. I felt a tidal rush of sadness. My husband, the husband I hoped wouldn't leave me. I wanted to take his round red fleshy face in my hands, kiss him and tell him it would be all right, and that we would be all right.

The boy brought over another round of drinks. We'd gone back to the local hotel, the Enniskane Arms. The lounge had yellow walls. The carpet, with its big swirly pattern, had a slightly sticky feel. A sign for 'Gourmet Food' hung over the carvery, which was closed, the stainless-steel bain-maries empty. There was a slightly musty smell in the room mixed with the stink of overcooked vegetables.

'Sure it's grand,' DJ had said, two evenings before, when the topic of where we'd go after the funeral came up. His house had been the obvious choice – but Mary wasn't gone on having people back to the house. She was a bit weird like that. She was on the excitable side, too, something to do with her thyroid. That was why she had the bulgy eyes.

'It's meanness pure and simple,' Karen had said, blowing out a cloud of smoke. 'They wouldn't give you the steam off their piss. Do you remember years ago when DJ came up to Dublin and stayed with you and you said that he ate an orange in his room because he was afraid he might have to share it with the kids?' Karen forgot very little.

Frank had wanted a sit-down meal but the hotel couldn't provide it for the numbers that were bound to come. Or, at least, that was DJ's interpretation of the matter. They'd laid on soup and sandwiches, sausages, chips and chicken wings, with a radioactive-looking sauce, and mini pizzas. It wasn't what Frank wanted but he was cute enough not to say anything.

The place was packed to the rafters. People had come from the four corners to pay their respects. And for the free gargle. It was nice, actually, everyone coming together to mark the end of somebody's life.

'Nothing like a good funeral,' Karen said, helping herself to a chicken wing and dunking it in the sauce.

She was like a mind-reader. 'I think I prefer them to weddings,' I said.

'I know what you mean,' she agreed.

Weddings could be nice – but they could also be very competitive. People getting married in foreign locations, brides flying here, there and everywhere to get their dress, pressure over presents, over-the-top hen and stag dos.

Frank had a pint of Guinness in his hand, and his brothers, cousins and half the county of Offaly were swarming around him. There were lots of country faces – there was a difference in them, I thought, from the way my da's face had been urban through and through.

'It's weird to see Dad in this context,' Ella said, suddenly beside me.

We watched him smile and shake the hand of some old fella. I felt a pang. It reminded me of the Frank I'd known long before he learnt to sniff Château Pétrus this and Grand

Cru that and to swirl them around his glass. Frank Lawlor had drunk pints of the black stuff.

Frank wasn't really the big man down here, just one of the Lawlors – a local boy done good for himself – in a place where people had known his father and grandfather. Frank had smarts. He'd never throw his weight around at home. He knew that you couldn't get too above yourself when you went back. Not where your people were known and where, despite your heavy watch and shiny shoes, you still, as Frank put it to me once when he was drunk, had 'the imprint of the enamel bucket on your arse' – when he was very young the Lawlors had had no inside toilet. Not that I was casting judgement on this. In our flats, my own family had shared a bathroom with two other families.

'These are Dad's people,' I added, smiling at my daughter.

'They're your people too, Ella,' Karen said, pulling her leg.

Ella's face tightened. It had been a bit of a shock for her to meet some of her relatives, to know that she came from the same gene pool. One fella had come to her in a shabby old raincoat – he'd looked like he was carved out of bog oak – and told her he was her cousin. Her bright, polite smile didn't reach her eyes, which told me she was rattled.

Frank had been good about going home to see his mother but he had mainly gone on his own. Once the kids had got a bit bigger they hadn't wanted to go.

'She's only teasing you, love,' I said to Ella, patting her stiff shoulder.

Ella and Dylan weren't used to being slagged, not like us when we were growing up when there had been no let-up.

'Yeah, I know,' Ella said, shrugging. She wasn't used to Karen's humour because she didn't really know her aunt. The strangeness of that thought hit me. Our family had been a tight-knit bunch, at least when Ma and Da were alive.

They'd have been stunned to think that my sister and my daughter were virtual strangers.

'Your ma tells me you're a total genius at school,' Karen said. Her accent was stronger. She did that around anyone she encountered from my current life – gave them a blast of 'Dublin in the rare oul times'. This, of course, was to wind me up and to draw attention to how uppity I'd got.

Ella rolled her eyes.

'Well, you are,' I said.

Ella pulled another face.

'She thinks I go on about it too much,' I said to Karen.

'Just like our ma so,' Karen said drily.

'Ma did not go on about me and school.'

Karen threw her head back and laughed. 'I've heard it all now.'

'Fair enough, your ma got the best Leaving Certificate that anyone ever got in our flats but Ma and Da, your grandparents that you never met,' she said, nodding at Ella, 'bored the backside off anyone who would listen.'

I didn't remember that. 'Ella's in a totally different league to me,' I said, feeling a burst of maternal pride. 'Straight As,' I added.

Ella crossed her eyes.

'Your mother was a genius at maths,' said Karen, 'and I'm not joking.'

'She's been drinking,' I said to Ella, pleased all the same.

'Don't mind her,' Karen said. 'She was a proper little swot and she was always teacher's pet at school.'

I was too. I loved school. Never missed a day if I could help it. When I was in primary I used to go in early – always spotless even though Ma had no washing-machine and no drier. I'd help the teacher get the classroom ready. I'd wipe the board for her and put out fresh chalk and feed the class hamster. I had been in my element. In secondary I'd been waiting outside the gates for the caretaker to open up.

I had loved having my own desk, seat and coat hook. I had loved the way the pens and copies, pencils, rubbers and toppers were yours. I came from a house where bodies were densely packed in and everyone 'borrowed' your things, so the order that had prevailed at school had been a dream.

I still remembered the pleasure I had derived from practising my writing on the blue and red lines, later from writing my name with a flourish on the front of my copies. And the praise I had received for all of this had been like a drug.

'She's very ambitious,' my class teacher had said once to a baffled Ma.

She was wrong there. I hadn't been ambitious at all. My hunger for approval had been confused with ambition. It was praise I was after. I had figured out that I was good at something – maths – and that I not only enjoyed it but got recognition for it too.

'That's some accent she's got on her,' Karen said, as we watched Ella drift over to Frank, who had beckoned to her.

'It's the school she went to,' I said defensively.

'How d'ye know ET was a Protestant?' Karen asked.

'Tell me.'

'Because he looked like one,' she said, and laughed.

'Very funny,' I said, smiling.

We'd sent Ella to a posh Protestant school where we'd paid a small fortune for the 'cultured' accent. It had been Frank's idea. A lot of our Catholic friends sent their children to Protestant schools because of their 'lovely, free, open attitude to education' – or because they were 'disillusioned with the Catholic Church' after all the sex scandals. These were some of the many reasons put forward. Frank had been more up front as to why he'd plumped for the Prods.

'That's a load of bollocks if I ever heard it,' he had roared one night at a dinner party, slamming his hand on the table. 'Go on out of that,' he'd said. I had been half admiring, half mortified. I had always had a split attitude to Frank saying the unsayable. Mainly I cringed, but my embarrassment was usually tinged with a sort of pride in his boldness. 'Let's call a spade a spade,' he had gone on. 'You're doing it for the same reason as us. Because you can't beat the Prods for the auld bit of polish and, like us, you're willing to pay for it now you've got a few shekels in your back pocket.'

There had been a chorus of indignant protest but Frank didn't care.

'Your parents wouldn't have dreamt of sending you to Protestant schools. Imagine you lot, with names like feckin' Maeve and Ciara, schlepping up to a Protestant school. Are you feckin' joking me? But, by Jaysus, Maximilian and Madison and Camilla, and whatever the feck you've called your kids, will be sent,' he'd said, and another storm of protest had broken out. Ciara had looked like somebody had poured a bottle of vinegar down her gullet. Any hint that she might be into reinvention or social climbing sent her into orbit.

'I know I'm right,' Frank had said afterwards.

Frank was never slow to point out what he considered to be other people's pretensions, even though he harboured quite a few himself, the sort of notions that had led him to consider a coat of arms for our house and the turrets. But that was fairly typical of human nature. It was easier to spot these things in other people.

'Ella's the head off you,' Karen said, jiggling the ice in her glass.

'Do you think?'

'Yeah, I do. Obviously not the colouring since you dyed your hair blonde but she's good-looking and brainy,' she said.

I found myself going a bit red. Karen was not known for lavishing praise.

'And she's a bit stuck-up like you and all,' she added.

'I'm not stuck-up.'

'Go on out of that, Mrs Bouquet,' she said, looking straight at me. 'You had a high hole on ya as far back as I can remember. You were always into being poshie. You had notions when you were in your cot.'

And look where that had got me, I thought, taking a slug of my wine.

'You must be very proud of her all the same,' Karen said, popping a stick of gum into her mouth.

'I am,' I said, feeling bad I couldn't think of much to say about Karen's lot. She had three kids. They were a fair bit younger than mine because, although Karen was older, she'd married much later. They were called Derry, Saoirse and Colleen Eireann, the names chosen on account of Karen's Darren being as mad into the idea of the Irish language as he was the dream of a united Ireland.

I'd sent them presents for birthdays and Christmas, and cash for Communions and Confirmations, but I knew very little about my nieces and nephew other than that they went to the school Karen and I had gone to in the Liberties. And that Derry was mad into GAA football and the girls were big into the Irish dancing. I'd been a crap auntie. I rarely visited them. And they hardly ever came to ours, mainly because I hardly ever invited them.

Karen was looking around the bar, her jaws moving rhythmically. 'This lot are some bunch of carrot-crunchers all the same,' she said, reaching for her wine. 'Would you look at that one passing behind Frank?' she said. I tried to shush her. 'Love,' she said, pretending to cup her hands to her mouth, 'the eighties called and they want their style of dressing back. Or that fella over there like some sort of natural-selection slip-up. I wouldn't be surprised if he waved at planes.'

Our family were Dubs back as far as you could go and we were brought up thinking that culchies were a bit slow, even though everyone knew that Dublin was full of boggers who basically ran the nation. It was particularly ironic that, as children, we were encouraged to think we were a cut above, given that we hadn't a pot to piss in. I mean, we weren't exactly a bunch of high rollers.

'Aren't you lucky Ella didn't take after them? They look like a pack of Munchkins.'

'Ah, they're not that bad, Karen,' I said. Secretly I was very relieved my daughter didn't take after that side of the family physically. Not saying anything but they were a bit vertically challenged and their noses were on the big side.

Karen stuck a finger under her eye and pulled it down. 'Would you go on out of that? That fella is no oil painting,' she said, pointing at one of Frank's brothers. 'And only a mother could love that face,' she said, indicating Frank's youngest brother. She cocked an eye. 'And would you look at DJ's chisellers there – with the snozzes on them, they look like the direct descendants of Cyrano de Bergerac.'

I thought of telling her to mind the language but that would have made her worse. Tell Karen to do anything and you were guaranteed she would do the opposite. Instead I popped back at her so that she actually coloured, 'They could have been your kids too, Karen.'

Getting Karen to feel embarrassed was some achievement. She and DJ had shifted at our wedding.

'Ah, here,' she said, nodding towards the bar, 'if you go on like that I'll need another large brandy.' She shook her head so that the black bits underneath her platinum hair were exposed. 'I can't believe I let Chopper Teeth suck the face off me. I must have been desperate.'

'Are you sure that's all you did?' I asked. She went puce again.

We looked at each other and burst out laughing.

'Listen, I'd rather shag the child-catcher from *Chitty Chitty Bang Bang* and that's a fact,' Karen said, still a bit flushed.

I eyeballed her mock-innocently. 'But back then . . .'

'Would you go on out of that!' she growled, half laughing, half scowling. Then her expression changed. 'Can you believe this bunch of muppets looked down on us at the wedding?' Her eyes narrowed to slits. 'Don't say you don't remember, Anita,' she said sourly. 'Frank's ma looking over at us like she'd smelt something bad. And the Brothers Grimm acting like they were some big deal *in their suits*,' she said, making a poor stab at a culchie accent.

We'd had a reception in the Shelbourne Hotel, which was a major big deal. All my older brothers and sisters had had their dos in pubs. Frank and his brothers had been stuffed inside suits like the cast from a second-rate Mafia movie. Da had been scratchy in a suit, his shoes scuffed, screwing up his face at the taste of the wine. I'd been mortified. In the end I'd relented and let him drink bottles of stout. Ma had been decked out in powder pink. She'd rented a hat. She'd sipped sherry until two bright pink spots to match her rig-out had appeared on her cheeks.

We'd had melon or chilled orange juice to start. Then chicken and ham. Late in the evening our uncle Robbie had had to be stopped from singing 'Her eyes they shone like diamonds' over and over again, the pint still in his hand as he swayed forward, his eyes shut, the remains of the wedding cake next to him. I shouldn't have let Uncle Robbie, in his blue serge suit, sing. I regretted it now. But I had felt raw, my skin exposed. I wanted the Butlers to be good enough for the Lawlors.

Our crowd had stayed on one side of the reception room, the Lawlors on the other. It was clear that, even then, the Lawlors had seen themselves as a cut above. Our gang were shite with money. They'd managed to get through the boom and not made a penny. Even my brothers and sisters who'd gone to America had done a fair job of sidestepping the American dream. The Lawlors, though, had made a few quid. Now they owned half of Enniskane. Back then at the wedding, they'd had nothing but a couple of stony grey fields and a broken-down Massey Ferguson tractor but they were the posh ones. Our mud hut is nicer than yours, that sort of thing. Ma and Da had retreated into themselves. Not able to deal with that. They were gentle people. They had real manners so they did. Ma, in her own old Dublin way, was genteel and ladylike.

'It's a long time ago, I can't really remember,' I said to Karen, so that I didn't egg her on. She could get bolshy with a couple of jars on her and I didn't want to be digging up old resentments. 'You and DJ did your bit to keep things cordial anyway.' That shut her up quick time.

Two old fellas were discussing football next to us.

'We've it all to do now . . .'

'We're going through a bit of turmoil all right . . .'

''Tis a dangerous carry-on when you start pussyfooting around players . . .'

'Darren would love this,' said Karen. Darren was mad into the GAA. 'Father Willy is delighted with himself anyway.' She nodded to where the priest was talking to Biba's chest. He was a small, colourless slip of a man, with a narrow papery face. 'I know where he'd like to stick *his* feckin' *willy*.'

63

'Jesus, Karen, would you keep your voice down?' She was like the bloody town crier.

'Get up on a gust of wind, I'd say,' she said, her eyes fastened on them. 'Look at him. He's like a dog in heat talking to Biba's tits.'

'Christ, Karen, sssh!'

Karen shrugged. 'Suitably named, that's all I'm saying. What do you make of your woman?' she said, puffing out a ring of smoke in her blithe yet assessing way. 'She's got a killer little figure on her. She looks fit as a butcher's dog.'

I said nothing. Biba Bailey was tall, tanned and blonde, with big boobs and gloss-covered lips that made a popping sound when she talked. She was very striking in a showy way. She'd turned up to the funeral, looking like the textbook young widow in an American soap, like she was playing a part. Short tight black dress like a bandage across her bottom, big black sunglasses, spiky-heeled black stilettos and a black handbag.

'I'd say Dylan doesn't know his luck,' Karen said, poking me in the ribs.

I slapped her away, half laughing. It wasn't something you wanted to think about, your son getting jiggy with a girl. When she'd flung her long bare legs out of Dylan's sports car, hips oscillating, I'd felt my breath catch in my chest. This was not the usual sort of girl Dylan had gone out with.

'She'll run rings around your Dylan,' Karen said, with that special knack of hers for knowing what I was thinking.

I watched Dylan put his hand on the small of Biba's back. He was on the short side, like Frank, built like a brick shit house – he spent hours lifting weights in the gym. His hands were like shovels, just like his father's. Ella had got the looks, but l loved my Dylan and his round open face. The baby whose tummy had been taut with colic so that I'd opened the

64

poppers on his Babygro and let him kick his fat little legs. The small sweet boy with the freckles on his nose who'd flung his arms around my neck and said, 'I love you, Mum.' The happy, messy, enthusiastic teenager, who had been my special boy. The young man I hoped she wouldn't hurt, with her suggestive sexy stride and skirt cut up to her bum.

I would try not to judge her. Frank's mam had done that with me: he had brought me home and I'd seen straight away that I wasn't what Kathleen Lawlor had been hoping for. I could still remember the look on her face, like she'd swallowed a wasp. It had hurt. Worst of all, it had felt like a judgement on Ma and Da.

She had been the cause of our first fight. Frank had asked me not to mention that I worked part-time as a hostess in a club in Leeson Street. I'd made some crack about how I was sorry I wasn't a big ignorant camogie-playing heifer from Offaly with thighs like pink hams.

I leant across for my drink. 'You've got to let kids go,' I said, drawing up a stool so that Karen followed suit.

'I'm surprised Ella isn't doing a line,' Karen said, crossing her walnut-coloured legs, 'lovely-looking girl like that.'

'She is,' I said.

The boyfriend hadn't come. It was too close to the exams, Ella had explained. He needed to study. You couldn't blame him for that, she had said, but I could see that she was disappointed.

'Your man has to study. He's doing law like her. The father's a judge,' I said, regretting saying it the moment it came out of my mouth.

And, of course, the boast wasn't lost on Karen.

'*A judge!*' she said, in the sarky way that made me feel like an idiot.

The lounge boy came up and offered us some chips from

65

plastic baskets. Karen took a handful, shoving them into her mouth. 'I'm starved,' she said. 'I'd murder a packet of Taytos.' Karen mainlined Taytos. 'Any chance of a packet of cheese and onion crisps?' she asked, handing him a note.

'It's all paid for,' he told her.

'Go mad so and make it two packets,' she said, and we both laughed.

'Could I get more wine, please?' I asked.

'Anita, do you eat anything?' Karen asked, when he'd gone and she was adjusting a gold hoop earring. 'You look like a lat.'

'Of course I do,' I lied. 'Wrap dresses are very forgiving.'

'Yeah,' she said, grabbing her spare tyre. 'I must get myself a magic dress so . . . You're hitting the hooch fairly hard,' she added, looking at my empty glass.

'I'm sad.'

'Right,' Karen deadpanned. 'I forgot you and Frank's ma were so close.' She was watching me out of the side of her eye.

'I feel bad for Frank,' I said. 'He really loved his mother.'

'God help him,' Karen said.

God help him was right, I thought, seeing Mam in front of me with her Yardley perfume, half-eaten packets of winegums, and small hard eyes, like rosary beads, lost in the dough of her pious face.

She gave me a penetrating look.

'Kathleen was his mother,' I insisted. 'Now that she's gone . . .' I felt a lump form in my gullet. I fattened my bottom lip. It was a major surprise that a bolt of lightning didn't come out of the sky and strike me down, big fraudulent cow that I was. I didn't give a rattling damn about Mam. 'Oh, Jesus,' I said, as a tear rolled down my cheek.

Karen was watching me closely now. 'Anita, are you all right?'

I wanted to tell her. I didn't want to tell her. She'd have run over and got Frank in a head lock – and, let's face it, she'd have been only too thrilled to do it. There was nothing to tell her anyway, I told myself. Frank and I were grand.

But it would have been nice to share with somebody how it felt to have the bottom falling out of your world, to have your mind roiling and seething with images of your husband's betrayal. It might have helped to share the shock of it. I wouldn't, though.

I raised a shoulder, then let it drop. 'I'm grand, Karen,' I said, wiping my face. 'I'm tired, that's all.'

Karen said nothing, still watching me as I stared at my empty glass.

We were staying with DJ and Mary. The Lawlor family place was a couple of fields over. They had closed it up so that its front was almost covered with brambles. Mam had moved in with DJ and Mary. It had been a condition of Frank building the house for them – a high price to pay for bricks and mortar, I thought.

The Lawlor family home had never been a warm house to go to. There had always been an undertow of things not said, everyone tripping over each other to please Mam. I would have said it was a tense house with lots of pregnant pauses in the conversation. Karen had remarked on it the time she'd been down. 'Christ almighty, they're fucking miserable, so they are. You'd have more fun in a nunnery.'

It had been an old farmhouse with the smell of damp and mice, and slug trails across the bedroom carpet in the morning. There were a few scrubby trees outside and some gorse bushes. Originally the Lawlors had a small-holding of marshy acidic fields, although to listen to DJ going on you'd be forgiven for thinking they were big ranchers.

I could visualize 'the good room', dark and smelling musty, the slightly moist carpet, the dining-room table and chairs that had never been sat at or on. In the corner there had been a display cabinet full of Aynsley china, and two big porcelain dogs on the mantelpiece over the unlit grate. And there was Mam's picture of the last pope – you felt he was eyeballing you no matter where you were in the room. The house was far bigger than Ma and Da's flat, but for all its china dogs and the conspicuously positioned set of *Encyclopaedia Britannica* – which was so clean you knew nobody had ever consulted any of its volumes – there was something very dour about it.

Don't get me wrong. It was like a palace compared to where Karen and I had been brought up. Our tenement flat was part of a row of once-fancy Georgian townhouses with beautiful plum-coloured brick and fanlights. By the time we moved in, it had become a warren of flats that had the reputation of being rough. It wasn't the whole story: there were plenty of decent hard-working people living there.

There'd been a big, draughty pitch-black hallway, with bare walls and a bare concrete floor, that smelt of pee and frying and rubbish. You couldn't have swung a cat in our flat. Karen and I had shared a bedroom with a thin partition separating it from the dingy little bathroom. We'd basically lived in one room. But there had been a steady flow of visitors and constant chat. Ma and Da were sociable. That was the thing that always struck me about the Lawlors' place: nobody ever visited. The few who were brave enough to knock on the door were frozen out and discouraged from returning. There was always a fault found with them afterwards. They stayed too long, talked too much. It was part of the reason Frank was so outgoing, I thought. And part of the reason he'd gone for me maybe: he was desperate for a bit of life and gas. Say what you like but Frank and I had had a lot of craic over the years.

I closed the curtains. Night time was scary in the country, with bats dive-bombing you and strange noises and the feeling that eyes were looking at you from behind every weirdly shaped bush. There was something creepy about it. And you couldn't call for help, like you could in the city. There was nobody for miles to hear you.

I sank into a chair, bleary eyed. I was quite pissed. Not as pissed as Frank and some of the crowd at the funeral, but well on all the same. I felt shattered with the strain of pretending I was crying for Mam and not for myself. I'd rot in hell, I thought, propping my head on my hand.

My eyes watered. The room was dusty, and it had been tidied hastily. Things had been fired into the cupboard I'd opened. Not saying anything, but Mary wasn't the best of houskeepers. To be fair, she'd done more than her share of running around after Mam. Mam had made a big stink about moving in with them but once she'd got her feet under the table she'd treated poor Mary like a slave.

I was uptight when it came to cleaning. No matter how much help I had, I always ended up going over it myself. I sterilized my J-cloths every night – which said spades about my psyche, according to Ella. 'Jesus, Mum, would you ever do something else with your time?' she'd said to me one day, when she'd come across me dusting the frames of our paintings. 'You're always prowling around the house with an aerosol gun of detergent like it's your mission in life. You'll be out scrubbing the front step next,' she'd said, in a voice tinged with a scorn that I'd found hurtful.

Maybe all kids felt superior to their parents. Maybe it was in the nature of the beast. Maybe it was the job of kids to do that and parents not only expected it but wanted it in a funny

69

kind of way. When I was growing up I would definitely have said that I wanted to be different from mine. That I loved them but thought I had something that would carry me away from them and from where I'd grown up.

DJ and Mary owned a three-storey modern house with a portico, Ionic columns and more verandas and terraces than you could count. There were seven bedrooms and seven en-suite bathrooms with Japanese *shoji* sliding screens dividing each room. DJ's fixation with bathrooms and bidets might have had something to do with the outside latrine. They had a gym in the basement and a hot tub out the back next to a monster patio. There was also a 'Rapid River Pool' designed specifically for exercise, although I was pretty sure DJ couldn't swim, and by the look of Mary, she wasn't exactly killing herself pounding up and down it. Anyway, DJ and Mary had really gone for it. But, then, Frank had built the house for free.

I wondered if Mary was half blind. Even allowing for differences in taste, the décor was unbelievable: peach walls and a pinky sort of carpet. Actually, that was an insult to the visually impaired.

A gleam of moonlight poked through into the room so that the edge of Frank's face was highlighted. He was asleep on top of the bedspread, fully clothed, his hand drooping over the edge of the bed. He'd swayed upstairs and fallen down too tired to do anything bar shut his eyes. I had slipped his shoes off. A gentle snoring sound came from his slack mouth.

Earlier Frank and I had shared a moment. It had been towards the end of the night. The crowd had started to thin.

'Do you remember, Anita, bringing Mam here for dinner after we got engaged?'

I did. Mam had sat in the front seat of Frank's new car – a

red Honda that he was so beside himself about getting that we'd practically had to have our picture taken with it. Mam had a headscarf on that we had given her, tied under her chin with a small tense knot. I couldn't remember what we'd eaten. I think the waitress had offered us blue or black wine, meaning Blue Nun or Black Tower. Maybe I'd imagined that. Either way it was some sort of gut-rot altar wine, which we'd been thrilled with.

Mam's mouth had been screwed up like a ball of paper. I had caught her throwing savage glances at my belly, desperate to figure out if we had another announcement to make. I'd worked myself into a sweat trying to find things to say that might catch her interest. It had been an uphill struggle. Mam wasn't having any of it. You couldn't charm Mam. She was a harsh woman, born at a time when means were limited and grim lives full of struggle had led to grim people like her.

Anyway, earlier Frank had laid his hand on my arm. 'I was so proud of you,' he'd said, smiling at me. He'd been proud showing me off to his mother.

I'd tried to fake a smile but I'd started crying again and Frank had thought the tears were for Mam. 'You're a great girl, Anita,' he'd said. 'You've been a great wife and a great mother. And a great daughter-in-law,' he added expansively, which was over-egging it a bit, but I wasn't about to query him when he was on this sort of a complimentary roll.

We did have lots of mileage on the clock, I thought. You couldn't just dismantle a life like that. I compressed my lips, my eyes lighting on Frank's phone. It had slid from his pocket onto the floor. It was on the carpet, kind of calling out to me. Normally he guarded it as if it were the Crown Jewels – which, in light of recent developments, made sense.

I stood up and crossed the room. He was out for the count, I thought, bending down to retrieve the phone. It was still on. My heart started to pound. It was a massive invasion to read someone's text messages – like reading their post. I stood there for a while, clutching the phone, debating with myself. There were sounds downstairs. Mary: maybe clearing away the last of the things. We'd had a cup of tea when we'd come back. She'd opened a packet of biscuits.

'They're gone mad with the hospitality, cracking open a packet of biscuits,' Frank had whispered into my ear. I'd burst out laughing and it had been like old times. Frank was funny. He had what you call comic timing. There had been times over the years when I'd almost wet myself at some of his impressions.

In some ways it had been a nice day. I had been glad of Frank's words. But he had betrayed me. I went into the bathroom and closed the door behind me. Avoiding my reflection in the mirror and my guilty eyes, I turned on the tap to cover the beeping noise of the phone. First I scanned the received messages. This took a while. There were around five hundred in his inbox. Frank was always on the blower. There was nothing much, just business stuff. A few about golf. One or two dirty jokes from a fella he knew – a contractor from Limerick. I was a bit surprised by that: your man looked like butter wouldn't melt in his mouth.

Next I turned my attention to Frank's sent messages. My heart was racing as I scrolled down. Then it nearly stopped: *Women r oft late. Big deal. Stop stressing n it'll cum. x Frank.*

My knees buckled. Bile and wine rose up in my throat. The phone fell from my fingers. I bent over the loo, shuddering and twitching, as I puked my guts up.

4

Time had passed and nothing had happened. The issue of Little Miss Big Knockers was receding like a boat crossing a distant horizon. A boat, once large and dominating the view in the harbour, that was now a tiny speck. I could feel it in my waters.

She wasn't pregnant, after all. Frank had lost interest. The fright had brought them to their senses. You couldn't be expecting a baby with another woman and stand there at the island – a lump of extortionately expensive granite floating in the vast ocean that was our kitchen – as Frank had done earlier, and squeeze oranges with your family watching you. We were sitting around the table. We were the Waltons. It was an achievement just to have Frank there. Normally he was absent, or jumping up and down from the table taking calls, often shouting things down the phone like 'See you in court, pal.'

I had come to an uneasy accommodation with Frank's fling. I wasn't engaging in self-deception. Frank had made a mistake. His affair had been recreational, not serious. He had had a mid-life crisis. Okay, I'd have preferred him to buy an even faster car or to take up bungee jumping or something relatively benign to get his kicks but I could live with it. I could forgive him, I thought, as he smiled at something Ella was saying.

'A stiff dick has no conscience,' as Karen rather crudely put it – and Jesus said forgive your neighbour, even if he was your fecking stupid husband swinging it about so that he deserved to have it chopped off, like that Bobbitt eejit in America.

Not that I was a member of the God Squad. I was never that gone on religion. When I was small I went through a pious phase of being devoted to the Virgin Mary, or Holy Mary as I had called her, because I was cast as her in our Nativity play. I sort of got my head turned. Next thing you knew I was erecting May-day altars in my bedroom.

'Oh, for feck's sake,' Karen had said, watching me put a jam-jar of flowers on a piece of grubby lace, 'you're not right in the head.'

During that time I had loved going to Mass with Ma, skipping down to the church beside her, Ma with her good headscarf knotted under her chin, me carrying her missal with the navy leather cover. Really, I got off on the melodrama. It was nothing to do with spirituality: it was about being girlishly pure and good – and a big lick-arse, as Karen would have pointed out. And I'd loved the iconography and the incense and the singing. Karen had only gone when the priest from the Missions came. The word would go round that he'd give a bit of a sex talk and the place would be packed to the rafters.

Now we were eating breakfast in the kitchen, like four ants in a football stadium. Frank was tired. He'd been on *Morning Ireland*, one of Ireland's most listened-to radio programmes, giving his view on the state of the economy and how his development was NOT in jeopardy. He'd sounded animated and confident, his voice manly and fearless, that of a thrusting alpha male.

He had been invited on because people had an interest in him – the size of the development he was doing, the sky-high price he'd paid for the land and the fact he'd bought it without having got his planning permission. And because, of course, he'd put himself about as a poster boy of the Celtic Tiger. He'd had his architect on the show with him – his 'starchitect'. He was an emaciated little English fella called Russell Bernard Owen who wore a uniform of distressed denims that had no doubt cost a fortune, with skinny-rib black polo-necks and the heavy rectangular glasses that seemed to be the face furniture of choice for big-shot architects like him. When they were together, he and Frank looked like a cartoon. Frank robust, red-faced and thick-necked, Russell Bernard Owen pale and reedy.

Russell Bernard Owen spoke in halting sentences, often leaving large gaps in the middle so that you expected him to come out with something great. This never materialized. He talked a lot about the 'autonomy' of buildings and about 'the feel' and 'touch' and 'soul' of things in a flat low monotone that forced you to lean in to hear him. Half the time I had no idea what he was jawing on about. Frank thought he was the man, though.

I had tried to persuade Frank to use an Irish architect. But he was having none of it. 'I want some international fella, some major big shit who's going to blow people's socks off. This will be *my legacy*, Anita.'

Frank was all about his legacy now. In the early years of our marriage he'd thrown up God-awful egg-box houses all round the outskirts of Dublin in which you could hear people breathing in the next room. Now he was all Le Corbusier this and Daniel Libeskind that and *my legacy*.

Russell Bernard Owen for his part talked about the need for 'private architectural patrons' like Frank. He said that for great iconic buildings to be built – and here he generally mentioned the Parthenon – men like Frank, 'forward-thinking visionary leaders', were required to take a risk on behalf of future generations. This, of course, had Frank's arse levitating off the seat with pride and his cheque book – or the bank's, depending on how you looked on it – wide open. It showed, I thought, that despite his vague, theoretical, artistic language there were no flies on old Russell.

When it came to artists – and Russell Bernard Owen was a very great artist, according to Frank – Frank seemed to lose his inbuilt bullshit detector. A sort of innocence seemed to take over this hard-nosed man from the bogs of Offaly. He thought artists were dreamy and from another realm. I thought Russell Bernard Owen was a ruthless little so-and-so who could have floated over from England on the hot air of his monumental ego – but there was no telling Frank.

So Russell Bernard Owen had puffed up Frank on the radio and talked about 'the philanthropy of building soaring towers and memorials', and Frank had been more than happy to run with the ball: 'We want to construct a landmark development that is iconic and global but retains local distinctiveness, a development for the citizens of Wexford and for their future descendants and for all of Ireland.' There was no doubt that those boys were all hopped on pride and testosterone and, of course, no small amount of bullshit.

I'd rung Frank after the interview. 'You did well, love.'

'Thanks.'

I knew that voice. It meant he was busy and to stop bothering him. I bit my lip. I had been working up to asking him a particular question for some time. 'Will the bank pull the plug on you, Frank?' This was a question the presenter had asked him. There had been a fraction of a hesitation, which had made my heart turn over, before he had peddled her some upbeat keep-the-flag-flying schtick.

On the phone to me he had sounded weary. 'No,' he had said. 'How many times do I have to tell you? They can't. It's like this, Anita. If you owe the bank a mid-sized amount it's

76

your problem. If you owe them the amount I owe, it's their problem. The bank has put in capital. Appointing a receiver is expensive and a pain in the hole. They'll play along with me but they won't be wiping my arse for me any more, that's for sure.'

'Come home, Frank, you sound tired. We're having breakfast for Ella.'

So, as the good, forgiving little wife I was, I'd dickied myself up, despite the early hour, put my hair into soft waves, worn a slinky jersey camel dress, doused myself in perfume and teetered around the kitchen in my toweringly high shoes – Maeve called them 'knock me over fuck mes' – with an apron tied around my waist.

I won't lie. I'd already had a glass of orange and champagne to get me in the forgiving mood. I'd stopped at that because Ella was going to the States and I was driving her to the airport. Then I'd baked some scones, which was a major stretch for me. I didn't cook much, which was ironic, given my kitchen with its glittering stainless-steel German appliances and giant silent fridge the size of a morgue. Plus it was the last thing I needed, given that I was committed to a bloody charity lunch later in the day that Ciara had roped me into. There was no way I was getting out of it because I was bringing the auction prizes. I'd pushed the boat out because my baby girl was leaving me and I wanted to make sure her send-off was a good one.

The scones hadn't turned out too badly, which was a surprise. I had been a complete dunce at home economics. The teacher had told me to sling my hook after the first year when the topic of subject options came up. And I wasn't sorry. My piece of material for sewing always got sweaty and grubby between my clumsy fingers. My buns never rose, only slumped to one side like the Leaning Tower of Pisa. She was

77

always very sarcastic with me. Then one day in class she'd gone too far.

'You'd know a *good* family by the state of their tea-towels,' she'd said, looking directly at me, her long, skinny face flushed. She'd been holding up my tea-towel. It was dirty because I'd spilt something on it in class. It had been spotless when Ma, the cleanest woman in the world, had given it to me.

I wasn't having her casting aspersions on the Butlers and certainly not on Ma. So I'd challenged her – spunky little bitch that I was back then – asking her if she was referring to me. She'd gone mental, shouting and screaming. She suffered from her nerves and started quivering like the strings on a violin whenever she got her knickers in a knot. Not long after that we'd agreed to part company, and I'd done art instead, even though I was lousy at drawing.

Not that I was overly exercised. Back then I was Miss Outstanding Performance in Mathematics. One of my reports had actually said something like 'She consistently produces outstanding performances in mathematics.' I had skipped around the place chanting it in my head like a mantra. *Outstanding. Outstanding. Outstanding.*

Anyway, that was far back in the mists of time. Now I was just happy that my husband hadn't run off with a girl young enough to be his daughter.

'Another scone, Dylan?' I asked, catching him mouthing something at Ella. I wondered how many times I'd used the word 'scone'. I was bandying it about like nobody's business, the subtext being, 'Do you see, Frank, what a wonderful homemaker your wife is? What a great little scone-baking treasure you have on your hands?'

'Nah,' Dylan said, waving a hand. 'I've got to rock 'n' roll soon. I'm meeting Biba.'

I should have known. He was dressed up to the nines, the

hair gelled. Frank went mental when he saw Dylan's products in his bathroom. 'Is he a fairy or what?'

Frank came from a different time when real men didn't use moisturizer and they certainly weren't tanned and smooth like Dylan. But Dylan had always been into clothes. There had been the sporty stage when he wouldn't wear anything unless it was nylon with a big sports logo. He hadn't been into playing sports, which had incensed Frank. It had been more about the look.

Then had come his 'homie' stage when he wore outsized rapper jeans down around his arse so that you could see his underpants. This had been a bad look for Dylan given that he was short. He had looked like he was swaddled, and like his clothes were wearing him. After that had come his I'm-in-the-band/with-the-band interlude when he wore T-shirts with the names of obscure musicians on them and his room perpetually smelt of dope and stale cigarettes. Which was why I didn't mind the latest incarnation, which involved expensive designer trainers and ultra-tight T-shirts, chosen specifically to showcase the muscles he'd spent long hours acquiring in the gym. Anything to kiss the bong and weed stage goodbye. I couldn't stand seeing him sitting around like a vegetable wolfing pizzas and anything else he could shove down his throat because he had 'the munchies'.

Dylan spent any free time he had with Biba. He stayed most nights in her flat in Castleknock on the north side of the city. Or else I'd get a flash of her blonde head darting down the black granite path to the coach house. They seemed to go out all the time if the media coverage they got was anything to go by. A picture of them at this opening, at that party, in a nightclub owned by Dylan's friend Jamie Deegan. How Dylan managed to get up for work in the morning I didn't know.

I looked at him and tried to suppress my annoyance. 'Your sister is going away for the summer, Dylan, so we're having a family meal. Can you not hang on for another hour?'

'Christopher's mother makes her own granola,' Ella chipped in.

We heard a lot about Christopher and his family, their likes and dislikes, the way they went to the theatre, the opera in Wexford, subscribed to the *New York Review of Books*, Christopher's taste for South American writers and vegetarian food, the fact Christopher's mother was 'a voracious reader' ... 'For fuck's sake, I haven't even met them and I know what Jesus brand of bog-roll they use,' Frank had hissed at me one night. It was called 'mentionitis'. Hard and all as it was to believe now, I'd once had a bad dose of it where Frank was concerned.

Actually, I was pretty fed up of hearing about them myself.

'Christopher said it's common to have your house too clean,' Ella remarked one day.

I had heard myself say sourly, 'You should be well in there so, given the state of your room.'

Ella's room was like a cess pit, heaps of clothes on the floor, half-eaten bowls of cereal, abandoned cups of tea, cotton buds dipped in cleanser and makeup on her dressing table. If Ma could have seen her granddaughter's room she would have had a stroke.

Now Dylan was using a finger to push up the end of his nose. 'That sounds spiffing.'

'Get lost,' Ella said, but her face creased with laughter. Ella and Dylan still got on great.

Then Dylan fixed eyes with me. 'Ella doesn't care if I split,' he said. 'She's only going for the summer. It's not like she's emigrating or anything.'

Ella was going to New York to intern with an organization

that worked for prisoners' rights. It was part of an Irish-American programme. She was one of ten gifted students chosen on account of the high marks she'd been awarded in her exams. 'I hope this doesn't mean she ends up defending a bunch of no-hopers for fuck-all money,' Frank had said to me privately. 'Corporate law is where the real dough is – the dogs on the street know that.' Secretly he was proud as Punch.

Christopher was going too. He was going to work in a judge's office. His father had arranged it. He hadn't been picked for the programme. And for all his supposed clever-ness he hadn't done as well as Ella in the exams.

'He's really super-bright, Mum,' Ella had insisted, when I'd asked. She got this defensive look when she spoke about him, as if she sensed I was trying to undermine him, which I probably was. 'He just sort of bombed in company law. He didn't get the mark he deserved. It was because he didn't see eye to eye with the lecturer. It was so unfair. He was penal-ized for having strong views.'

Oh, yeah, right, I'd thought. It was the lecturer's fault. I tried not to think mean things about Christopher, but there was something kind of controlling and cold about him. Ella had told me he'd put a *fatwah* on them texting each other too much because he felt it 'interfered' with his studies. Fat lot of good that seemed to have done him, I'd thought, enjoying feeling mean-spirited. But it was when I saw her looking into his eyes as if he was God handing down the Ten Command-ments that I wanted to scream. I wanted to say to her that men were great but they had a way of sidetracking you, of swallowing you. I wanted to say to her that in my darker moments I felt marriage and love meant the death of female ambition. I wanted to tell her that I and the whole world had drip-fed her romance since she was a small girl. I had read her stories about Snow White, Cinderella and Sleeping Beauty, all nice, passive girls who were rescued for being pretty and not much else. I wanted to say that, yes, I had watched *Pride and Prejudice* with her and gone all gooey-eyed over Mr Darcy coming out of the lake looking wet and masterful – but that at some point Mr Darcy would get sick of Elizabeth's 'fine eyes' and want his dinner on the table and his clothes washed.

'I don't mind if Dylan has to go, Mum,' Ella was saying, with one of her little shrugs.

'I mind,' I said, trying to catch Frank's eye but he was staring into the middle distance.

Dylan propped his head in his palm and sighed.

'Glass of Buck's Fizz, Frank?' I asked.

'No, thanks,' Frank said.

'Our daughter is going to America.'

'I've got to do some work,' came the flat response.

As I topped up my own glass – another tiny bit wouldn't put me over the limit – I saw Ella frowning at me. 'Are you not driving me to the airport?'

'Yes,' I said, my smile not slipping. 'A wee dram of Buck's Fizz won't hurt.' Silence. I decided to ignore the fact that my children were trading glances. 'I can't believe you're going to America to work with real lawyers, Ella,' I said, allowing myself to feel a glow of pride.

'You've done very well,' Frank chipped in, 'thanks to your hard work at your studies.' He threw Dylan a look in which I recognized the signs of potential strife. Frank persisted in comparing the children.

'He's different from her, Frank,' I would say to him. 'He has other talents.'

'A talent for sitting on his arse,' Frank would respond, with a sarcastic grunt.

Ella had always been focused. At four she would snap on her goggles and swim down the pool straight as an arrow.

Dylan would weave and bob and chat until the teacher gave out to him. She set herself goals and chased them down. He was more fluid in the way he approached things. That was how I saw it.

He was brilliant at art. His teacher had wanted him to go to art college. He had been a sensitive-looking man with glasses and a soft voice, which didn't impress Frank. 'He has real talent,' the art teacher had said to us, 'but he might have to do a portfolio course first. I'm not sure if he'd get straight into NCAD. He could, though, if he focused.'

Frank, with his enlightened views on masculinity, had been dead set against it. He had sat there with his big thick neck going redder, a vein twitching on the side of his temple, and I'd been petrified he'd let us both down and say something completely insulting. Thankfully, he'd saved his ire for me. 'Is that fella on drugs or what?' he'd said, when we'd walked back to our car. 'Is that what I pay private-school fees for? Art college is for shirt-lifters.'

Frank had an unreconstructed attitude to sexuality. If a man ordered a latte or wore a hat and gloves he got suspicious as to his orientation. There was also the fact – and he wouldn't have admitted this under pain of death – that he had been harbouring the hope that Dylan might follow him into the business, but even as a young fella Dylan had hated going out on site. Frank had bought him a little yellow hard hat and a box of pretend tools, but anyone with a pair of eyes could see that he had no interest. He'd far prefer to sit up at the table and draw buildings.

If that wasn't a runner, Frank was all in favour of medicine. 'It'd be perfect for you, Dylan. You're a people person. You'd have a great bedside manner.'

Dylan would give a lazy roll of the shoulder – the type he specialized in, which made Frank violent. 'Nah, Dad, I wouldn't get the points in a fit and I'm not into that whole saving-lives thing. That's just not how I roll.'

'You think that lot are into saving lives?' Frank would splutter. 'My hole. Look at Will – there's savage money to be made in fannies. If I'm ever reincarnated I want to come back as an obstetrician. Or an orthodontist,' he'd add, as an afterthought. 'There's serious moolah in mouths too. Those bunch of fuckers are daylight Dick Turpin robbers.'

There had been lots of fruitless conversations like that.

Dylan had said very little about art college after Frank had rubbished it. Big surprise there. And I hadn't said enough. I'd let it slide. After he'd left school Dylan had had lots of ideas about what he was going to do, some of them half-arsed business enterprises, fuelled probably by the frenzied sense of can-do that the Celtic Tiger economy created, that seemed to involve maximum glamour and minimum work. He'd been in a band called Dead End for a while. He'd seen no irony in the name, even though Ella had made plenty of attempts to point it out, and Frank had said, 'That would be about right,' when he was told. We'd paid a fortune for a drum kit and a guitar, and they'd practised in the coach house, attracting plenty of complaints from the neighbours and their cats. The boy who had been lead singer had sounded like he was being tortured. They'd never actually played a paying gig.

Then Dylan had decided to go travelling, which had ended in a monumental piss-up in Australia.

There was this push and shove between Frank and Dylan as they sparred. Dylan often set out to bait his father, yet he wanted his blessing. Deep down he wanted Frank's attention – look at me, Dad, look at me. That was what the job in stockbroking had been about. Dylan battled so hard for his approval yet Frank was blind to it. Frank wanted him to go to college and do something Frank wanted him to do, or to take over the business.

Sometimes parents envisaged their kids busting down the doors of worlds they'd never gained access to, like me with Ella studying law in Trinity. In other cases, the parent, like Frank, hoped that the child would be a chip off the old block and carry on their work. But there was a tipping point when your dreams became a burden to your children.

'It's just an internship, Mum,' Ella called over to me, in support of her brother.

'If Nana May could see you . . .' I said dreamily. 'Or Nana Kathleen,' I added hurriedly, before Frank could think I was casting aspersions.

Frank's mam would have listened to the news with her lips disappearing off her face. Then she would have dredged up some story about another young person she knew who had had the chance to ride shotgun with the President of the United States for the summer.

My ma would have been gob-smacked at the idea of her granddaughter studying law in Trinity College, never mind going to the States on an internship. Ma had cleaned houses, including for a big-shot judge who lived on Merrion Square. I had gone there once with her to collect her pay. It had been Christmas. We'd stood outside on the step waiting for the woman of the house to come out. It had been a big black door with a brass knocker and a Georgian fanlight.

The judge's wife was very posh with a cashmere sweater and pearls, but she'd been nice. She'd given me sweets and asked Ma in for a glass of sherry on account of it being Christmas Eve. Ma had gone pink and said no. She'd been thrilled to be asked but she was way too shy. Ma knew her place. There was no social mobility back then.

'Do you ever think you might become a judge?' I'd asked

Ella one day, just after she'd started law and I'd got a bit carried away imagining her in a wig and gown, saying in a stern Ella voice, 'Take him down,' which she would be very good at in my opinion.

She'd considered the question briefly before flicking her hair airily and saying, 'Maybe.' She had said it like it was no big deal that May Butler's granddaughter might be a judge.

Ella and Dylan's generation was so confident. They were praised all the time. They were winners. They had American-style confidence. They were all told they were great. Even if they came last in a race they got a medal. They were encouraged to talk about themselves and give their views. It was a different approach from when we were growing up. We had been afraid of our shadows. We had been told it was a sin to focus on ourselves. Ella and Dylan asked questions all the time – whatever came into their heads – while we had been told that asking questions was rude.

'So . . . *New York*,' I said to Ella, sipping my Buck's Fizz. I felt very emotional at the thought of letting her go, but I wasn't going to show it. I started humming 'New York, New York' Liza Minnelli-style, and clicking my fingers. Da da da da da.

Ella gave me a polite smile. She looked strained. Her guarded look had returned. When she was small she couldn't get enough of me. She copied the way I dressed, sitting up at my dressing-table, smearing makeup on her face, walking around after me in my high heels. When Frank and I were going out she would lie on my bed and watch me. 'You're very pretty, Mummy,' she would say. 'I want to be like you when I grow up.'

She'd got over that.

'God, Mum, isn't that dress a bit young for you?' she'd said earlier, casting her eye over me, her mouth pursed. I tried not to let it get to me. It was a teenage thing to think that you had invented the wheel, to be savage and conservative while thinking yourself radical.

But it rankled that there was no criticism for Frank about how he looked. Frank who had taken to wearing aviators and drove a red, phallic, mid-life-crisis car. Jesus, was I slow or what? How had I not seen the signs that something was up? Frank, who would have driven his car up the stairs to bed if he could have got away with it, had taken up jogging. I had watched him sweat his way down Shrewsbury Road – his softened body encased in nylon so that it looked like a German sausage – and not suspected a thing. I'd seen him do push-ups in the bedroom, gazing at his side profile in the mirror, tilting his head back and sucking in his belly, making a yeah-I've-still-got-it snuffling noise through his nostrils. And I'd never suspected a thing.

I watched Ella help herself to mixed berries. She was on the brink of having sex. I knew that lots of girls were sexually active much younger now. I'd been expecting it for years. But it hadn't happened. I just knew Ella hadn't. She was so knowing and worldly-wise sometimes that it shocked me. And in other ways she was innocent and unsullied. She was beautiful and serious and thoughtful. Christopher was her first real boyfriend.

I'd seen a nuzzle mark on her chest. I'd seen it when she'd stepped out of the shower wrapped in a towel. I'd sent her off to get the pill.

She'd gone scarlet. 'Oh, my God, Mum,' she'd said, crinkling her nose in disgust. 'That is *soooo* my private business.' She'd turned away from me. 'I know all that stuff from school.'

Frank would have a fit even now if he thought she was having sex. When he looked at her he saw a small girl with pigtails. One time he'd picked up one of her teen mags and started leafing through it until he'd come across tips for giving a great blow-job. He'd nearly had a seizure. Of course he'd blamed me. 'Jesus almighty, Anita,' he'd roared, as if I'd personally written the article. 'There are tips here for going down on a fella.'

Frank was very unrealistic about these things. He wanted her dancing at the crossroads like de Valera's maidens. He didn't know that she was going to America with Christopher. He thought she was heading off with a group of girls. Ella and I had agreed not to enlighten him. 'Dad has enough pressures at the moment,' I'd explained to her.

Like the possibility of having another family. Ella would have gone postal if I'd told her that. Daddy's girl.

'A chip off the old block,' Frank liked to say.

They were alike. She was her father's daughter with the same drive and determination. Dylan was like me. He needed to fill silences in a conversation. Ella and Frank could stay quiet and only speak when it suited them.

I should have let Ella loose on Little Miss Big Knockers. That would teach her. I had rung her a few nights before. Frank had been off playing golf with some buddies. I'd had a few. The kids were out. The phone had been clammy in my hand. My heart had been pounding. And I'd drunk-dialled.

Her voice had been like a punch in the stomach. 'Hello . . . Hello. Who's this? Hello?'

In the airport, the strip neon lights cast a jaundiced glow on our skins. I had a rictus grin stretched across my face like the Joker. Ella had warned me in the car, 'Do not make a big deal out of saying goodbye, Mum. I'm only going for the summer.'

I had gone into her room the night before. *Tucking in*, we'd called it, when she'd been little. She used to make a big production of it, insisting on all her teddies being kissed goodnight and the room being checked for spiders before she folded away her book. Ella always read until the last minute. Not Dylan. At bedtime Dylan had usually been bouncing on his bed. He would be half naked, zinging up and down, his chubby cheeks pink and shiny, until you had to bawl at him to get under the covers.

Ella was definitely a little nervous about going away. She had let me straighten the sheets and kiss her goodnight. I had badly wanted to climb in next to her and breathe in the scent of her freshly washed hair. But that would have been pushing my luck.

There was a knot in my stomach before I'd even abandoned the Range Rover in the short-term car park. A spool of images kept running through my head – a young Ella with a gap between her teeth grinning up at me; Ella in her school uniform at the Young Scientists' exhibition; Ella going to her first disco with a mouthful of metal; Ella standing on the stage at school being awarded a prize for the best Leaving Cert, with Frank's flash going off.

Christopher's parents were fine. I had talked too much, though, waggling my hands and burbling on at them, over-effusive. Inside I felt like I was crumbling. Ella and Christopher were almost checked in. My throat was tightening. The check-in assistant with the smiley eyes was handing Ella back her travel documents, her long red talons curled around them. Oh, Jesus, an ominous lump was forming in my throat. Ella's bags were being ferried away on the belt.

Frank hadn't come to the airport, much to our relief, given that we were keeping up the Ella-heading-off-with-girlfriends fiction, and he'd been too preoccupied to delve for details. He'd kissed Ella on the top of her head, his eyes misting over as he let her go when his lawyer Eamon had picked him up.

I had tracked him across the hall out the door. ''Bye Frank,' I had said, in an overly upbeat bright voice.

'Thanks for breakfast,' he had said, turning briefly. 'The scones were lovely,' he added gruffly.

Frank could surprise you like that. 'That was nice,' was what he usually said after a meal. Okay, he wasn't inventive with the compliments but he was no wordsmith. And he had seemed to mean it. He wasn't false. He had always been quick to put Mam in her box if she tried to undermine me, telling her how great I was.

'You're welcome, Frank,' I had said.

'I'll be back late tonight.'

Right. That comment had ripped the top off the well of neediness, insecurity and loneliness that was threatening to engulf me. 'Do you love me, Frank?' I blurted, as he walked towards the waiting car.

He stopped. Allowing his shoulders to drop, he gave a theatrical sigh before pivoting to face me. 'I don't have time for this, Anita,' he said, as if he were humouring a child.

My bottom lip quivered a little – although I was angry at his patronizing tone.

'Do you love me, Frank?' I asked again, the tears backing up behind my eyes.

Anyone who has to ask this question of their partner should know that the answer will not be good. I hadn't planned on asking it. This was bad timing. The moment was not about me. It was Ella's milestone, but it felt like mine too. Ella's leaving seemed connected to Frank's betrayal, to the end of an era.

He blew out his cheeks. Venomously, I decided he looked like a red-faced chipmunk. 'You may have all the fucking time in the world but I've a business to run,' he had added. Momentarily I hated him. 'That's how I pay for this house and the holidays and the clothes . . .'

The rest had been lost as I blinked back angry tears. I'd heard it a million times before anyway. It was the Great Provider Speech. The one that meant that you had no right to ask what you were asking, to complain, to make any further demands because of the life he had bestowed on you. 'You should be grateful, girl,' was the subtext. Not even the subtext actually: it was when his gratitude for all the dinners, child-minding and general support melted away.

He strode towards Eamon, who was waving at me. I wanted to hurl abuse after him. *We had a deal, arsehole, and I've kept my end up.*

There had been a deal. True, it was not written down. But there had been a deal. I would stay at home and rear the kids; Frank would go out and bring home the bacon. Frank had encouraged me to stop doing the books for his company after Dylan was born. He had been resistant to me working, partly because it was a status thing to have the missus at home – it showed the whole world you didn't need the second salary – and partly because he had wanted the children to 'have a good start'.

And I had gone along with it. I'd wanted to be there for the children. I was happy at home when they were small, even when we didn't have much money. And, yeah, when Frank started to make a few quid I liked being a yummy mummy, gliding along in my fancy car, done up to the nines, unloading my shopping, with my beautiful kids in the back.

Then it had seemed as if those times would never end. As if I would always be needed to help with a project on Germany or to drive somebody to their football lesson or to put together a costume for the Christmas play. And at the back of my mind I told myself that when the children got that bit bigger I would go to college. But time had gone on and the day had never come, and here I was in the airport waving my baby off to America for the summer with her boyfriend. *Her lover* – although it was hard to imagine Christopher, with his thin limbs and skinny jeans and protruding Adam's apple, cast in the role of the great seducer.

Ella was saying something to Christopher's mother now. She hadn't wanted me to bring her to the airport. 'I can get a lift with Christopher's parents,' she had said, *faux*-casual.

'Of course I'm bringing you.'

'It's no big deal, Mum,' she had said.

There had been a pregnant silence.

'You don't have to get all dressed up or anything. It's just going to the airport. And Christopher's parents aren't really like that.'

Like what? I'd wanted to ask, turning away from her so that she wouldn't see my face. What was the latest way I'd failed to live up to her expectations? And I wouldn't mind but Christopher's father, the judge, looked like something you'd mount on the wall. His head was huge. He had bushy eyebrows that nearly met in the middle and a bulbous nose. The mother was a large, outdoorsy woman with widely spaced eyes and a nice expression. Ella had said she was big into her golf. She was a generous size fourteen, maybe a sixteen down below. And, not saying anything, she wasn't very well put together. She even had a smear of lipstick on her snaggle tooth. It had been hard to see where they'd got Christopher from, a fact I had taken it upon myself to comment on.

'I don't know who Christopher takes after,' I had said, looking at him in his T-shirt with its '*Green* is the New Black' slogan. 'His colouring is so different.' When I got nervous I couldn't stop talking. Manic small-talk flew from my mouth. 'No, I just can't see the resemblance,' I had said, and went on and on, like an out-of-control train, until Ella had guided me away on some pretext. She had hissed at me, her fingers pressing into my arm, 'Mu-um, Christopher is adopted.'

I was mortified so I was. I clammed up then. I went from verbal diarrhoea to dumb silence.

The judge seemed a bit on the bossy side, writing the luggage labels for Christopher and generally telling everyone what to do, which I suppose was to be expected. He was from the class and generation of male that presumed it was in charge of everything. I could see Ella darting sidelong glances at him. She definitely wasn't used to being told what to do. Frank, for all his talk of *birds*, wasn't in practice that sexist. He thought that women could do anything men could do and probably better. 'They're harder-working and more focused,' he often said. 'You can get a better pound of flesh from them.'

Nobody could have accused Frank of not being pragmatic.

'A lick-arse of the first order, is what I heard,' Frank had said about the judge. 'He brown-nosed the Taoiseach something awful to get that judicial appointment.'

People in glass houses. Frank had had his lips permanently and surgically attached to the last Taoiseach's backside. He was devastated when the man was ousted from office.

Christopher's mother was holding it together, no problem. She was not a woman to lose her composure. Nor was she a woman who went in for cosmetic procedures. Her forehead had deep grooves in it. She was nice, though, very sympathetic. 'New York seems so far away,' she said, seeing my eyes water.

We were standing at the barrier to Passport Control. Ella and Christopher were saying their last goodbyes. I bit the inside of my cheek, trying to think of happy things. There were none. The tears spilt over.

The judge was issuing last-minute instructions. 'You can't bring water through,' he said to Ella, so she tilted her bottle to her mouth and started to gulp it back.

The tears were coursing down my face now. Ella looked away, embarrassed, as I delved in my bag for a tissue. She gave me a quick hug and a peck on the cheek. She raised her hand, her smile tight. ''Bye, Mum. I'll ring you.'

I nodded, unable to speak. I was starting to make strangled sounds, as I attempted to quell my sobs. Jesus, I thought. Get a grip, Mary of the Sorrows. I was acting like it was an American wake. The judge was looking at me out of the corner of his eye, as if I needed to be committed.

An older couple moved around me, casting me curious looks. A small girl dressed all in Barbie pink picked her nose and walked backwards staring at me so that her mother, a young woman with a slab of veiny white marbled flesh hanging over the waistband of her jeans, was forced to come back to retrieve her.

Through my blurred vision I saw Ella walking quickly away, and a terrible incommunicable grief welled up inside me. If she didn't go, nothing bad would happen. I felt that. And yet I wanted her to live the fabulous life she was going to have, the life I'd been planning for her. It was me who had taught her the alphabet and her numbers. She'd been like a little sponge. It was me who had fantasized about the exciting things she would do when I launched her into the world. The possibilities for her seemed endless. She could go anywhere and be anything on her terms. She would not make my mistakes. She would not end up like me, I thought, as the back of her head disappeared from view.

The rain was coming down in sheets. The man on the radio talked about low pressures and anticyclones and 'exceptionally heavy falls'. He said it was the wettest summer since records began.

I cried all the way home, manoeuvring my jeep through the sprawling traffic. Past the long row of small terraced houses in the northside suburbs of Dublin. The small slightly shabby shops, the takeaways and off-licences – *Booze to go* – and Internet cafés where you could phone home on the other side of the world at knock-down rates, and motorbike shops and tattoo parlours and television shops and furniture shops and foreign-sounding huckster shops, a money shop – *Cheques cashed on the spot* – and pubs with cheap plywood fronts and shabby paint jobs. Back over the river Liffey and towards home, where the houses became steadily bigger, the shops more upmarket, the restaurants more plentiful. The rain bubbled up through the gutters, running down the road in giant streams.

I was going to be incredibly late for the lunch. Ordinarily on a day like this – with so much to pack in – my heart would have been racing and I would have been making frantic calculations as to how I was going to get everything done. But now I didn't care. I just cried and cried. It was as if once the lid had come off I couldn't get it back on.

'Are you sure you're okay?' the judge's wife had asked, as we turned to leave the airport. 'I don't like to leave you like this. Can we call your husband?'

No, I had wanted to howl at her. *We'd probably interrupt him humping some young one.*

I was still crying a little when I got home. Ella would kill me for having made a show of myself. But how could I explain to her? How could I say to her that as she walked away I'd been struck by the emptiness of my life? I walked down the black gravel path that wound through the land-scaped gardens to the coach house on the off-chance that

Dylan was there. He had come and gone, leaving puddles of towels dumped on the floor. His bathroom was like something out of a top-flight spa. 'What did your last slave die of of?' I'd say to him sometimes.

'Happiness,' he'd shoot back, with a lopsided grin so that I couldn't stay mad.

He'd left the shower running. Dylan was careless about things like that. Ella wasn't much better, in spite of all her stated environmental credentials and her haranguing of Frank to introduce green building technologies into his business. They were part of the power-shower generation, I thought, switching it off. Frank and I were of the generation that got up early to put on the immersion heater so that we could have a lukewarm wash on the way out. My family had had weekly baths. The rest of the time Ma had given us what she called a 'cat's lick'. The kids told me to shut up when I told them stuff like that. I'm not sure they really believed me. They thought thrift was freakish. 'Yeah, right, Mum, and I suppose you walked to school in your bare feet.'

I was back in the house now – in the hall – sitting on the bottom stair. I knew I should move, but I just couldn't. The staircase behind me curved upwards towards the first floor. Light came through the big square skylight so that the oak panelling of the hall and the four giant Andy Warhol-style pictures of me were illuminated. There were other paintings – too many for the walls, bunched together as if we couldn't bear not to display our vast collection.

Frank bought art by the yard. So while he was bolshy in his declarations about knowing what he liked, he had a childlike reverence for artists and bought the expertise to help him choose paintings. That admiration was coupled with scorn for those who purported to know about art. We'd once gone to an art exhibition with Ciara and Will. This was the first time either Frank or I had ever heard of the artist even though Ciara, who'd done some history of art courses, had told us that, while not Warhol, he was 'the godfather of pop art'. Will had stood at a distance staring at a painting for a very long time before moving slowly forward and nosing right up against it as if analysing every daub. Frank had wanted to hit him over the head with a bag of hammers.

Frank was solution-driven. He knew he was locked out of a world he didn't know how to navigate. He didn't have the language and it was too late to learn, so he was going to conquer the terrain by owning more damn art than anyone else. He was a dealer's delight. They saw him coming.

I sat dumbly on the stair, contemplating a move into the kitchen. I didn't want to sit in the kitchen, my shrine to modern technology. I'd be swallowed by its vastness, by the silence hanging inside its stainless-steel perimeter. There was no life, no action there.

When the children were smaller the kitchen had been the nerve centre of the house, especially in the morning when it had been mental. The kitchen in our second house had been small with cheap modern presses and a breakfast bar because it was too small for a full-sized table. The counter would be covered with crumbs, blobs of butter and jam and bowls of sodden cereal. Questions had been constantly fired at me of the 'Where's my gum shield/maths copy/library book?' variety. Frank would have been going on about something or other. 'Just sort it out, Anita,' he'd say, if the kids started fighting. Then I'd usher them out to the car with orders to tie their laces, zip up their coats, promising to pick up this and drop back that, beeping the horn for Dylan, who would have run back into the house for something. A little later I'd have that moment of semi-relief when I, like the droves of other mothers, sprinted away from the school free as a bird for a couple of hours. There had been order and happiness and security in that morning chaos, I thought now.

The distant hum of the vacuum-cleaner came from the top of the house. Lena was upstairs. She was nice, Lena, in a matter-of-fact Polish way. She didn't speak much English, which was unusual for a Polish girl. We communicated in our own way and sometimes we even had a cup of tea together, although that seemed to make her a little uncomfortable. I wondered what she thought of us – a spoilt bunch of lazy so-and-sos who couldn't lift a teacup for ourselves.

I wasn't always spoilt. I had done my own cleaning and mended my clothes and made do. I had saved for things. I could hear the crunch of gravel as footsteps approached. Crouton started to bark. I had left the gates open. There were footsteps and then some junk leaflets fluttered through the door. They were for an Indian restaurant with Chinese sounding dishes. Through the mullioned window by the door I could see a Chinese man retreating. We'd had a meal from them – I'd rung before I thought. They were a Chinese restaurant trying to branch into Indian. The food had tasted weird.

This hall was as big as some people's whole apartments. The house was a shrine to Frank's success. I was proud of it, really. I didn't go along with that the-poor-are-happy routine, which some people – usually people with plenty – promoted. The poor and the meek did not inherit the earth. There had been plenty of proof of that in my neighbourhood.

Our local parish priest used to go on with that old codswallop while his soft, buttery bum spilt over the sides of his big, comfortable car seat. And he had a big parochial house and grand dinners. There were times, though, when I caught myself wondering if we'd got lost in our house, if we'd been drowned by its sheer grandeur and sense of expensively purchased isolation.

I stared at my handbag, slouching on the ground like a small snoozing animal. It was hand-sewn Italian calfskin and had cost a sinful amount. I had seen it in a magazine and tracked it ruthlessly, like a lioness stalking her prey, getting my mitts on it ahead of the posse so that I could produce it with quiet up-your-bum glee. It had seemed such a triumph, such a coup.

I wondered what time Frank would come back. I had considered going to him and telling him I knew about your woman but that it was okay. We could move past her. We were bigger and stronger than that. We could have counselling and get the old Frank and Anita back. With a bit of work and effort we'd be back in the new-couple stage, when we were in love with each other and ourselves. Back when the possibility of romance and greatness seemed to lurk around every corner, when I'd looked in the mirror and thought that the world was created for the two of us.

My mobile phone began to ring, its sound muffled by the leather of the bag. It would be Ciara, wondering where I was. She had left successive messages.

'Ring me.'

'Call me, babe.'

'I'm getting anxious.'

The lunch was in aid of Indian street children. Ciara was styling the show, which was why I'd been drafted to bring the prizes – it was all hands on deck in her first outing as a stylist for years. She had been a stylist in London, a chapter in her life that she frequently mentioned – kind of wistfully, I thought. She had styled photo shoots for *Vogue*. '*I* worked on an advertising campaign with Mario Testino,' she said sometimes, when she was pissed, thumping her chest with her fist as if she didn't quite believe it herself.

She'd met Will by chance, at the conclusion of a long,

unstable relationship with a narcissistic and sexy film director, who mainly seemed to make ads even though he was
always on the verge of becoming the next Scorsese or Taran-
tino. He had dumped her for the fiftieth time – enter Will,
stage left.

Will had told the story many times of how they'd met at a
rugby international, all reference to the unreliable ride of an
English director omitted. Ciara always carolled her lines on
cue. Show time! She would say, smiling prettily, something
like 'I had no interest in rugby – it was total chance I was
dragged along to that match.'

Will would beam. 'It was Fate, darling.'

Once he had said it was 'kismet'. Later when we were lying
in bed Frank's voice had come out of the dark: 'What the
fuck is kismet?'

Ciara would continue, 'Will rescued me from my life in
London . . .'

'She was running herself ragged shooting.'

'And here we are,' Ciara would trill, at which point Will
would hold out his hand to catch hers.

The London life had been packed away in the thorough
way Ciara did everything, but there were times when I
wondered if she had packed away an essential part of herself
with it, like a river forced to go underground. And whether
one day that river might burst to the surface and break its
banks.

So, because Ciara hadn't styled a show in years she was,
understandably, nervous. I was helping with the auction prizes
but only in an unofficial capacity. Ciara was on the committee.
After years of manoeuvring she had finally managed to muscle
her way onto it so that now she could officially 'put something
back' along with all the other wives of movers and shakers
who were involved. They included the wife of a television

presenter and, most desirable of all, the wife of the rock star – she was a beautiful woman with a serene aura, extremely grounded and exceedingly nice. Ciara had spent quite a bit of time chasing her down. She had proved more elusive than Ciara had bargained for, though. Ciara reminded me of someone pursuing a plastic bag blowing down the road, which stopped and then started again just as they were about to catch it.

If I let her down, Ciara would fillet me. Her Olympian social climbing would not allow for a friend's cock-ups. But although I was woefully late I did not answer the phone. Instead I laid my head against the off-white wall. My gaze swivelled to a photo on the table. It had been taken at the top of the Eiffel Tower by another tourist. Ella had been around eleven. Her jacket hung open to reveal a sweatshirt with a picture of a horse on it. It had been hard work to get it off her body. She had worn it to bed a number of times. Her teeth were encased in braces, and she wore a pink bobble hat. Dylan had been fourteen. He had spots between his eyebrows. Frank was wearing an acid green Puffa jacket that made him look chunky. I was smiling at something he was saying. I looked so much younger, I thought, eyeing my rounded cheeks. You could see our breath misting the cold Parisian air. I was scared of heights. My heart had been in my mouth as I climbed the steps to the top of the tower, trying not to look down through the gaps in the wrought-iron. I had counted to a hundred over and over again to distract myself.

We had gone to EuroDisney as well and grazed on transfats and sugar among the wobbling fat people buying mountains of overpriced merchandise positioned at the foot of every ride. Dylan had loved every minute of it. We'd stayed in an awful Wild West-themed hotel for a night, where we'd eaten breakfast in the 'Chuck Wagon', which Frank had secretly liked. Ella had dragged us back into the city to the Louvre where we'd seen the *Mona Lisa*. Dylan had pronounced it a 'heap of shite'. It had been a very happy holiday, I thought, feeling a twist in my stomach.

Frank had made a mistake. Men would be men. Sensible women turned a blind eye.

Again, I heard the sound of footsteps. These were shorter and sharper. A woman's tread, I thought, hearing the click-clack of stilettos advancing towards the house. A white envelope fell onto the mat, 'Personal' emblazoned on the front. It was addressed to Frank. I stood up and peered out the window.

Through the cascading rain I saw a flash of red curls under an umbrella. *Oh, Jesus.* I shrank out of sight. Every pore in my body felt alert. The air was being pressed out of my lungs.

I could yank open the door. I could shout that she was on private property. She would be wrong-footed to see me – the lady from the clinic. It might take her a while to make the connection. I could yell torrents of abuse at her. I could take a running jump at her and leap onto her back, grabbing fist-fuls of the Irish-dancing hair. I could wrestle her to the ground and spit in her face and shout things like 'Ho' and 'Slapper' and 'Whore of Babylon'.

Instead, I inched towards the window, quivering. Two spots of red burnt on my cheeks. She was walking away, the gravel crunching under her angry footsteps. She stopped and turned towards the house. She tipped her head back as if she sensed she was being watched. Her expression hovered between doubt and anger. Her mouth was set. Her skin was the colour of cream. She had so much hair. An image of Frank twining his fat disloyal fingers in it ran through my mind. She gave a pursed-mouth scowl, then turned away. She strode down the drive.

There was the sound of a car door being slammed, followed by an engine being turned on. I was a useless yellow-bellied coward, I thought, my chest heaving. Bending forward, I plucked the envelope from the floor, my hands shaking violently as I ripped it open. I felt a welling in my chest and the words swam in front of my eyes.

Dear Frank,

I'm having this baby with or without you. I don't believe in abortion and I cannot believe that you would even consider murdering our child.

I need to know if you are on board before I tell my parents. I intend to tell them before the week is out. They will support me even if you won't.

Fiona

I pitched backwards, a strong, silent scream building inside me.

5

Frank had gone AWOL. His phone was bouncing straight to message minder. Whether this was because he was dodging his distraught wife or his pregnant mistress, I didn't know. I left message after message, shrieking down the phone, my words jumbled as I wept angry choking tears into it. My legs were shaking under me like a pneumatic drill.

I had to go to the lunch. The auction prizes were loaded into the boot of my Range Rover, including a valuable piece of sculpture shaped like a tree that was so ugly Frank had said he would have paid good money to see it destroyed. Now, I thought, suppressing a sob, I'd like to wrap it around his head.

I had daubed my puffy face with makeup. I'd had a stiff drink or two – maybe even three, because the glasses were generous – but I wove my way towards town, hoping I wouldn't be stopped by the law for driving over the limit.

The fashion show was in progress when I got there. Slinking to my seat under cover of the relative darkness I saw that I had been demoted from the front row to the second – a sign that Frank's and my social star was dimming maybe. Not that I cared.

Ciara had fixed me with a tense, hypnotic stare when I'd arrived. 'Where were you?' she'd mouthed at me.

I had invented a story about a flat tyre, which she had only half accepted. She had eyed me suspiciously, her expression chilly. Normally this would have had me reaching for the vapours – or the wine bottle: I would not have crossed my style heroine Ciara, but now I really didn't give a damn. In the hierarchy of pain it was lower than the faithless-husband-and-pregnant-girlfriend scenario.

Later she seemed to relax anyway because it was obvious that the show was pretty slick. She sent me a text: *Think we've gt a hit on r hands!!!!* And she was probably feeling a bit more humane towards me because I clocked some photographer taking repeated shots of her in her seat. Ciara *loved* having her picture taken. Nobody would come near me, I predicted. I never let my picture be taken because I wasn't photogenic. It was something to do with my features. I looked sort of squinty-eyed in photos – like somebody's slow cousin. But I wouldn't be getting the chance to say no today anyway, that was for sure. Truthfully, I might as well have slung a bell around my neck I looked so thrown together.

I saw Ciara making for the loo and trailed after her – old droopy drawers.

'Let me in.'

She opened the door, checked that we weren't observed, and ushered me in. 'If someone sees us they'll make the wrong assumption,' she said, slamming the cubicle door behind us.

'Or the right one,' I corrected her.

'Really? You want some charlie?' She eyed me with surprise.

That was Ciara's little secret – the woman who got crushingly bored and escaped to the loo to pep herself up. The consultant's wife who, all week long, was about yoga and organic food and her children, and at the weekend could hoover the GDP of Bolivia up her beautiful nose. Ciara was like a Dyson. The habit dated from her London days. 'The most fun I've ever had in my life was in bathrooms,' she had said to me once, in a rare moment of coked-up candour.

Will hadn't a clue. More than once I'd heard him tell a

story about his college days — about how one summer in America he'd taken a toke from some surfers. Mad bastard, Will. If only he knew about his wife skipping off to meet her dealer. I'd gone with her once. My heart had been racing like a jack-hammer. We'd pulled into the forecourt of a petrol station. The dealer had driven up in a soft-top Mercedes. Ciara had hopped out and air-kissed him. He was tall and thin in an expensive soft leather bomber jacket. And next thing, boom, she was back in the Land Rover with 'the gear'. Mission accomplished.

'I'm high on life. I want to get even higher,' I said, watching her upend some fine white powder onto the downturned loo seat. She gave me an assessing look. It was the lumpen tone. And I didn't do cocaine. Charlie was not for me. Once you took some, it was like lighting a big fire that had to be stoked or it went out and left you cold and miserable. It was a beast that demanded to be fed. You wanted more and more and more, and it became the driving force of the evening. And it made me anxious. I didn't need to feel more uptight. I had cornered the market in that. Plus, to be totally honest — and I didn't often confront this truth — I was a booze hound.

Actually, what I needed was the sort of numbness and false confidence that coke could deliver. I needed to get obliterated.

Ciara efficiently chopped the powder up with a credit card — her wrist flicking backwards and forwards — as she marshalled it into two neat lines. One line was monster in comparison to the other. 'You go first,' she instructed me. 'The big one is for me simply because I need more.' She flashed me a druggy smile. 'Make it quick because I need to get back. This is very *bold*.'

Pressing one nostril, I bent down and snorted up the

powder, using the thin straw Ciara had given me. There was a risk of infection with notes, she had told me, as if *that* was the sordid part of the equation. I stopped and started until the line was gone. When it was Ciara's turn, she vacuumed up the powder with a deft movement, causing the line to disappear in zip time. 'Okay, better shake a leg,' she said.

I stood uncertainly in the middle of the cubicle so that she nudged me towards the door. And then I told her, as if I were reading the news: 'Frank is having an affair.'

Ciara gawped at me. 'Are you sure?' she asked, her eyes bulging.

I nodded.

'Oh, Anita,' she said, drawing her breath through her teeth in a sharp sigh. She reached out and touched my arm.

My eyes watered.

'God,' she said, giving me a quick hug. She drew back. 'I'm so shocked.'

She must be shocked. It wasn't like Ciara to dole out the hugs. Like, you could never have accused her of being affectionate.

She rested her hand on my arm again. Then she turned quickly back towards the loo and ran her finger along the lid – the drama of the moment put to one side. She rubbed her gums with the residue and cut her eyes back to me. 'I would never have thought that Frank would be unfaithful to you.'

'That makes two of us.'

Ciara gave a wince of distaste. 'Some opportunistic little tramp has got to him.'

I chewed my lip.

'Does Frank know that you know?' she asked, swiping some powder from her nose. 'Because if I was you,' she said, not waiting for me to reply, 'I'd consider carefully how I was going to play this.' The beautiful blue eyes gleamed. 'This girl may only be a flash in the pan. You don't want to destroy your marriage and your home for something that may not amount to a hill of beans.'

She didn't know about the baby incubating in Little Miss Big Knockers's homewrecking womb. I couldn't talk about the baby or I would crack like an egg. So I dredged up a dumb smile.

'Anita, you're strong. You'll get through this,' she said, injecting energy into her voice. It was pretty clear, though, that her *numero uno* priority was to get back to the show. And I wasn't strong. Ciara was on drugs. Literally.

When we got back from the bathroom, the models were sashaying up and down to the sounds of a rhythmic beat that caused my heart to thud. Some local celebrities had joined them on the catwalk. A barrel-chested celebrity chef with a mouth like a sewer stomped down with his trademark scowl. A well-known actor swaggered after him, swigging from a beer bottle with a libidinous grin stretched from ear to ear, then crossed to a constellation of leggy girls, who fluttered around him. He was permanently photographed in the papers with a bevy of good-looking young women in tow.

'Isn't he a complete ride?' the young one next to me hissed behind her hand. She was a television presenter with endless legs, big boobs and the boundless confidence of youth. She was on one of the lesser television channels, so not deserving of a front-row seat.

The actor had clean-cut, chiselled looks. I didn't think he was gorgeous, though. There was a dull expression in his watery blue eyes. I had seen him interviewed on *The Late Late Show* and thought he had a bad attitude to women. He was a real wham-bam-thank-you-ma'am merchant, something he boasted about in public.

For years I had come to these charity lunches and balls

and manoeuvred my way up the social ladder – with Frank's encouragement – but now I could feel a mini rebellion mounting in my brain. Damn Frank and damn the actor. Why should I say something nice about him? Why should I be forced to muster up a false show of enthusiasm? 'I think he looks like the missing link,' I said.

She blinked at me. 'I didn't catch that,' she said, her smile shrinking a little.

I repeated myself, and her smile melted right off her face. Then I added, 'I wouldn't be surprised if some scientist scooped him up with a butterfly net and took him to a lab for research purposes.'

After that, she angled her narrow back to me and ignored me.

The Round Room in the Mansion House had no natural light but they'd combated its cave-like quality with thousands of fairy lights twisted around white frosted trees. Pink muslin was draped everywhere. An oversized champagne glass decorated each table.

'It looks like Barbie controlled the decoration,' I said to Ciara, who shushed me and told me for the fiftieth time that she had had absolutely no part in it.

'Oh, I hope people don't think I had something to do with it,' she whispered, sinking her teeth into her bottom lip.

The room was a sea of fake tits and hair extensions and uninhabited-seeming frozen faces. The MC was a well-known drag queen. 'Aren't you all looking lovely, ladies?' she said, at the start of the lunch, her towering red wig swaying. 'I'd say there isn't a bottle of fake-tan left on any shelf in Dublin.'

Although I laughed loudly the remark went down like a lead balloon – no wonder, when half the room looked like they'd been dipped in Fanta. The mandarin-orange woman at the opposite side of the table from me – a bony blonde who was married to a well-known publican – actually glowed.

I didn't listen to a word of the speech. But it must have been a real tear-jerker because there were socialites and 'ladies who lunched' sniffing over their crème brûlée. The meal was over. All the desserts lay untouched as the waiting staff began to clear away the debris. 'The street children of India could do with some of this left-over food,' I said loudly, attracting a couple of vicious looks. I didn't give a rattling damn what anyone thought of me today – which felt strangely liberating, I thought, downing some more wine.

The auction was starting now.

'This is the ultimate charity fashion extravaganza in aid of a very worthy cause,' the MC was saying. She flung out her hand, her sequined turquoise dress riding up an enviably toned thigh.

'Great pair of old legs on her all the same,' I said, to my friend Maureen.

'Sacred Heart, I think she's a he,' confided Maureen, behind her hand, looking enjoyably scandalized.

Except when it came to financial matters, when she turned into a human calculator, Maureen could be a bit of a slow-poke.

'Come on, lad*ieeees*, dig deep for the street children of India.'

'The bids aren't nearly as high this year,' Maureen whispered. 'There was a bidding war last year for a case of Château Latour. It's definitely a sign of the economic slowdown. It's harder to get money out of people.'

Maureen was a placid, pear-shaped woman run to flesh – far better upholstered than any of our friends – with pineapple yellow hair in ringlets that no one over the age of seven should have worn. She was the *grande dame* of our group and I had parachuted her into our circle. Or, more like, Maureen had insinuated her way into our gang although it was mean to think like that. Older than us, she was more of an add-on really, and how welcome she was I didn't really know. Not very, was my guess.

She had been foisted on me by Frank, who knew her ex. Donal was a property developer who had left her for an Irish glamour model young enough to be her granddaughter. The model was a photogenic and publicity-ravenous girl with bouncy hair and dimples who was in the papers every second day wearing little more than a smile and hot pants. More often than not she was cocked up next to Dylan's girlfriend Biba. They were to be seen draped over car bonnets or on bicycles in bikinis or clinging to beaming, foolish-looking male politicians launching initiatives and drives.

It couldn't have been easy for Maureen, staring down the barrel of her mid-fifties – with heavy upper arms and a fondness for lurid eye makeup – to compete with the lineless golden youth of her successor. I was in Maureen's gang now, I thought, feeling my shoulders sag.

The MC minced across the stage, her hips oscillating. 'We're talking about dinner here cooked for ten in your home by some of *this world famous chef's team.*'

'Last year that would have sparked a bidding frenzy,' Maureen said.

She was right. I'd noticed reticence in the bidding at the last ball I'd gone to. Before, property developers like Frank would have leapt to their feet and beaten their chests, like atavistic stone-age men, yelling their crazily inflated bids in a way that whipped up the audience into an orgasmic frenzy. Two years previously Frank had bid against another developer for some prize – a golfing lesson with a pro, I thought, I couldn't remember now for sure. They had yelled out bid after bid, buoyed up by the whooping and hollering of the crowd. In the end when Frank won – or lost, depending on your perspective – I was surprised he hadn't scooped me up Tarzan-style and swung out of there on a vine, yodelling.

'The goodie bags aren't up to much,' Maeve remarked, in the put-upon voice that had become her speciality. She was seated on my right. It was the downturned mouth that marred her otherwise pretty face. She was just back from shopping in New York. 'Doing my bit to keep the American economy afloat,' she had said earlier, throwing back her lustrous black locks. Maeve had her hair blow dried every day. 'Ultan tells me that my credit-card limit is not a target I have to reach every month,' she added, with a glassy laugh.

Maeve did a lot to prop up the economy of many countries. She roamed the world shopping, and never seemed to tire of ferrying home even more stuff. She was forever trekking to New York with empty suitcases. Shopping was one of the few topics that could bring a smile to her face. Otherwise it was one moan after another. You could fly her to the moon and she'd say she found it a bit boring. At some level Maeve was profoundly dissatisfied with life and she wasn't going to hold back on sharing that fact. Often her moaning was very funny. Sometimes it was plain obnoxious and spoilt.

'Plus the entertainment is some singer off *You're A Star*,' she said, wrinkling her nose. 'Last year they flew in a band from Rome. And there was an aerial act. Remember those girls swinging from the ceiling on trapezes?' She scowled. 'And we got lobster ravioli. This year it's a slab of grey beef. Or mushroom risotto for vegetarians.'

'It's for a good cause, I suppose,' Maureen chipped in. Maureen was decent like that.

Maeve gave her a little smile. 'Of course. I was just saying,' she said, her dark blue eyes glinting.

Maureen would be requiring a food-taster in the future, I thought, watching Maeve give an angry little jerk of her head.

The Queen Bee, the patron of the charity and a doyenne of charity fundraising, was on the stage now thanking everyone. A teak-coloured fleshy woman with good legs, she was dressed in billowing peach chiffon. Her husband had made his fortune about thirty years previously, which meant that by Dublin standards she was old money. The waters parted for her wherever she went.

'. . . and, of course, a warm and sincere thank you to Mahaffy jewellers from myself and all the committee. Without your continued sponsorship all this would not be possible.'

'She's got very old,' Maeve hissed, behind her hand. 'Her neck looks terrible.'

A narrow-shouldered girl stepped forward to give the doyenne a bouquet. Someone proposed a toast to her. The audience stood up with their glasses, their heads all turned towards the stage. A chorus rang out throughout the room.

'To oblivion and beyond,' I called out too loudly, clinking my glass against another woman's, causing champagne to spill over the edge of the flute onto the tablecloth. She eyed me warily.

We'd floated up the road from the Mansion House to the Shelbourne on a river of champagne, dodging the rain with huge umbrellas over our heads. We were a motley crew, tottering along on high heels in our bright outfits, fairly pissed, our bit done for the street children of India. The bar – No. 27 – was in the shape of a right angle. It fronted onto the park – the tops of the trees were visible over the sea of heads milling about. A series of giant bold paintings depicting park scenes decorated the walls. Staff in starched uniforms fought to serve the scrum that was three deep at the black stone bar. The crescendo of sound floated up towards the ceiling.

There were suits. There were tuxedos and evening dress, a good crowd from the charity lunch. There were also acres of brown flesh and partially exposed breasts on display. The majority of people looked dressy. Old fellas were trying to crack onto younger women with their tits hanging out or the other way around, I thought, sipping my drink and watching a girl with blonde curly hair and a huge arse press herself against a guy in a pinstripe suit.

'You're looking at the last days of the Roman Empire,' a swaying man with bloodshot eyes and a Guinness moustache had remarked to us earlier. 'A chill wind is blowing, and we're all just about to realize it.'

When he had gone, Shannon said, 'He's that telecoms guy. It's kind of scary when you hear talk like that from a big gun like him. I remember he made megabucks when he floated his company.'

Maeve tossed her head. 'Yeah, but he lost it all again. He's smashed. Never mind him. Sour grapes if ever I heard them. You'd get sick of these harbingers of doom trying to talk the economy down and ruin it for everyone.' She twirled her champagne flute towards the light and hooted with laughter. 'Sure what economic slow-down?' she said, flashing a smile that didn't quite reach her eyes.

Maeve was a publican's daughter from County Galway and had an almost sexual relationship with money. Stories of the very wealthy made her want to climax there and then. She'd stick her head forward, a post-coital flush spreading across her chest and neck, her pink tongue jutting between her wet lips, all agog. Maeve's husband made serious cash but sometimes I thought that if Maeve reckoned he could net a bit extra from minding mice at a crossroads she'd have been all in favour.

We had a table in the corner. Ciara, who had been to the loo again, was now at the bar fending off advances from a large bald man in a navy blazer with gold buttons. He was old enough to be her father and salivating over her. She had introduced him as someone from 'the George sailing club', which was why she hadn't told him to go whistle. Will's family were head, neck and tail of the sailing club. The man was talking to her tits. I felt like going over there and setting him straight on a few facts of life. *Do you seriously think that someone like Ciara would go for you of her own free will, even if she wasn't married and you were a free agent, which you're clearly not with the big married head on you? Ciara wouldn't pee on you if you were on fire.*

Men were always desirable in their own eyes. They could have body odour and a belly like a stretched balloon tipping towards their toes, and they still thought that all women were dying to get on down with them. I'd seen it at parties, men in their fifties with wide arses doing air guitar and clutching at their crotch. And no matter how follicly challenged, over-weight, pigeon-chested or downright ugly they were, they never shied away from the task of running an inventory of women's faults.

It was getting late. The summer light had gone dusky. A procession of women had stopped to chat. We were all getting drunk, our faces flushed from the oceans of alcohol that were pumping through our charitable veins.

Ciara was tossing her head skittishly, talking too rapidly in staccato bursts. We had made regular trips to the loo, gliding past the rows of women rearranging their hair and makeup. Ciara's eyes had glittered, her crooked finger beckoning me into a cubicle towards a temporary nirvana.

Not a word from Frank, not even a text. A loud voice in

my head told me to go home, but I was still hanging in, powered by vodka, Moët et Chandon and long lines of white powder, seeking to postpone the moment of reckoning, the avalanche of pain that I knew was waiting. My heart was pounding from the coke. Thump, thump, thump. I had no idea how much I'd done. It felt like we'd been out for days.

'There's a very convivial feel in here,' Maureen said, slugging back another glass of wine. She was slumped in her chair. She had removed her coffee-coloured jacket to reveal a lace camisole that emphasized the pendulous slope of her boobs. There was a sheen on her forehead and she was sweating faintly through her foundation. Her fuchsia lipstick had bled outside the lines of her mouth.

Compared to me she looked good, I thought, catching sight of my face in a mirror. 'That's one way of putting it, Maureen,' I said, looking around the room.

Actually, people were locked out of their heads. Go home, Anita, I thought, watching a television presenter stick his tongue into the ear of a woman with a carmine mouth. His hair was insanely bouffant. I watched the woman giggle and pretend to swat him away.

'That's not his wife,' Maureen said, glaring at them as he breathed into the woman's hair. She was very down on infidelity – understandable in the circumstances. I was now very much on Team Maureen when it came to men playing away.

'You think?' I said, as the woman gave the long, low, hot laugh recognized the world over as a mating call.

'I do,' Maureen said. Maureen was irony-proof. 'I bet you he wears a ring that he's taken off.'

Frank wore a ring. 'I wouldn't say a ring would turn her off or put a stop to his gallop,' I said bitterly. Frank was a hypocrite. Frank was the husband I had comforted because his mother didn't get the last rites in time. Apparently this was a big deal, according to his so-called religious beliefs. This had come from the same man who had tried to inveigle his knocked-up twenty-something girlfriend into having an abortion.

Shannon was sitting on the window-sill behind us with Maeve. Ciara had rejoined us.

'Jesus, I forgot to say! Did you hear that one of Tracey Thornley's implants burst?' said Maeve.

'*Nooooo!*'

Tracey Thornley was not a close friend, but Frank and I had hung out with her and her husband a lot.

'Yeah,' said Maeve, 'she's had to have them both out. It's why she wasn't at the lunch today. I can't imagine what she looks like without those air-bags.'

Minus the large plastic boobs, Tracey would look like a rib with hair.

'She's so skinny she looks like she's digesting herself,' Shannon said, with a clear trace of envy in her voice.

'She's too thin,' Ciara said scrunching up her nose. 'She's what I call hooker thin. There's something kind of cheap about those concave inner thighs.'

Shannon shot her a look but said nothing.

To put Tracy's figure in context, she made Shannon look beefy. Maeve unkindly called her Karen Carpenter behind her back.

'I still can't believe Dermot gave her breasts for her birthday,' said Ciara, turning to Maeve. 'I mean, is that true? I'd be so insulted if Will gave me plastic surgery for my birthday.'

'Tracey told me without one iota of shame,' Maeve said. 'She seemed thrilled by it.'

'Tracey's nice,' declared Shannon. 'She wouldn't hurt a fly.'

'That wouldn't exactly be what you'd want written on your epitaph,' remarked Maeve.

They were probably all thinking the same as I was: that

Maeve was safe enough there. Not the kind of thing you'd point out to her, though. It would be like taking your life in your hands.

I wondered what might be written on my epitaph – 'She liked a drink'?

'Where do some of these guys get off,' Shannon sniffed, 'being so arrogant as to give their wives body parts for presents? It's kind of presumptuous.'

'I got my breast implants for *me*,' Maeve said. 'There's no way I'd be dictated to by Ultan.'

I had the mean thought that Ultan wouldn't care much what Maeve's breasts were like.

'Dermot is obsessed by Tracey's appearance,' Maeve said. 'I wouldn't be at all surprised if he calorie-counts her food. He even encourages her to wear those tiny dresses. She's a chattel to him.'

'She loves him, I guess,' I said.

Tracey had told me once in front of Frank and Dermot that she loved him so much she would have hacked off a leg for him, which had seemed pretty extreme. But who could say why a connection existed between two people? There was no legislating for the human heart.

'Is that Paul Hogan over there?' Ciara asked, telescoping her head towards the door. 'Who's that guy with him?'

'Hmm, he looks familiar.' Maeve had followed her gaze.

Some man was whacking Paul on the back and Paul was flashing his trademark Cheshire grin. As usual, he looked dapper.

'That guy Paul's got a lot of guts,' Shannon said. 'Jimmy banks with him. He can be a little obnoxious, I guess, but he's got chutzpah.'

'He's the man,' Maeve said. 'Ultan banks with him too.'

'So does Frank,' I added.

'Everyone banks with Paul,' said Maeve. 'Paul has done a lot for business in this country. Without the likes of Paul, loads of guys wouldn't have had their start.'

'How so?' asked Ciara.

'Because a lot of the older bankers made very conservative lending decisions in what were mainly traditional sectors. And they were snobbish. They looked after their own little circle. Light-touch regulation and flexibility have been the bywords of Paul's success,' said Maeve, sounding as if she was channelling Ultan.

Maureen sniffed. 'Donal would say that there's been a lot of reckless lending.'

You could rely on Maureen to puncture the mood.

'There's Dermot Thornley now,' I said, trying and failing to muster a smile.

For the earlier part of the day I had smiled robotically. Now a smile was beyond me.

Dermot Thornley waved at us, then disappeared into the mêlée.

Maeve swung her head around. 'Well, as Tracey's off getting her tits removed I wonder who he's here with . . . He's a total hound dog,' she added.

'When he's talking to you he has this way of making you feel like you're the only person in the room,' Shannon said. 'It's pretty effective.'

She was right. I had bumped into Dermot a couple of weeks before at a party and he had sat on the armrest of my chair, his arm encircling my shoulders, telling me how, with a fat laugh, he had always been 'a huge fan' of mine.

Maeve sat forward in her chair, a bold look on her face. 'They say that the Thornleys are into swinging.'

'You've gotta be kidding,' Shannon said immediately. 'That's total baloney, I'd say.' Shannon didn't like to speak ill of people, which marked her out as a bit of a freak in our circle.

Maeve was nettled. 'I was at a dinner party where I'm positive they were blooding me and Ultan out.'

We stared at her. The idea that anyone might consider a bloodless hermit like Ultan, with his narrow hips, a candidate for lusty activities seemed a long shot.

'My hairdresser told me she got a lift back from Marbella on a plane with some of Dermot Thornley's friends and it turned into an orgy. She said she was very relieved to get off safely. She had to lock herself in the loo.'

Maureen's eyes boggled.

'Well, it wasn't Dermot Thornley on the plane,' Shannon said.

'Show me a person's friends . . .' Maeve said. She tossed her head back. 'Anyway,' she said, 'Dermot Thornley came up to me at your party, Anita, and whispered in my ear, "I'd like to fuck you senseless against a wall."'

Ciara lifted her eyebrows.

Maureen gave a little shudder. 'Swinging, though!' she breathed, looking appalled – but obviously reluctant to let the topic slide. 'So sordid.'

'Oh, go on out of that,' Maeve said. 'You love it – sitting forward there, practically panting. You're desperate for the details.'

Maureen spluttered. 'I beg your pardon?'

Maeve baited poor Maureen too much but, to be fair, she had a point. I could visualize Maureen retelling the story. She loved gossip, particularly tales she could tut-tut at.

Ciara made a face. 'A very good barrister friend of Will's said there was a group of younger barristers who were very into it. I know them, actually. They're quite an attractive bunch. You wouldn't think they'd have to resort to that.'

Maeve had a saucy look on her face. 'It's a form of exhibitionism. It's obviously to get kicks.'

Ciara continued, 'Apparently some of the girlfriends and wives used to snog in open view of their husbands.'

'No!' said Maureen, her heavily ringed podgy hand covering her mouth.

Shannon tsked. 'I gotta say that's really stretching credibility.'

Maureen said primly, 'I think it's totally disgusting. Whatever happened to old-fashioned common decency?'

'It went out of fashion,' Maeve retorted, 'thanks be to God.'

Maureen made a face.

Maeve raised a shoulder and dropped it. 'Whatever floats your boat. It's a free world. I don't care if somebody has sex with the family Labrador once it's behind closed doors and I don't have to hear about it.'

Maureen straightened in her chair. 'Well, I don't know about you,' she said, her lips pursed so that her mouth looked like a lipsticked prune, 'but when I was growing up a sense of right and wrong was instilled in me. During Lent we went to Mass every morning and our father made us say five decades of the Rosary, every night. We held the Crucifix of the Rosary in our right hands.'

'That must have been fun,' Maeve said, her tone bone dry.

Maureen's lips were pressed together so firmly they nearly disappeared from her face. 'There's nothing wrong with family values.'

Maeve ignored her. 'If you ask me, what's right and what's wrong are a matter of personal opinion. Morality is relative.'

'I would have to say that I strongly disagree with you, Maeve,' Maureen said, looking riled. Ordinarily she was quite serene, but not where family values were concerned.

Maeve tossed her head. 'Being good is boring. Self-restraint is overrated.'

'I'll tell you what *is* true,' Shannon said, lowering her voice. 'I heard from a woman I know – she's divorced and I won't say her name – that mothers at the gym pay the French tennis coach for sex.'

'Really?' said Ciara, her eyes rounding. 'That guy's a gigolo?'

'That's what she said,' Shannon agreed, her eyes full of mirth. 'He coaches the boys but I've never got the impression he was a gigolo.'

Maeve had gone quiet. And her neck had gone crimson.

My response was vague. 'Hmm,' I said, avoiding Maeve's eye. 'I don't know, really.'

Maureen's mouth had fallen open. Her ample *décolletage* was flushed with alcohol and surprise. 'I find that very hard to believe. That *mothers* pay their children's tennis coach for sex.'

'Have you ever seen that guy from the rear?' said Shannon, with a dirty laugh. 'He's got buns of steel.' She was only joking. She would never stray from Jimmy. They had an extremely happy marriage. I watched Shannon readjust the giant bow in her hair. It looked insane. I'd overheard her telling a social diarist that she was dressed in an outfit by Chanel. Shannon always wore whatever was in fashion, with no regard for her shape or age. No outfit was out of bounds.

When she first came to Ireland she had dressed in a fairly neutral American, almost preppy, way. But bit by bit the clothes got more outlandish. She was now in her forties but she wouldn't go easily. She'd go kicking and screaming into the night, trussed up inside the filmiest and shortest of outfits. I'd once attended a wedding where she'd worn a see-through skirt.

'Shannon makes mutton look like lamb,' Frank had said,

after she had answered the door to us in what looked like a baby-doll négligée but was in fact a dress. 'Oh, I'm sorry we're too early – we'll come back when you're dressed,' he had joked. Shannon had mock-punched his arm.

The conversation had moved on and the heat had left Maeve's cheeks. Maeve, for all her love of free expression, was keeping the Frenchman more or less to herself. To my knowledge, she had only talked to me about him and had sworn me to secrecy.

I could hear Ciara talking about the benefits of hot-housing your children. 'You should spend a couple of concentrated hours each day doing mental maths with them . . .'

Maureen was talking to me now about her ex, something about the value of the shares Donal had given her as part of her settlement. 'They slumped yesterday by more than eleven per cent. Eleven *per cent.*'

Maureen's ex-husband's empire was rock solid. He had built up banks of land around Dublin thirty years previously and he came high up on Ireland's rich list. He was in a different league from fellas like Frank. Maureen had been given a very generous settlement – a large house in Blackrock, a villa in Puerto Banus, a flat in London overlooking Hyde Park, plus stocks and shares and a lump-sum payment that would mean she never had to work. But she went on poor-mouthing a bit. Partly, I thought, because she wanted an excuse to talk about Donal.

I tried to be patient with Maureen. I knew how badly she missed her husband and the status she felt had come with being married to him. But sometimes, watching her lips move, I found myself tuning out. I'd heard it all before. I could have written a thesis about Donal. And I wouldn't mind but the man himself wouldn't exactly have set the world on fire.

I'd seen Donal out one night in the Unicorn restaurant, acting like love's young dream with the girlfriend. He was not a man – say, like Will – whom you might have mentally cast in the role of seducer. Not that Will would be unfaithful, but he had the right looks for the part of dashing hero. Donal was mutton dressed as ram – with a dye job that was very obvious around the ears. And denims that made his arse look like a sack of puppies fighting. All he was missing was the earring.

The waiter edged his way between our huddle setting down an ice-bucket and a quartet of glasses.

'Whose shout is it, la-*diees*?' asked Maeve, shimmying her hips.

Maeve was a seasoned party girl – although recently there had been times when I'd thought she seemed a little jaded, as if the party might be going on just that bit too long.

'It's my pop,' said Shannon. 'Stick it on my tab.'

'Nope,' said Maeve, looking pointedly at Maureen, who was suddenly busying herself with her mobile phone. Maureen was a great woman for sitting on her hands. 'I'll get it,' Maeve said, still staring at Maureen who was oblivious of the looks she was attracting.

'No, this one's on me,' I said, dropping a credit card into the saucer. I told the waiter, 'We need a fifth glass, please.'

'Are you sure, hon?' Shannon asked.

'I'm sure,' I said. 'This one's on Frank.' Ciara and I weren't long back from having had a little toot. The coke was just hitting the back of my throat and nose and I felt myself burst into life. My addled brain was turning somersaults. 'I was just wondering what our teenage selves would say if they could see us now,' I said, cutting across something Shannon was saying.

I was so wired. I heard myself talking at the wrong speed, like a record being played too fast. My eyes panned the group. 'Do you remember the sense of possibility when you were young? The intense conversations you had with your pals about love and what you were going to do with your life? I mean, if the young versions of us could see us now, what do you think they'd make of us?'

Maeve refilled her glass, her eyes scanning the group. She gave a self-congratulatory smile. 'I'd say they'd think we'd done very well.'

'Do you think so?' I asked.

Her tone when she replied was a little defensive. 'Yeah, I do.' She gave an abrupt laugh. 'I would have thought that was obvious.'

'If you'd asked me ten years ago if I'd done well I probably would have said yes, but not now.'

'What's changed?' asked Shannon.

'Sometimes,' I said, running my tongue along my gums, which were numb from the coke, 'I feel that Frank and the kids have moved on, leaving me behind.' It was true. The soundtrack to my life had become the slam of doors as people stepped inside their bedrooms with cries of 'Not now, Mum.'

'I totally get that,' said Shannon, nodding. 'More and more I see the boys growing away from me. They're constructing worlds for themselves where I can't follow. They still love me, and sometimes they need me, but they want to break free too.'

Maureen piped up: 'I remember when that happened with my kids. Although, you know, I always had my golf and my bridge . . .'

'You also had a career outside the home once, Maureen,' I said. 'I never had that. I did the books for Frank's business until Dylan was born but that was all.'

Maureen, who had been a nurse, smiled. 'That was years ago,' she said, putting her hand on her throat. 'I couldn't imagine nursing now – I wouldn't have a clue.'

'You all had careers, other lives before you became mothers and wives,' I reminded them. 'I just wonder if sometimes you miss those lives.'

'I liked being a stay-at-home wife,' Maureen said. 'I felt that was where my duty lay. And I was good at being a homemaker. My children and my husband were the focus of my life,' she said, the corners of her mouth turning down a little.

A small solemn silence grew, as we pondered this truth. Maureen's husband had bolted. She had a son who lived in London and a daughter who was married with small children in Cork. Her daughter and son-in-law were good to her and Maureen went down to visit regularly, but it wasn't the same as having your daughter near by. The son seemed to come home when it suited him.

'I used to make my children's clothes,' she said, with a lopsided smile.

'I bet you were an awesome cook too,' Shannon said kindly.

'I was, actually,' Maureen admitted.

'You mean you are,' Maeve corrected her. 'You're not dead, Maureen.'

'Cooking for one isn't the same,' Maureen said, her eyes clouding. 'You don't get the same enjoyment out of it as you do cooking for other people. I mainly just have cheese on toast in the evenings or a boiled egg.'

After a pause Shannon said, 'Well, I'd be lying if I said I didn't miss being an attorney. I'd definitely like to be that girl again, in the slick suit and pumps.' It wasn't the first time she'd made this confession. 'Sooner rather than later,' she added.

'Really?' asked Maeve, clearly sceptical.

'Yeah,' said Shannon. 'Don't get me wrong, I've enjoyed being at home with the boys. I've been damn lucky to have the opportunity – Jimmy can carry us without a second salary coming in. None of my sisters have the option to be home-makers and I know they consider me very lucky. But all the repetition – and when they were younger putting up with that awful loser Barney,' she said. 'There were times when they were little I felt like I was going stir crazy. Especially in the mom-and-baby group. I found it hard to work out was it me or the other mothers – if it was that they were all on Prozac or that I needed to be.'

We all laughed.

'Maybe you were just going to the wrong group,' countered Maeve. 'I met some lovely girls in mine.'

Shannon shrugged. 'I guess I found it hard going from negotiating big sexy deals to discussing the logistics of freez-ing baby food in ice-cube trays. And that made me feel guilty as hell. But work was so damn ordered – a nice male world where everything ran smoothly and you could take refuge from home. When the boys were younger, Jimmy would say sometimes at the weekend, "I think I need to go into the office." What he really meant was "I want a break from this food-spattered mayhem."' She shook her head. 'I used to really resent him for that.'

'You still have your legal brain.'

Shannon frowned. 'I'd like to think so. I've been home for nearly ten years, though. Sometimes I feel my brain's gone to pot. And,' she said, with a rueful smile, 'I guess there is the possibility that while I've been wiping the heinies of the future generation my human capital has diminished. I don't know where the years have gone. One minute you're tying bibs on them, the next you're wondering when you should have the sex talk. I'm definitely going to look into going back after the summer,' she said. 'The problem is that I trained in a different legal system – as a US attorney, I'm not licensed to

127

practise here. I'd have to do a conversion exam.' She paused. 'I guess even if I was to get licensed, I'd prefer a part-time job, with lots of dough, so I still got to spend plenty of quality time with the kids.'

'Yeah, right,' said Maeve, drily. 'Wouldn't we all?' Then she said, 'I was happy to kiss Monday mornings goodbye.' Maeve had never gone back to accountancy after her first pregnancy. My hunch was that privately she had made the decision to give up the second Ultan Mohally had planted a rock the size of Skelig Michael on her finger. That had been seven years ago. Since then she had firmly planted her flag in the camp of the stay-at-home mothers.

'Your kids are still small,' I said. 'They're at a quite demanding stage.'

'That's not why I haven't gone back,' she said. 'I saw what happened in the office when women came back after maternity leave. Straight away they were on the back foot. It was just the way the system worked. And if Ultan or whoever wants to call a meeting for ten o'clock at night that's his right. And if some woman can't go because her kid has the measles and she's got to get home, well, that's nobody's fault but she's going to end up stressed out of her mind. She either misses the meeting or misses sitting with her kid. There was no way I was being marginalized like that.'

'I gotta say,' Shannon said, 'there's definitely something in what Maeve says. Corporate life is tricky for women. If you can't wield a golf club or do all the locker-room stuff with the guys you're at a disadvantage. But there are jobs I guess that seem more conducive to being a mom. Jimmy's sister teaches school in Kildare. She has three kids and she seems to have a pretty cool work–life balance.'

'Yeah, well,' said Maeve, 'I'm going to tell Madison when she grows up to pick something less challenging to do, not to bother killing herself. The best thing a girl can be is good-looking with a nice shapely arse. Nobody really gives a shit if she's good at Shakespeare or calculus. The currency of looks is far more important for women. You're better off teaching your daughter to avoid croissants.'

Yeah, that strategy had really worked for me, I thought, allowing a big mouthful of champagne to slip down my throat.

'You're kidding, right?' said Shannon. 'That's so damn depressing.'

Maeve shrugged. Then she said, 'The minute they put Max on my chest I just knew I couldn't go back.'

I saw Shannon and Ciara trade looks. 'You never get that precious time back,' she added.

This was a bit rich coming from Maeve, who spent a significant amount of her time shopping and slugging champagne between massages and private sessions with her Pilates teacher. And hot dates with the tennis coach.

'Maeve,' I said, fixing eyes with her, 'I can't believe you don't miss your career. I bet you were brilliant as an accountant. You're very clever and you love money.'

She threw me a vicious look.

That had come out wrong. I was riding the cocaine highway now, my manically paced thoughts insisting on being aired. A volley of words spewed from my mouth. 'Ciara was a stylist and not just any old stylist but one who worked with Mario Testino and *Vogue*.'

'God,' said Shannon, admiringly, 'that's so cool.'

Ciara's eyes glittered with narcotic pride.

'Ciara had ambition that propelled her from Navan all the way to London.'

'Navan!' said Maeve, her eyes assessing. 'I never knew you were from Navan.'

Ciara flushed a dark red. She *was* from Navan, a fact she

129

seemed to regard as the fourth secret of Fatima. And she certainly didn't have a Navan accent. She had three brothers but didn't mention them often. Her da was a policeman. I only knew that because we'd bumped into her uncle on Grafton Street when he was up for a GAA match. 'Podge' was a mountain of a man with a burst orange for a face who said 'persun' instead of 'person'. A nice, warm man but you'd never have had him down as a relative of Ciara's.

Ciara hadn't said much about him after we'd left him on the street, only that he was a garda like her father, which was how I found out what her father did. Her ma was a housewife, I think, but beyond that I didn't know. Their names cropped up rarely. And while she certainly had her parents, 'Joe and Marie', up to the house now and then, it never seemed to be when her friends were around.

Ciara seemed a lot keener on discussing her husband's crowd. A bit like Will himself. We knew all about the Whites. They sailed and skied and had houses in Provence and Italy and played rugby and generally seemed to keep the Irish medical system going with their medical genius. His old man and his granda had both been doctors, one playing rugby for Leinster, the other for Ireland.

'It's like death by fucking anecdote, listening to Will,' Frank had said once, after Will had rolled out a tale of his da's derring-do on the rugby pitch. 'Heir to a shit-load of self-entitlement and a shit-load of shit stories. Check my fucking pulse there to see if I'm still alive, will ya, after that last hilarious one?'

Frank never gave poor Will a break.

'I'm sure Navan is a great place,' I said.

'I've never been to Navan,' said Maureen, in a tone that suggested she thought this was a good thing.

'I grew up in a tenement flat not far from the York Street

buildings,' I said, to divert attention from Ciara, who looked like she'd swallowed a wasp.

Eight mascaraed eyes were suddenly trained on me. I, too, had been sketchy about my background. I'd been most honest with Shannon because I trusted her – but also because she was American and she probably didn't get what I was on about. Plus she'd been very open about her own background, which was blue-collar.

'Near St Stephen's Green. A five-minute walk from here. My mother was a cleaning lady and my father was a conductor.'

'In an orchestra?' asked Maureen.

'A bus conductor,' I told her. 'He was the one who used to stand on the bus and shout, "Fares, please,"' I said, in a broad Dublin accent that made Maeve and Ciara giggle.

Shannon snorted with laughter. 'I'm sorry – it's the way you said that.'

'It's grand,' I said. 'I had my wedding reception in this hotel. No member of my family had ever seen inside the door before except a cousin who was a kitchen porter. To my family it was as exciting as the moon landings. I've spent the last twenty years trying to erase my accent. This is how I used to talk,' I said, putting on the Dub accent again. I plunged my teeth into my bottom lip. 'Look at us,' I said. 'Shannon and I spend half of our life in the gym, pounding away on the treadmill on the road to nowhere . . .'

'I'd be like the size of a house if I didn't,' protested Shannon.

There was a chorus of dissent. When it had died down, I went on, 'We all shop a lot. Particularly Maeve and I.'

'I don't shop that much,' Maeve shot back testily, her back stiffening. 'I buy less than you but what I buy is more expensive.'

'Maeve, I'm surprised they haven't erected a statue to you

outside Harvey Nichols,' I said, which provoked more laughter. I set down my glass too quickly and champagne splashed onto my lap. 'And when you're not shopping you're talking about what you bought. Or shopping on-line.' I was sharing thoughts now that I should have kept to myself but my tongue wouldn't sit still. 'That big brain of yours goes to waste, Maeve. All that mental energy of yours ploughed into gossiping, trawling over the minutiae of other people's lives, dissecting them like insects. Would you not like to do something with your wonderful intellect?'

'Fuck off, Anita,' Maeve said, and Maureen's small sad eyes bulged.

There was a sort of clutching at my chest now but I was like a runaway train that couldn't stop. That was the thing about coke. When the effects wore off it made you lapse into a sullen silence and your greedy little brain could think of nothing but the next hit.

'And Ciara — it's a wonder she hasn't grown a third nostril.'

Maeve had once memorably described Ciara to me as 'compulsively perfect'. 'I've always been surprised that she takes coke,' she had said. 'You wouldn't think she'd risk the loss of control when she's so compulsively perfect.'

'Sometimes, Ciara,' I said, 'I think you take coke to anaesthetize yourself from boredom.'

'Sorry —' said Maureen, but Ciara cut her off.

'Jesus, Anita,' she said, her eyes flashing, 'you've gone too far. I'm very happy with my life, thank you very much.'

'I'm sorry.'

'I'm extremely happy being a mother and wife,' she said, her cheeks scarlet with anger. 'Just because you're unhappy — don't blame your bad situation on me,' she said, prodding the air with a long, slender finger. 'You're projecting,' she said, and the others swivelled their gaze to me.

'Frank and I are having problems,' I said flatly. 'Big problems.'

'Oh?' said Maeve, her eyes widening.

'I can't talk about it now,' I said. 'I just can't.'

Maeve looked either disappointed or annoyed, I couldn't figure out which. She was probably pissed off that Ciara had known before she did, I decided. I tried to catch Ciara's eye, but she avoided mine. 'I didn't mean you weren't happy with your life.' I was groping for the right words to make things better between us. 'I just meant that sometimes I wonder if you miss parts of your old life. You seemed so happy earlier when you'd styled the show. What I said came out wrong.'

'Don't you dare psychoanalyse me,' Ciara said, reddening again. 'I do not miss my old life as a stylist. Not in any way. I like being at home. It's a decision I made. Nobody forced me to do anything. I chose this life.'

'Different strokes for different folks, I guess,' said Shannon. 'Come on, guys, let's not be mad at each other.'

Shannon was very often the peacemaker. Along with me. Normally.

Maureen sat forward in her chair. 'What did she mean about Ciara growing a third nostril?' she asked Maeve.

Ciara tried to stare Maeve into silence. It didn't work.

'She's referring to coke,' Maeve said.

'Thanks a lot, Maeve,' snapped Ciara. Her face contorted. 'I'm pretty sure you've had the odd toot. In fact, I know you have.'

'Oh, well, off with my head,' said Maeve.

Maeve did coke only infrequently. Like me, she preferred booze. It was the illicit aspect of the whole thing, the procurement, the whiff of law-breaking that attracted her more than the actual hit. And she was more than willing to 'fess up to it because, unlike Ciara, she didn't care what people thought of her.

The usual politesse had completely broken down. Thanks to me, I thought guiltily.

'You don't seriously take *cocaine*, Ciara?' Maureen asked, her eyes boggling.

'Oh, God,' said Maeve, 'hold the front page. "Women In Cocaine Shocker". What planet have you been on for the last ten years, Maureen?'

'Maureen, I don't normally do cocaine,' I told her, in the spirit of honesty that seemed to be going around, 'but tonight I'm bombed out of my mind on it. I'm so high on coke I think my heart is going to leap out of my chest.'

Maureen, who was extremely religious, looked at us as if we'd just had a whizz in the tabernacle.

My heart was seriously racing now. *Rat a tat tat.* I put my hand on my chest as if that would calm it. It was an effort not to cry. 'I feel like I'm on the scrap heap,' I said.

Frank had been like the Pied Piper, I thought, feeling the tears build at the back of my eyes. I had listened to his call and dropped everything, immersing myself in complete and total Frankness. I had followed the sound of that tune unquestioningly for twenty-six years.

The aroma of Shannon's perfume hit my nostrils. It smelt of orchids, I thought. The pain in my chest was sharp now. 'What is there for me now? What happens to me now that my mothering is pretty much done?' And my husband seems to be gone, I thought, a lump forming in my throat.

No one spoke for a moment. Then Maeve snorted. 'You certainly know how to kill an evening, Anita, I'll grant you that.'

'In Christ's name, is this it?' I asked.

'Your nose is bleeding, Anita,' Ciara said icily.

'Are you okay, hon?' Shannon asked, half standing up and bending over me.

Bright red blood poured down my face into my lap. She yanked a napkin from the table and handed it to me.

'Jesus, Mary and Joseph,' I heard Maureen say. She was fanning her face with her hand. Then she whispered, 'She isn't having an overdose, is she?'

'It's only a burst blood vessel,' Ciara said stonily. 'Trust me, she'll live.'

'Has it stopped, Anita?' Shannon asked. 'Tilt your head back – that'll staunch the flow.'

'I only wanted to come out for a few drinks and do my bit for charity,' Maureen said, with a clenched face. 'I'm not able for this. Gigolos . . . and *swinging* and snorting *cocaine*.'

'Interesting how your first thought is for yourself, Maureen,' Maeve said, which even in my bloodied state I recognized as rich coming from her.

'You okay?' Shannon asked, resting her hand on my arm. 'We should go to the bathroom.'

'I'm fine,' I said. 'It's stopping, I think.'

Maureen said grimly, 'This country has gone to the dogs.'

Maeve made a rude snorting noise. 'Oh, drop the rose-tinted back-in-the-good-old-days schtick, Maureen. Multi-partner, multi-orifice sex might be new in Termonfeckin, but priests were beating people out of fogged-up Morris Minors a long time and it wasn't for playing Scrabble. I read *The Ballroom of Romance*. They did a lot more in those fields on the way home from dances than fumble.'

Maureen went to protest but Maeve cut her off rudely. 'Anyway, you'd want to come down off the HMG.'

'What's that?' asked Ciara.

'The high moral ground.' Maeve fixed eyes with Maureen. 'I know for a fact, Maureen, that your local chemist can't keep the Solpadeine on his shelves because you and some of your golfing cronies take so much of the stuff. I've heard about your coffee mornings where you're all popping it like nobody's business.'

'I beg your pardon . . .' said Maureen, two pink spots appearing on her cheeks. 'I certainly don't take Solpadeine.'

'But some of your pals do. And for your information, Maureen, the codeine in Solpadeine is an opiate from the same family as heroin and morphine so you could say that some of your friends are on the hard stuff.'

In spite of everything Ciara giggled.

'Anyway, I thought as a holy roller you'd know that "he who is without sin shall cast the first stone,"' Maeve concluded.

Maeve was pretty drunk, I realized, watching some of her violently coloured cocktail sluice onto her lap. She was drinking champagne and a cocktail at the same time. But she had a point, I thought, dabbing my nose.

'At least let me bring you down to the bathroom,' Shannon pleaded.

'Oh, good Lord, I'm not able for this at all,' quavered Maureen.

I stood up, the napkin over my nose. Tears stabbed at my eyelids. I could feel my bottom lip trembling. 'I'm not able for it either,' I mumbled, and began to push my way through the throng.

6

I thought I was having a heart attack. My heart felt like a mandarin orange being squeezed inside a giant fist. I stumbled outside through the hotel's revolving door, past the top-hatted doorman, looking for a taxi as torrential rain coursed down. People ran past, coats on their heads, laughing and talking. I thought my number was up and that I might never see my husband and children again.

You stupid, stupid bitch, Anita. The blood was pumping from my nose and down my front. I lifted my hand and a cab stopped beside me. 'St James,' I said to the taxi driver, trying to stay calm.

When he saw the state of me, he didn't want to take me. But I hopped into the back before he could drive away and, fair play, once he'd got going he thundered through the streets like Superman. We beat a path through the hordes of people milling on the streets, knots of wet revellers, the odd fella pissing on the side of the road, one or two puking, glammed-up girls with fellas' jackets on them, gardaí loading people into paddy wagons, all part of the usual Friday revelry in Dublin.

Up past Dublin Castle we went, past the graceful stone arches of Christ Church Cathedral, down Thomas Street, zooming past the Guinness brewery, bumping along over the Luas tracks and swinging into St James Hospital with a squeal of brakes. All your man was missing was the cape and the S on his front.

Accident and Emergency was like Armageddon. I'd have been better off dying of a heart attack. It was bedlam. If you weren't traumatized going in, you would be coming out. The marble-effect lino, orange plastic chairs and strip lighting made everyone look like jaundiced insects. It was like being on the set of *Shameless*. The whole place was like an ad for 'Say No to Drugs'.

'What's da story?' a man asked, as he sat down beside me, a bloodied bandage around his head.

My nose had stopped bleeding. Ciara had been right. The triage nurse said it was a burst blood vessel. But my heart felt as if a vice had tightened it. I was given a preliminary ECG. I was in no immediate danger of croaking it, which was good news. But I'd been put on the 'urgent' list. This meant, according to the nurse, that I'd only be waiting a couple of hours to be seen by a doctor. God knew how long those designated 'minor' would have to hang around.

The nurse asked me if I'd consumed alcohol or taken any cocaine. I knew why she was cross. I was clogging up the unit because of my stupid behaviour. And she was right. I could feel shame boiling inside me. But she had far too much attitude for someone in a caring profession.

'Are yis interested in buying any gear, love?' Bandage Man was asking me. 'Or any yokes?'

'No – no, thanks,' I said. I'd done enough drugs for one evening.

He didn't seem to hear me. He looked beyond me with the spaced-out gaze of the hardened drug user. Not that, under the circumstances, I was one to be throwing stones. 'Five yokes for twenty squids,' he said, fiddling with his gold sovereign ring and sniffing. His nails were bitten back to the quick.

'Sorry, no,' I said again.

'Ah – g'wan, love, they're A1,' he said.

'No, thanks.' Did I look like a user to a professional such as him?

'For fuck's sake,' he muttered under his breath, 'scabby bitch.'

A young fella – a complete head-the-ball with a baseball cap turned backwards – kept shouting down the phone as if there was nobody else in the room. 'I'll fuckin' swing for ya if you lay a finger on her, d'ye hear me, roight?'

Behind me somebody yelled, 'I've got rights. This is fuckin' ridiculous. I've been waiting for fuckin' hours. What's the story here?'

Maybe this was what hell looked like. My eyes roamed around the waiting room. People high on drugs and alcohol careering around in sportswear that had never seen any sporting action, their knuckles, necks and ears weighed down with cheap gold jewellery, tormenting the overburdened staff.

My heart was calming down a bit.

There was a scuffle. The man shouting about his rights was being ejected by two weary security guards. All in a night's work, their expressions seemed to say.

'Bastards the whole lot of yez,' he bellowed, digging his heels into the floor. 'Fuckin' bastards.'

The woman on my right – a huge mound packaged inside a flimsy polka-dot blouse – was cramming Taytos into her mouth with salt-encrusted fingers. Was she ultra-confident or the reverse, I wondered.

Then an old one in a pink and black tracksuit with sores all around her mouth schlepped up to me. 'Carly's me name,' she said, swinging her arse down next to me and leaning in on top of me – her breath stank of fags and booze. 'And friendship's me game,' she said, cackling.

I felt sorry for her but I just couldn't handle her, so when she turned to the drug dealer on the other side I moved seats. There was nobody I could ring, I thought, my eyes moist.

'Anita Butler,' said a voice.

I stared at its owner. He was short with sloping shoulders. 'Anita,' he repeated. I nodded.

'I thought so,' he said, squinting at me in a way I remembered. It made him look a bit slow. Actually, he was incredibly clever.

I stared at him slack-jawed. 'I don't believe it,' I said.

'Oh, my God,' I said, shaking his hand. It felt squishy and slightly clammy.

We had called him Animal, perhaps after the mad drummer in *The Muppet Show*. He had been called that before my time, the nickname following him down the years. Our naming conventions often meant that we nicknamed somebody their polar opposite. We'd had a teacher with poker-straight hair called 'Curly'. Animal's real name was Mr Stack.

He was wearing a shapeless tweed jacket with leather elbow patches, much as I remembered. It might have been the same jacket. Its shoulders were decorated with a sea of dandruff. He had a long nose with slit-like nostrils. An image of him walking across the schoolyard behind the grey metal fences, eating biscuits furtively – so he wouldn't have to share them – flashed into my mind. 'Give us a biscuit, sir,' we used to shout at him.

His skin was still pockmarked and the thick bottle glasses that made his eyes look abnormally big were smudged. He needed a haircut. And he still wore the big leather 'Made in Ireland' – *Déanta in Éirinn* – shoes.

'I wasn't sure if it was you there at first, faith,' he said, peering at me myopically.

'Have the years been so unkind?' I trilled, and instantly regretted it.

He didn't reply, just kept looking at me closely as if I was an alien fallen to earth.

'How are you?' I asked him.

'Erra sure grand,' he said, in his thick Kerry accent. Suddenly I was struck by a thought that made me feel damp with embarrassment. He would have registered the change in my speech. But there was no way I could revert to the broad Dub accent of my youth without sounding even more of a fraud.

'In here with a suspected broken arm,' he said. It was tied up in a tea-towel. 'And how are you yourself?'

'I'm terrible,' I wanted to howl. 'I feel so ashamed and so low and so hollowed out. I've hit rock bottom.' I had no armour left but, like General Custer, I made one last stand. I smiled at him, baring my expensively purchased boomtime teeth. 'I'm great, thanks,' I said, forcing my voice into a pleasant perkiness.

''Tis cat in here,' he said, looking around.

He was an out-and-out culchie. That I remembered. We used to take the holy piss out of him. And he used to give it right back to us. 'I'd never trust a Dub to watch my spuds boil,' he'd say, so that we'd howl with laughter. With his *Evening Press* and the Kerry football jersey he'd wear under the tweed jacket. '*An peil*', he called the football. He was always bursting into Irish. We teased him because we were mad about him. He was an inspirational man. A brilliant teacher. There had been nobody to touch him at St Fachtna's. He had believed in us. He was our own Mr Chips.

'What did you do with yourself?' he asked.

I stared at him dumbly. Then: 'After school?'

He nodded.

My stomach churned. The pause grew and stretched ahead of me accusingly. I was assailed by memories that I had done a good job of screening. 'Well,' I said, in a peppy little voice, wilfully misunderstanding him, 'I got married and had two lovely children. Dylan is nearly twenty-two, he's a stock-broker. Ella is nineteen, and she's just finished first law.' I gave him a brilliant purposeful smile. 'She's gone to America for the summer on a sort of a scholarship to do with prisoners' rights. My husband Frank is a property developer.' His eyes were completely unreadable. 'You might have read about him?' I said, instantly conscious that I'd referred to my husband and therefore to his success.

I did this a lot. It was my way of gaining recognition. I'd feel a pulse of pride when I saw the look in their eyes that seemed to say, 'Ah, now we're interested'. It was my only way of identifying myself in a public sense – my calling card. It was downright pathetic.

Animal was ominously silent.

'Frank Lawlor, the property developer?' I tried again, slightly indignant that he might not know of him.

He sort of nodded. I wasn't entirely sure. The big fishy eyes were still trained on me. He lacked social skills. He taught maths. Figures were his thing.

'What did you do *yourself*, though?' he said, squinting.

I looked down at his scuffed shoes. 'Don't ask me this,' I wanted to shout, heat creeping into my cheeks. In the world I moved in women didn't get asked this question. We were mothers and wives, end of story, some of us decorative, some of us not, but we didn't have to account for ourselves.

'I worked for a while in Brown Thomas,' I said, reddening. I had been on a makeup counter, which was considered the business back then. I used to sashay up Grafton Street in my nice clothes thinking I was the cat's pyjamas. 'And I worked as a hostess in a nightclub on Leeson Street,' I added, my tummy tightening. 'Those were the days,' I burbled, with a laugh.

Silence.

'You never did anything with your maths so?'

'No,' I said, glancing down at my hands. 'Leave me alone,' I wanted to say. 'Just leave me alone.'

He shook his head slowly. 'I thought we'd hear about you,' he said. 'I felt certain that we'd have news of you. About the things you'd gone on to do,' he said, sticking his tongue out between his teeth.

Then, when I'd thought he could twist the knife no further, he said it. The blood in my veins turned to lead. 'You had an exceptional gift for maths.'

Oh, good Jesus. I was winded. I'd limped into the hospital with my heart aching from a faithless husband, the humiliation of a suspected drug overdose, the knowledge that I had insulted my friends – and now this. It was like being hit over the head with a shovel.

'My mother got cancer just after the Leaving,' I said.

'I heard that all right,' he said, his eyes still trained on me. 'I was sorry,' he added.

A male nurse came out through a door labelled 'Triage'. 'Sean Stack,' he called.

'Looks like your ship has come in,' I said jokily.

'"Twas a pleasure to meet you, Anita. Take care of yourself,' he said. 'You've changed a lot, girleen.' He shuffled off, trailing the unmistakable whiff of disappointment.

The hospital let me go about six hours later. Walking outside, I blinked at the grey morning air. They had made me run on a machine and given me beta-blockers to slow down my pulse. The little arrhythmic seizures had tailed off. As an official waste of hospital resources, I was deeply ashamed of myself. My mouth was sandpaper dry. My head pounded from a hangover. I was jittery and fearful of the impending showdown with Frank.

He was waiting for me when I got home. I heard him

hawking before I saw him. I paused outside the door before entering the room to see him sitting on the floor. He was slumped against the base of the circular 1970s cream leather sofa. The bedroom furniture had been made by a fancy design team. Ciara, Maeve and I had flown to Italy armed with our credit cards – the unholy trinity of consumerism – whipping each other into an orgy of competitive buying, like junkies let loose over a mound of white powder.

Frank's shoulders were dipped. Even from where I stood I could see that his eyes were puffy and sleep-deprived. I caught sight of my reflection in the two-tone 1960s mirror – a 'find' that I had been directed to by the man who had overseen much of my buying for the house. When I looked at it now I thought it was ugly – if not as ugly as me. I looked like someone who had fallen out of the ugly tree and hit every branch on the way down. It was not a good look when you were trying to persuade your faithless husband to stay with you.

The rain lashed against the window panes. The pasty grey light infiltrated our bedroom, dappling the floor in sombre patches. Frank's meaty arms were folded across his squat body as if to protect himself. He was dressed in trousers and an open-necked shirt, brown suede loafers on his feet. In our early years he had been very keen on shirts and ties and waist-coats until I'd explained the rules of casual dressing to him.

He knew I was standing there. My pulse began to gallop again. He broke the silence first, his head turned away. 'Where were you?'

'Hospital,' I said shortly, feeling my heart accelerate.

He accepted my explanation without comment. There was no 'Look at the state of you', which said a lot. 'We'll need an ark if this keeps going,' he remarked, staring out the curved bay windows.

He was trying to talk about the weather. He and his culchie family never shut up about it, I thought, angry tears filming my eyes. 'Why, Frank?' I demanded. My voice had a rasping quality to it.

He looked at me briefly, then flicked his eyes away.

'*Why?*' I demanded, stepping further into the room. My voice rose an octave. 'Is it because I'm losing my looks, because I'm a depreciating fucking asset like all your other interests?'

Still he said nothing.

'Tell me, you *fucker! Tell me!*'

'I don't know why,' he said, his eyes directed anywhere but on me. 'It just sort of happened.'

I was shaking. 'Why did you do it? Was it the excitement, the freshness . . . the newness of her or what?' I was shouting now.

He ran his hand across his face. 'Christ, I don't know, Anita,' he said.

'It just sort of happened,' I parroted back to him. Then: '*You gave her a bracelet just like mine!*' I screamed. '*My* Jo Malone perfume!'

For the first time his eyes swivelled to meet mine.

'I met her when I was at Will's clinic. I sat next to her on the day of your fiftieth. She told me about her boyfriend and how he'd been finished with his wife for years. How they were just going through the motions,' I said. 'Then I worked out she was talking about *us.*'

'Anita . . . I'm sorry. I'm sorry.'

'Sorry doesn't cut it, fucker. Did you go out trawling bars and nightclubs looking for someone?' I asked, jabbing my finger in the air.

He pinched the bridge of his nose. It was slightly broken-looking, like a boxer's, but it was a nose I had loved. 'I met her through work,' he said quietly, lowering his head. 'She's an estate agent.'

'How perfect,' I said, with a hard, bitter laugh that nearly choked me. 'She's an estate agent,' I repeated. I was pacing up and down the room now, ranting like a mad woman. 'I gave up everything to be your wife,' I cried. 'I wanted to be a teacher.'

His hand was half covering his face. 'You *were* working in Brown Thomas when I met you,' he said.

'I could have gone to college,' I screamed. 'I met my old teacher last night and he said I had an exceptional gift for maths. I could have gone to Trinity College, Frank.'

'Nobody stopped you, Anita,' he said.

That wasn't true. *He* had bloody stopped me. I had been undermined by his success. He had used up all the oxygen in our marriage for achievement. Frank's career had always come first. Yet even as I laid the entire blame at his doorstep, I felt creeping doubt. 'Fuck you!' I shrieked. 'I had lots going for me,' I said then, my chest heaving.

'Nobody doubts that,' Frank said.

'Nobody doubts that. Nobody doubts that.' I mimicked his voice. 'The whole world doubts it.'

I was crying now, walking around in manic circles. 'I'm forty-five years of age. What am I supposed to do? I have nothing of my own.'

'I'll look after you.'

'I'm not a child, Frank.'

He said nothing.

Tears rained down my face. 'My identity,' I spat, my chest heaving, 'has been centred on being a mum and a wife. What am I supposed to do now? Am I supposed to just find myself a new identity?'

It was then that my eye was caught by the bags. They were standing at the bottom of the grey *chaise-longue*. The bottom of my stomach fell away. Feverishly I changed tack and began to grope for the right words that would make him stay. At that second I knew I would be prepared to live with the humiliation, to shed my dignity – I would be prepared to eat shit – if he wouldn't leave me.

'We can get past this,' I said, trying to make him look at me. 'I love you, Frank. I'm your wife.' My voice was pleading now. 'Don't go.' The tears were cascading. He was deliberately not looking at me.

'Anita,' he said, putting a hand over his eyes.

I put my bunched-up fist to my mouth. 'You wanted her to have an abortion. I saw it in the note.'

His jaw was clenched.

'You wanted her to have an abortion, which means you didn't want to have a family with her.'

'She doesn't believe in abortion,' he said.

'We can go for couples counselling,' I said, although even in my panic I knew that, with Frank, that was about as likely as a pig flying past the window.

He stood up so that we faced each other. I was desperate now. 'Do you remember the day we got married, Frank? How happy we were? Walking down the aisle after we were married, Mr and Mrs Lawlor . . . It was such a beautiful day even though it was November. The sun was shining but there was a bit of wind. The confetti blew everywhere.'

His eyes looked moist. 'Don't, Anita,' he said softly.

I was babbling now, like a drowning woman fighting to keep her head above the water. 'You helped me with my veil when we stepped outside. It blew in my face. Do you remember that, Frank? It was like we were in our own little bubble we were so happy.'

We'd driven off in his car. Just the two of us, the cans dragging along the ground, the 'Just Married' sign organized by

DJ, who'd been the best man. People on the street and in other cars had waved at us. I couldn't remember what we'd said to each other but I remembered that it had felt as if we were the only two people in the world.

'She's pregnant, Anita,' he said. His voice was very quiet now, almost inaudible. 'She said she was on the pill but she's pregnant . . .' His voice petered out. His eyes were wet. He lifted his shoulders as if galvanizing himself. Then he walked to the dresser, pausing mid-stride. 'I'm sorry,' he said, his back to me.

I watched him propel himself forward again. His fingers curled around the car keys. My face was as wet as the windows outside. My voice dropped to a whisper. 'Don't go, Frank. Don't go.'

He was positioned by the door now. I held out my arms, pleading. He was moving beyond me. My heart began to accelerate again. I grabbed his sleeve and started to sob. 'Jesus Christ, don't do this to me, Frank.' I tried to prise the keys from him, leaning in towards him, but he pulled away flinching. He lunged for his bags. Scooping them up, he ran out the door. I could hear his footsteps pounding down the stairs and dying away. The front door banged. A car door slammed. The engine roared into life. And then there was the sound of a car reversing out of the drive.

Part II

7

Karen was sucking the life out of a fag. 'So, how are you?' she asked, setting down the iron so that a little nimbus cloud of steam puffed into the air.

I rested my elbows on the kitchen table and nudged some crayons out of the way. I wasn't sure how to answer her. I was alone, rattling around in my house with Crouton, our dog. I felt like a displaced person, a refugee. Even Crouton seemed depressed, lying around in his 'I love Mutt Ugly' sweatshirt, with his head resting on his paws.

'I'm worried about Dylan,' I said.

Dylan had taken the news of Frank's leaving very badly. He had refused to see his father and wouldn't take his calls. Big surprise there. I believed that Frank and I loved our children equally – but there was Team Frank and Ella, Team Anita and Dylan. Roughly speaking, I shielded Dylan from Frank's disappointment, and Frank gave Ella the validation she required.

'It'll take time,' Karen said.

'Does Ella know?'

'No, thank God.'

We had decided not to say anything to her while she was so far away. Dylan had agreed to maintain the pretence. Still, considering the amount of publicity, I was surprised no one else had mentioned it. When she had rung from the States it had seemed incredibly weird saying, 'No, no real news,' when she'd asked if anything was up.

'And how are *you*?' Karen was watching me out of the corner of her eye.

How was I? I didn't want to tell my sister how I felt split open. How I was gripped by the nothingness of my life. How I replayed the scene of Frank running down the stairs, his receding steps echoing in my head, over and over. How I burst into tears spontaneously, sometimes sobbing as if I was in physical pain. How I had shocked myself with some of my thoughts – thoughts that had ambushed me in the middle of the night. Thoughts about smashing my Range Rover into a concrete wall. The sort of black thoughts that I would never have thought myself capable of.

Karen was wearing the usual face she wore for talking about Frank. She was in her element now that it was open season on him and she no longer had to make sly digs. She had a legitimate reason to hate his guts. She was dying for me to let rip on him. She had been good to me, though, far better than I deserved, disloyal cow that I had been. There were days when I saw no reason to get out of bed. When Karen had come over on her white charger, to find me mouldering in the sheets, she'd half coaxed, half bullied me to my feet.

'Thanks, Karen.' I had begun to cry as she'd handed me a glass of water and some painkillers.

'For what?' she'd asked. 'I'm your sister.' I had felt a fresh burst of shame for having sidelined her.

'I'll rip his head off,' she had said. And it seemed that the sentiment had stemmed as much from her upset for me as from her dislike of Frank.

Now I said, 'I'm okay.' I felt tired and limp all the time, even though I was doing nothing more strenuous than sitting on my backside staring into space – or staring into the bottom of a wine glass. I found myself waking with a fuzzy head and dry mouth. Splashing my face, I would resolve not to drink that day. But then as the hours wore on there seemed no compelling reason not to drink.

My friends had mostly gone away for the summer to their second homes. As soon as the holidays rolled around and the children had done whatever exams they were doing, there was a mass exodus from south County Dublin as they left for the season.

Ciara was stationed in West Cork, presumably battling it out in the rain, which was still of epic proportions although she'd made light of it. She had rung once to relate 'news', in a gay social voice, which let me know that she was still not over the things I'd said in the Shelbourne. They'd been body-boarding at Barley Cove where the waves were rough and amazing. Will had caught a lobster so she was making a fish soup with a recipe that Will's sister had given her, which involved roasting the lobster shells.

Frank and I had gone down there once. Will had spent a lot of his time visiting the butcher and the fishmonger on the pier and generally bellowing across the narrow street at some other chum down from Dublin on his holidays about 'the wonderful fresh lobster' he'd bought on the pier from a fisherman called Liam or Willy or Padjo.

'Never again,' Frank had said, on the drive back. 'It's no holiday if you're stuck freezing your balls off, looking out at the mist. Even the feckin' cows look depressed.'

Frank actually resented the way Will and Ciara went to West Cork. He was deeply suspicious that it was yet another way of asserting their poshness. 'It's just plain stupid trudging through the rain for a walk and pretending you're all happy campers when you could be off sunning your arse in a five-star abroad with waiter service.'

Ciara had said nothing about me coming down. Despite the banter about the lobster and the waves and the hot buttered scones in Adele's Tea Room, our conversation had been strained. I didn't blame her. I had implied that her marriage was boring and as good as accused her of being a drug addict.

All my friends knew now that Frank had bolted and was having a baby with somebody else. It was in this context that they had mostly forgiven me for my meltdown.

Shannon had gone home with the kids to the States to see her parents, as she did each summer. She texted me a lot, encouraging me to keep going and move on. She'd even suggested that I come with her to America, which was lovely of her, but I suspected she was relieved when I turned her down.

Maeve's appetite for gory details of the split far outweighed any ire she might have felt. She had suggested that I talk to a lawyer and fast. 'The word on the street, Anita, is that Frank has made a big mistake in trying to build those hotels, that he won't get the planning and that he's going to go under.'

Clearly the big bash we'd thrown for his fiftieth had failed as a PR exercise.

'You need to get a settlement sorted quickly. You need to be pragmatic.'

Well, Maeve was pragmatic. Underneath the pretty sexy surface lay thinly disguised ruthlessness. She had decamped to Northern Italy where they had a villa. It was outside Portofino near the rock star's place, a fact she tortured Ciara with. 'Oh, yes, she's just so lovely,' she'd say of the rock star's wife, and poor Ciara would go green.

In fact, Maeve didn't give much of a damn about them, I thought, although she said it was worth living near them to torment Ciara, who was hell-bent on penetrating their circle and was constantly finding ways to get closer to them.

It wasn't hard to imagine Maeve rehashing the whole sorry tale under the hot Italian sun. I could see her in my mind's eye, her face pulled into a suitably sympathetic shape: 'Poor

Anita. God love her, you wouldn't wish it on your worst enemy.' Maeve would use all those Irish ways of expressing sympathy at somebody's failure while relishing the chance to have a good old gossip. To be fair to Maeve, she had invited me to Italy, which she needn't have done. 'Don't be a stranger,' was what she had said, and I felt she'd meant it. Maeve was kind, in her own flawed way, and in spite of her lacerating tongue.

Maureen had gone to Marbella. Her villa was an enormous U-shaped palace with twelve bedrooms, but it was dwarfed by its gigantic neighbour, the ridiculously big villa of a Saudi prince. We had one near by, although not on that scale. It was in an Irish enclave, slightly characterless but with a pool and palm trees and a small staff of local people who came in each day to water the grass, make omelettes and clean the house.

Maureen had begged me to come out. At one point I had considered it. The news of our split – it had been reported in the social diary of one paper and in a tabloid on the front page, 'Developer Frank Lawlor Splits from Wife' – had travelled around our patch of Dublin, which gave me another reason for wanting to flee. But I couldn't face Maureen's excessive sympathy. She was ringing and texting me non-stop, encouraging me to talk about it. She was ruthless in her compassion. There was nowhere to hide from the headlamp beam of her fanatical, unrelenting sympathy.

'I know better than anyone what you've been through,' she'd said on the phone, so I decided there and then to stay put. I didn't want to offer my story up for dissection over lunch at the Marbella Club, to put myself forward as an object of pity. And I just wasn't up to faking happiness. You needed energy for that.

So there I was at home. I phoned Frank a lot, often in the

middle of the night, great storms of tears and curses raining down the phone at him.

'Anita, you're going to have to stop ringing me like this,' Frank had said one night, so that I had paused mid-rant. He had faltered, then added, 'Fiona is pregnant. She needs her sleep.'

Frank was living with her in Milltown. She had an expensive apartment – I wondered if Frank had bought it for her – but its value had tumbled, according to Karen, who made it her business to know these things and who read the property pages avidly. Karen was cute as the bees. She was mortgage-free, thanks to living in our parents' council flat. After Ma had died, Karen and her Darren had moved in with Da to look after him. They had talked about moving on but it had never happened. So now Karen was failing to keep the smile off her face as the chickens came home to roost for those caught up in the great gold rush that had been the Irish property boom. 'To quote Bessie Burgess,' she said one night, 'yez are all rightly shanghaied now.'

'Do you not feel any sympathy for people in trouble?'

She had shrugged. 'It's a rich person's recession. It's the little people like me who'll have to carry the can for the crap they've got the country in. Some people, like the bankers and – sorry to say, mentioning no names – some of the developers, are lucky we're not hanging them in the street. In fairness to my Darren, he mightn't exactly be Einstein but he did say unfettered capitalism would destroy the capitalist system in the end.'

I had thought of what Frank had said about Darren after he'd listened to one of his political monologues: 'Darren is a lipless pussy-whipped cunt who might get more workers' rights if he ever got up off his hole and did some work.'

Anyway, I had challenged Karen: 'Wasn't it Marx who said that, rather than Darren?'

Karen had smirked. 'There's hope for you yet. I see signs of recovery when you're getting that lippy. And you know your Marx. I wouldn't have you down as a Marxist.'

'Pots and kettles,' I had shot back. 'Not sure you'd make the best comrade either, with your annual holiday to Spain and your department-store job.'

'I'm lukewarm on Communism,' she'd served back at me – conversation with Karen was very often like a heated game of tennis, with balls banging across the net. 'Russian women didn't have it easy under Communism, queuing for bread and having to wear hickey clothes and crap eye shadow and having to stick crisps bags on fellas' willies with elastics instead of johnnies because they were too poor to get proper ones.'

Karen was inspecting me now. 'You look a bit tired,' she said.

I gave a short bark of a laugh. 'You think? I know I look awful,' I said. There were pouches under my eyes. My cheeks were sunken, my makeup slapped anyhow onto my face. I looked ragged in a way I had never looked before. I had always been vain, twirling in front of mirrors making faces, ploughing way too much effort into how I looked, polishing the surface. Now I had gone the other way.

'You don't look awful,' she said, too quickly. 'I just meant that you seem very down.'

I'd woken that morning to find mascara pooled in the creases at the corners of my eyes. My appointment for Botox and fillers had come and gone so the lines on my face – the number eleven between my brows, the brackets on either side of my nose – had crept back. I just didn't have the energy to get it done and I wasn't all that sure that I could afford it.

I caught my sister's eye. 'Karen,' I said, with emphasis, 'I know I look like Elvis in his later period in Vegas. When he had the cape and rhinestones and the puffy face.'

She spluttered with laughter. 'Ah, Anita, I didn't mean it like that.' She pulled on the fag again and exhaled.

I could barely see her through the smoke. We had grown up in a cloud of it, with Ma and Da puffing away like two wheezy chimneys, their fingers yellowed by the nicotine. They hadn't even stopped when they had chest infections. Da would have an inhaler in one hand and a lit fag in the other. Even when Ma was diagnosed with cancer she hadn't stopped. Karen had smoked from when she was about fourteen. And all my older brothers and sisters smoked. Not that I knew much about them. They'd all pretty much moved off by the time Karen and I arrived. They were fleeting presences that came and went occasionally, back from England and America. One up north. Another in Australia. They were of the age when people had left Ireland in droves in search of work – there used to be a national joke about the last person left turning out the lights.

Karen and I were like a second family to Ma and Da. Ma thought she was done when she had my sister Jacqueline. Then, fifteen years later, Karen made her appearance. She was called a change-of-life baby. When I came along six years later, I was called a bloody miracle. So really there was only Ma, Da, Karen and me at home, all smoking.

None of the Lawlors had ever smoked, apart from Frank, who kept it a deadly secret and was always on and off them. For a while, in the early days of our relationship, I'd enjoyed winding his family up, lighting cigarettes and taking long, hard, enjoyable drags. It was one of the few ways I could rebel. I'd given up when I'd fallen pregnant with Dylan.

'Another cuppa?' Karen asked, putting on the kettle.

'Lovely,' I lied. My tongue was hanging out of my head for a drink. I'd have sold my own granny for a glass of wine. I wasn't telling Karen that. She'd passed a few critical remarks about my drinking. People in glass houses, I thought. I'd said nothing about her chain smoking. We all needed our little crutch.

She put on the kettle. We were a family of tea drinkers. My ma had been able to do the housework with a cup and saucer balanced on her palm. Every single event in our lives had been punctuated with a cup of tea.

The raucous sound of Karen's daughter Colleen Eireann – a sweet-faced kid with two big bunches of black hair sticking out of the sides of her head – and her friend practising their Irish dancing in the hall drifted into the room.

'It must be lonely in that big house,' Karen said, still inspecting me.

'The mornings are the worst,' I heard myself say, in a flat, droopy voice. There was the awful moment of realization when I opened my eyes and it dawned on me yet again that he had gone. Images from the morning Frank left would run through my head. Me sinking to the ground, still in my blood-spattered rig-out, my cheek against the carpet. Still as a statue for hours. Like a dead animal that had been run over. Until Lena the cleaner had come upon me and had set down her bundle of ironed laundry on the floor, saying something in Polish that I didn't understand.

Karen unplugged the iron and folded up the board. I couldn't imagine ironing now. My mother had taken in ironing to earn extra money. She had ironed and cleaned for other people, then come home and done it all over again for us.

'In a funny sort of way I miss his snoring,' I said, my eyes focusing on the brightly coloured children's paintings plastered all over the wall. Karen's kitchen was very kidcentric, I thought, visualizing the smooth, expensive contours of my designer kitchen.

I also missed the chance to give out about the toilet seat not being put down. I missed him driving up at night and coming in the door, saying, 'Would somebody turn off a fucking light? This place is like an effin' lighthouse.'

Intending to change the subject, I said, 'You have the place very nice, Karen.'

Karen gave a little toss of her head but she looked pleased. 'I got a bit of stuff from Habitat before it closed down,' she said, lighting another fag from the last. 'Darren and me drove up north to Ikea a couple of times. And you'd pick up a good bit of stuff in the Arnott's sale.'

'You were always a great shopper,' I said. She was filling the kettle.

'And you were always terrible with money,' she said. 'Speaking of which, have you spoken to *him* yet about the house and money?'

I shook my head.

'I don't want to be getting on your case, but you need to know where you stand.'

The word 'money' made my ears ring. A sort of roaring in my head forced me to shut down the rogue thoughts that were trying to penetrate my brain. *You have no money now. You are dependent on your husband who has left you. You rely on his charity.*

'Our whole family were shite with money,' Karen added.

It was true. I had spendthrift genes. There was never any extra money growing up, we were always in the red, but on the rare occasion that fortune shone on us – like when Da won money on a Spot the Ball competition or on the dogs – the money had been frittered immediately. Karen was the thrifty exception. Karen always had a few quid stowed away. She was the Bank of Butler – even Ma would borrow from her sometimes to get a bottle of milk or a packet of fags. At one point Karen had even considered charging interest on her short-term loans. She could have had a successful career as a money-lender.

I meant what I'd said to her. She had the place like a little palace now. The whole building was different today anyway. The Corpo had totally rebuilt the flats so that the block was unrecognizable from when we were growing up. They even had solar panels on the roof, which had made Frank grumble, 'Yeah, and it's the likes of me that are paying for it,' even though he had every tax dodge going in the book – tax shelters, buying art, sticking stuff offshore, dosh under the mattress, you name it. When the Corpo had torn down the terrace and replaced it with brand new modern flats there had been some complaints from well-heeled objectors at the destruction of such a historic part of Dublin, but people like Karen and Darren weren't complaining. It wasn't easy living in a piece of history. And while I could understand why people were sorry to see the old terrace pulled down – the beautiful doorways and arches and Bakelite handles all gone – it was far nicer sitting in a bright front room than it was in the gloom of our childhood.

Now all the flats had central heating. And, of course, they had bathrooms and loos. I'd been about seven when we'd stopped sharing a toilet with two other families. Mrs Collins, who had lived next door and given out about everything from the government to the young people – like one uninterrupted monologue – was long dead and buried. The Keoghs, a large family, with children like steps, all with watery blue eyes and bad chests, had moved to Neilstown. It had been the policy in the seventies to move Dubs from the inner city to housing schemes on the periphery. Only a hard core of people had held out. Our family was one of those.

'They're not feckin' ethnically cleansing us,' my da had said. 'It's those feckin' culchie civil servants who want to deport us from our own city.' It had been a subject he'd felt strongly about.

Karen had boards on the floors. Her walls were painted white, which gave the illusion of more space. The old Belfast sinks were gone, which was a pity in a way, but there were bookshelves with books on. That had been a surprise. Karen and I had not grown up with books. I had made sure that was not the case with my kids, but I had not expected to see books in Karen's.

'You're staring at the books,' Karen said, following my gaze so that I coloured. 'Surprised to see them in my house, are we?'

'No, not at all,' I lied, the flush spreading.

Karen looked at me coolly. 'You were always a desperate liar.' Then, blowing out a ring of smoke, she said, 'I might never have read but that doesn't mean I don't want my kids to read.'

There was a pause.

Then she said, 'I heard this American one on daytime telly going on about how you had to give your kids the keys to lots of doors by giving them an education, and that once you'd done that, it was up to them if they wanted to go through those doors.'

She made a *moue*. 'She had frosted lipstick and a big hickey perm. And she spoke in that slow, dozy drawl that makes Americans take all day to say stuff that could be wrapped up in two seconds and which makes you want to shout at the telly, "Piss or get off the pot." But what she said kind of hit a chord with me.'

I felt a sort of shame. I had always equated Karen's insistence on remaining 'authentic' as her not wanting to get on in life. Unlike me.

There was a rattling sound, followed by a loud thump.

Karen ran over to the door and yanked it open. 'Colleen Eireann, keep it down a bit,' she bellowed. 'Good girl.' Then, more softly, in a voice that held a smile: 'Good girl, India-Jade, pet, you've a grand high kick there. You too, Colleen Eireann. You should get your auntie Anita to dance for you. She was the all-Irish champion back when you two weren't even twinkles in your daddies' eyes.'

'What does that mean?' came a giggly voice.

Karen retracted her head and winked at me. 'Never you mind,' she said, closing the door behind her. 'Colleen Eireann takes after her mother,' she said, rolling her eyes, 'at dancing.'

'You weren't that bad,' I said.

'Ah, lay off with the praise or my head won't fit out the door.'

Karen was great. The only time I had smiled in the last month was when I had been with her.

'I had two left feet and two thighs like big pink Limerick hams poking out under my costume,' she said. 'Of course, you were great. Ma used to spend hours sitting there at the *feis* with her knitting, waiting for her little chicken to scoop the first prize so she could go home and sew you another costume.'

An image flashed into my mind of me scudding across the stage in my heavy black battering shoes, my sausage ringlets bouncing, my arms rigid, counting time – *a haon, dó, trí, ceathair, cúig, sé, seacht* – full of it, packaged inside one of the elaborate Celtic costumes that Ma had spent hours embroidering for me.

'Poor Colleen Eireann,' Karen sighed, 'she's like a baby elephant.'

No question, Colleen Eireann was built like a Sherman tank. She didn't get that from her parents. Karen was curvaceous and she was carrying a couple of pounds but she certainly wasn't fat. And Darren was like a glass of milk in a tracksuit with a thin moustache – or Ronnie, as we called it growing up. Karen was probably feeding Colleen Eireann too much fattening processed food, I thought, and immediately felt guilty for being so judgemental.

'I haven't the heart to tell her,' Karen whispered. She poured the water in on top of the teabags. 'But they'll have to reinforce the stage if she keeps going. There,' she said, setting a cup of tea in front of me. She plonked the milk carton on the table. There was no jug, I thought, and batted away another judgemental thought.

'Why were we never that close, Karen?' I asked, watching her blow on her tea.

She considered my question for a minute or so. 'Because,' she said, swivelling her head towards me, 'you got to be the Virgin Mary in the Nativity play at school with a blue cloak and a Tiny Tears doll cuddled up in your arms. And I got to be a donkey.'

I laughed. 'Seriously,' I said.

'When you left home, Anita,' Karen said, fixing eyes with me, 'you made it as plain as the noses on DJ's children that you weren't coming back.'

It was true. I'd wanted to better myself. At least, that was how I had seen it. Growing up I'd often had guilty dreams of belonging to a richer, more glamorous family. Sometimes sitting in the cinema, sucking bonbons in the dark, staring up at the screen, I'd dream of belonging to another family. I'd concoct all sorts of scenarios where it would be discovered that there had been a mix-up of babies at the hospital and that I really belonged to a rich flaxen-haired man and his beautiful bow-mouthed wife who spoke like something off the BBC and brought me home to live in a big house with

164

white muslin curtains and a large garden with a dog called Lassie. I wasn't particularly imaginative.

I had loved my parents but I didn't want Ma's nervousness or Da's jaunty whistling, which gave the impression he thought he was cock of the walk, but was just a cover for his lack of confidence.

I wasn't sure how to explain my flight. There probably wasn't a way that didn't make me sound like a snobbish disloyal, ungrateful little bitch. 'Ma and Da worked so hard,' I said, feeling my way.

Karen said nothing so I continued, 'Life was such a struggle for them.'

Our parents had always been burdened by want. Ma had twelve pregnancies, four miscarriages and eight kids. Their lives were about the daily grind and duty and sacrifice and loving their family and their country. It was all about survival.

'Sometimes, Karen, I felt as if Ma and Da always expected the worst. That it sort of became their default setting. I think I wanted to get away from that.'

Karen stubbed out her cigarette and shook her head. 'They adored each other. That's why Da followed Ma to the grave.'

Technically Da had died of a brain haemorrhage. But he'd really died of a broken heart. He'd had a stroke not long after Ma went so that the left side of his body had been paralysed. He had lain in bed with his frozen limbs and thick slurred speech, dealing with the double whammy of Ma's death and the stroke. There had been talk of recovery and rehabilitation but I'd known he wouldn't last long.

It was not too sentimental to say that Ma and Da proved that true love existed. Frank used to say sometimes that men married birds for their looks and that birds married men for their money. I wasn't sure if he was joking. But I knew that Ma and Da had loved each other.

I had another stab at explanation. 'Ma and Da knew their place. I remember going down to the doc with Ma and watching her kowtowing to him – yes, sir, no, sir, three bags full, sir. I hated watching that, the way she sort of put up with him patronizing her.' I'd hated the way that, like pricked balloons, Ma and Da would deflate around school teachers or others they thought were authority figures. They scrambled for formal language they didn't have, and let themselves be totally intimidated.

Karen gave a derisive sniff. 'That doc was so full of it. One time Ma went to him with her chest and do you know what he said to her? He told her it would do her a power of good if she went out sailing.'

'No!'

'Yeah,' Karen said. 'He pointed to the photo of himself on his boat that he had hanging behind his desk.' She put on a mincing voice, and an image of the tall doctor with the leathery, flushed face and red-rimmed eyes floated into my mind. 'Sailing is wonderful, Mrs Butler. I'd highly recommend it.'

I laughed. 'I think he was an alcoholic, you know.'

'*Really?*' Her voice dripped sarcasm. She made a face. 'He was a complete pisshead. His breath was always minty but it was only masking the booze. He should have been struck off.'

'That's why Frank was so attractive to me,' I told her.

A sceptical look spread over her face.

'He never would have put up with that. He just wouldn't take it. When I had Dylan, the consultant was very good but he was a bit short with us. Frank told him where to get off. Frank never knew his place. He just went out there and took what he wanted.'

It was true. Ma and Da had never seemed to imagine

anything outside their own existence. For Frank, the world was his oyster. Karen was conspicuously silent so I decided to change the subject. I reverted to the earlier part of the conversation. 'I was a stuck-up little cow, wasn't I?' When I was young I'd cottoned on to the fact that adults loved me. They thought I was pretty and good and sweet. I'd made a career out of being pious and grubbing for approval.

Karen arched an eyebrow. 'I cannot tell a lie. Lookit, there was a pair of us in it,' she said, beginning to unwrap what looked like a cake. I watched her plunge a knife into it with more force than was necessary.

She set a plate in front of me. 'It's called cake,' she said, handing me a fork. 'And eating. You should try it some time. And, no, it's not organic,' she said. 'And it's not fat-free, dairy-free or from some Fancy Dan shop. It's a Tea Time Express cake from Dunnes, which you once thought was the dog's . . . It was hard being your older sister.'

'Bet you it's not so hard now,' I said, giving a stagey laugh.

She ignored this. 'You were good at everything. School, dancing, debating . . . I was practically slung out of school every second week for going behind the bike sheds and smoking.' She gave a big dirty laugh. 'For learning about biology in the practical sense.'

'You were cool,' I countered, 'with your eye-liner and frosted pink lipstick and your flares. Listening to music with your pals in our room with your posters stuck all over the walls.'

'Right,' she said drily.

'You were so funny. Everyone wanted to be around you.'

'Karen the character,' she said. 'I'll never forget at the end of first year old Bugs' – the principal – 'coming into the classroom with her big buck teeth stuck out in front of her and her clipboard calling out the names of the different streams, dividing us up into groups. My name got called out first. I got up off my chair trying to keep the smile off my face. I thought I was clever.'

'You *were* clever,' I said firmly. And she was.

Karen continued, 'Then she called out another name or two and the doubts started to creep in.' She looked at me. 'They weren't exactly Mensa material. Then Jean Murphy's name got called and I knew the game was up. My ears started buzzing and ringing. I thought there was some mistake. I saw Jean Murphy lumbering across the room with her pasty face and her heavy breathing and her knuckles scraping the ground and her too small eyes, God love her, and I knew that was it. I was in with the thickos.'

She puffed out her cheeks. 'It still hurts in a way,' she said, with a crooked smile. 'Isn't that fucked up?'

I said nothing.

'It felt unfair to me. I was sick with glandular fever in first year. I missed a good bit of school so I did crap in my summer tests. That was me washed up for ever. After that I sort of switched off for good. I barely went to school.'

A memory crawled into my mind then of the man from the Department of Education at our house, wondering why Karen wasn't coming to school. Da and Ma had been mortified. It had almost been as bad as having the law to the door. Karen had walked in from school – or wherever she'd been – swinging her bag over her shoulder, her school skirt cut up to her bum and the tie half-way down her chest, unaware that Da was waiting for her. He'd whacked her across the face – Da, who'd never laid a finger on us and who was trembling himself. A ghost white Karen had lifted a hand to the spot on her cheek, which was stinging red. Ma hadn't spoken all night. Da hadn't said much more.

'On the scrap heap at the age of twelve and labelled a character. "She's some bleedin' character that one." "Karen the character", that was me. Give someone a label and they'll live up to it. It's why I *never* label my kids.'

'You're the successful one now, Karen,' I said.

She rewarded this remark with a sceptical look.

'You've got a great marriage, gorgeous kids, a lovely home, a career.'

'I like my life, I suppose.' Then she said, 'I was so jealous of you. Ma and Da were so proud of you. They practically levitated off the ground when they heard you were head girl.'

My throat constricted. That was not how I remembered it. Ma and Da had seemed pleased enough but they hadn't seemed all that interested. They had not pushed me. They had not asked me about my plans.

'And when that bogger maths teacher said you should go to Trinity . . .' Karen said, and I felt as if an electric current had been shot through me '. . . Ma practically had to be sedated she was so excited. When you got the scholarship I thought she was going to have a bleeding heart attack.'

I shook my head. 'I came home and told Ma and Da that Animal said I should go to college and they gave me a very cool reception.'

'Would you go on out of that?' she said. 'They were beside themselves. I mean, they mightn't have gone on about it but it was so obvious. They probably didn't know what to say. It was like telling them you were about to travel to outer space. And we weren't the sort of family to discuss our "feelings".'

That was true, I thought, closing my eyes. There had been constant chatter in the flat but very little discussion or real talk. Things were routinely pushed under the carpet. There had been no mention of my brother Keith skipping off to England after he'd been arrested for receiving stolen tellies. I'd only heard about it years later from Karen. The commentary on our uncle Robbie's roaring alcoholism was confined to 'Ah, sure Robbie's fond of an auld drink.' Our auntie Mary went 'for a little holiday' every now and then. There was no mention of the fact that she was periodically committed when she threatened to throw herself out of top-floor windows.

Karen crossed the room, bent down and opened a cupboard. 'I found some old stuff belonging to you,' she said, turning around with a small battered cardboard box in her hand. Her tone became teasing. 'The letters you wrote to Sellafield complaining about the plant,' she said, setting the box on the table. 'Copy books. Reports. A glowing reference from Bugs, which I would pin to my chest if I was you.'

I stared at her.

'Ma kept it all.'

It was hard to believe that Ma had kept the reports she had so fleetingly glanced at. 'Why are you giving me this stuff now?'

She let a shoulder drop. 'I did a big clear-out. And it's not like you don't have the space,' she said, her tone suspiciously casual.

'Ma kept my school reports,' I repeated.

A cloud of smoke was hovering in front of Karen's face. 'She probably burnt mine out of shame.' Then she said, 'I was surprised you never made it to Trinity. You were that poor bogger teacher's great white hope. What was it he used to say? "If some day one of you walks the ten minutes up the road to Trinity College and goes through the gates, my life's work will have been worth it."'

Her comment hung in the air, like lead in my veins.

'You made such a song and dance about your studying. With your special desk and lamp and highlighter pens and study plans tacked up on the wall. I tried so hard to distract you but no way were you looking up. There was more planning went into your studying campaign for getting to college than there was for the Normandy Landings. I never got what made you change your mind. One minute you were going to college, the next you were taking a year off, and that was it,' she said, snapping her fingers.

The room had closed in on me. I felt claustrophobic.

'Why, Anita? Why did you not go to college? I've never asked you.'

'I have to go, Karen,' I said, standing up.

She looked at me dubiously.

'I forgot. I have a man coming to do some painting,' I lied, pushing back the chair.

'Don't forget your box,' she said, thrusting it into my arms.

The rain was ceaseless. It was as if one giant cloud was parked over Ireland. The rain fell and fell and fell. Nobody had ever seen anything like it before. At least, not since records began.

When Karen would yank open the curtains and attempt to strong-arm me out of bed with 'On your feet, you lazy bitch,' I'd shoot back, 'At least you can't say it's a lovely day.'

The rain bounced down from the green rows of newly planted poplars in Frank's 'development'. 'It's not a bloody development, Frank,' I'd roared at him, 'it's an estate.'

I was parked next to a clump of densely spaced plants. My usual spot. I was like Stan in the van only without a plan. I had been out here many nights. Driving down the Stillorgan dual carriageway under the flyover, past the entrance to UCD, a little tipsy from wine, over the limit for sure, my SUV finding its way like a homing pigeon. Parking my car like now, watching the lights on in their apartment, picturing them inside, imagining my husband, the father of my children, lying with another woman, a baby growing in her tummy. My knees grew weak at the thought.

At night my grief and anger would condense. I would

float through the house, which had taken on the quality of a morgue, the silence ringing in the large, shadowy rooms, the quiet closing in on me. That was when I would swing up into the Range Rover and head for the dual carriageway.

The development was reasonably new, and as property prices had started to go south, marketing techniques had become ritzier in a bid to attract buyers. There were giant hoardings running around the houses, which showed photographs of gorgeous young women and total rides of young fellas sipping champagne and looking sexy. The tag line at the bottom announced, in large bold letters, 'Where elegant people live elegant lives in elegant surroundings'. I had to stop myself placing my hand on the horn and keeping it there to rouse the elegant people from their elegant sleep in their elegant development and let them know about my coruscating inelegant pain.

A taxi drove up, splashing through the puddles, and disgorged its passengers, a couple who looked the worse for wear. It took the fella a couple of minutes to find his money. The girl ran into the darkness, her step unsteady. The car door slammed and the taxi took off.

Three young fellas on a bike sailed past, oblivious to the rain, laughter burbling from them. They were college students, I thought. One looked at me and laughed again. I was like a mad woman in my nightie with a cardigan thrown over it. A slant of yellow light from the streetlamps hit my face. Mad, drunken thoughts were coursing through my mind. I could drive up to their apartment and shout out the window so everyone in the vicinity could hear me. 'Come out you here, you fat, red-faced bastard and you curly-haired Whore of Babylon you, I'll give you elegant living.'

There were times I found myself gripped by a grief that bowled me over. It was surreal to think of Frank starting out again in an apartment with a new baby on the way, loosening his tie at the end of the day and throwing himself down on the couch, the remote control firmly in his grip, with a different woman trying to wrestle it from him.

I'd sat at home that night, eyeing the box Karen had foisted on me. There had been copy books at the top. I'd stared at the fat round girly handwriting, in which I'd shared my thoughts on nuclear power and emigration. I had been surprisingly politicized. There was a dog-eared faded clipping from the paper about the young student who had won a coveted maths prize. A photo of Ma, Da and myself at the prize-giving caused my eyes to moisten. Ma, in her blue coat and headscarf with her chapped hands firmly clasped around her bag, was looking shyly at the camera. And although you couldn't see it in the grainy shot, I knew that the face powder she wore would have been caught in the fine lines fanning about her mouth. There was Da with his slight stoop, smaller than I remembered him, in his suit, his shoes a bit too big for him, and me sandwiched between them, with a cheap bag and shoes and a wary but pleased expression.

When I told them I was going to defer my place in college they had accepted it without comment. By then a small lump had been found under Ma's arm – a small, savage lump that would cost Ma a breast, her hair and then her life.

The reference I had sought from Bugs when I was looking for work in Brown Thomas made my heart turn over. 'Anita is a natural leader, accepting of others and generous with her time. To any future employer I would describe her as the kind of person who has the rare combination of independence and reliability . . .'

The girl in the letter was a phantom. I switched on the engine. She was long gone.

8

The summer had ended and the rain had stopped. But although the oppressive black cloud had moved away it had swiftly been replaced with a cloud of another type: a financial one. Right through the interconnected villages that made up Dublin, people could talk of little else than the recession. Would we all end up living in cardboard boxes? How long would it last? Which sectors would be worst affected?

Frank was not exempt from this talk, and Dylan had told me that his name was being bandied about as somebody likely to go bankrupt. The Irish banks were said to be under-capitalized – maybe even at risk of going under – due to reckless lending to property developers like him. Even if Frank was to get his planning permission, it was by no means certain that the banks would lend him the rest of the money he needed to finish his development. Karen had ordered – that was the only word for it – me to talk to Frank about money. 'You cannot continue to bury your head in the sand, Anita. You're not an ostrich. You have no job, no pension. You need to wake up – and fast. Frank will have given personal guarantees left, right and centre. You know what that means? That Frank personally will be the mark for the repayment of all those giant loans he took.'

She couldn't understand how I could know so little about the family finances. But after I had given up doing Frank's books I had retreated from all such practicalities into a child-like state of ignorance. My card worked when I put it in the wall. Frank was generous and never reined me in. Beyond that I didn't ask. I was forty-five, with a child's understanding of my husband's finances. I felt as if I had been asleep and that now I was struggling to open my eyes and deal with what the daylight had brought.

Sooner or later I had to work my way up to the money conversation.

Frank came and went, dismantling his life with me bit by bit. Sometimes I ignored him, shutting myself in my room so that he hammered on the door begging me to come out.

'Fuck off, you dirty, cradle-snatching bastard,' I'd shout, until he went away.

Other days I trailed him around, saying things to twist the knife in his back and make him feel bad about having left me. I could have changed the locks, of course. But that would have been no more than a symbolic gesture and he might have objected. The house was in my name, I thought – but could I be absolutely sure about that? Frank had said a lot of things that had turned out not to be true.

This particular day I followed him down the stairs to the office in the basement. He looked grey-faced and jowly. I watched him plunge his thick fingers inside a filing cabinet.

'How deep will this recession go, Frank?' My breath caught in my chest as I waited for his answer.

He gave a short bark of a laugh. 'The party's over, Anita, that's for fucking sure.'

I hightailed it out of there. I didn't want to know any more. If he'd sat me down and started to lay it on the line, I probably would have put my hands over my ears and started shouting, 'I'm not listening.' The subject made my stomach knot. Frank had two houses to run now, two women. His business was shaky. I didn't work. I had no money stashed away. Basically I just didn't want to face the music.

*

There was no sign of Frank, although I knew he was coming to Dylan's party. Dylan and Biba were sharing a twenty-second birthday party in a nightclub, the Branch, on South Anne Street. Why Dylan wanted me to come I didn't know, but he was angry with his father and protective of me.

Frank would not be dissuaded from attending. 'I'm coming to his birthday, no matter what,' Frank had said, digging in his heels. 'I'm his father.'

I hadn't bothered to point out that Frank had missed years of Dylan's birthdays. And Ella's.

Whether or not Frank was bringing Fiona Keane, I didn't know, but the thought made me sick with nerves. I was running to the toilet every couple of minutes. And I was scared stiff about how Dylan might handle it. There would be drink taken, which would increase the likelihood of, at the very least, a heated exchange of words.

'Having a baby at his age,' Dylan had exploded, when he'd heard that she was pregnant. 'It's disgusting.'

While Frank's feelings weren't exactly top of my list of priorities I didn't want things to get worse between Dylan and his father so I tried to lighten his mood a little with a bit of black humour. 'Old people do have sex,' I had said, but he had just stamped out of the room.

The Branch was a sort of HQ for Dylan and the moneyed kids he hung around with. A sort of flotsam and jetsam of scenesters, wealthy south County Dublin kids – the perma-tanned pampered Celtic cubs – and what passed for celebrity in Ireland. It was owned by Jamie Deegan, the son of our neighbours. Jamie was a pal of Dylan's, and Ella had met up with him recently in New York.

The Deegans lived in one of the biggest houses on Shrewsbury Road. They had an outdoor pool, the entire floor of which was a television screen so that Ted Deegan –

a striking man with close-cropped hair – could watch the telly when he was doing his laps. The Deegans led a glamorous life, a social rung above us, although it would have driven Frank mad to hear it put like that. While we went to Marbella or stayed in the Sandy Lane in Barbados, the Deegans existed in a more rarefied world of private islands and private jets. We had been to their house for a party when they had invited all the neighbours they were not fighting with. Ted Deegan seemed to sue and be sued by even more people than Frank. Our road was a hotbed of cross-litigation, people suing each other over inches of ground, boundary walls, which showed that Frank was not the only one with the peasant obsession about land in the blood.

The Deegans' party had been an eye-popping high-camp extravaganza – an *Arabian Nights* party. Flowers had been flown in from London along with jet loads of sand from the Middle East. Staff had been employed for a couple of weeks in advance, making props and creating lighting and decorations. Maria Deegan had come swaying over the lawn on a real camel.

Ted owned a large insurance company that had expanded aggressively throughout the boom years and the Deegans were said to be billionaires, even though Ted had once lost everything by being a Lloyd's Name and had had to start again. He hung out with a senior Irish businessman who was long divorced from his wife and was said to keep a stable of young girls around the world.

Occasionally rumours swirled about the Deegan marriage. It was said that Ted had been caught by his wife in the pool house shagging their cleaner. It was also said that Ted had been seen trapped on top of the electric gates of their house, moving backwards and forwards for hours as his wife caught him attempting to scale them after he'd been out tomcatting

177

around. Maria, a petite woman with kohl-rimmed eyes, was supposedly having an affair with Ted's pal, the senior Irish businessman, right under his nose and *le tout Dublin* knew it. There were plenty of people who said she was about thirty years too old for the businessman, whose tastes ran far younger. Either way the Deegans were still together.

Biba had advertised her birthday as a sort of PR stunt, inviting media types and people from within the fashion industry – 'to increase her profile,' Dylan said. Biba was all about her profile. She got paid for turning up at promotional photo calls scantily clad. The more she got her mug in the paper, the more 'jobs' she stood to get.

Karen and I were arriving when a Porsche pulled up outside the nightclub with a squeal of brakes. Its tinted windows precluded us from having a gawk inside until the door swung open and a grinning Dylan and Biba hopped out sporting matching his and hers tans. The car, which I didn't recognize, may have been Jamie Deegan's.

They sashayed up the red carpet, waving at the two or three waiting photographers. Apart from the odd sighting of a Premiership footballer or some minor pop star from England, the Irish paparazzi had to make do with snapping barely known local people from the worlds of television, modelling and the media.

Biba led Dylan by the hand, tossing her head like a pony and looking upwards from under her eyelashes in that flirty way of hers. She threw her arms out so that her short dress rode up her thighs.

'Jaysus, wouldn't you love to yank it down?' Karen hissed, from behind her hand. 'She's so full of herself I'd say she's starring in a movie in her own head. Look at her stopping there. I'll tell you what she's doing. She's mentally hitting the pause button on the scene and checking her angle.'

We trailed after them — avoiding the carpet — to the top of the queue, as instructed by Dylan, where a lipsticked girl with a clipboard spirited us inside. She stamped our hands before ushering us up a couple of flights of stairs to what looked like the top floor of the building. We were then passed to a bosomy platinum-haired young woman who plonked us at a table.

'It's the VIP suite,' Dylan told us proudly, hunkering down to our level.

'I've news for you, Dylan, pet — there are no VIPs in Ireland, apart from Bono,' Karen told him, but her voice had been drowned in the music so Dylan just nodded, delighted with himself.

We were seated behind a velvet rope, our table — along with a couple of others — on a dais so that we were raised above the rest of the crowd, like sheep inside a pen. 'I feel like a complete eejit up here,' I remarked to Karen.

'I feel great,' Karen said, beaming from ear to ear. 'Sitting up here rubbernecking,' she added, in her unique blend of sarcasm and enthusiasm. 'It's great seeing how the other half lives.'

'Yeah, on credit,' I said drily.

'Jaysus, I never thought I'd hear the day. It's like hearing Imelda Marcos saying she's giving up shoe shopping.'

I shrugged.

'That dress is fab on you,' Karen said.

I shrugged again. She had selected a vivid turquoise dress in duchesse satin for me. I'd stood, limp and uninterested, in front of my walk-in wardrobe while she had rifled through it. 'You need to be looking hot in case that fanny has the cheek to show her puss,' she had said.

'You can take what you want too,' I had told her, flicking my head towards the clothes.

'Are you serious?'

'I'm deadly serious.'

'Happy days,' Karen had replied, rubbing her hands.

She had come in what could only be described as a rig-out, a creation of her own devising, involving a corset that hiked her boobs up, and fringing — a sort of Annie-Oakley-on-acid outfit. She was also wearing cowboy boots. And since we'd arrived she'd applied even more makeup. 'An old door needs a lick of new paint,' she had said, snapping shut her compact when she caught me watching her.

'Oh, my God, Mum, what does Auntie Karen look like?' Dylan had said, eyeing her doubtfully when she'd slipped from her stool and teetered off to the jacks.

'Not a word about your auntie, Dylan,' I said, in a sharp voice that caused him to swing his head towards me. I rarely spoke like that to him: I talked softly, using one of the long list of pet names I'd had for him since he was a baby — he gave out about it but secretly he loved it. In other words, I was the real Irish mammy who thought her boy walked on water. 'Your auntie Karen is brilliant.'

A young girl dressed in hot pants with endless legs and a thicket of hair burnt up the dance-floor below. The surrounding men were hypnotized as she threw back her head in a pose of mock-ecstasy. The club was a sea of writhing bodies, bumping and grinding. You could almost smell the pheromones in the air.

'Get a load of him,' Karen said, when she got back, nodding towards a bare-chested young man showcasing his rippling muscles. 'Christ!' She set down her drink and gave a lusty laugh. 'In our day fellas only shuffled onto the dance-floor just before they played "Amhrán na bhFiann". And only when they were pissed out of their heads.'

The atmosphere seemed very sexually charged, but I was

being middle-aged – you always thought things had been more innocent when you were younger.

'At least this lighting is our friend,' Karen shouted, pointing to the dimmers. 'I wouldn't stand down there if you paid me,' she said, gesturing to Biba beneath us, illuminated by strobe lights.

Biba had flitted from person to person, like a bee between flowers, having her picture taken. Now, briefly stationary, she was talking to an incredibly big man. Built like a monster, he was in a tight T-shirt, chosen to highlight his beefed-up trapezoids. He looked vaguely familiar, I thought, watching him smile at something Biba was saying. He was a sportsman, possibly rugby. The bold diagonal stripes of Biba's dress flashed as she leant over to whisper something into his ear. I watched them disappear into the shadows at the rear of the floor.

'I wouldn't trust that one as far as I could throw her,' Karen said, taking a long noisy sip of her violently coloured cocktail. 'She's an operator if ever I saw one. Aren't fellas awful fecking eejits the way they think with their dicks?' she said, twiddling the umbrella in her drink. 'I mean, they're so basic in their thinking. You'd wonder if in a scientific sense the evolution of women and men was different. If the developmental process didn't go as far with the fellas. And speaking of thinking with your willy . . .'

I followed her gaze to where Dylan was threading through the crowd with Jamie Deegan. At least there was one young person I knew. I didn't recognize most of the crowd, apart from the girl Maureen's Donal was seeing – to my relief, Donal was nowhere in sight, although if he had popped up in the middle of the dance-floor doing air guitar I wouldn't have been surprised. Many of Dylan's friends seemed not to be there. But, then, I could see that the party was largely a PR exercise.

I watched Jamie push a pair of sunglasses back into his hair. He had chiselled cheekbones, a deep tan and a vivid purple shirt. He was a golden boy and it seemed he always had been. He'd been brilliant at rugby, captaining the Senior Cup team in his rugby-obsessed school, which in certain circles guaranteed him a free pass for life. When his team had won the Holy Grail that was the Senior Cup his mother had hired a suite in the Four Seasons where the team, high on their victory, had got higher on champagne.

I had met Jamie the other day. He slowed down his antique sports car – a beautiful old Aston Martin that I presumed had been supplied by his old man. Ted Deegan collected cars. Jamie had told me about meeting Ella in New York. They'd gone for a drink in some bar in TriBeCa where, according to Dylan, Jamie – or his family – had a big one-storey loft apartment. It had been 'cool' to see her, he'd said, running his hand through his hair. No, Christopher hadn't been with her. She'd seemed in good form. He hadn't said anything about Frank and me splitting, I knew. Dylan had told me he had warned him to say nothing.

He was, he'd said, dividing his time between Dublin and New York where he was trying to get another nightclub established. His patter was steady and he was charming, full of beguiling bonhomie, but if you tuned into what he was saying it didn't add up to much.

Regardless, people orbited around Jamie like planets around the sun. Dylan was one of those planets. I could see why Jamie was keen on the relationship: he got both Dylan's unqualified admiration and his cash as Dylan seemed to be at Jamie's night-club on an almost constant basis. What Dylan got out of the relationship I wasn't sure. He had always been biddable, even as a child. If somebody he admired had told him to jump off a cliff, he would have done it with a good-natured dopey smile.

Jamie sat down at a low table at the far end of the VIP section on which there were buckets of champagne. Dylan had followed him and was now telling him a story. Jamie rewarded him with the slow, lazy smile that almost certainly drove girls wild. I had a pang then for the lolloping, cheerful, affectionate puppy that was my son.

Dylan was now accepting delivery of two more champagne buckets. The knot of people swarming around him held out their glasses. Drinks had arrived all night, seemingly unordered, ferried to their table by a beautiful Slavic girl with a wide mouth and a hanky for a dress.

'Who's paying for all of this?' I asked my sister.

'You are,' retorted Karen. 'He likes to live in the fast lane like his mammy and daddy.'

Frank was almost certainly bankrolling some of it. He would have given Dylan money for his birthday. Dylan had good prospects but he was very junior in the stockbroking firm, no more than a bag carrier so far. Biba and he had gone to visit Jamie in New York for a weekend and stayed in a trendy hotel in the Meat Packing District. There had been a holiday to Ibiza. And there seemed to be endless socializing, much of it involving driving around in fast cars swigging champagne. Or hanging around in Jamie's penthouse in the Docklands doing God knew what.

'You should see Jamie's pad, Mum,' Dylan had told me one day. 'It rocks. It's all glass and has this totally amazing view of the docks. His mum got a top interior architect from London to do it. The roof slides back so that you can see the sky. Plus he copied the fire out of a James Bond movie.'

Now Dylan caught me looking at him and gave me the thumbs-up. These kids were boomtime children, with their perfectly straight and whitened teeth. They were confident in restaurants and five-star hotels in a way that we, their parents, had never been. You could argue that nothing really changed, that drugs might come in and out of fashion but the mating rituals were basically the same as they had been in our day, that hair and clothes were better, but only through better nutrition and access to global influences. From birth these young people had known nothing but good times and a world of full employment. They had a sense of entitlement and the expectation that everything would go their way. But times were changing. The financial stormclouds that were gathering showed no sign of blowing away.

I was worried about how my son would fare. Underneath the quick smile, the easy patter, I knew he was drifting. Dylan was no more suited to being a stockbroker than Frank was to being a ballet dancer. I should have been more vocal. I should have helped my son to express the artistic talent his teachers had talked about. And to find real confidence, I thought, watching him being air-kissed by a pretty raven-haired girl with a wild-eyed expression that signalled she had taken something stronger than booze.

Frank was darting nervous looks in our direction from the other side of the room. I had converged on him and Little Miss Big Knockers as I was going to the loo. They were just arriving. We had stared at each other, speechless for a few seconds.

'Frank,' I had managed eventually.

'Anita,' he said, as if he'd seen a ghost.

It was a holy miracle. For the first time in his life Frank Lawlor was dumbstruck.

'That's me,' I'd said, nailing a horrible smile to my face, 'the woman you were married to for all those years.' A lump had formed in my throat. I was not good at being nasty. I was a born people-pleaser programmed to be nice, to seek approval, to burble sweetly.

So many times I had rehearsed this scene in my head, where I was majestic and menacing and beautiful in an older, slightly windswept way. Where I, Anita Lawlor, née Butler, took control of the scene. I had obsessed over this woman, wondering what she wore, what she ate, if she'd gone to college. I had thought of doorstepping her at work, of confronting her or ringing her parents.

Now I had stood stock still and reddened. I'd forced myself to swivel my gaze to her. 'Yes, that's right,' I said, hearing the tremor in my voice. 'I'm the woman from the clinic. It was my husband you stole.'

Heat had come into Fiona Keane's round cheeks but she was not quelled. Feeling damp under the arms I tried to stare her down but she had met my eye. She'd led Frank away like a guilty pet pig. I'd wanted to shout after her, 'And by the way labour is every bit as bad as they say.'

I had my back to them now. Karen threw poisonous looks at them every now and then. 'Hark at love's young dream,' she said. 'It was brazen of your woman to come. The little trollop.'

'Brazen' was a good word for her. Fiona Keane did not make you feel good about young women. She made you think of a generation of self-absorbed, hard, ambitious girls, who would do anything to get ahead. But it was not good to think like that. Down that route lay Maureen and her bitter-lemon thinking. There were lots of lovely young women like Ella who were not unsisterly and predatory.

That said, I knew that Fiona Keane had insisted on coming. Frank would not have wanted to provoke Dylan by bringing her. Nor would he have wanted to hurt me more. He was a selfish, unfaithful man but he was not unkind.

'I'd say Frank's shitting himself that I'll go over there and throw him a few digs,' Karen said. 'He's been looking at us a lot.'

'The irony,' I said, slugging back my drink. 'He was never so attentive when we were together.'

'Can you believe Frank is slipping the mickey to a chubby bird?' Karen remarked.

'Karen.'

'Sorry,' she said, looking at me apologetically, 'but she's not the best-looking.'

'She's pretty,' I retorted.

'Not a patch on you with her big head of Fanta hair.'

Karen was loyal.

'She's young enough to be my daughter.' Fiona Keane was twenty-five. 'She's got a career and a womb that will produce babies.'

Karen snorted. 'She has Frank tricked out like God knows what,' she said. 'He looks sinister in that flowery shirt. Like a child abuser or something.'

Frank's shirt was a mistake. It would have suited somebody of Dylan's age. His rotund middle-aged body was not designed for that sort of gear – it made him look paunchier and it was pinching his neck. His fitness regime seemed to have slipped.

She cupped her hands to her mouth. 'Frank! The oldest swinger in town called and he wants his shirt back.'

A striking young couple at the table next to us eyed us doubtfully.

'Frank! A village has lost its idiot.'

'Stop it, Karen,' I said, batting her arm.

'Well, she's not showing yet,' Karen said.

She was like a reporter on the front line of a battle, relaying bits of intelligence back to HQ.

'She's only about twelve weeks. They were seeing each other on and off for about six months when she got pregnant.'

'That's some going.'

'Frank said she was on the pill.'

'She was on her hole.' Karen jiggled the ice in her glass. 'No woman ever gets pregnant without meaning to.'

'Do you really think that?'

'Not when they've only been "going out" for six months.'

Frank had claimed he'd broken it off with her. And then one night she'd turned up in the Shelbourne bar. A couple of bottles of Moët later he'd gone back to her place where, 'in the elegant surroundings', a sperm had met an egg.

'Don't allow yourself to feel sentimental,' Karen advised. 'Frank did the dirt on you and got a girl not much older than your son up the pole. Keep that to the forefront of your mind. You're in the same boat as Jerry Hall. Take a leaf out of her book and get on with things. You didn't see her moping around the place. She got out there and looked fabulous.'

'I don't feel like Jerry Hall,' I said, feeling exhausted by the thought.

'Think of Diana sitting in front of the Taj Mahal looking lonely and miserable. Remember how things took off for her when she got shot of His Royal Jug Ears.'

'Look how it ended for her.'

'You were stone mad about Di,' Karen said, not willing to concede the point.

I had been.

'You got the Di haircut and you even tried to tilt your head down and look up from beneath your lashes in that shy Di way,' she said.

'Yeah,' I said, dredging up a half-smile. 'You said I looked like somebody who waved at planes.' God, I was achingly sad. I wondered if Frank was remembering, as I was, the night we had met in the nightclub on Leeson Street where I'd worked as a hostess. I had a mental picture of a much slimmer Frank, his hair still dark, standing by the bar, a bucket of overpriced wine in front of him, illuminated by ultraviolet light. He had asked me straight out. There had been no messing, no fear that he'd get knocked back. His self-belief had shone like a beacon in those dark days when Irish people were used to being poor and accepting second best. His confidence that he was going to go out there and take the world by storm had been attractive. And the fact that he hadn't been tanked up. Other fellas would sidle up to you at last orders and ask you what you were having, glassy-eyed or trying to be the last one left with you when everyone else was gone. Then they'd sort of fall on you. Frank, in his shiny suit, had asked me out for dinner. We'd gone to a restaurant on Dame Street called Nico's. It was my first time eating pasta. The waiter had had to come out and show me how to twist it around my fork. I had thought Frank was so sophisticated.

He'd lived in a flat in Rathmines with a couple of fellas from Offaly. Eamon his solicitor had been one of the gang. The sink was full of dishes. There was always the smell of a fry in the place. And the drinking was savage. Some of the lads ended up working for Frank – they hadn't progressed due to the boozing. I didn't sleep with him for ages. He'd asked me to marry him after three weeks and I'd accused him of just trying to get the leg over.

I pretended to be casual but I was stone mad about him. And he loved me. So how did you go from burning love and desire to something less intense and then to something so far in the opposite direction so that you could do what Frank had done? Maybe thousands of failings, omissions and unkindnesses carried you away from each other so that other people, like Fiona Keane, got a chance to come between you.

'He wanted her to have an abortion.'

'I'm very surprised at that,' Karen said, her lips thinning with distaste. 'I thought Frankie boy, being a devoted foot soldier of the Vatican, was against that sort of thing.'

Like me, Karen was an atheist. We got it from Da, I think. He didn't mind Ma going down to the church and doing her thing but he was a great devotee of James Connolly and Marx and the fella who got offed with the ice pick so he hadn't been too gone on religion. 'De opium of de people,' he'd say, after a few bevvies when he started to get expansive.

'Well, Frank told her he could arrange an abortion for her,' I said.

'Which makes him a fucking hypocrite into the bargain,' she said, her lip curling. She wagged a finger. 'I remember him full well lecturing me on how abortion was murder at the time of the X Case.'

I said nothing. I didn't want to get into a debate – Karen was very militant about a woman's right to choose. In the X Case a little girl had become pregnant when she was raped by her neighbour; Karen had patrolled the streets campaigning pro-choice. She said that people had thrown things at her on O'Connell Street and shouted, 'Baby-killer!' Karen, of course, had given back as good as she got – 'Say that closer to my face, you inbred cross-eyed fuck' – and some of her fellow campaigners had felt obliged to ask her to rein it in.

My shoulders sagged. 'It shows in a way that Frank didn't really want to be with her.'

'No, he just wanted to bone her without any consequences,' Karen said, her face hard.

'He gave her the run-around, which was why she came to the house with the letter. It showed he wasn't committed to her.'

'Which is just lovely behaviour,' Karen said sarcastically. 'Let's not give him a clap on the back for that.'

'It shows,' I persisted, 'that he was dragging his feet about the whole thing.'

'There's no point in thinking like that now,' Karen said briskly. 'That sort of logic is self-defeating.'

'I almost hope he loves her,' I said, after a minute or two. 'Otherwise it all seems so pathetic.'

Karen made one of her scoffing noises. 'He doesn't love her. He looks like a trapped animal. I'd say she hunted him down. Zoned in on him in a weak moment and told him he was the fucking devil and all while opening her legs. He doesn't know what hit him. About to be put on diaper duty at the age of fifty.'

'Frank didn't change nappies for Ella and Dylan.'

Karen snorted. 'This one won't stand for that. One look at her face would tell you so. He doesn't know what's hit him. And serve him right,' she said, with venom. 'Don't you dare go feeling sorry for him or I'll swing for you.'

The wine had started to work on me and I was feeling maudlin. 'I was prepared to forgive him, you know,' I said, suddenly tearful. Equal parts of love and fear had driven the decision.

'You'd have said you forgave him but you'd have grown to hate him. And what the hell would you have done with your woman and the baby?'

A rogue tear ran down my face.

She biffed my arm. 'Come on now.'

'Let's have another drink,' I said, wiping my eyes with the back of my hand.

Karen sprang up out of her seat and, extending her crossed hands, went to pull me up. 'Come on, chicken, we're outta here.'

*

I took the Rangy. It had been in a car park on St Stephen's Green. Karen never said not to drive. I suppose it hadn't entered her head that I could be so stupid, so reckless. Driving over the limit had become a habit. When I thought of it later I found it hard to believe that I had been so selfish. My thinking was that it would take less than five minutes to get home.

I drove down Lower Baggot Street. It had begun to rain, driving down in sheets, splashing off the windscreen. The wipers struggled to meet the challenge, comedic in its intensity. I turned on the radio to hear that earlier in the day people had turned back on the M50, unable to continue driving into the city such was the deluge. The emergency services had been called. It was thought that motorists had checked into hotels.

Frank and Little Miss Big Knockers had left just before us.

'Slinking off to your lair,' Karen had said, quite audibly, as Fiona Keane passed us, her shoulders thrown back defiantly. 'She's an able dealer,' Karen said to me. 'I've met a lot of Kerry people in my time, and while I'd grant you they're very clever, they're mad for money. Those Kerry people would take the eye out of your head. They're cute as the bees.'

'She's from Limerick,' I'd said.

'Those Limerick people would take the eye out of your head,' she'd shot back, without missing a beat. 'Give all your relatives down in Stab City my regards,' she'd shouted after Fiona Keane.

Frank had loitered next to us briefly, as if he was planning to say something. Karen had eyeballed him like an attack dog so he had settled for a limp wave.

'Even his hand looks guilty,' Karen had remarked, with a derisive snort. She'd yelled after him, 'Congratulations, Frank, on having your own grandchildren.'

I started. Jesus. There was a bang. My heart accelerated as I corrected the wheel. The Rangy had migrated to the left. Dammit, I thought, feeling nauseous. I'd clipped a parked Fiesta. I hadn't seen it. It was fine. I'd nudged its wing mirror. No harm done. Nearly home.

There had been no scenes between Dylan and Frank.

When we were leaving I'd hugged Dylan for longer than was necessary. He had craned his head back and asked me if I was okay. 'I'm fine, pet,' I'd said, smiling brightly. I was trying hard not to upset him, jumping out of bed if I heard him coming into the house, trying not to be needy, so that he wouldn't blame his father more and feel burdened by me. 'You were brilliant with your dad.'

After a cursory nod Dylan had ignored Frank and Little Miss Big Knockers. It must have been a new experience for Frank to be invisible. He was not used to being sidelined socially in favour of me.

'Thank you,' I had said, leaning forward and pressing my cheek to my son's.

I had felt him stiffen. 'Why did he have to bring *her*?' he'd asked, pulling back from me, his face contorted. 'He's a loser.'

'Please don't speak about Dad like that, Dylan,' I had said softly. 'He's still your father and he loves you very much.'

Dylan had shaken his head in a way that told me he was trying not to cry. It made me want to howl.

'Go have fun, my pet,' I had said, etching a deliberate smile onto my face. I had aimed for a jaunty, upbeat tone. 'Happy birthday!'

I was on Pembroke Road now, scudding through Ballsbridge past the white circular American Embassy on my right.

There had been no scenes.

'Anita,' Karen had said, underneath her umbrella, a plume

of her smoke floating up into the ether, 'leave the grog alone when you get home.' She'd asked to come with me. 'We can have a pyjamas party.'

'I want to be on my own, Karen. Thanks, though.'

'Okay,' she'd agreed reluctantly.

We'd stood in silence as Karen had pulled hard on the fag. 'Thanks, Karen,' I'd said. 'I just need to . . . sleep.'

She'd looked at me. 'No more booze.'

'No more booze,' I'd echoed, clamping on a false, perfidious – an Ella word – smile. I was already hearing the sweet sound of the bottle being uncorked.

I was turning into a liar, I thought, inching forward and waiting to exploit a gap in the traffic. Booze was making a liar of me. My eyes swam with tears. The visibility was terrible. I saw my chance. Gunning the accelerator, I swept right taking the corner too wide. The Range Rover reared forward, like a huge metal stallion, mounting the footpath with a huge bump. There was a crashing sound of metal crunching against wrought-iron railings.

Switching off the ignition, I sat crouched over the wheel, stunned. My head fell back against the seat. I swivelled it to the side. There was a faint ringing in my ears. I don't know how long it was before I saw a car with markings slide up to the kerb on the other side of the road. A man jumped out of it. He had a rain jacket. He was putting on his hat. I stared at him, shadows flickering in my head, as he strode across the road. I was a little dazed. There was a sharp rap on the window. He was beckoning to me to roll it down. I leant forward to find the button. It took me a minute or two to find it. Everything seemed in slow motion.

'Please step out of the vehicle, ma'am.'

He was stationary in front of me. His lips were pursed.

Still I didn't move.

'Step out of the vehicle, ma'am.'

The tone had gone from firm to insistent. Oh, God. He was barking at me now.

'Ma'am, I'm afraid I'll need you to step out of the vehicle and take a breathalyser test.'

9

I got one call. I rang Frank. He had come charging into the station on his white steed with his *consigliere* Eamon in tow. Now we were standing on the steps of the Donnybrook garda station, the Three Stooges. It was the early hours of the morning. Frank was grey-faced, his lips a worrying blue that I was trying to ignore. He had damp circles under his arms and there was a faint sheen on his forehead.

Eamon's sallow skin looked yellow under the streetlights. His bald patch gave him a monkish appearance. He was a small, slightly nervy man, with a high-pitched laugh that was nowhere in evidence now. We'd known him for ever.

Frank lit a cigarette. He was back on the fags. Eamon smoked like a demon too. I watched them, Mutt and Jeff, friends since childhood. Two boys from Offaly – from the same tribe – done good. Eamon was a clever Offaly boy – from even humbler circumstances than Frank – who'd the Christian Brothers to thank for his education. He'd studied law at night. He had the same political allegiances as Frank and was in the tent everyone wanted to be in at the Galway races with his small blonde wife, who was dwarfed by the massive feathers she had stuck in her head, which made her resemble a cockatoo. She'd bought it with her mother in tow for a second opinion – country girls let loose with big wedges of the cash that Eamon had been salting away.

I was fond of Eamon. He was a decent old skin in his own lick-arse fox-faced way. He was what passed as a friend for Frank. Frank knew everyone, he was gregarious and outgoing, but he was essentially a lone wolf. He had fallen out with more people than I could keep track of so it was a miracle that he and Eamon had been friends for over forty years.

Of course, Eamon was a yes-man, like most people Frank had managed to work with successfully. Frank's thin skin and psyche did not allow for criticism. I'd often wondered privately if his Dubai-style resort scheme had happened in part because he surrounded himself with men who were not prepared to shout, 'Halt.'

Frank gave him an awful time, leaving messages at six in the morning – 'Answer the fucking phone, Eamon.' Or he would bellow, 'Can I do it or not?' Eamon definitely earned his money. But he'd made plenty out of Frank. And when the good times had rolled there had been plenty of dough to go around. So, Eamon would have jumped off a cliff for Frank.

Eamon was godfather to Ella. He always remembered her birthday and Christmas, and came to the house with unimaginative but generous presents. You could see, though, that he couldn't quite get over his luck at being *a solicitor*, just as his wife Carmel hadn't got over the joy of marrying one. Of course it had been Karen who had pointed that out to me, years before. 'I'd say the pair of them get down on their knees every morning and thank Holy God for making Eamon a solicitor,' she'd said.

Anyway, fair play, Eamon had got the finger out in the station. He'd swung into action, asking questions in a crisp tone, taking notes, pushing up his sleeve to check the time, demanding to speak to the member in charge, like a small, determined dog with a bone.

I'd been driven to the station in a paddy wagon. A paddy wagon. They'd shoved me into a cell. The door had swung shut and I'd started to weep self-pitying, fearful tears. I was a forty-five-year-old pisshead housewife, sitting in a cell in a dress too young for me, waiting for my ex-husband, who had left me for a girl young enough to be our daughter who was pregnant. I was in jail. This was rock bottom.

'Well, I suppose we've done what we can,' Eamon was saying, darting another glance at his watch.

That was the one thing about Eamon. He spoke in riddles with references so veiled that I never had a clue what he was on about. He wouldn't have told his right hand what the left was doing, which made him just the sort of boyo to be Frank's solicitor. If you asked Eamon the time of day he'd tell you he'd get back to you on it.

The two men were eyeing me warily – *the crazy lady* – as if they didn't know what the hell I might do next. I'd never had so much attention from the pair of them in years. I was staring at them, challenging them to say anything to me, when I felt a surge of weird energy.

If this was rock bottom, I thought, watching Frank light another fag, I could handle it. If this was rock bottom the only way was up. My head was pounding. I felt tired and sweaty but strangely alive. It was as if I had gone so far beyond the pale that I felt fearless. I was 'Anita the outlaw'.

The irony was not lost on me. The woman who had spent years manoeuvring her way up some invisible social ladder, getting her children to play with the right children so that she could insinuate herself with the parents, working out the correct place to holiday, trying to get into the right golf club, even though she didn't play golf, the kids into the right tennis club, observing all the little rules, sucking up to people she didn't particularly like, being nice to people Frank had decided she should court.

I stared at Eamon. He looked like an undertaker. But, then, he always did. His suits, which probably cost a fortune, always looked too big for him, as if he'd found them in a charity shop. He shifted from foot to foot, looking like Eeyore the small grey donkey in *Winnie-the-Pooh*. It wasn't much of a stretch to imagine him standing by a graveside with a suitably sepulchral look, wringing his hands professionally, as the coffin was lowered into the ground, or backing a hearse to the door of a church.

At this moment Frank didn't look much better.

'Nobody's died,' I said, taking a deep breath. Then I started to giggle. The giggles turned into gales of inappropriate, rollicking laughter. I saw a nervous smile flicker on Eamon's face. It was quenched entirely when I kept on laughing. Eventually I was doubled over.

'Jesus, Anita,' Frank said.

'Jesus nothing,' I said, gasping, 'I've really done it now.'

Eamon's eyes darted to Frank.

'Back away from the crazy lady,' I wheezed, wiping my eyes. They were silent.

'I'll drive you home,' Eamon said, still eyeing me doubtfully.

Frank put his arm around my shoulders, presumably to steer me in the direction of the car, but I shook it off. He coloured and Eamon looked away in embarrassment. It was quite clear from his face that he wanted to be anywhere but embroiled with Frank's dipsomaniac ex-wife.

'You'll drive us *home*. *Home*,' I repeated, and Frank flinched. 'We no longer have a home.'

'You stay here sure,' Eamon said, edging cautiously away. 'I'll bring the car around.'

'The last time I met yourself and Carmel was when we spent that weekend in Dromoland,' I said to Eamon, so he was forced to stall.

Frank and I, Eamon and Carmel, with a couple of Frank's

business associates and their wives, had spent a weekend in Dromoland Castle, set in the lush green fields of County Clare. Dromoland was sixteenth-century and beautiful, with chandeliers, patterned carpets and heavy brocade curtains. There were stiff linen tablecloths and heavy silver cutlery, and through the window of the dining room you could see a lake and ancient trees. It was slightly kitsch maybe but the best of Irish.

Frank had been paying for the whole jaunt – nobody could accuse him of being ungenerous – and he had enjoyed playing 'mine host'. He and the other men had come trooping down the stairs to go pheasant-shooting, tricked out in check shirts, silk waistcoats, sleeveless pullovers, their plus fours tucked inside heavy green socks with feathers. The atmosphere of the place, it seemed, had gone to their heads.

There had been a line of Range Rovers and Land Rovers parked on the gravel outside. I had made some joke about us being used to living *in* an estate rather than *on* an estate, which had caused Frank to look annoyed. It had obviously been a fantasy of his that he should be a gentleman shooter. We, the wives, had watched them truck over the lawn, in tweed caps and brogues, rifles over their shoulders, delighted with themselves, Robin Hood and his band of Merry Men.

'Don't they look impressive?' Carmel had said, clasping her hands to her chest.

One of the men's voices had floated back on the breeze, followed by a burst of laughter: 'Don't let him be fookin' rushin' ya.'

We women were supposed to beautify ourselves in the spa and trail around the gardens – which were based on designs by the fella who'd planned the gardens at Versailles – chatting until our menfolk came back. Carmel had talked a lot about the Royal Family – in a way that suggested she was their intimate – so it seemed fairly certain that she, too, had been overcome by our surroundings. Over coffee – the girls having a gay time – she had said things like 'What a terrible burden for Wills to carry,' and 'I think Harry will find it hard to deal with the discipline in the army.'

They were a nice bunch of women, although at one point I had half thought of drowning myself in the lily pond. Instead I had drowned myself in booze.

'I stand corrected, Eamon,' I said. 'The last time I met you was at Frank's fiftieth. It doesn't really count, though, because I was bombed out of my mind. I'd just discovered that Romeo here was slipping it to Juliet.'

Eamon didn't know where to look so he settled for staring at the pavement.

'For fuck's sake, Anita,' Frank said, a pulse twitching at the side of his head.

'The truth hurts, Frank.'

'They don't teach you this in Blackhall, Eamon, I'd say, when they're teaching you to be a solicitor,' Frank observed. 'How to deal with a valued client's drunken, irate, crazy ex-wife. You get the car.' He ground out the cigarette under his foot, his jaw clenched.

We watched Eamon scuttle off. I turned to Frank. 'I'm surprised she lets you smoke. I thought that generation was very health-conscious.'

Silence.

'Sorry about all this, Frank,' I said, wanting to needle him further. 'I hope I didn't wake *Fiona* up. I know she needs her sleep.'

Frank said nothing.

'This will be in the papers, I suppose,' I said.

'If it goes to court,' Frank said, closing his eyes and pinching the bridge of his nose.

'It's going to court, Frank,' I said flatly.

'I'll hire a top barrister,' Frank said, 'the very best.' He looked slightly askew. His shirt was crumpled and the stubble on his face left a bluish shadow.

'Did you not hear what Eamon said?' Heat had crept into my voice. 'It's a *strict liability offence* meaning that once you're over the limit you're convicted. I blew into the bag. I was two times over the limit and, ta-da, case over. They even,' I said, rummaging in my handbag, then waving a piece of paper in his face, 'gave me a printout to prove it. And there isn't a stroke you can pull to change that, Frank.'

'I have a cousin a guard in Tullamore . . .'

I wasn't listening to him any more. Eamon's car looked very phallic, much like Frank's, I thought, watching him glide up to the kerb. Was there something in that? Two short-arsed men driving around in mobile penises?

Frank was trying to put his hand on mine. I felt a tsunami-cised rush of indignation. 'You have no right to do that,' I barked. I could feel the fury bubbling up inside me. The bloody cheek of him.

Eamon's meagre little features peered out from behind the wheel of his Mercedes, like a small anxious baked bean. I strode to the edge of the kerb with my hand raised, transported by my anger. Catching the eye of a taxi man, I climbed into the back seat of the cab. 'I'll make my own way home,' I shouted, poking my head out. 'And you can go to fuck with your uncle in Tullamore, Frank.'

They were gawping at me now.

'Cheers, Eamon, regards to Carmel,' I added, and the taxi took off.

I O

It was a week since I'd been carted off to jail in a paddy wagon. Now I was being carted off to a prison of another sort. Shannon and I were going to Dundrum shopping centre to meet Maeve for coffee. And Maureen was coming.

Maureen had rung me and I had sort of said where I was going and she had sort of tagged along. 'Oh, that's perfect. I need to get a baby present for my friend Louise's daughter. Did I tell you about Louise? She's my golfing friend, plays off a handicap of . . .'

I didn't want to go – and not just because I wasn't in the humour for Maureen. The shopping centre was in the middle of a built-up suburban area. I'd never been that gone on the suburbs: they sprawled on for ever in a way that left me feeling uncertain. There was something so definite about the tenement flats where I had grown up in terms of their location and your identity: you were such and such from the Coppinger Street flats off St Stephen's Green; everyone knew your mother, grandmother, great-grand-mother, great-great-grandmother and so on. Our house in Shrewsbury Road, detached and set back from the road behind its electric gates, also had a firm sense of territorial markings although more in a dare-to-come-onto-our-land-and-a-sniper-will-blow-your-head-off sort of way.

Talk, talk, talk. Maureen was in the back seat of Shannon's great big metal beast, rabbiting on. So far we'd covered her ovaries. Maureen's ovaries had been our close friends for years. We'd also received an update on her sciatica – she

never had anything as low level as back pain, always sciatica
– and her reflux. We heard that her grandsons in Cork looked
like Donal 'around the eyes'. But if Our Lady had appeared
to Maureen she would have looked a lot like Donal.

Maureen had the absolute confidence of the bore that
what she had to share with the world was eagerly awaited. If
you'd stuck her under a tree and gagged her she'd have kept
going. She hadn't always been that bad. It was loneliness, I
thought, which was why I tried hard to be tolerant. She didn't
get the attention she needed so she had to make guerrilla
attacks on people to get it.

What would Maureen have said if she'd known about me
being slung in a cell? She wouldn't have liked it. The confession would certainly have stemmed the ceaseless flow of
medical revelations. She might even have withdrawn some
of her sympathy. That would have been a relief. Maureen
was kind, but her mournful little smile, undershot with some
thing strangely upbeat, depressed me. It made me want to
leap about and holler and whoop and do the jitterbug and
shout, *I'm alive, I'm alive.*

Shannon was gripping the wheel glumly – Jimmy had lost
a lot of money on shares. The markets had gone mad. Dylan
had said – mouthing someone else, I was sure – that 'all the
old certainties' had 'been debunked'. He parroted what was
said at work. Sometimes he spoke in the swinging-dick lingo
of the alpha male, some of it pretty sexist and reeking of a
machismo that just wasn't him: 'Share prices went up and
down like a whore's knickers.'

We were meeting Maeve in Dundrum. I was trying not to
dream of wine. I was off the grog for one week, which
equalled one hundred and sixty-eight hours, or ten thousand
and eighty minutes. Not that I was counting.

After the garda station I'd gone home and drained every

last bottle down the sink. Frank's wine cellar in the basement was still intact, but I'd flushed the key down the loo. Or tried. It was still lying at the bottom of the bowl, daring me to shove my arm down and retrieve it. I'd thought about doing that. But I hadn't. Yet.

Since I'd decided to abstain, my desire for gargle had ballooned. I was practically hallucinating about a glass of wine. I'd have sold my body, slept with Maureen's Donal in exchange for one, as Maureen talked on about Donal having 'the foresight to de-invest'. No, I wouldn't go that far. A disturbing image of Donal's round white bottom bobbing up and down like a penny apple in a basin of water invaded my mind.

One website I'd consulted had suggested making a list of the reasons you had to give up the sauce. I'd actually had a stab at it. My half-written list had been on the pillow and was stuck to my sweaty cheek when I had woken up the following morning. *So that I don't* . . .

1. . . . crash cars
2. . . . spend nights in cells
3. . . . make scenes in airports
4. . . . end up in hospital with suspected drug overdoses
5. . . . over-share with my friends and insult them
6. . . . have to be dragged out of bed by relatives
7. . . . suffer from constant wine flu
8. . . . have to pretend to be bright and breezy in the morning when I feel like dry retching
9. . . . blot out reality

Listening to Maureen, I added a tenth.

10. . . . become a custodian of the past

Maeve would want to drink at lunch. I had no idea how I

might dodge the issue. Would I have to go around and say to people, 'I don't drink,' in the heavy tone that telegraphed you shouldn't ask why?

I had only really started to hit the bottle towards the end of Ella's school years. Initially, staving off boredom had been a large part of it. Then maybe the reasons had shifted. I began drinking to avoid looking into the gaping chasm that was opening up in my life. And once my life had become less regimented, without the school pick-ups and drop-offs and vaguely supervisory role of the teenage years, I'd had more opportunity to drink. Was I an alcoholic? Like your typical problem drinker, I suspected my eye had sought out the information on the web that I wanted to find: 'But having a drinking problem doesn't mean that you are alcoholic or that you have to abstain from alcohol. Most people who experience problems from drinking choose to reduce their consumption to moderate levels rather than to abstain.'

'I don't really think that you're an actual alkie,' Karen had said, expelling a spiral of smoke thoughtfully. 'What?' she'd asked, catching sight of my face. 'You asked . . . You drink too much, though. It's hard to tell when we're a nation of functioning pissheads.'

I would abstain for the moment. But I would take it one day at a time, not making any grand promises to myself. If I ended up cracking and swigging madly from a bottle, I'd start again. I would learn to live for today.

Maureen burbled happily on: 'And I know it isn't patriotic but maybe it's time to move money offshore, as Donal says.'

'What money?' I heard Shannon mutter.

Shannon manoeuvred her great big jeep down the narrow lane to the maze of car parking spaces in the bowels of the hulking great shopping centre.

'I mean, Donal says that the Irish banks may not be able

to deal with their huge liabilities. Their loan books are in real trouble, thanks to the excessive culture of lending to the developers. No offence, Anita.'

'None taken,' I said shortly.

Frank's name was cropping up in the news as one of the guys who might have contributed to taking Paul Hogan's bank down.

Maureen followed her comment by leaning forward and squeezing my shoulder. Inwardly I sighed. She began to talk about Ted Deegan. Something about 'contracts for difference' and 'share price movements'. Maureen could easily have taught the Central Bank a thing or two but it was beyond me.

'Ted Deegan bet on shares going up. Now that those shares have pretty much collapsed he's said to have lost well in excess of a billion on them.' The kernel of what she was saying seemed to be that he was in financial difficulties.

'It's so confusing in this car park,' Shannon complained, taking her ticket from the machine and swivelling her head indecisively. 'Trying to park is such a pain in the ass. It's like a goddam maze. I don't really care for this mall,' she said, scowling.

I had never seen Shannon like this before.

When the car was parked the three of us trotted down the main concourse, our heels clicking along the marble floor.

'Donal is driving a Harley Davidson around,' Maureen was saying darkly. 'He thinks he's in that movie *Easy Rider*. You know – the one with the men in leather jackets and unbrushed hair who do nothing but drive around all the time.' She bristled. 'He told Donal Junior that he finds it very *mind expanding*.'

Maureen was like a car jammed in gear, chugging along, unable to drive freely. Her life was a memorial to something that no longer existed.

'Gee, it's so quiet here,' Shannon remarked.

And it was. Normally the place would have been teeming at this time. But on this day – in a week when the global stock markets had plummeted and governments, including ours, had moved to prop up the banking sector – tumbleweed might have blown through the atrium.

'I'll see you in Harvey Nicks,' Maureen said, at the foot of the escalator.

'See you later,' I said, gathering from Shannon's face that she was as glad as I to have a little breather from her.

Shannon and I left the centre and crossed the square, past the fountains, to the Harvey Nichols glass-cube café. It was home from home, with its incongruous orange plastic furniture and large vases of lilies. We the stay-at-home mums had flocked here like starlings after we had left our precious cargo at school. There was a uniform. In winter we tucked our jeans into riding boots; in summer the jeans were white and the footwear sandals. But we always had sunglasses pushed back above our shiny Botoxed foreheads, regardless of the season. Today we were few in number. The café was half empty. A sort of eerie pall hung over the place. Voices seemed lower, hair less bouncy – even the large soft leather handbags that littered the floor seemed to slouch, as if to say, 'RIP, our day is gone.'

I wolfed my entire scone and pictured a headline in the paper: 'Woman Eats Whole Scone In Harvey Nichols Café'. Maybe it was because I wasn't drinking, but I found myself much hungrier. Shannon's scone lay in front of her. She had cut it into four quarters, eating roughly half of it before pushing the remainder away. Suddenly she zoomed her face in towards mine. Underneath the layers of makeup, she looked pinched. 'Jimmy's under so much pressure. Obviously, being a stockbroker, he played the market. He borrowed money from Paul Hogan's bank to buy shares. The shares are worthless. Now he owes the bank and he owes them big.' She exhaled noisily. 'And work's really hard for him. He's in the private client department. There's nothing happening for him. Bonds are where it's at now. The private client work has almost totally dried up. And clients are jumpy.'

She bit her lip. 'One guy came into the office and went crazy. He did a sort of Michael-Douglas-falling-down impression. He'd lost three million over a six-month period on the back of advice they'd given him, and when they sent him a bill for forty thousand euro he went ape. It tipped him over the edge. He ran around the place threatening to kill himself.' She shook her head balefully. 'I mean, he was legally obliged to pay – stocks go down as well as up – but Jimmy felt awful. Now they have bouncers discreetly tucked away in the lobby in case it happens again.'

'Ireland has turned into Russia,' I said. Frank had told me a story about a well-known developer who had been beaten up for not paying his subcontractor – in another version of the story he had been beaten up by the Russian Mafia to whom the subcontractor had sold the debt. It might or might not have been true but it gave a flavour of the stories doing the rounds, and reflected how Ireland had changed.

Her shoulders drooped. 'Jimmy's not eating.'

It was hard to imagine the buoyant double-chinned Jimmy off his food. He had seemed to get fatter as Shannon had shrunk, as if he had swallowed some of her. That happened with a lot of the husbands and wives we knew. The men grew bigger, their stomachs steadily distending towards their toes, while the women shrank, their lollipop heads seeming to grow larger.

'He's not sleeping, he's hollow-eyed – I'm really scared for him. I tried to get him to take sleeping tablets but he won't. He just lies there, looking at the ceiling. If things get really bad they might let him go.'

'But he's a partner, isn't he?'

'He set up the firm. But they won't be prepared to carry him for ever if the private client work doesn't pick up. And in his game he has to appear chipper and confident all the time. It's kind of crucial. There's no room for self-doubt. Show your soft underbelly and you're gone. Negative thinking is contagious. At least, that's how they view it in stockbroking. They fear it like nothing else. You have to talk the talk and walk the walk. And Jimmy has lost his confidence. Hell, I'd say the kids can see it in his eyes.'

Her face collapsed. 'He won't get another job. He's over forty. Stockbrokers burn out. They have a shelf life. Who'd take him on?' Her gaze seemed to turn inward. Then, after a slight pause, she said, lowering her voice, 'We're still finishing off the house. It's gone way over budget. The designer ordered carpets and fabrics and all sorts of things that weren't okayed and which have to be paid for now. We're tied into buying an apartment in Dubai and the realtor says we can't back out at this point. We're obliged to complete or they'll sue us for the purchase price. We're in serious shit.' She grimaced. 'And the worst of it all is that there's nothing I can do to help.'

'Hi, guys.' It was Tracey Thornley.

'Hey there, Traccy,' Shannon said, nailing a wafer-thin smile to her face.

'Look at you!' Tracey trilled at Shannon. 'You look great – you're so skinny!'

That was Tracey's stock greeting. Tracey herself looked emaciated – all tiny limbs and big eyes. And now, with her deflated chest, she had a bony clavicle. 'Oh, my God, how are you?' she asked, in the manner of someone addressing survivors of a nuclear disaster. 'It's so dead in here,' she rocketed on, without waiting for an answer. 'Where is everyone?'

Her eyes, which looked as if they had been stitched back – Maeve insisted they had – flicked around the room. Tracey had once had a good job in television but now she was the ultimate trophy wife. She turned her attention to me. 'Anita, I'm *sooo* embarrassed,' she carolled. 'I've been meaning to call you.'

'It's fine,' I told her.

She stooped to give me a quick hug, which made both of us feel super-awkward. When she had straightened up she folded her arms across her chest. 'How *are* you?' Her voice dripped an almost theatrical concern. This still happened: women would be smiling and chatting and then their eyes would alight on me and they would become funereal.

'Great,' I said brightly.

Tracey continued to look at me, radiating sympathy so that the smile nearly cracked off my face. It was like a game of Chicken, I thought, wondering which of us would look away first. She caved before I did. She switched to being perky again, which was her natural mode. 'It's weird what a difference a couple of months can make – we're all recessionistas now.'

She was still clearly in the dark about how much trouble the economy was in and, by extension, most of us. It was no laughing matter. But conversation had always rattled out of Tracey, like bullets out of a machine gun. When she had moved on, you were always hard pressed to remember one thing she'd said.

'Do you remember when this place opened?' she asked, shaking her expensively highlighted head. 'It was the big thing.'

I did. I'd come up for a nose with Maeve. We'd stood at the back of a queue that had turned out to be made up of thousands. The media had been there. When the doors had opened we'd been pushed forward in the scrum, barrelling through the doors like eejits, providing the journalists with their shots of the happy shoppers ready to spend their loot. The local clergy had been there, too, to bless the centre.

'We'll all just have to soldier on,' Tracey said, with a game little smile.

Although Tracey had once been beautiful she now resembled a wax doll or maybe a mannequin. Her over-plucked eyebrows gave her a sort of bald look, like a newly hatched chick. The fillers she'd had – or maybe the surgery – had altered her expression. She had a sort of puffy look around the nose. Her skin had seen too much sun but it had been stripped back and sanded. There was a thin line, I thought, between self-preservation and pride in one's femininity, and a crazy maniacal determination to hold back the years at whatever cost. Where exactly it lay was debatable, but Tracey Thornley, I felt reasonably sure, had crossed it a long time ago.

Now she gave a conspiratorial smile. 'I've just bought a bespoke Zagliani bag. Naughty me,' she said. 'I'll have to hide it from Dermot.'

Shannon had an odd look on her face and remained conspicuously silent so I felt obliged to say something. 'They're made from python skin and injected with Botox, aren't they?'

Tracey nodded and twittered on for another couple of minutes, before taking her leave. La, la, la, la, la, la, la. Shannon kept her eyes fastened on the menu.

'Ciao,' Tracey said, blowing us an extravagant kiss. Although originally from Howth, she always said, 'Ciao,' very loudly when you were saying goodbye to her, like she had Italian connections.

'Have a good one,' Shannon said, her face tight. '*Not*,' she added, when Tracey had tick-tacked off.

The warmth had drained from her face and she was bristling, which was not like her. Normally Shannon was smiley and good-humoured. The fact that she didn't bitch about people was one of the things I loved about her. Now she looked really riled. 'She's got to be kidding. A Zagliani bag!' she said, her face flaming. 'They cost a small fortune.'

'The Thornleys obviously aren't feeling the pinch.'

It had become like a competitive sport, wondering who was suffering as a result of the downturn and who had remained unaffected.

'She's nuts if she thinks she can bleat on Marie Antoinette-style about Zagliani bags. Say what you like, Anita, but it's bad taste,' she said, looking aggrieved. 'That sort of conspicuous consumption is going to pall very quickly, the way things are going. Bling is dead.' Her mouth bunched at the corners as if it was being yanked back by a bridle. 'Jimmy played a bit of golf with Dermot and those guys bet enormous dough on their rounds. Like twenty big ones a pop. And Jimmy says they're all laughing at us now in Brussels and abroad, saying that financially we've been like the Wild West, that we live in a banana republic. Screw Tracey,' she said.

I was flabbergasted to hear her swear – Shannon had the American thing of not cursing so she spent a lot of time being appalled by our bad language.

'I don't know what Jimmy and I are going to do. I'm really scared.' Her shoulders sagged. 'Hell, I don't even know if I got licensed to practise law here whether I'd get work. The word on the street is that there has been a huge evaporation of legal work and that my area, mergers and acquisitions, is on a major slowdown. I'd be surplus to requirements, Anita.' She gave a brittle laugh. 'And I'd thought the world would be waiting for my contribution.'

'It's the recession,' I said.

'I was emailing a girl I used to work with back home. The American banking system is in ruins too. Do you think it's, like, a coincidence that the whole show was run by men high on life and testosterone? Maybe if they'd had more women at the higher echelons of the banks we mightn't be looking at the train wreck we're faced with.'

Some of us had gone along with it, too, though, I thought. We had colluded by not asking any questions, happy once the money landed in our accounts. Shannon and I had been part of that high-rolling, high-spending gang. We could have piped up and said no in our own way. No use in saying it now.

Shannon stared at the table. When she looked up she wore an expression of panic. 'We may have bitten off more than we can chew. We couldn't sell the house if we wanted to – or, at least, only for way less than we borrowed. The bottom has fallen out of the market for houses like that. I've let the au pair go and the cleaner, I don't buy clothes, I don't go to the beauty salon . . .' She heaved a deep sigh. 'And I've cancelled the gym membership.'

That was seriously hard core – and told me everything I needed to know.

Shannon gave a small smile. 'I shouldn't be whining,' she said. 'You have your plate full too.'

I shook my head. 'You're not. You never do, Shannon,' I told her. 'You are one of the most positive people I know.'

'Not any more,' she said ruefully. She looked despondent. 'It's just I don't know what we're going to do. And I know I shouldn't say this but I'm completely bushed from stress and

I'm bushed from the kids. I'm not used to doing so much housework and child-minding.'

It was funny, I thought, how, bit by bit, with prosperity your norms changed so that you didn't even notice it happening. And then one day you woke up and you'd come to expect certain things. You didn't think it was weird to have au pairs and cleaners even though you didn't work outside the home. You didn't laugh people out of court, as you once might have done, for hiring party planners or even people to decorate your Christmas tree. And you didn't think it was weird that you hadn't touched an iron or mopped a floor in at least ten years.

Her lips parted. 'And the worst is, because I can't get a job there's nothing I can do to help my husband,' she repeated. She straightened. 'There's Maeve.' Her eyes flicked to where Maeve was striding along, her shoulders weighed down with bags.

Shannon lifted her hand to her. Maeve waved jauntily at us. 'Not a word, especially not to *her*,' she said, through gritted teeth, before producing a bright, social smile.

Maeve, who was dressed in a leather jacket with a big diamond cross around her neck, flopped back in her chair. 'Sorry about that,' she said, snapping her phone shut. 'It was the bloody au pair. I have to draw her a picture if I want her to do anything.'

Maeve was in perky mode. Her smiles were girlish, by Maeve standards anyway, and her skin had that post-coital glow. She'd just seen the French tennis coach, I decided. The glow certainly wasn't courtesy of her husband. Maeve said that she often paraded around the marital bedroom in underwear that would have made a whore blush, bending over and licking her lips and striking exaggerated seductive poses, but that Ultan never seemed aroused: he just kept on reading whatever balance sheet he was engrossed in, his mobile phone head-set on. 'How I conceived my babies I don't know,' she'd drunkenly confided once. 'Their conception should be on a par with the Virgin Birth.'

Maybe Ultan Mohally was gay. He was not particularly effete. Nor was he *per se* unattractive. His features were in the right place. But there was something sort of neutral about his sexual aura. However, my taste ran to beefy, lusty, spear-chucking types, like Frank, with steak-eater handshakes. Men who savaged their food, alpha-male carnivores who, in a primitive, antediluvian – this was a favourite Ella word – way, would get you and your children to high ground if there was a flood.

'Anyway, as I was saying, it's the speed at which this down-turn has come that's most remarkable,' Maeve said, sitting forward. 'The important thing is that we keep spending,' she added, blowing the surface of a decaf skinny latte. 'We need people to consume or the economy will contract. The more we save, the worse it is.'

'You're certainly putting your money where your mouth is,' Shannon said, nodding at the defiant sea of shopping bags around Maeve's ankles and giving a tight smile.

Maeve's smile was breezy. 'Always happy to do my bit.'

Frank had said that Ultan and Maeve were grand, that Ultan had been too cute to invest his own money in the giant deals he put together for his clients.

I had not been shopping in a while. There was something so utterly bizarre about that. I was a professional drift shop-per. Normally I would shop a couple of times a week. I shopped on-line. I was known by name in all of the shops, big and small. I planned my wardrobe seasons ahead. I was a marketing man's wet dream. When my cooker wasn't quite working or maybe smelling a little, I replaced it. When my fridge struck me as too small or my freezer as too big, whoosh, it was out the door. If the décor in my living room needed pepping up I started *de novo*.

Maeve and I had that in common, that and the drinking. I wanted to say to Maeve that the thought had struck me – very late in the game – you could be buried alive by shopping. In fact, I had said it: that night in the Shelbourne when I was off my head on coke. She had told me to fuck off then and was probably taking the view that all the things I'd said that night had been the ramblings of a woman who was out of her mind. She would certainly tell me to fuck off if I raised the topic again when I was stone-cold sober.

You could be deadened by the endless round of acquisitions, until wanting to consume became your main rationale for moving forward. And you never won the battle – that was the tyranny of acquisition. It was like trying to run across quicksand. The hole just kept getting deeper. You never managed to fill it with stuff.

Instead I said, 'Maureen seemed to suggest we should be saving.'

'Yeah, well, Maureen probably has her Communion money still under the mattress,' Maeve retorted.

'She always seems quite financially astute to me,' I said.

Maeve harrumphed. 'Well, I'd say now that Maureen has never heard of John Maynard Keynes. It's our patriotic duty to shop,' she said, flicking freshly blow-dried hair over her shoulder. It was anybody's guess what percentage of her life Maeve spent in a hairdresser's chair. She continued, 'John Maynard Keynes gave an infamous speech in 1931 on the radio, telling housewives that it was their patriotic duty to spend.' She put on a booming voice: 'He said that if you do not buy goods, the shops will not clear their stocks, they will not give repeat orders, and someone will be thrown out of work.'

There were times like this when you got flashes of the other Maeve, the smart, professional woman she must have been.

'It was a brilliant speech, actually,' she said, her eyes darting to her watch. 'He said something like, "Oh, sally forth, housewives of Britain, and lay you in sheets and towels" . . . And he was right. It's time for a drink, ladies,' she said.

Maeve routinely drank at lunch. She was brilliant at holding her booze so it was hard to tell when she'd been drinking. She would have had to drink all day and all night before you could tell she'd been at it. She was always up for demolishing a bottle or two. 'Midweek, I'm only one bottle a day,' was her joke.

That sort of drinking snuck up on you. Maeve and I were no different from the women who had drunk in the tenement flats I'd grown up in. But the appearance of money somehow masked the fact you were a lush. Drinking wine with 'the girls' seemed benign and fun.

'We'll get a bottle,' she said, turning to look for a waiter.

'I'm driving,' Shannon said.

'You're always driving,' Maeve said acidly, so that a faint flush appeared on Shannon's face. Shannon didn't drink much, which drove Maeve crazy. She hated non-drinkers, which made you wonder how she dealt with her abstemious husband.

'I'm collecting the kids,' Shannon said, sounding defensive.

'Why can't your au pair do it?' asked Maeve, beckoning a waiter.

My eyes met Shannon's in a split second of understanding. She wasn't going to share the fact that she'd let her au pair go. 'Count me out of the wine too, Maeve,' I said, scrunching my toes in my shoes.

The remark distracted Maeve, as I'd intended. As her dark head telescoped towards me, Shannon shot me a look of gratitude. 'I might have a piece of cake instead,' I said, toying with the menu.

That was an incredibly stupid thing for me to say, if I was hoping to keep my new-found sobriety under the radar. I might as well have announced that I was planning on lighting a crack pipe. Nobody we knew ate cake – apart from Maureen. I felt as if a giant camera was zooming in on me for a high-definition close-up.

The waiter came to a halt by our table.

Maeve, still eyeing me, said, 'I'll have a *glass* of the Sancerre.'

My mouth started to water. Two opposing voices in my head began to slug it out.

One glass won't kill you . . .

No, you can't. One glass will lead to another bottle . . .

You don't know if you're an alcoholic . . .

You're fooling yourself again . . .

You only live once . . .

You'll end up carrying little bottles around in your handbag and pissing yourself like poor old Mrs Keogh who lived next door to Ma and Da used to do . . .

'Have a glass,' Maeve pressed me. 'Go on, for God's sake.'

'I can't,' I said, trying to keep my tone light. An American website I had consulted on drinking said that saying no got easier the more you did it. It suggested practising refusing drinks politely. 'Say something clever,' it counselled, and gave examples, like 'I'm performing neurosurgery in the morning' or 'I don't need any more hair on my chest.'

Americans had a different sense of humour, I reckoned. Whoever wrote that had almost certainly never lived in Ireland. And needed to get out more.

The waiter continued to hover. 'That's fine,' I told him, mustering a weak smile.

Maeve looked profoundly dissatisfied. 'Are you not drinking or something?' she asked belligerently, her eyes now two blue slits.

I shrugged my shoulders and tried to think of something suitably evasive yet satisfactory to say. 'I'm going out later,' I managed.

Maeve scowled.

Not drinking in Ireland would be the opposite of fun. Non-drinkers were viewed with suspicion, if not downright hostility. I know because I'd had those feelings myself. Non-drinkers or, worse, teetotallers, were up there with holy rollers like Frank's mam, flat-footed people with long faces and halitosis and bad hair and sinister Pioneer pins prominently displayed on their lapels. Karen had said that in Ireland the people without a glass in their hand were the problem.

'I may as well have asked Father Matthew for lunch,' Maeve said grimly. She was just about to add something when her eye was caught by a woman passing the café. She craned and swivelled her head. 'Her daughter Mercedes is in Madison's kindergarten,' she remarked. 'Would you look at her still hanging onto the summer?' The woman was dressed in a pair of light-coloured jeans and a T-shirt. Maeve was encased in the season's latest.

'She probably can't afford new winter clothes,' Shannon said glumly.

Scenting news, Maeve swung her shiny head around like a heat-seeking missile. 'But you and Jimmy are grand, aren't you?' she asked, her eyes narrow and assessing.

'Of course,' Shannon lied, mustering a brave little smile.

'Oh, my God, don't look now,' Maeve instructed us, flicking

her eyes to the left, then averting them again. 'Check out Lisa O'Sullivan.'

A heavily pregnant woman walked by in a smock and leggings.

'She's exploded. The poor thing. She's on her fourth, I think.'

'She looks very well,' Shannon remarked.

'She does,' I agreed, although the woman looked like a bloated marshmallow.

Maeve pulled a face. 'I hope for her sake it's water retention and not cake. I don't get people who just eat and eat when they're pregnant. That whole eating-for-two thing is a myth, and you only have to lose all the weight you gain afterwards.'

Shannon nodded. 'I'd agree with you there.'

'You were tiny when you were pregnant,' Maeve told Shannon, her eyes still tracking her quarry. 'But you hired a personal trainer to keep you thin, didn't you?'

Shannon nodded. 'And I watched my diet. I didn't actually wear maternity clothes until the last month of my third trimester.' She sounded proud.

Even in pregnancy being big was *verboten*.

'I'm not being mean,' Maeve said, which meant she was definitely about to be, 'but I think Lisa's got kind of old-looking.'

There was no limit to the appetite for this kind of conversation. I just didn't have the stomach today for the usual conversational treadmill of weight, ageing and other women. I liked meeting for coffee. Usually there would be a part of me that didn't want the morning to end because I'd be spat out into the long day stretching ahead. But walking back across the concourse from the coffee shop or trailing through the centre, I often felt strangely flaccid, tired from the chatting, the perennial discussion of other women's thighs, arses, life choices – the emptiness of it all, really.

There was something enticing about our non-stop chat – it was like opting for the bright colours of a sugary bun but after you'd eaten it you felt low and tired as you crashed down from the high. Today that feeling had kicked in sooner. I felt like leaving now.

'She's got three kids under the age of seven,' Shannon said. 'I guess she's bound to look a little frazzled.'

'I think she looks her age,' I said then.

'Exactly,' Maeve said, her eyes resting on me.

'What's wrong with looking your age?' I said, thinking again how I'd love a glass of wine.

Maeve looked at me as if I'd decided to blacken my arse and run around the café shouting heresies.

I continued, 'Why should it be such a crime to look your age? Why do we hate ourselves so much? Is it innate or are we taught it?'

'Christ, how much coffee have you had?' she asked, her eyes popping. 'This is what happens when you don't drink.'

'Seriously,' I said, 'I've hated myself for years. I've always wanted to be taller. I've always wanted a rounder, firmer arse, a greater distance between my knee and my ankle. When I was a little girl I didn't love myself but I was happy. Then one day I woke up and I was dissatisfied. I knew all my physical faults. And the only thing that seemed to make me happy was spotting other women's.'

Maeve mimed incredulity.

I sighed. 'We spend so much time trying to prop up a building that's only going to fall in the end anyway.'

'That sounds kind of defeatist,' Shannon said, frowning. 'I mean, would you stop cutting your hair, or applying lipstick?'

'Sometimes I wonder if we should just say no. To ourselves,

221

to society . . .' I ventured. 'Maybe we should accept the fact we'll never look twenty again and plough some of the energy we expend on trying to look young into other things.'

Shannon scrunched up her nose. 'How is this movement going to start? Who's going to be first to say that they're not going to diet any more or get Botox or what-have-you?'

Maeve said, 'Women have been adorning themselves since the start of time. It's an intrinsic part of being feminine.'

'But they haven't necessarily had their skin sandblasted off,' I countered, 'or had the fat sucked out of their thighs or their forehead shot with poison or their faces cut open and stitched back.'

Maeve gave a dismissive flip of the hand. 'Bodily discontent is the hallmark of our age,' she said. 'It's the reality of the time we live in.' She drank half her wine in one swallow. 'There is a bright side to all of this. We're the generation who can buy replacements for anything we don't like. We can buy new boobs, new faces . . .'

'I gotta go,' I said, standing up.

Maeve looked put out. She never wanted any social gathering to end. And her powers of persuasion were considerable. Maeve was a spider and you were the fly being lured into her web. She kidnapped you. It was like some form of Stockholm syndrome. You started out committing to one drink or a coffee and the next thing you knew it was midnight and you were falling out of Residence, the private members club.

'Why?' Maeve demanded. Her mouth had pursed and curved downwards.

'Ella's coming home in a few days,' I said, scooping up my bag. 'I have a couple of things to do. Sorry,' I said, trying to ignore Shannon: she looked trapped.

''Bye,' Maeve said tersely.

"Byeeee,' I said, and escaped outside into the bright clear day, resisting the urge to break into a gallop.

When Dylan came into the den, his gym bag banging against a sturdy hip, I was seated on the sofa. He was on his mobile – to Biba, I thought. I waited for him to finish. He was in a bad mood with me anyway.

I had been there for some time, my arms wrapped around my ribs. The room had cost a fortune to decorate. A guy recommended by Ciara as having 'a good eye' had guided me. He had 'curated' the space for me. 'I'm going for a modernist temple,' he had said, advising on varying shades of dove grey, which I liked. 'I want the aesthetic to be strong but relaxing.'

I had actually listened to that kind of bull. Now I found that the urge to drink was threatening to overpower me. I'd unfurled a foot, which was now tapping the floor. I could turn to religion in my quest to battle the booze. Ma's faith had always been a great comfort to her. She had not rammed it down people's throats, like Frank's mam had done. She had been a quiet, true believer. Maybe I could prostrate myself on the altar like one of our neighbours used to do when I lived with Ma and Da and Karen. The eldest Keogh boy with the watery blue Keogh eyes and the bad Keogh chest had got seriously into religion, praying to God in a pose and manner that had seemed almost sexual.

Of course, Karen had picked this up straight away. 'He's as gay as Christmas,' she had hissed at me one night, when we were sent down to the church with flowers. 'A good ride would sort him out. There'd be less of that praying and beating himself across the chest and hair-shirt carry-on. And what's wrong with two fellas doin' it?' she'd said, tonguing her chewing gum into the other cheek. Karen had always been ahead of her time.

Dylan had dropped his voice. 'Okay, love you,' I heard him say. Inwardly I made a face. Outwardly I was careful to keep it neutral.

He let his bag drop. It clattered onto the floor.

'Hi, love,' I said, smiling brightly.

'Hi, Mum,' he said, giving me a quick peck. His cheeks were flushed from the gym. It was hard for Dylan to keep the weight off. He had the Lawlor tendency to pork up. His body was quite taut, but despite all the push-ups and circuit training he would eventually go the way of Frank, I imagined.

'How was work, pet?'

'Crap,' he said. Hovering near the door he began fingering the lapel of his jacket.

Dylan's job was not going well. I knew the signs. After the initial burst of enthusiasm, he stopped wanting to talk about it and then the shit would hit the fan in some guise or other.

'I'm moving out, Mum,' he said, squaring his shoulders as if anticipating a fight.

My first thought was for myself. I was seized by a momentary panic.

His eyes met mine, then moved away. He locked his jaw defiantly. 'I'm sorry, Mum,' he added, deflating a little. 'I don't like leaving you here on your own. But if you won't let Biba move in, I have no choice. I'm moving into her place.'

Dylan had wanted Biba to move into the coach house.

'It's not a good idea,' I had said. 'The timing is wrong.'

'What do you mean?' he'd asked, a flicker of apprehension in his eyes.

'Just with the separation,' I'd said, 'and the uncertainty over Dad's planning. Everything's up in the air.'

I still had not sat down with Frank in any meaningful way and talked about money. My brain got jammed when I started to think of what might happen. I found it impossible to imagine a new life. I had also told Dylan that it was unwise to settle down too young and that he should sow his wild oats.

He had raged at that. 'Sow my wild oats?' he'd said, eyes boggling. 'What mother says that to her son?' He had jabbed the air with his finger accusingly. 'You just don't like Biba!'

No shit, Sherlock. I wasn't going to say that, though. So I had stuck to my guns, which meant that since then, on the rare occasions that he was in, Dylan had hung over his meals sullenly, slouching around the place as if I was public enemy number one. He was used to getting his way with me. He was not used to me saying no. I had always been a soft touch. It was uncharted territory for us both.

Now more heat came into his cheeks. 'We're very serious about each other,' he said, looking acutely self-conscious.

I was suffused with a mixture of love and sadness. I stared at my foot, which I was still tapping. I did not need a drink, I told myself. I could handle this situation without alcohol. I did not need to be numbed. I had to let my baby boy go. My baby boy was a twenty-two-year-old man. My baby boy and the over-perfumed party girl with the cartoon sexiness. I had thought he might never move out of the coach house. That it would be a case of till death did us part. That was what I had sort of hoped for, in a guilty, stifling Irish-mammy way.

'If you let her move in it would be different,' he said.

'You wouldn't go, you mean.'

He nodded, his eyes sliding away from mine guiltily.

I did not particularly like Biba, with her decorative smiles, which seemed insincere. Maybe she was lovely. Maybe she and I were just one more link in a long chain of mother-in-law and daughter-in-law battles. I would not be browbeaten, though.

I forced my voice into a pleasant neutrality: 'It's your decision, Dylan, just as it's your life,' I said, trembling a little. It *was*

225

his life, I thought, and stood up. I patted his face. 'Don't look so worried,' I said, producing a smile. 'You're going to be a northsider.' This was my half-arsed attempt at a joke. I blew him a kiss. 'I'm going out with Auntie Karen. See you later.'

11

The sun was beating down as I drove the Range Rover out of the gates. It had cost as much as the price of a small car to mend. I had queried the bill with the mechanic, who had looked at me as if I'd grown an extra head. I had never even read the figure before, never mind questioned the amount. I drove out of his garage and decided I should sell the thing. It was becoming like a relic from another age.

I was on my way to the airport. Ella was coming home. She knew about Frank, thanks to some little cow who had Facebooked her to see if she was 'hanging in there' after the sad split of her parents. There had been ructions on the phone. It had taken all my strength to persuade her not to jack in the job and come home to strangle her father. She knew nothing about the cluster of cells, living somewhere around the Stillorgan dual carriageway, that was fast turning into a new brother or sister.

I had considered taking a Valium. I hadn't, though. I could see where my subconscious was going with that – give up booze and take up swallowing Valium instead. This time I was a couple of steps ahead of my true nature. Some people were like that: if they ate chocolate they ate too much; if they exercised, they overdid it. I was a Butler. And Butlers were weak-willed, undisciplined, addictive types. But I was waking up with something approaching mental clarity. For the first time in ages I glimpsed new shoots. I was like Lazarus risen from the dead, I thought, edging my way into the afternoon traffic. I was in charge of a reclamation project of sorts. If

227

the Dutch could reclaim all that land from the sea, then maybe I could reclaim part of myself.

Ella had come zigzagging across the airport floor, her laden trolley refusing to obey her.

'Hey, Mom,' she'd said, almost breezily. I eyed her: she normally called me 'Mum'. She had allowed me to hug her but didn't really hug me back. Her fists were clenched, I'd noticed.

'No Christopher?'

'He got a different flight,' she'd said shortly.

'Oh.'

'We broke up. I don't want to talk about it.'

'I'm sorry.'

That was a lie. Long, thin, intense face aside, and snout cockily tilted upwards, he wasn't the worst. But I was in my backside sorry. I'd stuck on a regretful face, though.

'Don't pretend, Mum.' Her going native hadn't lasted all that long. She cocked an eye at me. 'I know you didn't like him. And you were totally right,' she'd said, giving me the ghost of a smile.

Now we were speeding along in the Range Rover – Thelma and fecking Louise. And there was still no mention of Frank. It was eerie. My maternal radar beeped furiously. This was not good. 'We should talk about Dad, love,' I ventured. Obviously there was a part of me that could have listened to her all day jabbering on about America but I was concerned too.

'Not now, Mum,' she said, her face turning to flint. 'I'm bushed. And I don't want to talk about that disloyal pervert,' she said venomously.

'Don't speak about your father like that.'

She began to talk about the internship. 'It was great. I mean, it was kind of demanding but it was great. This other intern, like, discovered that this man who had been on Death Row for twenty years couldn't have committed the crime. The evidence had been overlooked by the trial lawyer, who was some sort of alcoholic, and that was, like, a major rush, a sort of realization of what lawyers can do. I didn't unearth anything like that,' she said, letting a shoulder drop a little, 'but we all felt kind of part of it.'

Her accent hadn't changed, but the rhythms of her conversation were definitely more American.

She frowned. 'I'm not sure I'd like to make criminology my life. It could get sort of depressing. And I'm not sure if you can ever really change things at a systemic level.'

Pathetic, but when my daughter spoke like that I wanted to broadcast her over a Tannoy.

'What that girl did was exceptional. The legal system itself is basically fine. Criminality is a broader issue to do with poverty and lack of advantage in society.' She had loved New York. 'MOMA was one of my favourite places. It just had so much energy. I spent a lot of time there, looking at the paintings and just soaking up the atmosphere. Even the building was glamorous. There were so many amazing places to hang out in New York. I think this bar called Schillers was probably my favourite. It did great cocktails, although I couldn't actually drink them because they are so incredibly up their arses about minors not drinking.' She pulled a face. 'It was *soooo* annoying. It really did my head in at times. Anyhow it was cool in a laid-back kind of way. Jamie Deegan brought me there actually. I saw him a bit. He lives in this amazing loft in TriBeCa. Surprise, surprise,' she said, rolling her eyes in her trademark ironic way.

She was silent for a moment. Then she said, her expression softening, 'Yeah, Jamie's actually not that bad. Better than I thought.' She was toying with her scarf. 'He's quite witty. And he said he liked MOMA a lot. I mean, you wouldn't really think it, what with him having been such a rugger bugger at school.'

Ella had always been allergic to the rugby scene. 'And he's very sort of . . .' she stuck her bottom lip out '. . . energetic, I guess, would be the word. He's a doer, you know.'

I was hearing a lot about Jamie.

'Of course, Christopher hated him but that's not an indication of anything,' she said, the muscles around her mouth tightening. 'I mean, Christopher hated everything.'

I said nothing. Inside I was doing a dance and singing happy songs. *Yee-ha, bye-bye, Christopher.*

She burbled on for another while until I stopped her, my heart suddenly leaden. 'Ella,' I said, 'I have something I need to tell you.'

She had made me drive her directly to Frank's offices. There had been no reasoning with her once I'd broken the news of the baby. 'I want to talk to him!' she had shouted. After that she had said nothing. She had sat in the passenger seat with her fists balled, staring out the window in deathly silence.

I had waited in the car. Karen had rung me to find out if I'd told her. 'Oh, he's in big trouble so,' she had said. 'You know what girls and their daddies are like.' Karen had no idea just how bad a time Frank was in for with Ella. She didn't really know Ella. You didn't mess with our Ella. Ella had even been extremely strict with her dolls growing up. Those dolls had had a terrible time.

Now Ella was running out of the building with Frank after her. He was shouting something but she didn't stop. She was hell bent on reaching the car. Her face was contorted with a mixture of fury and determination. She groped for the door handle. 'Drive!' she said, slamming the door.

Frank was cupping his hands around his mouth, moving forward. He caught my eye, a regretful lame-dog glance that said, 'What do I do? Tell me! How do I make it right?'

For one second we were briefly united as parents. But then the moment passed. I felt like rolling down the window and asking him where he had thought the affair would end. Had he reckoned he could sail off with his girlfriend and get her pregnant without collateral damage?

I felt so sad for my lovely daughter. And also a little for Frank. Ella had had him on a pedestal. And now he had tumbled down.

'Mum, *drive!*' she yelled.

So I indicated and we pulled out, leaving Frank gazing after us like a distressed goldfish. All-powerful Frank, who, with the broad shoulders, no neck and bowling-ball head, now looked small and diminished in the rear-view mirror, a middle-aged man in a shirt who had fucked up. There's no fool like an old fool.

Ella was motionless, making no sound.

'Ella.'

Nothing. I braked and pulled into the side of the road, swerving as I nearly side-rammed a car I hadn't seen. The driver put up his finger and beeped, as he had every right to do. Putting on my hazards I leant over and tried to circle my arms around her shoulders, but she twisted away from me. 'Ella,' I tried again. I could feel a stinging in my own eyes. 'Ella,' I said, cupping her face with my hands.

It was then that the dam burst. She started to cry, great big sobs that shook her whole body. I tried to comfort her again. This time she didn't push me away. Her words were half muffled as she turned her silky head and her lovely Ella smell into my chest. 'She's six years older than me!' she cried.

And although my heart was breaking for my daughter,

part of me was relieved. Ella was very self-sufficient emotionally while Dylan had always been clingy. She had relentlessly applied logic to every situation. When one of their hamsters had eaten the other and Dylan had bawled over the blood-spattered cage, Ella had delivered the line that we should have read the book on hamsters. When she found me watching made-for-television movies about mothers dying of cancer and leaving behind telegenic, strangely well behaved children, she cast me withering looks. And, of course, she was right. But there had been times when I'd wondered if she was a little cold. Times when – and I'd instantly quelled this scary thought – I'd wondered if she might be a little like Frank's mam. The thought had scared the bejaysus out of me, which was why I was glad to see this outburst of emotion.

'Oh, Mum,' she said, clinging on to me and allowing me to tighten the hug.

Later we sat in the kitchen. The ridiculously big kitchen. Future generations would excavate our homes and marvel. Sociologists and anthropologists would ask, 'Why did they need so much space?'

It was more like an art gallery than a kitchen. All white with one bold accent of neon pink – one painted wall. The lights were dimmed. The evening had drawn in. We were sitting at the island, sharing a lasagne. I was struggling not to calculate the fat and calorie content. We were drinking sparkling mineral water. If Ella had noticed I wasn't drinking wine, she hadn't mentioned it. I said nothing. I was making no prognostications or claims for myself. *One day at a time, sweet Jesus.*

Ella was perched on a high stool, one long leg tucked under her bottom. There was some colour in her cheeks now. That was the thing about youth: it was resilient. She was hurting but already she was moving forward. 'I can't believe Dylan would move in with Biba so soon. I think she's a user, Mum. And Dylan doesn't see it.' She railed against the stupidity of men. Christopher had been very lazy, she said, her face darkening. 'He spent his days on the sofa watching shit TV,' she said, with disgust. 'Half the time he didn't even make it into work. He thought he was all brooding and into existentialism but actually he was just idle and into pizza.'

She had darted me a sideways look. 'And, Mum, like, I don't want to shock you but he was a total stoner. He spent most of the day lying around like a vegetable smoking dope.'

I nodded as if I was struggling to take on board this shocking information. God help her head. If she only knew – not just about Ciara and her little nose straw or loads of the other people who had come to our parties over the years but about her uncle Keith who had been a total dope-head before he ran off to England for receiving the stolen tellies. Or Karen and Darren who in their salad days had been well into smoking weed. Or me – and my inner smile receded pretty quickly when I thought of this – ending up in hospital with a suspected overdose. Or, and I was in the horrors at this thought, my forthcoming drink-driving charge.

It was true that I had always felt the hypocrisy of delivering the 'Just say no, kids' lecture when a significant proportion of the people I knew, and even palled around with, kept half of Dublin's drug dealers and publicans in business.

Inevitably the conversation drifted back to Frank. Ella's face crumpled a little when she spoke of him. She said she hated him, but it sounded hollow.

'He's your father,' I said, 'and that won't change. He's been a good father and he loves you so much.' I was like Mother Teresa. But what I had said was true. Frank loved Ella. And Ella loved him.

I didn't want people saying bad things about him anyway. Maeve had started to run him down and I'd stopped her. It didn't help me if people badmouthed him.

'Are you leaving the door open for him?' Maeve had asked, with her uncanny ability to get to the nub of the matter.

I had shaken my head, not really knowing the answer. I didn't think so, but you couldn't just trash an entire marriage, a whole life. I had said something like that to Ella when she asked me if I hated him.

'You love somebody deeply, spend more than half your life with them, you don't just wake up and stop,' I had told her.

'How could he do that to us, Mum? How could he?' she asked, clamping her hand to her forehead.

I wanted to say to her that life was complicated. It wasn't like a maths problem with a definite outcome or a legal essay with a defined start, middle or end. Frank had betrayed me and I was sad. But that hadn't made me stop loving him.

'He's so having a mid-life crisis. That's so obvious. It's pathetic,' she had said, her eyes moistening. 'You think a twenty-five-year-old would go for a fifty-year-old if he wasn't rich? Dad's deluding himself. She's into him for his money. She totally wouldn't go for a guy of Dad's age if he was poor.' Her brow knitted. 'Dad's a cliché!'

Frank's number flashed up on the phone. Then Maeve was calling me. Then Ciara's name appeared on the screen. They'd have to wait, I thought, turning off the phone.

Ella was in her room on her phone. I could hear her voice dipping and rising. Gut instinct told me she was making a transatlantic call. And that the recipient of the call might be a young male neighbour of ours, one Jamie Deegan. I cleansed my face and drifted to bed, feeling strangely happy.

When I turned my phone back on, there was a cacophony of beeps as successive messages assaulted me.

Maeve: 'Where the hell are you? Ring me, for God's sake. Have you seen a paper? It's the Thornleys. You're never going to believe . . .' There was barely contained glee in her voice.

Ciara: 'Ring me, Anita. I presume you've heard about Dermot Thornley.'

Maureen: 'It's terrible about those friends of yours. It's hard to believe that anyone would behave like that . . .'

Shannon: 'God, I feel so sorry for Tracey. I feel so bad for bitching about her and the bag – although looks like some of our buddies may have bought that bag. Remember, innocent until proven guilty. He's only being investigated . . .'

Karen: 'Looks like one of your cronies has been caught with his mucky fingers in the till. Do not pass Go, straight to jail.'

After I'd tried, and failed, to get Frank on the phone, I drove to the garage, a coat thrown over my pyjamas, to get a paper. There on the newspaper rack, in the late edition of a tabloid, was a picture of Dermot and Tracey clutching glasses of champagne at some charity event underneath a screaming headline. Dermot was being investigated for misappropriation of client funds and for false accounting. A number of complaints had been made to the Institute of Chartered Accountants.

Maeve, when I rang her back, sounded positively energized by the news. 'I've just heard that the Fraud Squad are involved.'

I could picture her nostrils flaring like the skirts on a Spanish dancer. 'Oh, God,' I said. 'I wonder what this means for Frank. He's Frank's accountant.'

'I hadn't thought of that,' Maeve said, slightly chastened now.

Another shot of Dermot showed him climbing down from a helicopter in a linen suit with a mobile phone clamped to his ear, a self-satisfied Celtic Tiger grin stretched across his handsome features.

'It's all right,' Frank said wearily, when I finally got him. 'I didn't invest with him. He did my accounts, but I never gave the stupid bollocks any money to invest.'

'How come you didn't?' I asked.

'I never trusted him,' Frank said. I thought of all the dinners we'd eaten with Dermot and Tracey, all the laughter and bonhomie and back-slapping and social interaction, clearly founded on mistrust and falsity. 'But he was good with the banks and I couldn't get rid of him because he knew where all the bodies were buried.'

And I had no doubt that, over the years, Frank had buried a *lot* of bodies in his business.

I thought then of the Thornleys' lavish lifestyle, of the Bentleys and the Aston Martins and the helicopters ferrying guests to glitzy parties in marquees and the bands flown in to play at them and Tracey and her python handbag. 'What will happen to them, Frank?'

'I don't know. But if half of what's being said is true, he's not going to be a very popular man around town. They'll skin him alive.'

If Dermot had stolen money, people would understandably want to see justice done. But others would enjoy seeing him go down in flames. Irish people did not appreciate boasting. It didn't matter what a big, swinging dick you were, you had to be publicly humble or they would wait in the long grass for you. You had to hide your light under a bushel. Tracey and Dermot had flaunted their success: they had dangled their good looks and good fortune under people's noses and they would receive little sympathy.

'There's no difference between what your mate did and some fella from our flats smashing through a window and grabbing some ciggies except your man did it on a bigger scale and probably to some of his friends and family, which is just lovely,' Karen spat, 'so don't even try to excuse him. Just that your mate Dermot has a white collar and the right accent and went to the right school.'

'Innocent until proven guilty,' I said, parroting Shannon.

'Right, yeah,' she said, and rang off.

12

Ciara was baking Christmas cakes. I had called in to see her on the way home from school. There had been a number of vans parked in her drive. The work on her house and gardens never stopped: there was always a small army of people renovating, painting, decorating.

I had only been there about twenty minutes and already I wanted to beat a retreat.

'I got rid of the Mercedes,' she had confided, as she ushered me in past the new shining Toyota Prius parked proudly on the gravel. 'I know I only had it a couple of months but four-by-fours have had their day. I was back in London recently, doing some last-minute Christmas shopping.' Ciara's Christmas shopping had been done for months. Her presents, every year, were chosen and wrapped, ready to go. She did Santa at the start of September. 'Nobody drives them in Chelsea any more.' She gave a little laugh. 'They practically spit on you. It's the new zeitgeist,' she said, 'with the environment and the recession and all that.'

And all that. I watched her stir the cake mixture.

'I'm sort of mixing a Nigella recipe with a Rachel Allen one,' she said, giving me a brilliant, purposeful smile. The rock star's wife had given her a tip about Christmas cakes. 'She said to soak the fruit in Marsala instead of in brandy,' Ciara said.

Of course the rock star's wife was very public about her support for the environment, I recalled. An image of the gleaming Prius popped into my mind.

'She's very sophisticated, actually,' Ciara confided, 'but then she's bound to be with all the travel and exposure to different people.'

Ciara dried her hands on a tea-towel. I could feel her scrutinizing me. She was trying to figure out my look, I decided. And there wasn't one. I had put away my elaborate frocks and skyscraper heels. They had been consigned to the past. Now I wore jeans and casual tops. I no longer went to charity dos. Such occasions were thin on the ground anyway.

'What will you do with yourself,' Karen had asked, 'now that you're no longer eating full time for Africa?'

Ciara was dressed in a number of different shades of grey, which made her look more willowy than ever. A pretty flowery apron in the fifties style accentuated her slim middle. There was a strand of hair plastered across her forehead but she looked radiant, like an ad for domesticity. She was so perfect. If she had glided forward on castors I wouldn't have been surprised.

She sifted flour into the bowl, careful not to spill any around the sides. 'How are things with you?' she asked.

There was a note of false, almost aggressive brightness in her voice. She was speaking in exclamation marks, her smile too wide. There was tension in the kitchen among the tea-towels, Christmas cakes and the cup cakes Ciara had baked earlier and decorated with coloured sprinkles. Female friendships were complicated, predicated on all sorts of rules. There were hierarchies, leaders and underdogs. It wasn't all Hobnobs and kind words.

I had broken the contract between Ciara and me by quietly revolting. I had been the underdog, the compliant sidekick, while Ciara was Top Dog. That was the basis for our relationship. When she looked at me, things about me, deficiencies, made her feel good. She shared tips with me in the knowledge that I'd never really nail the look properly. She was always ten steps ahead.

I gave her unquestioning admiration – punctuated by the occasional stabs of envy – and tried to copy her. She saw her wonderful self reflected back in my adoring eyes. Now I was going my own way and she had picked up on it. Outwardly it was all business as usual but we both knew that the ground had shifted.

'I'm good,' I said. And in a way I was. At night I went to bed and slept. I was less jittery. And I did not wake up with wet cheeks. It was a start. And I could sense that I was gaining in confidence.

We were back to the subject of the rock star's wife. Ciara was now upending dried fruit into the bowl. 'Remember I mentioned about her son, little Kitson . . .'

She had snared the rock star's wife's son. I had done it myself, actually, used my children as social passports, as a way to net certain people and make them part of my social circle, however tangentially.

'He's coming to Jack's party.' Ciara tried to play it cool but she couldn't keep the big grin off her face. 'Kitson and Jack get on so well. He's such a sweet little boy. He's very sensitive, like Jack.'

Jack was a pleasant little blond-haired boy with a blank face who hid his light behind a bushel, if his cerebral talents and artistic bent were as marked as his mother said they were.

'But then *she*'s such a lovely person. We agree, I think, on the importance of a down-to-earth approach when you're raising children.'

Ciara was so grounded – with her blow-dries and her colonic irrigation and her maternity nurses and her yoga and her diets.

'Speaking of not being grounded,' she said, puckering her

lips, 'can you believe the facts that are coming out about Dermot Thornley?' She tutted.

'It's not great,' I said.

'It was on the news this morning that the Fraud Squad are involved.'

She'd said it in a supercilious way that made me want to needle her. 'What does your father think of it all?' I asked her. She stopped stirring the fruit into the cake mixture. 'He must have an interesting perspective as a garda.'

There was the fraction of a pause as her eyes slid away. The smile had congealed on her face. 'I didn't really discuss it with him,' she said, and resumed stirring.

The silence bristled with things unsaid.

When she looked up again she said, 'I know he was Frank's accountant.'

'Yes,' I said. She was getting no information from me.

Another silence grew.

Then Ciara said, 'The whole thing is so ugly. I wonder if Tracey was in on it.' She spooned the batter into foil-lined tins and surveyed her handiwork.

'She wasn't,' I said tersely.

'Oh?' she said, her neat head cocked.

'Shannon says Tracey's completely floored by what's happened.'

Ciara looked unconvinced.

'She also said that Tracey's doped up to the gills just to help her cope. That it's like she's woken up in the middle of a nightmare.'

Ciara raised her eyebrows sceptically and I felt like smacking her.

She sighed. 'It's all such a mess at the moment,' she said. 'Will had a very funny joke the other day, a little bit naughty.'

'Naughty'. She hadn't used that word when she was growing up. Like me, she had adopted a new accent and a new vocabulary to go with it.

'What's the difference between Ireland and Iceland?' She paused briefly. 'About six months and one letter,' she said, putting her fingertips over her lips in a *faux*-penitential pose and giving a merry laugh. Was she totally oblivious to other people's feelings?

Ciara was so competitive that even now, when many of the people we knew well were in meltdown, she was enjoying a moment of *Schadenfreude*. 'Messud's has shut down,' she said suddenly. Messud's was a Michelin-starred restaurant that Will and she loved. 'It's very sad.' She widened her blue eyes. 'It makes you thankful for what you've got.' She positioned a rogue strand of hair behind her ear. 'We've been fortunate in that Will was very cautious about his investments.'

Frank would be sorry to hear that. I also thought that Ciara was beginning to sound more and more like her husband.

'He invested a certain amount in MM but nothing significant. Ultan Mohally was pretty persuasive, I gather, but Will had the good sense to resist when he came back looking for us to invest more money.'

Frank had said that Ultan Mohally was a deal-maker rather than somebody who used his own money. 'That's the way it was until a couple of years ago,' Maeve had later told me, groaning. She said Ultan was leveraged up to his eyeballs. 'I think it just got to the point where he couldn't resist. They were buying properties so fast and flipping them and making so much goddam money he wanted a piece of the action.' Now Ultan was making cuts in the firm. 'His partners are in a rage with him because they're saying it was he who drove most of the big deals that resulted in them being so highly leveraged. Not that those snivelling turncoats weren't delighted with him when times were good. They thought he could walk on water.'

Ultan was into Paul Hogan's bank for a billion.

Ciara's daughter Camilla had been doing some homework in the corner at the circular Saarinen table. She got up and announced that she'd finished. 'Good girl. Go and do your piano practice,' Ciara instructed her. 'Forty-five minutes – put the egg-timer.'

Ciara piped classical music through the rooms her children played in. She fired mental maths at them. She played French tapes in the car. 'They're like sponges,' she had said once. 'It's a shame not to take advantage of that.'

Camilla heaved her shoulders and let out a dramatic sigh. 'I did thirty minutes this morning, Mum. And I had theory today. *Pleeeease*, Mum,' she begged, jigging up and down.

Ciara put on a disappointed face. 'Camilla, when you're on grade five that's what's expected. You know that. I'm not willing to discuss it.'

Camilla slouched off. A minute later strains of music were wafting in our direction.

'She's very annoyed,' Ciara confided, 'that she didn't get a main role in the Christmas play.' She gave a tight smile. 'She's got a part but with no singing. It's very galling. I mean, I know you shouldn't say it about your own but she's very musical. I hate it when things are unfair. It's the unfairness that kills you. I wouldn't mind but I just think it's very hard on her. I've had some *issues* with the teacher in question.' She rolled her eyes as if it was no big deal but I knew full well she'd probably considered taking a contract out on the music teacher's life.

'We're going skiing in January,' she said brightly. 'I'm really looking forward to it. We've just finalized the details.' She said they were hoping to meet up with the rock star and his wife

– they would be in Zermatt at the same time. But I felt sure there wasn't a chance of that happening. Ciara opened the oven door, popped the cake tins in and turned to smile at me triumphantly. 'We're also going to drive over the border to France and have a look around. It's a great time to snap up something,' she said. 'Lots of Brits and Irish are being forced to sell.'

I'd go home soon, I thought. I had nothing to say to Ciara. Our friendship had run its course. We'd never been what you could have called intimate. Or it had been a false sort of intimacy. I could see that now. You could never get beyond a certain point with her. It was like trying to penetrate a fortress. I had no knowledge of her interior life. She was beautiful and stylish. She had flair and panache. She knew how to dress and how to make her life look like something out of a magazine. But she was all style and no substance. She was restless with new enthusiasms, constantly shifting her paintings around her house, mastering new hobbies, then moving on. She mastered people too, made them hers, before her vaulting social ambition propelled her to set her sights higher.

I knew deep down that at the core of her perfectionism lay a lack of confidence. She was searching for social validation. And I wasn't interested any more. I no longer needed her approval. I did not want to copy her. And at that moment I realized, with a mixture of sadness and surprise, I didn't even want to listen to her.

Frank was outside poking around when I got home. It was nearly dark. He was hunched over what appeared to be a drain. He'd stopped coming into the house unannounced. I'd had to lay down some ground rules.

It turned out that he was cleaning the drains. It took a lot not to laugh: Frank – who wouldn't have changed a light bulb when he was living with me if I'd got down on bended knee, who got workmen in to do everything – was now cleaning the drains. Was it an eagerness to please, a desire to be near his wife and children? The children, who became mutinous and mute when their father was around so that I had usually ended up rescuing the conversation in spite of myself. I didn't know.

There was a silence now, as if Frank were unsure what to say next.

I broke it. 'Any word from Dermot Thornley?'

'Zip,' Frank said, his face darkening. 'He's not taking my calls. The whole thing is a huge pain in the arse. Not what I need right now. The fucking Fraud Squad will have been all over my files. Anyway, at least the stupid bollocks doesn't have my money.' He looked gloomy. 'I'd heard rumours about him, you know. I asked him. And he looked me straight in the eye and told me it was all complete bull.' He sighed. 'You never know who to trust, do you?'

I gave him a hard look. 'No,' I said shortly, so that he reddened.

There was an awkward pause, which I sort of enjoyed. Then he asked, 'You touch base with Tracey?'

I shook my head. 'I didn't want her to think I was ringing because of you. I also don't want to be rubbernecking. Shannon's in contact, I think. I'll text her in a while when the dust settles a bit.'

'God love her,' Frank said. In his own deeply flawed way, he was fundamentally decent. 'The planning decision is out next week,' he said. There was doubt in his eyes.

'There's nothing you can do now,' I said. 'What's done is done.'

He nodded, but he still seemed uncertain. 'You're looking very –'

'Lined,' I butted in.

He shook his head. 'You look well, Anita.'

My expression was pinched, I knew. Frank Lawlor could stick his banter and his charm and his charisma ten feet up his arse, I thought, glaring at him.

He faltered. Then he said, 'You've stopped shooting all that shit into your face.'

I raised a shoulder and let it drop. When I spoke my tone was dismissive, discouraging. 'For the moment.' I pursed my lips.

'The more casual look suits you,' he said, his expression hovering between nervousness and something I couldn't place. He ploughed on: 'The jeans and that . . .'

I bit back a smile. Frank the fashion adviser. He had a cheek to be trying to compliment me but it was funny all the same. And while I felt a pinprick of pleasure at the remark I didn't puff up as I would have done before. Compliments were no longer my life blood. 'I'd better go,' I said, beginning to move towards the house. 'Dylan broke up with the girl-friend,' I told him, turning back briefly.

Biba had dumped him. 'It's not you, it's me,' she had said, according to Dylan. 'I need some space.'

My son had looked helpless and bewildered. Part of me had done a jig of delight, the other part had wanted to storm over there and rip her head off for hurting my boy.

He had also lost his job. In a manner of speaking. 'Like, they asked for people to come forward for voluntary redun-dancy and I decided not to, so they basically pushed me off the cliff.'

It was a classic Dylan performance. He moved out of home and took on the expense of a flat and then, forgoing the chance of voluntary redundancy, ended up getting canned. So the prodigal son had come back. Now he was spending his time in the coach house, his Heartbreak Hotel, strumming his guitar and listening to Tom Waits-style music, between making raids on the fridge and strewing his dirty laundry on the floor.

'What's your plan?' I'd asked him, pushing the button to raise the blinds in his room. I was ankle deep in pizza boxes and Coke cans. My foot actually sank into a sodden bowl of breakfast cereal. There were life forms proliferating in the room, I was sure, whole eco-systems. 'Jesus, Dylan.'

The smell was fetid – of socks, sweat, and boy things I didn't want to analyse. It was more of a lair than a room. Dylan was panned out on the bed. He opened his eyes to a slit, managing to make it look like a major feat. I'd toed him on the chest.

'Mu-uuum.'

I'd torn his quilt off.

'What sort of a plan?' he'd asked, raising himself up on one elbow and looking as if I'd asked him to reveal the meaning of life.

'A plan as to what you're going to do with yourself. Job-wise, I mean.'

He hadn't got an answer for me so I'd told him to let me know once he'd formulated a plan. And to make it sooner rather than later.

'Not the worst thing,' Frank remarked now. 'I wasn't very gone on Biba.'

'Me neither,' I admitted, 'but he liked her. He's mooning around the place.'

'No sign of a job?' Frank asked lightly.

I shook my head.

'He could maybe work with me. I might be able to find him something to do.' There was humour in his eyes.

'He could,' I said, surrendering to a meagre smile, 'but I don't think that would be a very good idea, do you?'

It was strange. We spoke more easily now that we were

separated. There was a truce of sorts. I no longer shouted at him. I felt more detached. I had moved through the various stages of grief to some sort of acceptance of what had happened. It was Frank who seemed to be driving much of our communication.

'Dad is like a bad smell,' Ella had said. 'He won't go away. We see him more now that he doesn't live here. He made a decision to choose her,' she'd added, with the absolute conviction and certainty of youth, 'so he should move on.'

'Dylan won't talk to me,' Frank said. He looked sad and deflated. Old. 'I didn't have much of a relationship with my old fella growing up.'

I nodded.

'He was a quiet sort of a man. He worked in the local distillery until the year I was born.'

'I never knew that.'

'After that he was more of an odd-jobs man. A *gobán saor*, he used to call himself. Bottom line, he worked about half the time and then at half tilt. There was no fight between us as such but we never had two words to say to each other. I never got him and he never got me.'

There was a pause. Then he said, 'He was just happy to scrape by. I hated the way we had no car so that you'd have to hitch a lift in and out of the town, hoping that one of the neighbours would take pity on you and slow down when they saw you struggling along with the messages. I couldn't understand why my father never seemed to mind. Maybe that's what drove me all these years.'

This was as reflective as I'd ever heard Frank get. He didn't do navel-gazing. Action, not talk, was the answer to every problem. 'Just get the finger out' and it'd be fine.

'I've often worried that Dylan's a bit like him. That he inherited a genetic lack of drive. I had so many goals when I was his age. I had hunger in my belly,' he said, touching the mound of his stomach. 'Fuck it, I worked picking fruit, bumping up and down drills until my back was aching and my paws were stained pink from the effin' strawberries. I'd have shovelled shit from one side of the road to the other if I'd have made a few bob out of it. I wasn't too proud. I did that so my son wouldn't have to. You were a schoolboy, then you were a man. There was none of this faffing about trying to find yourself. You could find yourself at work.'

I gave a weary sigh. When I put my hand up, like a garda halting traffic, Frank took the hint. 'I've heard it all before, Frank,' I couldn't help adding.

He looked hurt. After a short pause, he said, 'I don't understand Dylan.'

'You have to let him be his own man, Frank. You can't force people to be what they're not.'

He gave a fretful shrug. 'I just want the best for my son.'

'I know,' I said, thinking I didn't have the energy for this man. I'd often thought that Frank sort of plugged into you, sucked you dry and then moved off. To be successful you had to be utterly focused – you had to be dead selfish. Frank was good at that.

'He won't take my calls,' Frank added.

'Give him time. You look like shit, Frank.' I hadn't planned on saying that. It just sort of slipped out. Old habits died hard.

He gave a bark of a laugh. 'I'm tired. We're like lepers now.'

I looked at him questioningly.

'Developers,' he clarified. He named a well-known politician. 'I met him in the street the other day and he was looking over his shoulder, afraid that he might be seen with me. The same fucking boyo was leapin' over tables to have his picture taken with me in the tent at the Galway races not two years ago.'

I remembered. The man in question was a smirking slee-veen who stood for nothing except staying in power. There was a whole tribe of them who had re-zoned land for devel-opers, drunk with the bankers, awarded contracts and carved up the spoils for those who were in the inner circle.

Frank gave a derisive little hiss. 'Hypocritical little fucker.' His forehead cleared. He formed a deliberate smile as if to say that this was no big deal.

I felt the urge to needle him. 'From hero to zero,' I said.

His smile melted away.

'That was uncalled-for,' I said, feeling mildly regretful.

'I deserved it,' he said, a little pompously. 'Of course Eamon's worrying like an old woman that we won't get the planning.'

That was Frank's indirect way of admitting he was anxious. Show no fear. Admit to no emotion. That was the Lawlor way. Kathleen Lawlor had done some job on her sons.

'You must be worried yourself,' I said, unwilling to let it go.

He didn't answer. Then, deflecting as only Frank could, 'If only I'd known that the whole world was going to go tits up.'

This seemed to suggest that he had been the hapless victim of circumstance. I wasn't letting him off the hook like that. His property gamble could not be laid at the door of larger forces outside his control. 'It was a big punt you took all the same,' I responded. I would not add that, according to Dylan, his stockbroking firm had devalued Frank's Wexford site by as much as seventy per cent.

Frank didn't seem to take the point. Instead he said, 'It was some fucking ride, what?' He shook his head. 'Watching the likes of me going over to London and buying the place up. We were riding the crest of a wave,' he said, clapping his hands together.

'Save it, Frank.'

'If only we'd known that the sub-prime crisis in America was floating towards us all the time like a silent iceberg.'

I didn't want to get pulled further into the conversation. But I couldn't let that bull go unchecked. 'Some might say, Frank, that you went on the roulette wheel with other people's money. Money,' I said, heat rising in my face, 'that Paul Hogan and his bank lent you so that now the taxpayer has to bail out the banks and pick up the tab for the recklessness of developers like you . . . and the greedy, incompetent bank officials. Lots of ordinary people will have to pay higher taxes and will probably lose their jobs.'

Frank looked surprised, then bitter. I was taken aback, too, by the volley of words that had poured out of my mouth.

'Christ,' he said, sounding riled, 'say what you think, why don't you?' Two sharp discs of red had appeared on his cheeks. 'And I'm to blame for all that, am I?' he asked stiffly.

'No,' I said, folding my arms across my chest, 'but don't try and blame America for everything.'

We stared at each other.

'You and your cronies have played your part. Paul Hogan writing loan cheques for you and Ultan Mohally and the Deegans and Jimmy . . .' I drew myself up. 'What the hell got into us, Frank?'

'Jesus, Anita,' Frank said, giving a tight smile. 'Is this some sort of Pauline conversion on the road to Damascus? You certainly knew how to spend it when the notion took you.'

The chilly evening jabbed at my face. 'I know,' I said, my voice quick and edgy, 'that I went along with you for the ride, happy to burn through the cash and to take helicopters when we could have driven cars and buy so many clothes that I could do with an aircraft hangar to house them. But there's no point in being delusional any more,' I said. 'That's what not drinking does to you. It brings things into clearer focus.'

'It's good you're not drinking,' he said.

'Why did you never say anything much about my drinking?'

Frank gave a harsh laugh. 'Are you going to lay that at my door too?'

I shook my head. 'Of course not. I just wondered if it ever worried you – if you even noticed.'

'I noticed, I suppose,' he said slowly. 'A lot of the time I just thought you were having a bit of craic. And lots of us were drinking too much, maybe, having too much of the auld craic.'

That much was true. Looking back now, it seemed as if there was a time when popping champagne corks was the soundtrack to our lives.

'Do you think you have a problem?' he asked.

I shrugged.

He returned to safer ground – the state of the country. He'd always been good at talking about himself or things that interested him. 'If the banks had stopped lending five years earlier they would have stopped the Celtic Tiger in its tracks and there would have been a mini revolution. Greed got us a lot of things we didn't have before. Irish people were sick of having no arse to the seat of their trousers.' He was on a roll now. 'I just wanted to build a classy development,' he said, 'a high-end group of buildings using world-class design, giving people proper luxury. I have every crank this side of the western world criticizing my development. It's just pure fucking snobbery. The likes of them, they get all fucking exercised by the starving children in Africa but they can't stand a fella like me from Offaly doing well.'

I pantomimed a yawn and Frank looked a little startled. I didn't care. When he veered into self-pity, it was boring. And I wasn't indulging it. 'Anyway, on the original subject of Dylan,' I said, 'I think he planned on working with Jamie Deegan but that hasn't come to pass. Jamie doesn't have anything for him to do – or, at least, nothing Dylan is willing to do. I have a feeling Jamie offered him bar work, which Dylan said no to. It was something Ella said.'

I paused. 'You shouldn't give him any more money, though. If he's broke it will focus his mind.'

'Fine,' Frank said, eyeing me strangely.

'He has to get over this idea of starting at the top of everything. He needs just to get an ordinary job and lower his expectations.'

Frank stuck out his bottom lip. 'I'm not sure lowering his expectations is what I'd advise my son to do.'

I gave a short bark of a laugh. 'That's exactly what we all have to do, Dylan included. It's time to recalibrate. It's back to Planet Earth.'

Dylan seemed worryingly convinced he was destined for great things without any evidence to back it up. Like I said, it was bad that our generation had been afraid of our shadow by comparison, but with Dylan the pendulum seemed to have swung the other way a bit too far. My son seemed to have caught the American bug of self-belief to the point of lunacy.

'You certainly seem very fired up,' Frank remarked, still studying me.

'Yeah, well . . .' I petered out mid-sentence, unwilling to explain myself further. 'By the by, I think Ella may be seeing Jamie Deegan – but, for God's sake, don't say anything.'

Frank frowned. 'I always thought Jamie was a bit of a smart Alec.' He made a regretful clucking sound. 'I quite liked that guy Christopher.' Waves of suspicion radiated from him.

'Frank, you're warming up to Christopher because he's gone. You always liked Jamie when he was Dylan's friend.'

'Sure Jamie's a talented kid, he has gumption, but there's something sort of . . .' He searched for the word but didn't find it. 'There's something about him. I can't put my finger on it.'

'It won't last,' I said, amused.

I had seen Ella and Jamie at the door, laughing and clowning around. It had been in the early hours and their shushed giggling had woken me. I had peered down at them briefly. Ella had pushed him away, laughing coquettishly. He had pulled her towards him then, and I had moved away from the window.

Another day I'd been trundling down Georges Street on the bus – 'very woman-of-the-people' had been Karen's comment – and I'd seen them walking along hand in hand. Ella was talking and Jamie was listening with a look on his face that told me she was delivering the lecture and he was the audience.

Ella had said nothing about Jamie so I was keeping my beak shut. We were getting on far too well.

'There are still rumours hanging around Ted Deegan,' Frank said. 'There's talk that he used some of the insurance deposits to buy shares. I doubt it myself. Ted is too fucking smart for that.' Frank had always secretly admired Ted Deegan, in so far as he looked up to anyone.

'Who knows?' I said. 'At this point anything seems possible. I'm going inside.' I turned away from him.

And just like that he dropped a bomb.

'Fiona lost the baby yesterday,' he said, to my retreating back.

I stopped in my tracks. It took me a moment or two to digest the words. 'I'm sorry to hear that,' I said, pivoting around and trying not to show that I was rattled.

His face was unreadable.

'Should you not be with her,' I asked, my voice neutral, 'instead of here cleaning drains?'

'She's gone home to Limerick to her parents,' he said tonelessly. 'That's what she wanted.' His mouth sagged downwards. 'She had to have a dry labour.'

'That must have been very hard on her,' I said.

He nodded.

I visualized Fiona Keane with her magnificent hair and cocky young face and found that I felt a little sorry for her. And for the baby.

'Why don't you loathe her, Mum?' Ella had asked me. 'I don't get it.'

It had taken me a while to frame the answer. 'Because,' I had said eventually, 'I need to conserve my energy for myself.'

'I'm sorry, Frank,' I said, my tone briskly sympathetic.

'I'm not sure that I am,' Frank said, running his hand across his face. 'God forgive me,' he said, blessing himself.

The comment hung in the air. Frank compressed his lips. 'Why should *you* be sorry?' he asked.

'I wouldn't wish away a human life,' I said, pushing my hands into my pockets.

We stared at each other.

'I feel bad for her,' he said, 'but she's young. And I didn't want another family.'

We were straying into dangerous ground.

'I had one,' he said, rounding off.

The moment stretched out.

'Anita, I don't know how the fuck we got here. I don't

know how I'm living in a flat the size of a shoebox with a girl young enough to be my daughter who I don't love.'

I gave a harsh laugh. 'I have a fair idea.'

'Fiona took my number for business reasons. She sent me a couple of texts, some stupid joke about developers. Then I texted back. It was nothing major, just a harmless bit of flirtation.'

My voice was cool but my face was anything but impassive. 'You were always a lousy judge of character.'

He ran his hand across his face. 'One afternoon I was in a meeting, bored senseless listening to Eamon go on about some judicial review, and she texted me.'

'Why are you telling me this now?'

'I want to explain to you.'

'I don't care, Frank,' I said, which wasn't strictly true. The masochistic part of me wanted to hear how it had come about. 'It's water under the bridge.'

'I texted back and asked her on the spur if she'd like to meet for a beer. She said she didn't drink beer, she only liked Chablis. I was bored. My nuts were in a vice with the planning. She made me feel good about myself.'

I snorted.

'So then I fired one off about how we could share a bottle of Chablis in her place.'

'And then you had to sleep with her,' I snapped.

'Seemed the next thing I knew she'd met me at the airport to tell me I was going to be a daddy and I'd left my wife, the only woman I've ever loved.'

'You're a hard case, Frank,' I said, feeling my throat tighten.

'I don't love her. I don't even fucking fancy her.'

'Don't,' I said, averting my face. I folded my arms across my chest in a defensive gesture.

'I'm so sorry, Anita.'

I ignored this. He was not drawing me into his shit, putting me under his Frank spell. 'See you later,' I said, in an artificially sprightly winding-up voice.

'Anita,' he begged.

I turned – and I shouldn't have. Through the gloom I could see that his eyes had misted over. His shoulders were hunched. There was a droop to his head and he looked hollow-eyed and hollowed out. And although I tried not to, I softened. The spectre of Frank and Anita could not be so easily banished. I'd been with this man almost all of my adult life. Was that what happened when you married so young? You failed to envisage a universe without some version of you as a couple? *No*, I thought, with renewed energy. We had gone too far for that. I would not be sucked in again.

The children would most likely be there, I thought, looking towards the house. I was fairly certain I'd seen a tuft of Dylan's hair popping out from behind the drawing room shutters. They wouldn't be happy to see Frank. I didn't want to be caught in the middle of their silent war. Frank had made his bed.

The exchange had caused a picture of a glass of wine to worm its way into my head. Frank had acted like a total prick. He had betrayed me and I would never forget it. But I had this constant back and forth about how I should treat him, and he was still the father of my children. A man who, in some respects, had been a good father and husband. He had bankrolled us all for years. Whether he could continue to do so was seriously debatable.

Karen had been like a dog with a bone. 'You either talk to Frank about his finances or you go to that little runt of a solicitor Eamon or I – so help me God – will go to both of them. I'm blue in the face from telling you, you have to get the finger out and face the reality of what's coming down

257

the tracks. You've had enough time to adjust to the separation.'

So Frank was being very generous. But then Frank had always been generous. He would have given you the shirt off his back. It was one of the things that I had loved about him. The fact he was so profligate, so devil-may-care. When I first met him I was in the habit of weighing my expenditure – I had no choice. Frank had soon eased me out of that habit.

He'd said our house was 'ring-fenced'. This information had not been good enough for Karen. 'You need to understand why the house is okay and what income is coming in and from where, and what portion you can expect to get.'

My eyes scanned the darkened garden. Karen was right. We had not talked about our finances except in the loosest and woolliest of terms. It was time to stop hiding from the truth. 'I've time for a cup of tea,' I said, feeling a cold sensation in the pit of my stomach. 'A quick one.'

He looked like all his Christmases had come at once.

'Frank,' I said, wanting to make things clear, 'don't get any ideas.'

He shook his head eagerly.

'I mean, don't read anything into this. It's just a cup of tea.'

I pushed the key into the lock with more force than was strictly necessary and made myself turn and look him in the eye. 'And we need to talk about money.'

13

I had planned on walking. Walking was my new thing. When I felt like a drink, I pounded the pavements like a mad woman, bombing along with my arms swinging like those of a goose-stepping soldier. I had cancelled my gym membership. I had no interest in attracting curious, pitying looks, having the same half-conversation over and over again, peddling plati-tudes and dodging questions. It was too expensive anyway, and too redolent of the past.

I preferred being out under the urban skies, walking along Sandymount beach, with the red and white striped Pigeon House chimneys, like something a pop artist might have constructed, to my back. I'd thread my way through the seagulls resting on the sand, the changing cityscapes strangely exhilarating, marching to drown the longing for some gargle.

'Heil Hitler,' a spotty teenage boy had shouted at me one evening, so that his gaggle of mates had roared with laughter.

Karen was waiting for me one night when I swung into the drive, peering out the drawing-room window with her nose pressed up against the glass. She opened it and stuck her head out, flicking ash onto the gravel. 'You're like horse dung, on the road day and night.'

Frank would have had a mickey fit to see her smoking in the drawing room. 'She'd have the place turned into Corona-tion Street in two seconds if you let her,' Frank had hissed once, when he thought he was out of Karen's earshot.

Karen had been sitting out the back, sunning herself with

her T-shirt rolled up, and her shoes and socks off. 'You'd want to be careful, Frank,' she'd shouted through the door, 'shackling yourself to bourgeois bullshit like that. You didn't grow up with it. And never underestimate the Butler ears. We can hear the grass grow.'

Well, Frank could go whistle. He was gone. And Karen was around, breathing life into the place.

Anyway, I'd been about to leave when I changed my plans. I got the crazy idea to cycle. I was officially gone mad. I hadn't swung my arse onto a bicycle seat in twenty years or more. But down I went to the basement, sifting through old exercise gear, countless crazes of Dylan's, including kayaks and skateboards, until I found Ella's bike, with a basket on the front and gauzy white ribbons tied to the handlebars.

I set off. It made me feel foolish, light-headed and giddy. I had to stop myself ringing the bell. A middle-aged woman – ex-lush (hopefully) – on the loose, attempting to start a new life. Today I was going to see Animal. The idea had been rumbling inside me for some time.

It was another beautiful day. There was the odd wispy cloud floating across the sky, but otherwise it was crisp, clear and sunny. I cycled into town, sticking to the side of the road, walking my bike across some junctions, too chicken even to dream of weaving in and out of the traffic. Down St Stephen's Green, onto Dame Street, then puffing my way up – I wasn't sure how to change the gears so I left them – past the neo-classical beauty of City Hall on Parliament Street, my favourite building in the city, then the majestic Christ Church and into the more derelict surroundings of Thomas Street.

Our old school was in the Liberties, off Thomas Street. It was near the Guinness brewery, not far from one of the few remaining pawnbrokers in the city, near where Frawley's used to be. We used to get everything there, from our school uniforms to our Communion outfits to our knickers. Ma also used to buy from the traders outside, who sold knick-knacks and odds and ends, big packets of washing powder, granny clothes, cheap makeup, Easter eggs at Easter and Christmas decorations at Christmas.

I passed a knot of junkies huddled around cans of what I thought was cider, their features gnawed away by skag or something else. A young fella in a hoodie called something out to me. He was standing next to a stream of thin liquid, pale in colour, his back to a wall covered with graffiti.

Mickser luvs Sharon.

Anto is a cocksucker.

Our school seemed greyer and more decrepit than the one in Memory Lane. It was a rectangle shape, like a big block of cheese turned on its side. You could get depressed just looking at it. It was like somewhere you'd do time. It was painted a different colour now but it still had the familiar grey tatty look about it. I walked in the gates and I was transported back: the smelly toilets, rough bog roll that scratched your backside and carbolic soap. I could visualize the headmistress with her buck teeth scouring the corridors for miscreants, doling out slaps and ear cuffs without breaking stride. She was a strong, formidable woman, a real feminist. She wouldn't have seen herself as such but she was. She had encouraged the girls to be strong and independent, not to take any crap from fellas.

I walked through the schoolyard, which was empty, and chained my bike to the railings, fleetingly wondering if it was wise to leave it there. It was Ella's and bound to be expensive.

Up the stairs I went, with butterflies in my stomach, lugging the spectre of my big fat failure and flunk-out behind me. When I had won the scholarship to Trinity, the headmistress had bragged about it to the entire school. I had been dragged in front of Assembly and the students were made to clap for me and my great success. There had been a piece in the local free-sheet with the imaginative headline, 'Local Girl Wins Scholarship'.

Most of my old teachers were bound to be retired. The headmistress was long gone, prematurely dispatched by stress and overwork. I inched my way up the stairs feeling like a teenager, as if I was about to be pounced on and required to account for myself.

I was outside the principal's office. I knocked. The headmaster answered. He seemed very pleasant, and a lot less formidable than our headmistress had been. She had been scary in a good way. He looked at his watch. The class was just over. 'Mr Stack' had a free period afterwards he said, consulting a giant wall planner. 'Nadine,' he called out, to a chubby, round-faced kid who was passing his open door. He told her to escort me to the classroom.

After throwing me a smile Nadine trudged along silently. She had backcombed hair, like a giant bird's nest. Our headmistress would not have stood for that. She had been old school and unsympathetic to personal vanity. Her approach had been brutal but undeniably effective. She had also been devoid of irony. 'You bully, you,' she'd shout, thumping ten bells out of a pupil half her height who'd been caught hassling someone.

The smell in the large brick building was the same, I thought, as I followed my silent guide down the narrow corridors. We passed what appeared to be still the cloakroom and a blast of teenage-girl smell wafted out, a sort of saccharine sweetness underlaid by something earthy.

'It's here,' Nadine announced, her plucked brows lifting a little. I was aware that my breathing was a little shallow. I was *sooo* nervous.

I thanked her and leant against the wall. I could see Animal's oddly shaped head through the small pane of glass in the door. He was talking about the Remainder Theorem.

'The Remainder Theorem states that when a polynominal f(x) is divided by $(x - a)$, the remainder is f(a).' All his years in Dublin had not taken the edge off his bogger Kerry accent. Karen used to do a very funny impression of him. She was a brilliant mimic. Nobody was safe. I dreaded to think how she'd done me over the years.

Animal's voice had a winding-up quality. He was telling them to take down their homework.

It had all seemed doable when I was working in my nice safe cocoon. Into school, back home to Ma and Da and my little desk. Being told I was 'a great girl so you are' by my headmistress and the teachers – the praise had been like oxygen to me. And then I'd gone on an organized tour of Trinity for prospective students and it had all fallen apart.

I jumped as a loud bell rang and interrupted my dreaming. Any minute now the students would pour out of the class-rooms like a herd of wildebeest. My stomach lurched. Animal was staring out the small window at me, like some sort of myopic sea creature. I could see recognition in his eyes. The door was opening. He was beckoning to me. He was saying hello, I was saying hello, and then he had ushered me into the classroom.

If Animal was surprised to see me he didn't show it. He pressed his damp hand into mine. His manner was as usual deliberate and slow, as if he had all the time in the world. He introduced me to the class. 'This is Anita Butler,' he said.

I stood at the front, fiddling with my handbag.

'Is that your girlfriend, sir?' a bold strap with hair in her eyes shouted. There was a spasm of laughter.

Animal ignored her. He was an old hand at that sort of banter but I had gone bright red. 'Anita is an ex-pupil. She was once head girl of this school.'

I could feel a sea of inspecting eyes. These girls were only a year or so younger than Ella. And I knew they were unforgiving in the way they dissected you.

'Anita was one of the brightest maths students ever to pass through the gates of this school,' he told them. 'She won a scholarship from Trinity College to study maths.'

I flushed, squeezing my toes inside my shoes.

'Ooh, very nice – *Trinity*,' came from somewhere at the back of the class in a strangulated parody of an English accent. 'Anyone for cricket?'

This produced more laughter.

'Nobody has done that in this school since, to my knowledge.'

'That's for fucking sure,' the girl with the hair in her eyes shouted. Animal told her not to swear.

Our headmistress would definitely have yanked that hair out of her eyes, I thought, watching her lean over and mouth something at a heavy-chested girl in another desk.

'What's Trinity like?' asked a pretty girl, with long eyelashes.

The accents were strong Dub, not marooned in mid-Atlantic like the bored, tonally flat voices of Ella's friends.

I glanced at Animal but he was silent. 'I didn't go,' I said, after a minute. My feet were welded to the ground. My mouth ran dry.

'Why?' came from the back of the class.

I paused. 'Because . . .' I trailed off. 'Because I bottled it.'

'Why did ya bottle it?' It was the hair-in-her-eyes girl again. She was leaning back in her chair with her arms behind her head. She reminded me a bit of Karen. Caustic and all front but whip-smart.

'I was scared.'

'Why were ya scared?' she shot back.

'I went into Trinity to see it and I was overwhelmed.' I paused to slow myself down so that I didn't start to talk my head off. 'I didn't know anybody who had gone there.' I halted again trying to pick my words. 'It was amazing – but it was all too much for me, the beautiful architecture, the sweeping grey buildings, the students with their backpacks looking to me like something out of another world. It was too foreign to somebody like me.'

'It's down the bleeding road,' said someone. There was a rumble of laughter.

On the tour I had been one of a little constellation of students following the guide around. The others had plied the guide with confident questions – or so it had seemed to me. I had listened to the rhythmic thud of balls in Botany Bay where the students played tennis and felt a clutching at my sides. *What the fuck was Anita Butler doing thinking that she could fit in here? She was smoking crack if she thought there would be a place for her somewhere like this, with her accent and her background.* That was how it had felt.

We had visited the Long Room, in the Old Library – the description underplayed the beauty of the soaring timber barrel-vaulted ceiling and the ancient hand-bound books that lined the stacks and gave off the pungent but pleasant scent of leather and privilege. There had been marble busts lining the room of notables like Jonathan Swift.

I had not been able to open my mouth. We – the little knot of students and our guide – had gone for coffee and I had not uttered a syllable. I had sat there like a speechless lump in my cheap clothes, foolishly silent and damp under the arms, drowning as the pressure built in my chest. By the time I had trailed back over the cobblestones of Front Square and through the hallowed gates into the other Dublin, my face had been tomato red and I felt I had failed some sort of test. I'd run home to St Stephen's Green and the safety of my bedroom, where I'd lain on my bed and told myself I would defer. The diagnosis of Ma's cancer had given me an out.

'I thought it wasn't for people like me,' I said.

'It's for poshos,' came a voice from the back.

'She's a posho,' said Hair-in-her-Eyes Girl.

'I'm not,' I said, smiling. 'I'm originally from the Coppinger Street flats.'

'She is on her . . .'

'Well, you don't bleedin' live there now.'

'True,' I said. 'But I grew up there.'

'The big bleedin' accent on ya,' said Hair-in-her-Eyes Girl so that everyone, even Animal and I, laughed.

'My ma is from the Coppinger Street flats,' said someone.

'We'll give you a medal,' said a girl with a messy ponytail.

'You should have gone,' said the pretty girl with the long eyelashes, only half meeting my eyes. 'If yez got a scholarship.'

'You're right,' I told her. I wouldn't tell them, I thought, about how I had planned to but that motherhood had intervened. About how those fabulous precious years of looking after my kids had rolled by in one long lovely blur until, hey presto, I was middle-aged and staring down the barrel of a lonely life by myself. I wouldn't say that being a wife and a mother was wonderful but you had to watch out you didn't go down a cul-de-sac from which there would be no coming back. I did say, 'You should always – *always* – take the chances you're given in life.'

Animal gave them permission to go then, so they stuffed their books into their bags and fled.

It was just him and me now. He stood there, rocking back and forward on his toes, like he'd always done, listening.

'It was too far for me to travel,' I said.

He pressed his lips together. 'That makes me sadder than you'll know, girleen.' He pinched his nose and sniffed. 'Trinity is ten minutes away but it may as well be in another galaxy. And not all that much has changed,' he said, with a little shake of his head.

'So I owe you an apology,' I breathed. 'For being off-hand in the hospital. But more for not thanking you for all that time and effort you ploughed into me.' He raised a hand to stay me but I barrelled on, colour flooding my cheeks. 'I feel I wasted your time,' I said, my eyes watering.

His gaze seemed to turn inward. Then he said, 'If I'd only picked up on it at the time.' Suddenly he looked his age. 'I'm glad you came back.'

I was eating pasta for the second time in twenty-four hours. I had officially gone crazy. There had been a lot of wisecracks and elbowing in the ribs. We were having a nice time.

'You need to lose that American accent, sis.'

There was regular mention of Jamie Deegan, I noticed. I was listening but my thoughts drifted back to Animal and the classroom. After a while I turned to the kids. 'I went back to my old school today,' I said, setting down my fork.

'Why?' asked Dylan, swivelling around on his stool.

'I bumped into my teacher during the summer. Once upon a time he wanted me to go to Trinity to study maths.'

They looked at me round-eyed.

'I had the marks and I got a scholarship.' If I'd said I'd had the option of a job as a hula-hula dancer they would have looked less surprised. I told them a bit about Animal but they didn't really get how inspirational he was.

'He sounds like he has personal-hygiene problems,' was what Dylan said.

'Oh, my God, why didn't you go to Trinity?' Ella demanded.

'Because I didn't have the confidence. Going to Trinity was like travelling to outer space to me.'

'Because you were, like, from a poor family?' Dylan asked, as if being poor was some sort of rare disease.

'Yes. I didn't know anybody who'd done something like that.'

'That's so weird,' said Dylan.

They had no real grasp of the invisible hurdles that some-times existed as a bar to advancement. And my family's poverty was exotic to them. Trinity was exotic to the kids I'd spoken to that day, although they wouldn't have let on that they gave a shite. My background was unthinkable to my kids. I had more or less written the memory of Ma and Da out of the picture.

'When I was growing up we didn't have our own toilet. Not till I was seven.'

'Where did you go to the loo?' Ella asked.

'We shared with two other families.'

'Shared a bog?' said Dylan, clearly disgusted.

'Yeah – with the Collins family and the Keoghs. Poor Mrs Keogh,' I said, smiling.

'Poor Mrs Keogh' was a refrain of our childhood that was guaranteed to reduce Karen and me to gales of laughter. When -ever her name had come up Ma would heave a sigh and say, 'Poor Mrs Keogh.' Mrs Keogh was perpetually convalescent. She suffered from every complaint known to the medical profession and a few that hadn't been discovered, which wasn't exactly a major fecking surprise when you thought of her twelve freckle-faced, adenoidal kids and her lazy-arse husband who, with his permanent squint, wouldn't get out of the bed except to drink or to go down the bookie's or to the labour.

'Your grandmother May was from Creighton Street on the quays. There were nine girls and three boys in her family. They were very poor. When the boats would come into the quays, as they did back then, my uncle Billy would take whatever he could get off them – bales of material, whatever. Ma used to say about her brother Billy, "He was a robber." Ma's house backed onto the Tedcastle yard. They'd remove bricks from the wall and take coal in. One time your grand-uncle Billy got up a ladder and fell over when he was taking some coal. He lost his card for the labour so he had to root through the coal to find it.'

'What's the labour?' Ella asked.

'Signing on.'

She still looked confused.

'Social welfare – the dole,' I said, again struck by their utter unfamiliarity with the world I had grown up in.

'It all sounds very Dickensian,' Ella remarked.

'Whatever that means,' said Dylan.

'It means like out of a Charles Dickens novel, dum-dum,' she told him. He mock-punched her.

'Your great-grandmother, my grandmother, used to wash clothes in a washhouse on Townsend Street.'

'Why?' Dylan asked.

'Because she loved washing clothes,' Ella deadpanned. 'To make money, Dylan!' she added, rolling her eyes.

I nodded. 'When Ma was a small girl she used to bring my nana down a flask of tea. And Nana would take off Ma's clothes while she was there and wash them. Ma only had two sets of clothes. One for school and the other for Sundays.' My children's eyes were wide. 'My grandfather used to pawn his suit on a Monday morning and hope that he would be able to make it back by Friday for Mass on Sunday. If he didn't, he'd go to Mass in another parish.'

Dylan blinked. 'God, that sounds rough.'

'They actually did all right by the standards of the time. At least they had fires in every room.' I thought of the pretty girl with the long eyelashes. Her name was Janice. Animal had asked me to take her on for extra maths. 'Janice needs encouragement, girleen, just like you.' He'd smiled. And before I could argue with him about how I was too busy, about how I wasn't capable, I found myself saying yes. And I felt better than I had in years.

14

Shannon's eyes moistened when she saw me. She gave me a hug. 'It's so nice of you to stop by,' she said, brushing dry lips across my cheek. 'I know that Frank's planning decision is out today.'

It was D-Day for Frank. I'd been up since early morning – jittery. The kids were anxious too. Ella had come into my bedroom before she left for college and set down her back-pack. 'What are the odds of Dad getting it?' she'd asked, standing at the end of the bed, her teeth sunk into her bottom lip.

Dylan had played it cooler. He'd hung around the kitchen rubbing his eyes and yawning theatrically, apparently half reading *Rolling Stone*, a cup of coffee by his bare feet – I'd noticed his toenails needed cutting. The very fact he'd surfaced before noon was singular in itself. 'To what do we owe this honour?' I'd asked, shooting him a sideways look. He'd gazed at me blankly so I'd explained: 'You're up *so* early.'

Half smiling, half scowling, Dylan had gone back to his magazine. Then, as I was on the cusp of leaving, I heard him say, 'Do you think he'll get it?'

I trailed Shannon into her kitchen. It dwarfed mine, which was some achievement. It was in the main part of Shannon's new house, which was a floating glass and steel box surrounded by interconnected satellites, accessed via thin glass corridors. The house, which was all about 'spatial innovation', had won countless architectural awards and had been featured in maga-zines all over the world, as had been predicted.

271

It was impressive certainly, striking, with its tensile steel and polished concrete, but there was something a bit anodyne and anonymous about it. When you sat in it you felt over-exposed, as if you were in the middle of a public space or somewhere sort of institutional.

'It's like being on the *Starship Enterprise*,' Frank had hissed, the first time we'd visited. 'I keep expecting a voice to say, "Beam me up, Scotty."'

'I miss the cleaner,' Shannon said wryly, as I attempted to quell the sound of the light sabre I had stepped on. The polished concrete floor was strewn with the accoutrements of boyhood – balls and trainers and electronic things that pulsated and flashed. When I trod on the sabre there was a loud burst of light and a syncopated harsh sound.

We were seated at a high wooden breakfast counter with bar stools, which opened onto a wooden deck and pool area that was still under construction. The kitchen was bounded by two enormous walls of glass. Through one I could see Jimmy's Aston Martin sitting outside, hunched on the gravel, bird shit on its window, as if it had been abandoned. On the other side, near the foundations for the pool, I saw a small digger perched forlornly on a mound of earth.

'I can't believe you're teaching,' she said, with a watery smile.

'I can't either.'

'You don't get paid, right?'

'No,' I said.

'It's a shame,' she said.

'I'm not qualified. I'm just helping out.'

'That's real good of you.'

It wasn't philanthropic. I was gaining from it most. At first when a student had come to me for a lesson my voice had sounded thin and reedy. And sometimes there was a tremor in it. Or it was too loud. It took me a while to modulate it to a point at which I felt comfortable. My legs had throbbed like a pneumatic drill. I'd had to stop my hand shaking. I'd felt dry-mouthed and light-headed.

Sure I still had bouts of nerves when I stared at a page and the figures swam in front of my eyes, but being mathematical didn't really leave you. I read maths books that Animal had given me and familiarized myself with the Junior and Leaving Cert courses. I had been very rusty obviously but the cogs in my mind had started to work again. It would be hard to describe the pleasure and optimism I took from those lessons without sounding like a mawkish git.

It was the gradual return of my confidence that was the most extraordinary thing. It was like Shannon had said: you could run a home, boss your family around, be this all-powerful Supreme Being, particularly when your children were small, but in some ways you lost your place in the big bad world

Now Shannon gnawed her bottom lip. She had got so thin she looked like her own initial.

'Listen to me going on about your job in terms of money. It's just . . .' She trailed off.

'I understand,' I said, noticing her chewed fingernails.

Jimmy had been let go from his stockbroking job.

'I don't know what to do. And Jimmy isn't coming up with any constructive solutions. He just sits there in that goddam chair of his, channel-jumping like a couch potato – as you saw.'

On my arrival Shannon had ushered me down the thin glass corridor connecting the kitchen to the den. The centre of the room was sunken, like something from the 1970s. Jimmy was dwarfed by the giant television screen he sat in front of, in the half-dark on a chesterfield sofa that jarred with the modernity of the room. He had insisted on bringing it from his old house, much to Shannon's chagrin. The air smelt stale. Jimmy was unshaven and grungy, his hair standing on end, his face creased from sleep. And for Jimmy – who was a short, robust, thick-bodied man – he looked thin.

He blinked at the football match, turning only when we called him.

'Hey, Jimmy,' I had said, injecting warmth and life into my voice.

He had rewarded me with the ghost of a smile that didn't reach his blue-ringed heavy-lidded eyes and a half-wave. There was no lift in his voice, no sign of the breezy, ruddy, affable alpha Jimmy, with the easy smile and the exuberant manner. No banter and no hug or bullish Jimmy behaviour. I tried hard to mask my shock.

Shannon and Jimmy's youngest son, Evan, whooshed into the room and plucked at her arm. His nose was running and he looked cold. Shannon swiped at his face with a piece of kitchen paper. 'You look frozen, Evan,' she scolded him. 'Where's your sweatshirt?'

It was a little chilly, actually. The under-floor heating wasn't working properly, Shannon had said. 'The contractor has gone bust. I couldn't afford to sue the son of a bitch anyway,' she had said, with a dazed, unhappy smile. 'Oh and the architect on the project is in Chapter Eleven – you know, administration or examinership or whatever the hell you call it. If only we owed the bank way more money we wouldn't be in this hole. We owe too much but not enough for the bank to have to play ball with us,' she said. 'We're expendable.'

We could hear thumping sounds from another room, followed by a chorus of shouts.

'Mom, Charlie won't stop hitting me. And Noah took my ball,' Evan said, 'and they won't stop wrestling.'

274

Shannon looked harried. She watched her son clamber up on a stool and nab a biscuit. He was a lovely child, plain like his father but with Jimmy's zestful charm. Or Jimmy's *former* charm.

Shannon sighed. 'With three boys, it never stops.'

The strains of Jimmy's match wafted down the corridor.

'Jimmy won't even do the school run,' she said. 'He doesn't want to be seen at the school gates. He thinks there's a stigma. He feels like a social leper.'

'He could go down to Coffee Society in Ranelagh, maybe,' I said. 'Frank says it's HQ for property developers who have nothing to do. I'm sure a stockbroker would be welcome.'

She gave a small smile.

'Actually, I'm not joking,' I told her. 'Frank goes in there himself. I'm sure he'd be delighted to see Jimmy.'

'If I could only get him out of that chair . . . All those years I was complaining and bitching that he was never here. And now he's here I want him gone. There's irony in that, I guess.' The tip of her nose had gone red. A loud thumping noise filtered through to the kitchen. 'I'll be back in a second,' she told me. Evan followed her, trailing crumbs.

I walked over to one giant wall of glass. Shannon and Jimmy had bulldozed the original ivy-clad period house. Its old-fashioned garden had also been torn up. The lupins and sweet peas, lavender and poppies were being replaced by a multi-level garden with a giant rockery of cartoon propor-tions – 'still under construction'.

Beyond the rockery would lie what one magazine had referred to 'as a series of structures that from a design perspective' would 'give the impression that they could be taken away at any time'. What their function would be was unclear. But for the moment these structures were like giant empty husks staring accusingly at the house.

Shannon returned holding a plate with Jimmy's half-eaten sandwich. 'He just picks at anything I put in front of him. Jimmy who once vacuumed up whatever you put in front of him. He's stopped playing golf. He won't go for a pint. He won't come out with me. It's like he's stopped living.' Shannon's mouth twitched. 'I read that suicide rates are going up with the downturn. I'm afraid he's going to do something crazy, like swallow a handful of pills.' She put her hand over her mouth.

I could see her eyes welling and thought she was going to cry. 'Ssh,' I said to her. 'That's crazy talk.'

'I'm sorry,' she said, when she had composed herself.

'Jimmy would never do anything like that,' I said firmly. I put my hand over hers.

'I think he just feels utterly helpless. He thinks he let his firm down. Before he left, he had to cold-call people, hunting for work that didn't exist. He feels he was let go because he didn't keep it together but they closed his section because the private client work just dried up. Worse still, he feels he let down his clients. So many clients lost money, in many cases their life savings, and Jimmy thinks *he* ruined their lives. I tell him that's crazy.'

Her expression hardened. 'In the end he just couldn't get the work so he got canned. They didn't care that Jimmy had worked his butt off for years and made the firm so much money.' She sounded bitter now. 'Jimmy helped found that firm. It was all about the bottom line so Jimmy had to go.' Her face contorted. 'I met one of his former colleagues with his wife. He and Jimmy were so tight. She asked me how things were. I just stared at her. And then she started telling me about the vacation they were planning, how much it cost. I wanted to say to her, "You're kidding, right? You're telling me about your fancy upscale vacation and I'm worrying how

276

we're gonna pay the basic bills?" The husband, the son of a bitch, only tried to rein her in when he realized how bummed I was. I swear to Christ I was like an inch away from telling her what I really thought. We used to go for dinner with them. They came to our kids' christenings. Jimmy founded the firm with him and that guy, the husband, just turfed him out, discarded him like an old shoe.'

Dropping her voice a couple of octaves she said, looking stricken, 'He'll never get another job in stockbroking. He's too old. He dropped the ball. That's it. *Finito.* We have three kids under the age of fourteen. And a giant mortgage.' She looked around her. 'This house was the pinnacle of our achievements. And now it's like an albatross around our necks. We may lose it. And sometimes I want to scream at Jimmy, "Get out there – pump gas, if that's what it takes. Be a man."'

I saw another flicker of anger in her.

'Sometimes I feel like he's turned into a sort of loser. That's awful, I know,' she said, visibly struggling not to cry. '"For better, for worse, for richer, for poorer – right?"'

I leant forward to touch her shoulder.

'And it's not like he didn't support me for years. I know he's depressed. The doctor said to give it time. I just think that a man sees his worth as bound up in his job and when he doesn't have one . . .'

'It's the pressure,' I said, feeling a lump in my own throat. 'The strain of financial worries is so hard.'

'You can say that again,' Shannon said. She exhaled noisily. 'People tell me, "It's only money – at least you have your health." Well, I guess they generally have some dough.'

'If I could help you I would,' I said.

When Frank and I had talked about money he had finally come clean. There were bristles on his chin so he'd looked like Desperate Dan, uncared-for, and I was quite glad about that: she clearly wasn't making a good fist of it. But then his face had caved in and I'd felt sorry for him.

'I'm breaking my backside to keep all the balls in the air, Anita, but I'm afraid I'm starting to drop them one by one,' he had said. 'I'm robbing Peter to pay Paul.'

I had seen his hands shake a little. And he had gone a really bad colour.

'I'm trying to service the interest on the loans. That bollocks Ultan Mohally is chasing me down, looking for more dosh to refinance the shite we all bought into with MM at his fucking suggestion.'

I had felt dizzy then and a little sick. I was forced to run through, as I did at regular intervals, the list of reasons I had for not hitting the bottle. 'I've stopped spending, Frank,' I'd said, 'but I'll find ways to rein it in more. And I'll talk to the kids.'

'We'll be grand. Don't worry. Just it'll be a bit tight for a while, like.'

Our home was fine, thank God. He'd been telling the truth about that. He had transferred it to my name years previously. 'Neither God nor man can touch it,' he explained, 'not the bank or any creditors. They can't even register judgments against it.' Other stuff might be taken, he said, the house in Spain, paintings, the boat we'd barely used, which had been sitting up on a pier collecting rust since Frank had ripped its propeller out driving over rocks. 'I shouldn't have bothered my hole calling the Coast Guard,' he said. 'I should have let it sink so I could collect the insurance money.'

The helicopter was gone. Frank had often worried it was on the small side anyway, insisting on parking it away from the likes of Ultan's, hiding it behind trees. All those things that were supposed to give pleasure – the pile of toys we'd accumulated to keep the Frank and Anita roadshow on the go – would be no more. It was fair to say that I didn't give a fiddler's.

'I do my own hair now,' I said to Shannon, touching my head in an attempt to make her laugh, 'as I'm sure you can see.'

She gave a bleak smile.

'If it's any comfort, I've gone right through the household expenses and slashed and burnt. I tried to sell my Range Rover but I was getting peanuts for it. Nobody wants those gas guzzlers now.'

Shannon said nothing for a while. When she spoke she said, 'It's the shopping in Lidl I hate most. Please don't tell anyone that I'm shopping there.'

I smiled. 'I've been shopping in Lidl too.'

Karen had been scathing about my first trip there. 'You'd swear to Jesus, Anita, that you were like some sort of pioneer setting out into the great unknown.'

I'd worn dark sunglasses although it was winter.

'Why don't you go the whole hog,' Karen had said, 'and wear a false moustache too?'

'It's a change, that's all,' I had told her, avoiding Karen's bald eye.

'You need to get over yourself,' she had said. And she was right.

I could hear a door clunk.

'Jimmy going to the bathroom,' Shannon said. 'The only place he goes, these days.' She made a mournful face. 'My mom would have tanned my ass if she heard me saying something like that about a shop like Lidl. She raised a large family on the income my dad brought home from the auto-parts shop he worked in and here am I whining. I shouldn't whine,' she said. 'At least I'm not poor Tracey Thornley, right? At least I'm not married to the friend-to-the-stars "fugitive" accountant.'

Tracey's husband Dermot had absconded under cover of darkness. Nobody knew where he was, although Dublin was awash with speculation. He was believed to be moving around Europe. Someone said they'd seen him, 'bold as brass', in London. It was reported that a warrant had been issued for his arrest and that international police agencies might be used to track him down. The telephone wires of Dublin and, in particular, our small patch were burning up. Stuff like that was pure gold in terms of gossip.

'Poor Tracey,' I said sadly. 'It doesn't bear thinking about.' The girl had been nervy at the best of times.

'She's gone down the country to stay with her parents,' Shannon said. 'I spoke to her. The media made it impossible for her to stay in the house. I even heard that there were non-media people outside it taking pictures.'

'Weird,' I said.

'I suspect friends are melting away like snow,' Shannon said.

She was being discussed constantly in hushed tones. I knew the drill. She would be stared at when she came into a room. Then they would look away quickly, while stealing sidelong glances, like people slowing down to stare at a car crash and driving reluctantly away for fear of being seen to be ghoulish. I'd been there. But for Tracey it was much worse. The coverage of Dermot and Tracey's fall from grace had been extensive.

'We should meet up with her when she comes back,' I said, 'invite her to do something.'

Shannon fixed her gaze on the middle distance. When she looked back at me she was a little wild-eyed. 'Why did I ever let my career go?'

'You had three boys,' I told her. 'You worked crazy hours.'

She shook her head. 'You never think your life will turn out like this.' She rubbed her fist over her mouth. 'If only I had a goddam job.'

It was a bright, cold afternoon. The sky was devoid of clouds. Everything had glistened but now the afternoon light was beginning to fade. Girls had been playing basketball outside in the grim yard so that high-pitched girlish shrieks of delight and calls of 'defence' floated up to the window. I'd been over and back to the window a couple of times, watching them, their thighs pink and white in the cold. Now the teams were roaring down the corridors, whirling and eddying, laughing and calling after each other, joyful and giddy.

Lauren and I were doing battle with algebra. Specifically we were attempting to solve quadratic equations. 'The thing is, Lauren, just in the same way as with linear equations, the solutions to quadratic equations may be verified by plugging them back into the original equation and making sure they actually work.'

Lauren nibbled the end of her pen in frustration. She heaved a heavy sigh, her heart-shaped gold earrings swaying. 'It's so hard, miss.'

'Satisfying, though, when you work it out,' I said.

She made a little face. Lauren was a different proposition from Janice. She was a stouter girl with ironed hair and a touch of acne, whose optimism and eagerness could suddenly give way to dark sardonic looks. She swerved from one to the other, shadows flitting across her sunny face if she didn't succeed at the rate she wanted to. She was very clever but highly strung.

'What would you like to do?' I had asked her, the first time we had met.

'Get the fuck out of here,' she had said, flashing me a smile that was part naïveté, part worldly-wise and knowing cynic, 'if you'll excuse the language, miss.'

She lived alone with her father, who worked for the corporation collecting refuse. Her mother was dead. Animal didn't know how.

Lauren fidgeted in her chair, restlessly shifting position. Even now while she was frowning at the page, her head propped in her palm, she was adjusting herself so that she was considering the problem from another direction.

'She's very bright,' Animal had said, 'but her concentration isn't the best.'

I moved to the door. Peering out the small window I saw that the basketball players were mingling with the school band, who had been released from another classroom. Although they bled into a big swarm you could tell the children in the band from the basketball players not only because of their clothes but because the musicians were paler and less robust.

I meandered back to the main window, darting a glance at my watch. There were papers and leaves blowing across the empty yard. It was a depressing place. I stared at it, not really focusing until I sensed Lauren's eyes examining me. 'You're very spaced today, miss, if you don't mind me saying.'

'I'm sorry, Lauren,' I said, flashing her an apologetic smile.

I'd found it hard to concentrate all day. When the headmaster had waylaid me earlier next to the graffiti-covered wall to invite me to the Christmas staff party I'd found myself twitching as I waited for him to finish.

Now my phone vibrated on the desk. Lauren's dark gaze was on me as I dived for it. Frank's number was flashing up. 'I'll have to take this,' I breathed.

*

Frank hadn't got the planning. An Bord Pleanála had rejected the scheme in its entirety. The decision of the board was unanimous. Frank's development would have 'destroyed the coherence' of the area, they said. It represented 'gross over-development' of a site of scenic rural beauty.

The evening edition of the paper, which I bought on the way home, screamed, 'Lawlor Vision in Ruins'. There was a shot of Frank on the nine o'clock news walking down the street in a three-piece suit and a camel coat. Eamon was scurrying alongside him, looking sepulchral in his shiny shoes.

Ella and Dylan and I watched the footage of Frank coming out of his offices. I tried to watch closely the effect it would have on my children, to see if it might change their attitude to him. Would they swallow their anger with him? They'd both refused to ring him after Fiona Keane lost the baby. Nor would they ring him that morning, as I'd suggested, to wish him luck in advance of the board's decision.

'Down but not out' was the soundbite Frank called out, as he barged through the phalanx of waiting reporters, snapping shut his phone. He followed this up with a magisterial wave.

An androgynous reporter yelled at him, pointing a mic in his face, 'Is this curtains for you, Mr Lawlor?'

Frank scoffed at the suggestion, absorbing it without a flinch, theatrical in his unconcern. 'Not a bit of it,' he dead-panned, all cavalier bonhomie. 'These are broad shoulders,' he said, tapping his collar bone so that we got a flash of his Irish Celtic harp cufflinks sticking out from under his jacket.

Mam used to talk a lot about 'the broad Lawlor shoulders' and 'the Lawlor steel'.

Frank paused. 'We have a new plan in the works already,' he said, clasping his hands behind his back. He was sucking in his stomach, I was fairly certain. He tilted his head, his eyes meeting the camera's lens squarely. 'It will be on a smaller scale with less capital expenditure and a shorter building time.'

Frank's face looked a little doughy. The lighting bleached some colour from it. But he remained buoyant throughout and the smile stayed fixed.

'Poor Dad,' I said, stealing glances at my children.

They made no acknowledgement of what I'd said. Ella's head fell back against the cushions, her face tense. Dylan was hunkered down by the edge of the sofa, making a sucking sound between his teeth. The idea, I decided, was to project casualness, as if to say, 'What do I care?'

'Never say die,' was Frank's parting shot before a lugubrious Eamon ushered him into a waiting car.

'Your dad's a fighter,' I said lightly, my eyes fixed on the screen. 'The winners in life are the ones who pick themselves up after failures and disappointments and get back on the horse.'

Dylan threw me a sidelong glance that I pretended not to see. His suspicions were founded: this lecture was directed at him.

'Dylan needs a good root up the arse,' Karen had said one day. And she was right.

I didn't go too hard on him. He was more vulnerable than Ella, who had processed Frank's betrayal of us and seemed to be getting on with her life. The very vehemence of Dylan's reaction – jeering at Frank behind his back, wanting to scissor him out of family photos – pointed to a greater hurt.

Ella plucked a cushion from the sofa and hugged it to her chest. 'It's the end of Dad's dream,' she said. 'That's basically it.'

'What happens now?' Dylan was staring at the television.

'I'm not sure,' I told them. 'It's all a bit up in the air.'

We'd had a short conversation on the phone earlier, Frank and I. He'd sounded a lot flatter than he had on the TV. 'I'm sorry, Frank.'

'I'm sorry too, Anita girl,' he'd said.

'Will the banks foreclose?'

Frank had offered a bone-dry laugh. 'Who would buy the site from them now? I'm not sure there's much appetite for big projects at the moment.' He had sighed heavily. 'My guess is the bank will get me to run the site for them, to develop it or sell it off or what-have-you. They took equity in it a year ago. The decision is as much a slap in the face for them as for us.' There was the sound of a match flaring and extinguishing.

'It must be a big shock.' I could hear him gulping a drink and then exhaling.

'You could say that.'

Another gulp.

'Sure fuck it, the site was probably non-viable with full planning permission anyway. The bank wouldn't have given me the money to finish it in this climate. You were dead fucking right what you said, Anita. I went to the bank with a set of costings and revenue projections that turned out to be halfway up my arse. And Paul Hogan was a bigger feckin' eejit to go along with it. There was a pair of us in it and a few more besides,' he said.

I could hear him blowing smoke out through his nose.

'It wasn't the only way I was reckless. Anita . . .' He was faltering.

'Don't, Frank,' I had said, pre-empting him.

He had ignored me. 'Anita, I got swept along.'

'Frank!' I said, to cut him off.

But he had continued: 'I tried to break it off but the fecking thing kept rekindling . . .'

I heard a woman's voice in the background then. She sounded shrill.

'Christ, am I allowed have a fag after the day I've had? What? I'm on the phone to – listen . . .'

The reception had become muffled then, as Frank put his hand over the phone. Little Miss Big Knockers and he were arguing, that much was clear.

'I'm wanted here,' he had said, turning back to the phone.

'You'd better go so,' I'd said, unable to resist the dig.

Now I said to the kids, 'The Lawlors are from tough stock, and your dad will be all right. You've good Offaly genes,' I added, teasing them.

'And Dublin ones,' Dylan said, with a sly smile, 'what with Uncle Billy robbing off the boats.'

Ella and I laughed. Dylan hunched his shoulders and looked pleased with himself.

A short fat man in a pin-striped suit with springy curly hair, half-moon glasses and a presidential air succeeded Frank on the news.

'Who's this arsehole?' Dylan said, frowning.

'He's a barrister who represented a group of objectors to Dad's scheme,' I told them. 'Dad hates him.'

'Yes, yes,' the barrister was saying, in a stentorian voice, looking like the cat that got the cream. 'One hopes that this decision marks a watershed, if you will. That it signals the end of developer-led development in this country and that so-called' – his short pug nose lifted as if he'd smelt something particularly odious – 'iconic signature buildings are at an end. Proper sustainable development is what we need in this country . . .'

Ella lifted her eyes from the screen. 'Screw him,' she said, setting down the cushion. She inched her bum to the edge of the sofa and folded her slender arms across her body. 'Dad has *cojones*,' she said, fixing eyes with a glum Dylan. It was a Frank word, and I watched the set lines of her mouth soften a little. 'I'm going to ring him,' she said, her eyes sliding away to the other side of the room.

15

I'd kept it simple. We'd had spiced beef and potato salad, with cheese to follow. Maureen was casting around for crackers. She looked chunky in a peach dress with a shot of silver, her hair puffed out like a golden mushroom. 'Would you mind?' she murmured to me, dabbing her mouth with a spattered linen napkin. 'It's silly but I need crackers for cheese.'

Maureen was a little rattled, I thought, by the untidiness. Her house was always pristine. Mine was certainly not as clean as it used to be. Lena, our cleaner, had gone home to Poland. Her husband had lost his job in construction. They wouldn't be coming back. And I wouldn't be replacing her. I couldn't afford to. Not really. And while I was a demon cleaner, I found I had less time, or maybe inclination.

We were four. Me, Maeve, Maureen and Tracey Thornley. The get-together was ostensibly to revive our defunct book club. *Brideshead Revisited* was the book. Really, I'd wanted to host something small for Tracey without letting her know. I did not want to make a *cause célèbre* of her, collecting her to my bosom as some people did with newly anointed victims, hoping to gain a ringside seat for the drama. I had equivocated about ringing her, unsure what to do, when she didn't reply to my text. But then Shannon had told me she had 'died a social death – it's like she's toxic.'

So I had rung her. The poor girl had jumped at the invitation. 'But Dermot was Frank's accountant,' she had said, her voice tired and broken.

'Means nothing, Tracey,' I told her. 'You're a different person.' I had debated then about saying anything else for fear of implying anything or seeming like I was sitting in judgement. But I had added, 'And just for your information, Dermot didn't invest on behalf of Frank.'

The court of public opinion had condemned her to social limbo. She might be a curiosity but that would fade and then she would be left to rot. Dermot was a pariah who had stolen from his own and she had become one by extension. Unless she broke with him totally she would not be rehabilitated. And it was said that they were still in contact. Despite everything, she seemed to love him.

Now that she was here she wasn't saying much. Her hair looked like it had been professionally blow-dried, which wouldn't have suited those who expected her to look repentant. She was extremely subdued, though, which might quell their ire, a ghostly shadow in the corner with the book propped listlessly in her lap, the manic chat silenced.

It was as Shannon had suggested to me: Tracey seemed to be doped up to the gills, speaking as if she was coming out of an anaesthetic. I had wanted Shannon to come as she got on best with Tracey, but she had pulled out at the last minute, leaving a brief message: 'I just can't, hon, I'm really sorry.'

It was hard to strike the balance with Tracey, to welcome her but without marking her out with undue fuss. And it was difficult to know what to say. There weren't all that many conventional utterances to take refuge in. *Sorry your husband's a crook who defrauded all and sundry, left you and your offspring and didn't even have the balls to face the music.*

Maureen had taken Tracey under her wing, thrilled at the prospect of having somebody to sympathize with. Not that Maureen was short of candidates. Currently she had an embarrassment of riches in that department. She was positively

289

chipper. There were lame dogs everywhere ready – or not – for kind words.

There was me, of course, with my husband who had not only left me but was in a precarious financial position. Maureen had also made a perky little comment about lovely refreshing non-alcoholic drinks, which let me know that my giving up the hooch had not slipped under her radar. Maeve persistently told me I was mad to have quit.

'You like a drink – big deal. I hope to God this restraint isn't part of the new national mood for self-flagellation.'

In general people said nothing, which led me to the conclusion that they had thought me a complete pisshead and were fearful of embarrassing me by drawing attention to my new sobriety.

The news had gone around about Jimmy's losing his job and his marbles. Maureen had come back from a visit to Shannon – a visit that had not been solicited and I knew hadn't been well received – saying 'The poor girl looked a wreck,' and 'in time' would 'hopefully accept' that 'nobody forced Jimmy to borrow the money for the shares'. If she had been put out at Shannon's slightly ferocious acceptance of her good wishes she hadn't said anything except that she seemed 'very down and a little tense'.

'I wanted to strangle her,' Shannon had seethed. 'She went on about her blimp of a son losing his job in London. She said how hard it had been on him walking out of his firm with a cardboard box of his belongings. He's not even thirty. He has no family. They have so much money. For Christ's sake.'

With Shannon's permission, I had asked Frank to put out feelers discreetly among his contacts and see if there were any jobs going for a person of her talents. And I had asked Maeve to consult Ultan. Maeve would have set about it quietly and without talk. For all her retailing of gossip and her love of the salacious, she was not a real bitch.

'Anything at all,' Shannon had said.

Ciara had talked a lot about inviting Shannon out, about 'doing something for her', but that had come to nothing, which was why I hadn't bothered inviting Ciara to the soirée. I was done with her.

I handed Maureen the box of crackers for her cheese. Her eyes widened a fraction. She did everything by the book, consciously genteel to the last, cutting crusts off sandwiches, covering trays with cloths, adhering to all the little rules and constructs. She didn't do boxes. She would get over it, though. She had Tracey.

'*Brideshead* is very zeitgeisty when you think about it,' I ventured. 'It heralds the end of an era, the end of an economic class.'

Maeve shot me a sarky look but otherwise there seemed no great enthusiasm for the discussion. Tracey looked stupefied. In our own ways we were all contending with things. Only Maureen was undented. 'I like to be transported by a book,' she said, with a small frown. 'This didn't do that for me.'

She was working up to something.

'I have to say,' she said, making a little fist, 'that I couldn't get the "homosexual" relationship between Sebastian and Charles that you were referring to, Maeve.'

'What a surprise,' Maeve responded, with a roll of her eyes. She was wearing scarlet shoes. There had been menace in her voice.

Maureen sank back in the armchair. 'I understand that Sebastian was a homosexual.' She tented her fingers. 'And that Charles and he had a wonderful heart-warming relationship. But it was platonic.'

'Oh, come off it,' Maeve said, making a sort of snuffle. She tapped her fork against her plate. She was in a filthy mood. She had complained that the bank was spying on them and that Ultan had put a moratorium on shopping. Now that there were huge loans to be paid back, any excessive expenditure would not be tolerated by the bank and could be traced on credit cards. 'Which means that I have lost the will to live.' Continuing now, Maeve said, 'All that eating peaches and talking of gazelles and unicorns and gambolling about with no clothes on – it doesn't take Miss Marple.' Then she said, 'Sebastian and Charles were bum chums.'

A crumb appeared to lodge in Maureen's throat. She coughed and spluttered, her chest heaving. 'Frog in my . . . throat,' she managed, her face crimson.

'Pat Maureen on the back, Anita,' Maeve instructed, looking bored as the coughing fit crescendoed. She began to pick at a mince pie morosely. Then she decided to chip in again. She spoke in an impatient staccato voice: 'I found the end mawkish and unconvincing. When Lord Marchmain recants. He was a lifelong atheist – I mean, that's why he ran away from his wife because he was sick of her pious bullshit.'

'Faith is a wonderful thing,' piped Maureen, who had recovered.

Maeve oozed sweetened bile. 'We'll all have to find faith now that the boom is over and we're all in deep doo-doo. It won't be just our Polish cleaning ladies and Filipina nannies going to Mass any longer.'

Apart from Maureen, Shannon was the only one of us who went to Mass. That was another thing that had surprised her when she'd first moved to Ireland. 'I thought you guys had such a strong belief.'

'You also thought we listened to traditional Irish music, and were disappointed we didn't dye the Liffey green for St

Patrick's Day and wore clumps of shamrock and sang rebel songs,' Maeve had told her acerbically.

'It's an awful thing to lose your faith,' Maureen said.

I held my breath, waiting for Maeve to unleash a shit storm.

'I can't be sure but I think it was the systematic abuse of small children by those beacons of priestly moral rectitude that led to me losing mine,' Maeve shot back, with an airy smile, her bright red talons waving, 'and the repeated cover-ups by the Church and total lack of remorse,' she added, flicking her luxuriant dark hair.

Maureen's mouth formed a thin line.

It was then that Tracey piped up. 'I can see that faith could get you through things.'

She sounded almost sleepy, I thought.

Maureen was solemn. 'Sadly, there have been lots of mistakes made by the Church. But,' she said, cocking her head at a jaunty angle, 'there are lots of wonderful things about Catholicism. Like the notions of redemption and forgiveness. Everyone deserves a second chance.'

Tracey mustered a feeble smile, her narrow shoulders seeming even slighter and more fragile.

'Everyone deserves a second chance,' Maureen repeated, as if we hadn't heard her the first time.

Maureen was a good person in spite of it all – the medical revelations, the ceaseless Donal stories and the absence of tact. 'I couldn't agree more,' I said.

'Hear, hear,' said Maeve. She looked surprisingly chastened.

16

I walked to Maeve's house. The weather was unseasonably mild. White skittish clouds scudded across the sky, propelled by a strong fresh breeze, and I had to pluck strands of hair out of my mouth. It was energizing. I felt peppy. More than peppy. I felt happy. All around me there was carnage, failing banks, higher taxes, businesses going bust, people losing their jobs, friends struggling – and I was as happy as Larry. Mrs Cavalier. My timing stank.

Maeve lived on Raglan Road, the historic street immortalized in Patrick Kavanagh's poem. She and Ultan had a beautiful period house located off the street up a flight of sweeping granite steps. Ultan had lobbed on an enormous extension the size of the original house. It was a series of lofty interconnecting rooms full of *objets d'art* and antique furniture that Maeve had paid an arm and a leg for, no expense spared. She had got rid of some of the heavier masculine furniture that had come with the house and replaced the traditional gilt wallpaper with a pale blue silk.

In the past Maeve had employed armies of people to help her do it up. She had perpetually been in the process of extending and renovating, decorating and adding new touches. This was all on hold now, thanks to the financial tsunami that had hit most of us and the bank's new attitude.

Maeve had the taste of a footballer's wife. Today she was wearing black leather leggings tucked into knee-high boots and a floaty leopard-print kaftan. If she had had to walk to a clothes line – about as likely as her landing on the moon – she'd have done it in full makeup, diamonds and a co-ordinating high-octane sexy outfit. When it came to the house, though, she had shipped the taste in, consulting a team of designers every step of the way.

She had summoned me. She had been like a virago all week. The sheriff had come to their door. 'He said that he was seizing goods on foot of a warrant to satisfy some judgment against Ultan. I rang our solicitor and he said to say that the property was the subject of dispute and that the sheriff would be held personally liable if he seized goods belonging to someone else, so I followed him around shrieking like a banshee, telling him that half the stuff belonged to my parents, which is bull. Of course it'll be all over the blasted papers.'

And it had been.

Maeve had sensed my hesitancy when we were on the phone. 'It's okay,' she had said, her tone sardonic. 'You can relax, Father Matthew. I don't want to drink with you. I can't drink anyway,' she'd said, and I presumed she was sick. 'It'll be paper hats and Club Orange all the way. I just need the lend of your ears.'

Maeve stood on the top step, pressing the button for the electric gates. Everything was big, I thought, looking up at her. Her high heels were big. Her hair was big – it was backcombed off her face. The house was big obviously. The Mercedes parked outside on the gravel was big. The wreath on the hall door was disproportionately big. The tree inside the gates was big. And the perfectly decorated Christmas tree nudging up against the drawing-room window was big. The window itself was big. It was the House of Big.

'The kids are at the panto with their nanny,' she announced, beckoning me in. She looked a little ragged. 'And Ultan's in New York.'

Maeve led me through the mosaic-tiled hall past an outsize

tree – not the one pressed up against the drawing-room window. It was perfectly decorated in black and white. We crossed under a glittering chandelier to the 'library'. It was a walnut-panelled room with a marble fireplace, Oriental rugs and floor-to-ceiling bookshelves lined with antique classic books that had been bought in a job lot by a dealer in antiquarian books for their gravitas, according to Maeve. Maeve didn't read all that much any more. And Ultan never read anything that wasn't on a balance sheet.

The room was beautiful in an ostentatious way. Prominent in it was a giant photo of Ultan and Maeve, Madison and Max, their eyes gleaming as they stared at the camera, their mouths apparently stretched into expressions of bliss. Ultan looked embalmed. He was wearing a violent purple short-sleeved shirt, his stab at casual. I don't think I'd ever seen him in anything but a suit before. Maeve said he never did dress-down Friday at work.

Now Maeve looked pale and drawn despite her fussy makeup. Her sexy smile had lost some of its wattage. She was hovering by the fireplace. 'I've something to tell you.'

The luxury in the room was stultifying. The sofas were overstuffed, the cushions a little too plumped, the paint job too perfect, your feet sank into the carpet, and there was something strangely deadening about the atmosphere.

She squared her shoulders. 'I'm late,' she announced, with a flat smile that had none of her usual edgy fizz. I was uncertain of her meaning until she followed up: 'I've been puking in the loo. All the usual signs.'

Okay.

She strode over to the mantelpiece and picked up a large vase of calla lilies. Her boobs possibly looked a little plumper. Other than that the tensile leanness of her body had not yet been blunted by this new life.

'I can't stand their smell,' she said, spinning around and putting her hand over her mouth. She stalked to the door, the heavily perfumed smell trailing her, opened it and shoved the vase out into the hall. She closed the door resolutely behind her, and jammed a thumbnail between her top and bottom teeth. The scent lingered on the air and she fanned her face with a hand. She smiled grimly. 'As I haven't had all that much sex with my husband – once, in fact, over the last six months – there's every chance I'm having a little French baby.'

My eyebrows shot towards my hairline. 'What are you going to do?'

She mustered a shrug. 'I haven't a clue. Glass of wine?' she asked, pointing to a bottle standing on the walnut sideboard.

I shook my head as the familiar longing hit the back of my throat.

'Christ,' she said. 'Have a bloody drink, won't you?'

'No. Thanks.'

'Well, you won't mind if I do.' She tacked on, 'Although your shitty disapproving look says otherwise.'

I raised my hands in mock surrender.

'I've cut down big-time,' she said defensively.

I wanted to believe her.

'Tea, coffee?'

I shook my head.

'A glass or two won't kill it,' Maeve said, as if she were trying to convince herself, 'worse luck.' She poured some wine, then flopped down into a silk-covered armchair. Tilting her chin at a defiant angle, she gave a half-hearted smile. She had small pouches under her eyes. 'What a mess.'

'How far gone are you?'

'Two months,' came the gloomy reply. She gave me a withering look. 'And I'm sure. There isn't a pregnancy test left on the shelves in Dublin 4.' She stared moodily into her wine, twiddling the stem of her glass. The sleeves of the kaftan fell back to reveal her sculpted naked forearms.

'Are you going to leave Ultan?' I asked hesitantly.

She gave me a savage look. 'Are you joking? Ultan would eviscerate me,' she said.

I thought of his shark's eyes.

'He leaves me to my own devices, but if I publicly humiliated him his fury would have no bounds. And he would never let me leave with his child, particularly not if it's a boy. Ultan didn't get where he got without being hard core. You do not fuck with Ultan Mohally,' she said. I could see the anger rising in her. 'I'm just not prepared to be poor – do you see?'

That was the thing when your life became bandaged by wealth: when beautiful things and baubles were bestowed on you, it became increasingly hard to visualize any other way of being.

She was staring resentfully into space, her mouth pursed. 'There are paternity tests you can carry out on unborn children in the womb. I'd have to go to Britain. They don't do prenatal paternity tests here because it's a service for women like me who've played away and are likely to abort if the baby isn't their husband's.'

'Are you thinking of having an abortion if it's not Ultan's?' I said, my tone neutral.

'No, as a matter of fact,' she said, with asperity. 'I wish I could but I don't think I could go through with it.'

I didn't think I could either. My feelings were ambivalent, though. I'd had Ella primed from when she was about fourteen about what to do if she had an accidental pregnancy. This was when she barely knew what sex was. I'd had a lecture that I delivered over and over as if on a loop.

You shouldn't be sexually active until such time as you are emotion-

298

ally mature enough to deal with the consequences, but if anything happens, don't tell anybody, not the boy, not your best friend, and not your father.

Although now I knew about Frank's cynical pragmatism on the subject I needn't have issued that last directive.

Ella used to put her hands over her ears.

Come home to me and we'll be on the first plane to London. Thousands of Irish women do it every year, but you'd have to keep it a deathly secret. Certainly it's a major decision but it's not the big deal everyone makes it out to be. If you do it in time it's just like bringing on a period. But you mustn't tell any of your friends I said this. This is just between you and me.

I couldn't stomach the idea of my daughter 'getting caught'.

Maeve gave me a pained look. 'I meant what I said to that holy roller Maureen about morality being relative. And I'm pro-choice. But it's the early training. You never really get over that sort of Catholic indoctrination – abortion is murder and all that. I mean, intellectually I know that, at this point, it's only a ball of cells, but if I was to go to England I'd chicken out.'

She set down her wine glass on a coffee-table and sighed. 'The nuns would be delighted to know they got to me about something.'

Irish people were funny about abortion: uptight as hell and sometimes downright wacko. It was the sort of thing that started mini wars between people and unseemly name-calling and slanging matches even between our public representatives, who were not beneath shouting, 'Murderers,' at pro-choice politicians.

Officially, there was no abortion in Ireland. It was a criminal offence for a doctor to perform one on Irish soil, although I'd heard it said that if you knew the right doctor you could easily get a D and C and, bingo, the contents of your uterus would be scraped out and nobody would be any the wiser. Otherwise you skulked off to England or the Continent, another member of a guilty, faceless band of women – or you clamped your teeth together and got on with it.

I'd seen a female senior counsel loudly gnashing her teeth over the subject at a party of Ciara's and attracting wrathful looks from Will and other guests. 'The Irish monomania with female reproduction is wearing,' she'd said. 'It's all about controlling women. My God, giving a foetus a right to life in the Constitution equal to that of a grown woman is an outrage. I'll tell you something for nothing. You wouldn't find that happening if men had babies.'

'Are you going to tell the Frenchman?'

Maeve shifted in her chair. 'I don't know. I'd have to have Pierre's written permission for the paternity test. And then if the baby was his I'd be afraid he might want it. I mean, could I trust that he wouldn't make a fuss?'

He was a gigolo. I wouldn't say that, though. This was a time for silence.

'He's French, but he's Catholic,' she went on, 'which I know means very little over there but he might get funny ideas. You just can't be sure. The whole thing is a total cock-up,' she said, rubbing her temples with beringed fingers.

'You could go back to work, Maeve,' I said. 'You're so well qualified. If you wanted to leave Ultan.'

'Right,' she said. 'You think I'd get taken on in this climate while pregnant? Anyway, do you think I want to go back and be patronized by some jumped-up little peon in a suit who's younger than me but has passed me out because I've been off having babies and who thinks he's God's gift?' She shuddered. 'Not a chance.'

'Could you work with Ultan?'

'What – and leave him?' Maeve said, sounding exasperated. 'Oh, hey, there, Ultan, I know I've cuckolded you and humiliated you and left with your children but could you giz a job?'

'I didn't think,' I said. 'You're right.'

'Anyway,' she said, 'Ultan isn't in a position to give anyone a job. I presume you know they're trying to refinance certain projects. It's a complete nightmare – they have to make cash calls on syndicate members and you can imagine how well that's going down.'

My stomach tensed. Frank was a member of certain syndicates with Ultan's firm. I immediately thought of the soothing, magical powers of a drink.

'People aren't taking the calls. They're basically telling MM to whistle for it.'

'If they don't have it, I guess,' I said, feeling awkward, and then I forced myself to ask, 'Do you mean Frank?'

'It's between them,' she said shortly. 'Nothing to do with us, Anita.'

In her screwed-up way, Maeve was loyal.

'The yacht and the jet have gone. And the helicopter. Everything is up for sale except the house in Portofino, because the latest is that we may have to go and bloody well live there and ride this thing out.'

'I'm sorry, Maeve.'

'Not half as sorry as I am. Portofino is grand, but full time? Christ.' She sighed. 'I get it. If we rent this house out, it'll look like we're making some sort of effort. Anyway, there's another reason I can't cut and run. I'd get half of nothing. I'm just gonna have to hang in there. If I'd half a wit I'd have siphoned some money off for myself and set up a running-away fund.' She threw her hands up. 'Some accountant I turned out to be.'

'Do you ever think, Maeve,' I said, my heart racing a little at the torrent of abuse I might draw on myself, 'that we've made a holy hames of things?'

Maeve was looking at me darkly. 'No,' she said tersely.

'I sometimes find myself thinking,' I said, 'that what the commentators are saying is right: that we have brought our country to its knees and that our kids and our grandchildren will have to pick up the tab for our foolishness and greed.'

Her eyes rested on me. 'I hope, now you're off the sauce and you're teaching the underprivileged, that you're not going to turn into a pious Holy Mary,' she said, with a tight smile.

I looked at her sadly. It was true that since I'd stopped drinking I had gained a lucidity that was not always welcome.

'Because I'll tell you something for nothing, I'm sick of being expected to wear a hair-shirt. So I had a good time. I'm tired of people looking at Ultan as if he's a pariah. I'm actually scared to go shopping. The other day I bought an Yves Saint Laurent scarf and I was frightened to be seen with the bag on the street. I put it into a cheaper unbranded one. They'll be lynching us next.'

There was a national mood of anger. Sometimes when I walked into the staffroom and sensed a remark dying away I wondered if they resented me for what they perceived my ilk and I had done to the country. In the main, though, I found my colleagues kind.

'Although, Christ above, that's the least of my worries,' she said, patting her stomach. She exhaled noisily. 'I keep thinking that Ultan and his family are very dark, dark-skinned and dark-haired. My whole family is dark. Would anyone be any the wiser? Statistics show that up to twenty per cent of men may be raising kids that aren't their own.'

I remembered going to the funeral of my uncle. His widow

and son had stood by the graveside, mourning him, incon-
solable. Next to them had been my uncle's best friend. My
cousin – the son – and the best friend had shared the same
distinctive flame-red hair, milky white pallor and spattering
of light brown freckles. It didn't take Sherlock Holmes, as
Karen had said in the pub afterwards.

'Do you think I could pull it off?' she asked. 'Shakespeare
said it was "a wise father" that knew "his own child". I mean,
the baby wouldn't come out coal black or anything, would it?
Pierre is very dark-skinned.'

I thought of the Frenchman with his shifty movie-star
looks and insolent smile slinking around the gym. How could
I possibly know? Did Ultan not have a say in this? Or even
the Frenchman?

'I don't really know,' I said. 'Either way,' I forced some
life into my voice, 'regardless of whether you go ahead or
terminate I'll do whatever I can to support you.'

There was giddy laughter in the air. Karen was hanging a
bauble towards the upper mid-section of the tree. With her
freshly applied tan she was unseasonably brown. Her breasts
were cantilevered so high that they were nearly touching her
chin. She was decked out in a scarlet silk blouse that made
her look extra buxom. We were all wearing Santa hats. Karen
had insisted.

'Come on,' she'd said, jamming one on Dylan's bolshy
head, 'it's that or a set of antlers. You're looking very well,'
she'd said to me. 'You're losing that ironed-face look.'

'Jaysus, thanks very much,' I'd shot back at her. We'd both
laughed at the language and the way I'd said it.

Karen blinked. 'The tree is lovely, very tasteful – too tasteful, if you ask me. When Anita and I were growing up we
had plastic Santas and flashing neon lights and big gaudy

Christmas decorations that were highly flammable and you could see from space.' She popped a chocolate into her mouth. She'd brought two boxes of Quality Street and a tin of luxury chocolate biscuits, which we were all lashing into, Karen in particular: she had given up cigarettes. It was really strange not to see streams of smoke coming from her nostrils.

'Great,' she said, foraging again. 'I'm going to be a fat non-smoker. The best of both worlds. I'm definitely going to beat this thing, though.'

She was covered with nicotine patches, and when her mouth wasn't filled with chocolate, her jaws were furiously clamped on nicotine gum. At least there was no haze of smoke to provoke Ella's wrath. Ella who hated smoking – *What kind of simpleton smokes when the information about how bad it is for you is out there?* Ella had become a little less spiky recently, although it was probably a question of degree.

She'd been late arriving home from college. She was seeing Frank, I thought. Instinct told me so – and the way she had not quite met my eyes when she apologized for being late. Actually, Frank had mentioned it. I had said nothing to Ella in keeping with my new policy of minding my own business. She had come in and let her bag fall to the floor, its contents disgorging. She had brought sweets for Karen's girls.

We were a motley crew, Ella, Dylan and I, Karen and her two girls, Saoirse and Colleen Eireann who – their chatter punctuated with giggles – were frisky and lovely.

Shannon hadn't come. I'd asked her and the boys to decorate the tree with us but she'd backed out at the last minute. This had become her norm. 'I could lie and say that one of the boys is sick,' she'd told me on the phone, 'but I won't. I'm just not up to it. I don't feel like performing.'

Darren had dropped off his family in their Ford Mondeo,

his taxi plate down off the roof, and I'd seen a nosy neigh-bour – a stalwart of the local Neighbourhood Watch brigade – peering through her gates as if she was wondering whether to ring 999. She'd once, in the course of a rambling story about taking a wrong turn and having to slam on her central locking, referred to the back of St Stephen's Green as 'Injun territory'. The story had centred on some 'corner boy' in a hoodie eyeing her bag on the front seat. It was a shame, I thought, watching her stare at Darren, that he hadn't stopped to show her his 'tats'.

Karen's son, Derry, had opted to stay with his father at the last minute, his head bent over his mobile phone, his thumbs flying across the key pad.

This was the first time we weren't having our tree profes-sionally decorated in I didn't know how long. Last year we'd sent out a Christmas card of the four of us seated under a giant tree touching the roof, with an enormous star on top that looked like a UFO. Frank had been darting glances at his watch, anxious to be away. I had been quietly pissed.

I wouldn't have minded a Christmas drink. But I was managing. I had to reiterate the positives to myself periodi-cally, like a mum telling her children in a bright, upbeat voice why leafy vegetables were good for them. It was corny but I had to do it. I'd look in the mirror and say to myself, 'My name is Anita and I don't miss vomiting in the morning. I don't miss headaches. I like the improved relationship with my children. I enjoy a new-found sense of mental clarity. Yeah, you go, girl.' I sort of had to pretend that I was a get-up-and-go, kick-ass American and not a booze-loving Irish person who liked to rationalize her drinking – there was always a good excuse for a drink – and drown her sorrows in the bottom of a glass.

Anyway, Christmas was different on a lot of levels this

year. 'We're approaching it in a different way,' I'd told the kids. Dylan had put a hand over his face and groaned.

We'd been in the family room.

'It doesn't have to be as materialistic. It really doesn't. We don't have the money we had and it's unseemly to be splashing out when so many people are losing their jobs.'

Dylan had flipped over the back of the sofa. When he resurfaced he had said, 'Mum, please don't ask us to make homemade presents or anything loserish like that. Like, I know there's a recession on but I'm beggin' you.'

'Hard times,' Ella had said humorously, and Dylan had crossed his eyes.

Ella had surprised me. She was coping unbelievably well with our more straitened finances. She'd even found herself a job in the stacks of the university library, reshelving books.

'Well, it's not exactly like you're asking her to live in penury, now is it?' Karen had said, when I'd relayed this information to her.

Ella had been kind to the girls, taking Saoirse upstairs and giving her some T-shirts – the pre-teen had been delighted. Colleen Eireann was dressed in a noxious Barbie pink dress, covered with sparkles, but she was chattering and laughing, totally unabashed by her cousins or surroundings. She reminded me of Karen. There had been no acclimatizing for either girl: Colleen Eireann had simply remarked that the house was a 'mansion' and that theirs would have fitted into our kitchen. It was said without envy or rancour.

Karen had a great rapport with her kids. That much was clear. They were bright-eyed, clever children, whose needs had been taken care of and who had been brought on and nurtured by a devoted mother. Saoirse was reading *Little Women*. She and Ella had discussed it, Saoirse going a little

306

shy but Ella coaxing her. They agreed that Jo was their favourite character.

Ella had finally come clean about Jamie Deegan. 'We're seeing each other,' she'd said one night, later leading him through the door and producing him like exhibit A, her cheeks reddening.

You couldn't have accused her of having a type. Jamie seemed to be the exact opposite of Christopher. Where Christopher was chippy and deliberately down-at-heel, Jamie looked as if he'd polished himself – his teeth were a set of blindingly white delft. I wasn't sure if he'd been to college but I'd stopped myself asking. With Christopher I'd more or less requested a complete set of academic results before he'd even had his coat off for the first time.

Christopher, it seemed, was but a distant memory. He'd turned up at the door one day with his strange springy walk, presenting himself in that humourless way of his, and I'd felt myself warming to Jamie even if he seemed like something bang out of a toothpaste commercial. Christopher had been wearing a short-sleeved T-shirt pulled down over a long-sleeved one, his donkey jacket – a judge's son in a Corporation worker's jacket! – hanging open, a woolly hat pulled down over his face.

I'd hidden behind a curtain in the drawing room, my head cocked, my big old snout twitching. Old habits died hard. The only thing different was that now I was smart enough not to reveal that I'd been playing the detective.

'I want my books back.'

'Fine.'

'It's not like that slow-learner nightclub owner you're going out with will be reading them.' This was said with a knowing sneer.

Oh, God, I thought, wincing, waiting for the comeback. I wasn't to be disappointed.

'With good reason, *Christopher*. Half of those books are arcane, turgid, obscurantist rubbish, notable only for their desire to be incomprehensible.'

Wow. Ella rocked.

Then she had said, in a real up-your-bum, hoity-toity voice, 'The hallmark of good writing is not only its universality but its simplicity.'

Game, set and match to my girl. I slunk away feeling half sorry for Christopher.

I'd been watching Jamie like a hawk, but he didn't seem to be distracting Ella from her studies. If anything, the poor boy seemed in awe of her intellect. He didn't seem to know what had hit him. He was preoccupied. His nightclub plans in New York were on ice, the swishy Deegan pad in TriBeCa was up for sale and his dad had his hands full. Ella had said very little about Ted Deegan's rumoured troubles, only that she thought things were a bit fraught business-wise. I hadn't pried.

I had told myself that if Ella did deviate a little from the straight and narrow and kick back it would be no harm. I would keep my big mouth shut. I was relieved, though, when I saw that she was keeping her focus.

Around Jamie Ella seemed to lighten up. He had none of Christopher's grinding moral superiority and Ella was a little less intense and self-consciously cool. It was refreshing to be free of her signature ironic detachment. Now she was poking Dylan in the back with an angel figurine. He was studiously ignoring her. She switched to elbowing him in the side. He pulled his hoodie over his head. She advanced on him with a big smile and muscled him backwards into a chair so that he landed with a thump, protesting loudly, his hood falling down. Karen's kids giggled. He tried to look huffy but a grin crept across his features and betrayed him.

Biba was going out with the rugby star we'd seen in the nightclub. Dylan was livid. 'I never saw it coming,' he'd said. 'Rugby is such a gay game.'

'It's very homoerotic,' Ella had volunteered loyally.

'Yeah, shoving your head up next to some other guy's arse, sniffing his butt cheeks. Taking group showers afterwards. Benders.' Dylan had snorted. 'He thinks he's such a beast. He did that stupid ad for those stupid ladders that old dears use to get to the top of a cupboard, some stupid sponsorship deal.'

Everything was 'stupid' in Dylan's world at the moment. He might have been a little put out, too, by Ella's appropriation of his friend Jamie. He hadn't said anything but you could see it: there was a faint bang from him tonight – he was not as dedicated to his ablutions as he used to be. And that was an understatement.

'You're acting like a depressed person,' I'd heard Ella hurl at him. 'I can help you with your CV.'

He had righted himself and was dunking one of Karen's biscuits into a cup of tea now, his shoulders hunched. His eyes were puffy and he was sleeping too much. His clothes were rumpled.

'When are you going to find a job?' I'd asked him again that morning, looming over him like the Antichrist. He'd had a blanket around him. 'What are you doing?'

'Playing X-box,' had been the bald response.

'Are you not too old to spend your day playing games?'

This had been greeted with a wall of silence.

Then he had said, 'You can make serious money if you design a game and pitch it perfectly. There are actual competitions with prize money. And in America gaming tutors get paid.'

'We don't live in America, Dylan. And you can't spend

your life slack-jawed in front of a monitor. I need you to get a paid job while you make up your mind about what you want to do . . . Jesus, Dylan, are these crisps I'm crunching on?'

'Sorry.'

'What about getting off your arse and looking for a job?' I'd asked, thin-lipped.

'There aren't that many going in stockbroking, in case you hadn't noticed.'

'Then look for a job somewhere else – behind a bar or as a waiter.'

'I can't see myself as a waiter, Mum,' he'd said, his voice dripping sarcasm – I'd wanted badly to swat him. 'I'm not exactly a minimum-wage type of dude.'

'Your grandfather was a bus conductor and your grand-mother was a cleaner. Your great-grandmother was a washerwoman. Your father worked his way up from basically nothing. Are you saying that work is beneath you'?

He'd looked a bit taken aback. Then he recovered himself: 'Like, it's great and all that you're not on the sauce any more, Mum, but I think you need to chill.'

That was the first time he'd mentioned my 'drinking'. 'Thank you for your good wishes, Dylan . . .'

'Ah, Mum, don't be like that . . .'

'Thank you . . .'

'I actually mean it. It's great you're off the hooch.'

'Thank you, Dylan – and I actually mean that you need to get a job. Any job. You can't continue to live here and not contribute. Ella has a job in the library and she's in full-time education.'

He went to open his mouth but I stayed him. 'If you want to go to college I'm sure Dad and I would find the money, but you'd still have to get a part-time job.'

'Stop, Mum,' he'd said, rubbing his eyes with the heels of his hands.

For all his sunniness Dylan had always been prone to self-dramatization. He was really going for it big-style at the moment – Oh, woe is me, I have no job, no girlfriend, the world does not understand me, et cetera. He was either sequestered in his room or he slouched dolefully around the place as though he had a huge load on his broad back. Ella had taken to calling him 'Atlas'.

Karen had let him have it right between the eyes. 'You'd want to get up off your arse and find yourself a job, Dylan. A big able-bodied fella like you sitting around . . .'

Frank had been more understanding, which confirmed my suspicion that he would do anything to mend fences with his son. 'Should you bring him to someone?' he had asked. 'In case he's depressed?'

I'd been dead surprised at that. Frank, I'd thought, came from the kick-up-the-arse school of psychology. Then he'd followed up with another revelation about his father. His father had 'suffered a bit from depression', he'd said, in that distinctly euphemistic Irish way, which could have meant Mr Lawlor had had anything from mild blues to weekly electric-shock treatments. I'd spent so many years with Frank and that was the first time he'd ever said one word about it.

But, then, Frank had more or less rewritten the script of his childhood, editing and omitting where necessary. I knew that these were defence mechanisms, that Frank's emotionally austere background had been parlayed into something much more befitting the Waltons. I grasped that when he said to people he would 'never be too proud to work any job', the assertion was underpinned by an insecurity about where he had come from and a determination to present his origins before they could be laid at his door.

311

The idea that Dylan might be depressed frightened me. I watched him closely, not sure whether to coddle him or, indeed, administer the kick up the arse. He did not need counselling, my gut instinct told me. He needed work. He was marinating in a stew of his own self-pity. He needed to realize that the world, as Karen might have said, did not smell of fresh paint. And that we did not have a right to be continually happy.

'Only a fool is always happy,' I said to him one day, as he lay on the sofa listlessly, feeling sorry for himself. 'We all have our ups and downs. It's how you navigate the downs in life that counts.'

I'd been quite pleased with that little speech. Not that Dylan gave much of a response. I'd told myself I wouldn't do it but I found myself comparing him to my students and their life chances, the level of determination that some of them displayed. I wondered if Frank and I had succeeded in raising a young man who was constitutionally allergic to work.

As I said, with sobriety came a certain mental clarity. With the clarity came realizations, not all of them welcome. Had I infantilized Dylan? As a parent you were supposed to set your children free. You were not to cleave them to you and use them as a buffer against reality, against your life and what it did or didn't have in store for you.

I'd stumbled across a sketch Dylan had done of Biba, a study, really. It had been buried under a pile of dirty clothes. Done in pen and ink, it caught her perfectly – the knowing look in the eyes, the slightly hard prettiness. It was neither savage nor sentimental. It was good. It was a ray of hope.

Now Colleen Eireann tunnelled through the cluster at the foot of the tree with a decoration in her hands. She was all hopped up on sugar. 'Can you put this at the top for me?' she asked Dylan, jigging up and down on the spot.

'Sure,' he said, taking it from her and reaching up.

'No – over there, next to the big red bow,' she said, arms flailing like chubby windmills. She instructed him in a bossy, sibilant voice that, again, reminded me of Karen.

Dylan fought to keep the smile from his face but he couldn't resist her cuteness. My beloved lazy strap of a son, whom I would have to get heavy with.

It could wait until after Christmas, I thought, returning Karen's smile.

I was sitting in my bed, looking at past exam papers, when Ella waltzed in. I took off my reading glasses – I needed them now: first stop reading glasses, next stop incontinence pads and Zimmer frame. I would become more and more decrepit. I tried to redirect my thoughts. I didn't allow myself to think like that any more.

Ella sank into an armchair and drew her knees towards her chin. She was dressed in a T-shirt and knickers, her hair in a messy ponytail, and munching a chocolate biscuit, her iPhone clutched in her hand. I had not given her my preoccupation with weight, I hoped. But how would I know? Maybe she weighed herself in secret and went without food and hated her lovely body. I didn't think so – I didn't believe her sense of self-worth was enmeshed with her weight – but it was hard to know.

There was a slight preamble about Karen's girls. I knew by the *faux*-casual set of her shoulders that she was working up to something.

'You were great with your cousins,' I told her. 'I'm so proud of you.'

The remark hung between us but it didn't sag. And she didn't brush the comment off. There was a warm silence that made my insides go gooey. I hummed a little tune in my head – 'My Girl'. Belt up, Anita. But, no, I was right to be happy. I had this sense that Ella and I were not far off being allies. I didn't want to dwell on it too much for fear of sabotaging it, but there had been a definite shift between us. Ella had decided I wasn't all that bad.

'I saw Dad today,' she said, twirling a strand of hair around a finger, her eyes sliding from my face.

'Great.'

'You don't mind?' she asked, scrutinizing me. 'I thought you might think it was disloyal.'

'Don't be ridiculous,' I said. 'Sure Dad has been here for a cup of tea. You've seen me talking to him.' I was delighted. And I wasn't surprised: the bond between Frank and Ella was so strong.

She gave me a smile that I wished I could frame. Sad, I know, but true.

Ella leant against the armrest and shifted in her chair so that I knew she had something else to say. Then she got to the point. 'She left him, Mum.'

'Oh.' I blinked at her. I'd thought something like that might be coming. Things had not been right there, I had sensed. Frank had been angling to come back, but I had given him short shrift. In true Frank style, he'd raised the subject repeatedly until I'd had to bawl him out. 'No,' I'd said to him one day, 'it doesn't work like that. You've had your fun and then you want to come waltzing back to the little wife who's waiting? I'm sorry, Frank, but things change.'

After that, I hadn't heard from him for a couple of days. But then he'd been back like a bad smell, banging the same old drum.

'I met *her* once,' Ella confessed, flushing, 'by mistake.' Her voice became acid. 'They were in the supermarket playing happy families. Cornelscourt. I was on my way back from Dalkey.'

An image of the scene drifted into my head. Poor Frank, I thought, suppressing a smile. He would have been terrified. Ella had always been able to quell him with a glance.

Her mouth twisted into an ugly shape. 'She had a tight top, and *boobs* and big hair and too much makeup. She was so obvious-looking, Mum.'

I shook my head. 'I've seen her too. But you don't need to run her down like that. Would you have accepted her any more if she'd had beautiful clothes and a figure you admired and you liked her look?'

'No,' she admitted, and shoved out her bottom lip.

'Well, then, it's not really relevant.' I didn't like Fiona Keane. I didn't like the way she had behaved. And there was a part of me that had tagged her the Whore of Babylon, that had tried to find her wanting in loads of ways and pass judgement on her perceived flaws – chunky thighs, wide hips, small eyes – but there was another part of me that did not want my lovely daughter to participate in the routine kicking that women doled out to each other. 'I'm just sick of the constant negativity that women display to each other,' I told her.

'Fair enough,' Ella said, putting her hands up, 'though I wouldn't exactly have had you down as Germaine Greer, Mum.'

I smiled and shrugged my shoulders.

There was a pause. Ella never gave up a fight easily. Sure enough, she concocted another way of making her point as I'd known she would. 'Dad went for her. That's all I meant. She was such a tired, jaded cliché. I'd imagined something else.'

I decided to park the subject. There were things I could have said but not to my daughter. I wouldn't speak of the classic masculine weakness that was as old as the hills. I wouldn't say that men responded to youth and nubility no matter what age they were. That even when they were in their dotage their age-spotted old heads swivelled to greet a pair of bouncy boobs or shapely hips, that they retained the desire to fertilize fresh, untilled soil, that they still thought with their appendage when they could no longer hold it to pee.

'I played my part in the breakdown of the relationship too,' I said. 'It mightn't look like that from the outside.'

'The drinking, you mean?'

I felt a little winded when my daughter named the fact of it so casually. 'Yes, partially. Although you might argue that the drinking was a symptom rather than a cause.' I paused. 'There are loads of wonderful things about my life. I'm a lucky woman. But I've been unhappy with aspects of it. I drank for lots of reasons I'm unravelling now. Sometimes people get stuck in a rut or a way of thinking and find it hard to beat their way out. They get lost. Drinking can become habitual.'

She nodded. She was listening intently. Enough of that, I thought. She didn't need to be made old before her time.

Then she said, 'It's good you're doing something with yourself.' She traced some shape on her knees. 'I don't know. I'm still a kid basically.'

'You're a young woman,' I corrected her.

She pulled a face. 'Anyway,' she said, 'I see Lainey's mum and Pia's mum and I just kind of think that I don't want that life. Climbing in and out of their four-by-fours with their perfect hair and nails and their rictus grins.'

'Like me, you mean.'

She gave a noncommittal shimmy of her shoulders. 'Not like you now. Like you before. If you read Tennessee Williams you get that whole Blanche DuBois thing, faded belles clinging to their beauty. I guess I don't want that to be a narrative of my life. Lots of girls I know do, but I don't.'

Oh, the wonderful naïveté of youth. Life didn't always go to plan. The years rolled on and suddenly you found yourself in a place you'd never thought you'd be. Of course I didn't make these banal observations. She wouldn't have believed them anyway. And it was good that my daughter was so spunky.

'About my drinking, Ella,' I said. 'I don't know if I'm an alcoholic. I know that I've been drinking too heavily for some time. So I've decided not to drink for a while.' I braced myself for what was to come, for the closed-in look her face got.

But she just smiled at me and said, so that I almost felt short-changed, 'Good.'

'I just wanted to say that I'm very sorry. I hope in time you can forgive me.'

'Sure,' she said.

As in, *End of.*

But then she said, letting her leg dangle down from the armchair, 'Christopher called you a lush.'

'Did he now?' I said, feeling hot at the thought.

'I whacked him across the face.'

'Oh, Ella.' I was torn between being appalled and delighted.

'It was when we were breaking up and I wouldn't change my mind about dumping him. He got rebarbative about my family.'

I could imagine that all right.

She snorted. 'He also said that you matched your art to your furniture.'

'Maybe he was right,' I said. He probably was.

'It's not the point,' she said. 'The thing about Christopher is that, for all his liberal claptrap, he resents social mobility.'

I smiled, delighted as always by my daughter's brightness.

'He cares about women making baskets in South America

and tea pickers in India but he's totally mired in snobbishness.' She went on, 'He's a self-righteous, hypocritical pain in the arse. You can totally tell he's going to end up in the Kildare Street Club, like his father, with a big fat cigar in his hand, sipping claret.' She snorted. 'He's already been there. Claimed it was an exercise in post-modern irony.' She added, with a grin, 'As Dad might say, "My hole."'

Changing the subject, I said. 'What did you say to Dad and Fiona Keane when you met them?'

'Not much. I cut her dead. I was pretty cold, I guess.'

So it had been as I imagined. Ella would have been flinty-eyed, with a ramrod back, as stiff as if rigor mortis had set in. She would have been the Queen of Mean.

'Afterwards, when she'd gone out to the car, I asked Dad if he was olfactorily challenged.'

I raised an eyebrow.

Ella waved a hand in front of her face. 'She reeked of perfume.'

We smiled.

'It didn't take her long,' Ella said, two vertical lines appearing on her forehead, 'to leave once he didn't get his planning. Now that he's poorer.'

'She lost a baby,' I said gently. 'Don't forget that.' When you were a mother you were obliged to say even-handed things. You had to say things like *respect your teacher* even though you privately thought the teacher was an uptight snooty cow who needed to get with the programme. Or: *I'm sure you'll benefit from the experience* when you thought the obligatory activity in question sounded boring as hell. Mothers had to say dull, commonsense, fair things.

Ella rearranged her slender limbs. She was beautiful in a refined blue-stocking sort of way. There was something sensuous about her, too, though. It was the fact she was so buttoned up, I thought. It was not hard to imagine boys wanting to undo her. She dressed in a simple way that offset her looks. She had none of the coarseness I'd had when I was younger – an image of Karen and me floated into my head: in our white stilettos, ankle chains and lemon mini skirts, with large cheap black plastic belts slung around our middles. But Ella had always had money – although money didn't buy taste, I thought. Nor did it explain her poise. She'd got that from Ma. Ma had had natural poise.

'Do you think you might take Dad back?' she asked, chewing a knuckle.

The question wrongfooted me. Ella leant her supple young body towards me. She could see my surprise at her *volte face*. 'I know what I said before. But, Mum, maybe he just made a mistake.'

I looked at her sadly. 'It doesn't work like that, Ella.'

'But do you love him?' she asked, that expressive brow furrowing.

Her tone was a little imploring, I thought. She wanted me to love her father, to take him back into the familial fold. But maybe children always wanted their parents to be together, no matter what age they were.

'Of course I love him. I've been with him so long. He gave me you. But it's not that simple,' I said.

'Oh,' she said plaintively.

She was waiting for me to speak. There was still hope in those eyes. I considered how to frame an answer. Ella would be like a dog with a bone. That was what a teacher had said about her once in a positive way: that when it came to understanding something or mastering a problem she was dogged. I didn't know what the answer was. I considered various options. Possibilities came to mind, many of them unsuitable for her ears.

I love your father, but I'm not sure I'm in love with him any more.
You cannot just skip over a betrayal like that.
I can breathe now.
For the first time in years I have space.

I hated that term 'space'. It came from the same selfish, egocentric lexicon as 'because I'm worth it'. But the fact remained that even if I had been able to forgive him, Frank took up a lot of oxygen in our relationship.

I have carved out a life for myself. It's not much but it's a start. I feel excited and hopeful. I feel me. So I think that would probably have to be a no.

My daughter was watching me. I groped for the right words. But just then divine salvation came: Ella's mobile burst into joyous life. Saved by the gong.

Ella smiled, her head revolving the other way. It had to be lover-boy. She got up and walked around in little circles, laughing lightly. A faint pretty flush began to spread from her neck towards her face. Then she was smiling at me. 'Later, Mum,' she mouthed. 'Cheers.'

Wriggling the fingers of one hand at me, she sashayed towards the door and I blew her a kiss. The circle of life went on.

I didn't know how I felt about Frank being deserted by Little Miss Big Knockers, I thought, turning out the light. I slid down in the bed. The knowledge provoked conflicting emotions in me, too complicated to unravel.

17

Ella roared down the stairs that she was coming. I was standing in the hall with my coat on, waiting for my children. We were going to Mass. Frank had got his wish and had made it back into the house after all. But he'd done it by ambulance.

The call had come when I'd been at my Christmas lunch with the staff from school. We'd been in a restaurant on Georges Street. The waitress had just set down baskets of bread. Animal was not there so I had felt a little self-conscious. He'd gone home to Kerry for the holidays. 'That wouldn't be my sort of craic,' he said, blinking at me with a sly smile. 'I'll be walking on the beach in Ballyferriter.'

I'd been eyeing the wine with a sort of longing and trying to concentrate on something the young English teacher with the sticky-out ears was saying when my phone rang. Frank had had a heart attack. Hurling an explanation at the English teacher, I'd dashed out onto the street, my arm outstretched, a roaring in my ears. I was halfway to the hospital before I realized I'd left my bag and coat in the restaurant.

The taxi man was very kind when I explained I'd no money. 'Don't you mind about that, pet,' he said, when I told him I would send him what I owed. 'We'll say a little prayer for your husband,' he'd said.

So we did. Me, the big cynic, saying Hail Marys and Our Fathers and Glory Bes all the way to the hospital. Apart from my brief pious stint as a child, I'd been completely disconnected from religion since I was a teenager. But as soon as the shit hit the fan I went scuttling back, which said

321

something. Maybe that I was a dyed-in-the-wool hypocrite prepared to use religion as a crutch, or perhaps that old habits died hard and, no matter how you disengaged from your traditions, you never really left the tribe you'd come from.

I'd followed the tiles on the floor to the ICU, dazed and frightened. *Don't let him die, please.* I knew then that I loved him and that I had never stopped loving him. The idea of him dying was too much to bear.

When I got there Frank was hooked up to an ECG machine. The ICU nurse was nice, a big, fleshy woman with a shelf for a chest and nicotine-laced breath. But she was kind and adept at handling traumatized relatives. It had happened when he'd been in the shower. First he'd thought it was heartburn. Then it had got a lot worse. Finally he'd managed to crawl to the telephone. My mobile had been off. 'You were the person I rang,' he had said. 'I thought I wouldn't get the chance to say goodbye.' Tears rained down his face and my eyes filled. 'I wanted to say I was sorry.'

He had been distressed then, of course. We'd spoken a little over the following five days. Gradually he'd become more bluff. But he had been rattled by the episode and I could see he was less certain of himself.

He spent five days in the hospital. Karen had dropped off flowers. I'd come across her in the lobby, arguing with the woman behind the reception desk, a solid-looking citizen with widely spaced bulging eyes – she had been bristling. 'Verna' was written mutinously on her badge.

'We can't do that,' Verna had been saying.

Tilting her head, her hip cocked out, Karen shot her a sceptical glance. 'So let me get this straight. I can't bring the flowers up. And *you*' – this was said in a vehemently accusatory tone – 'won't bring them up for me. So what would happen if I sent flowers via a florist? Would the delivery man have to dump them on the hospital steps and throw a stone up at the patient's window to alert them to their presence or would *he* be allowed the honour of bringing them up?'

'He'd be allowed bring them up,' Verna said, folding her arms across her chest, as if in anticipation of the onslaught that was to come.

'Well, that's just plain stupid,' Karen snarled. 'What makes him more qualified to walk up the stairs with the flowers than me or you?'

'You're missing the point.' The woman drew herself up to her full height. 'This is hospital policy.' Her chest seemed to expand as she added, 'These are *the rules*.'

'Verna, I fear that *you* are the one missing the point. Rules are only guidelines,' Karen shot back. 'They're there to be broken.'

'In your opinion,' said the woman.

Karen had met her match. They'd have been there all day.

'Come and say hello,' I said, tapping Karen on the shoulder.

'Anita,' she said, latching onto me and nearly hugging me to death, 'you poor chicken.'

'You mean poor Frank,' I had mumbled into her hair, my eyes filling with tears.

She wouldn't come up, though. 'No,' she'd said, shaking her head. 'I'll leave the man in peace.'

Karen just hadn't wanted to come up, that was the long and short of it. The relationship between her and Frank was too strained. And maybe Frank wouldn't have wanted to see her either, when I thought about it.

In a strange way, those were a special few days. The kids came and went. We were not a particularly tactile family – well, Dylan and I were touchy but the other two weren't – but we talked about stupid stuff. Frank and I talked. In some ways we didn't say very much. We stayed away from the dangerous topics and yet there was an intensity to our conversation that had been lost a long time ago. Everything was heightened by the fear that Frank might die. Time seemed to be suspended. The world shrank to what was in the room. It was just Frank and me and the kids.

Then Frank was discharged, and some of the magic slipped away. The ordinary entered the frame. Life seeped back in.

'I want to come home, Anita,' Frank had beseeched, sitting forward in the bed on the day before he was released. He'd reached for my hand with the blunt slightly podgy fingers that were so familiar to me. 'Please.'

I had looked at him then, and thought of how once I would have died for those attentions. The passing of time changed things. Some things came too late maybe. People were not dispensable, though. I told him he could come home for a while, that he could stay, we would look after him, but beyond that I couldn't say.

Now he was installed in a guest room. His face had fallen a little when he saw where he was being directed but, wisely, he'd said nothing. If the kids had questions surrounding his status they'd kept them to themselves.

Men came and went, trooping up the stairs to the room, murmuring and chatting, the odd rumble of laughter floating down the stairs. It was mainly contractors, developers, advisers, cronies. And, of course, Eamon who had become a regular fixture.

Frank's face was a pale moon hovering in the centre of the mound of pillows but there were distinct signs of recovery. 'You can tell Ultan Mohally to stop calling me looking for moolah. He can shove his cash calls up his bony arse. Tell him Frank Lawlor said to get up the yard. I can't give what I don't fucking have.'

He'd started to get saucy too, asking for things, making us run around. I'd had to strike a balance between looking after him and not letting him take over again. 'We'll have to get you a bell, Frank,' I said to him one evening, exasperated. We'd both laughed.

A leopard didn't change his spots. At some fundamental level, Frank believed that everything and everyone could be bought, and that wouldn't change. Anyone who thought otherwise was smoking crack. The bottom line was that Frank Lawlor – son of Kathleen – respected the buck and thought he could buy his way in and out of situations.

'It's Florence Nightingale you need, Frank,' I said to him another day, setting down yet another cup of tea.

'It's you I need.' He made cow eyes at me.

I won't lie. I felt conflicted. Like a lot of women I was a sucker for feeling needed. There was something, maybe, about the female engineering that allowed us to slip into the carer role. And yet there was a little part of me that was cynical. Maybe Frank had really hit the nail on the head when he mentioned 'need'. Maybe need was driving him back.

It would be a slow recovery, the doctors had said. A combination of factors had led to the heart attack. Both Mam and Frank's father had met their Maker, thanks to their hearts packing in the game. Most of the Lawlor brothers were on medication for their hearts. The Lawlor family history of dickey hearts played its part. Frank's diet had not been the best. And of course he'd been under overwhelming stress, however much he tried to deny it. 'Sure I'm grand,' he kept saying. 'I'll live to fight another day.'

A nice smell was wafting from the kitchen. Dylan was in charge of cooking. He was glad to be given something definite to do, a way he could help his father. He was awkward around him. Frank was effusive and Dylan was polite, but he stayed away from the room as much as possible. When he was there he was guarded. And yet I could see that he wanted to help. He had been very upset when I'd first told him about the heart attack. He had turned away from me because his eyes were filling with tears. In some ways he'd seemed to take it harder than Ella. She had been upset, too, of course, and frightened, but once the initial shock had worn off she'd focused on the medical side of things, haranguing the doctors and taking notes.

I had appointed Dylan chief cook and bottle-washer. The cleaning part was haphazard at best. But he was producing lovely meals, poring over the Jamie Oliver books I had given him. We'd had lasagne and chilli con carne and spaghetti Bolognese – but everything involved meat and Ella had started to complain. I'd smacked her back. 'Let him have this one thing he's good at. Please don't criticize or make fun of him. You're so good at everything.'

'I'm crap at cooking.'

It was true. Although she ate enough, Ella had very little interest in food, which she viewed mainly as fuel.

'Please, Ella. He needs to feel he's contributing.'

So, Dylan solemnly and proudly carried the meals – fresh healthy meals – up on a tray each day to Frank, who became instantly enlivened on seeing him. He was pathetically grateful to him. 'This is fucking lovely,' he'd say. What he really wanted to say, I thought, was 'I love you, son, and I'm sorry.' But he was an Irish fella so he stuck to the meal commentary. Frank had been humbled a little but I had no doubt that the Teflon-coated Frank would reappear in time – if he didn't die first. I felt a catch in my throat at the idea.

'Make it up with your father, Dylan,' I had said. 'This

experience teaches us that we never know the time or the day. Imagine if Dad died and you hadn't resolved things with him.' I was becoming a regular little sermonizer.

Dylan nodded, but maybe Frank had left some things too late. I thought of Dylan on Frank's back playing 'horsey' when he was small, the boisterous shouts – it was a sad thought that they might never be close again.

Now I pulled myself together. We had to get going. 'Come on, guys.' When this yielded nothing, I bellowed again, my voice echoing around the hall. 'We're late,' I cried rapping on the banister.

The church in Rathmines was big and grand, in the Greek style with a portico and copper dome and an inscription on the outside pediment: *'Mariae Immaculatae Refugium Peccatorum'* – Mary Immaculate, Refuge of Sinners. Originally built in the nineteenth century, it made you think of times when big congregations required big churches and the hierarchy was hell bent on constructing symbols of the faith with the repeal of the penal laws. And sin was big in Ireland.

I'd been told that the Mass on Christmas Eve was a family service and particularly lovely, and so it was. The children from the local schools put on a Nativity play. Ireland – and Mass – had changed a lot since my day. Mary was a little African girl, Joseph was Asian. Dotted through the crowd were people I recognized: the CEO of a publicly listed company, a senior counsel, Ciara's Filipina nanny, who gave me a merry little wave. It seemed very democratic. Mass, the beach and the park were the three places left in Ireland where you couldn't pull rank.

The music was beautiful. A soprano sang 'O Holy Night'. I craned my head back. She was small, dwarfed by a too-large coat, and had mild mousy features, but her voice, powerful and sweet, had filled the church, soaring up towards the big dome, its echoes lingering after she had finished. My breath had caught in my chest and it had been a struggle not to cry. I was flanked by my children. My heart burst with love and happiness and sadness and, most of all, gratitude for what I'd been given in life.

I'd asked Shannon to come with me, but she wouldn't. She had been advised the previous weekend by their GP not to leave Jimmy on his own. 'The doctor said he was a suicide risk,' she'd said, sounding defeated. 'He's going to counselling, which we probably can't afford, and he's on medication.'

They were coming over as a family on Christmas Day. I prayed for Jimmy, and I offered a few up for Shannon as well.

Ella was a bit hesitant, unsure of the procedures. She'd rarely had occasion to go to Mass because she had been to a Protestant school. Frank and I had ended up at their shindigs, mumbling our way through Protestant hymns, grouped with all the other Catholics, feeling a bit awkward.

It was one of the few things in which Frank had dared to go against Mam, in choosing to send Ella to the Prods. I'd been amazed that he would thwart her like that. But he hadn't been able to resist the lure of the perceived polish, such as it was. Mam had clawed back some authority by insisting that Ella receive religious instruction outside school and make her First Holy Communion and Confirmation. Dylan knew exactly what to do because he'd gone to a Catholic school. Frank, like I said, was up for paying the Prods to give our daughter a veneer of sophistication. But he had departed from this well-thought-out educational philosophy when it came to his son and heir.

'You want the Protestant polish for the girls but that's fuck-all use to boys. Boys need to be in with the fellas who are going to run the country, and that's not the Prods. Rugby-playing Catholic schools and the benefit of the old school tie are what's called for.'

Dylan wasn't quite running the country yet, I thought, shooting his scuffed trainers and messy hair a sidelong glance.

'Well, that went well,' Ella said, when we were funnelled out in the stream of people spilling onto the steps.

'There was no bolt of lightning to strike us down,' she elucidated, a small smile playing around her lips. She hadn't wanted to come. 'You're just doing this because you're afraid for Dad. That he might die,' she'd said.

'He won't die,' I'd said forcefully.

'You're using religion as a prop.'

'Would that be so bad?'

She'd changed tack. 'I'm not into that whole whore-Madonna dichotomy, handmaiden of the Lord thing that the Church peddles to women.'

'You're coming,' I'd said, encircling her shoulders with a firm arm.

She had enjoyed it in spite of herself. She had been visibly moved at 'O Holy Night' although she'd tried to tough it out.

I searched the throng for Dylan and saw him talking to a knot of young men he'd gone to school with. He'd be all right, I thought, watching him throw his head back and laugh at something a blocky little guy with a cheeky freckly face was saying.

The parish priest was shaking hands with the congregation. 'Good night, Father, and a very Happy Christmas to you.'

Cries of 'Happy Christmas' rang out through the still crisp air.

Mary, the Mother of God, zigzagged through the crowd, her pretty little face beaming, a diminutive figure in sky blue, her parents tracking her proudly.

I gathered my children and we headed for home, to where

Frank the prodigal husband was waiting. And to where Dylan insisted his special Christmas Eve repast was drying out on the cooker.

There was some mumbo-jumbo on the television. I'd turned the sound down. Dylan was making us tea. 'Bring us in a couple of biscuits too,' I'd told him, and he had grinned.

The day had been quiet, except when Shannon and Jimmy and the kids had popped over. They'd only stayed for an hour or two. Frank had been shocked by Jimmy, who had sat clutching a beer with a vacant look on his face. 'Jesus Christ, Anita, he's a shell.'

Shannon had broken down briefly in the kitchen. 'I feel,' she had said, struggling to regain control, 'as if I'm grieving for Jimmy. I feel like a widow. That he has died but there's been no funeral, no proper grieving.' She had practical concerns too. The kids' school had put on a talk about 'Raising children in a post-affluent society' but, she noted bitterly, its management hadn't offered her any help in managing the fees and she'd had to withdraw her three.

The only thing I could offer to do, I thought, was mind the kids. There was no date night any more. Shannon and Jimmy had always gone out together on a Thursday, and with friends at the weekend. She said she would try to go away for a day or two if she could organize company for Jimmy. His brother might come to stay with him. He had no interest in going anywhere. But she needed a break.

I could hear the gravel crunching. It would be Karen and Darren. They were calling around for a Christmas nightcap. I had presented it as a *fait accompli* to Frank. I would not have Karen pushed out of my life now. 'End of', as Ella liked to say.

Frank was resting in his room, worn out by the day. Or it

might be Ella, back from the Deegans', I thought, cocking an ear. Jamie had called over for her. She had been thrilled by his present, which had been far too expensive. I'd said nothing, but wondered if Ella's gift to him had been as costly. I hoped not.

I started as the front door banged open. Ella came barrelling into the drawing room, screaming and sobbing. I was unable to make sense of what she was saying. 'Ella, please,' I begged, crossing the room, 'slow down. I can't understand you.'

Ted Deegan had been floating in the swimming-pool when Ella and Jamie had found him. He'd shot himself in the head. Ella had talked about seeing him bobbing up and down, his eyes wide open, illuminated by the pool lights, which had switched on as they had walked around the periphery of the pool.

Maria Deegan had been out, said to be with her lover, her husband's best friend. Ella confirmed the truth of the rumours and media reports that had been circulating for the last few months: Ted Deegan had lost a fortune betting on contracts for difference. There were other more unsavoury rumours swirling too, such as those that Frank had touched on, but they remained unsubstantiated.

When Ted Deegan had gone broke before, as a Lloyd's Name, he'd had a nervous breakdown, Jamie told us, but it had been hushed up. 'We kept it inside the family.' This time that wasn't possible. Even American and British networks picked up on the story. The Irish papers bore screaming headlines.

Tycoon Found Floating Face Up In Pool By Son and Girlfriend
Tragic Tycoon Victim of Recession

There were pictures of the Deegans at social events, including a shot at their *Arabian Nights* extravaganza culled from an old social diary, with Maria Deegan in a sexy aqua-marine Arabian princess costume. The Deegans were described as 'conspicuous spenders' and said to be 'a main-stay of the Dublin social scene'. Another, showing Maria positioned between her husband and the senior Irish busi-nessman with whom she was having an affair, had a suggestive caption about the 'close personal friendship' between them all. There was a shot of Ted Deegan congratulating Jamie on winning the Senior Cup. There was even a side-bar panel connecting the Deegans with us, citing the relationship with Ella, which infuriated her.

'How dare they?' she spluttered, her eyes filling with tears.

I didn't like to point out that the Deegans were public people, and Jamie had a certain profile too, although he seemed to have spurned that kind of thing since he'd been going out with Ella. Dylan and Biba had graced many a page. And, of course, Frank had stuck his head above the parapet time and time again, saying 'Look at me.'

It was the day of poor Ted's burial. Although it was morn-ing, the light was already fading, it seemed, from the slate grey sky. Ella and Dylan had walked over to the Deegans. 'I just need to get through this, Mum,' Ella had said, recoiling from my hug. 'See you at the church.' She'd squared her shoulders and wiped her eyes.

I'd stolen over to the window and watched my children walking out the drive, Ella's spine resolute in the black coat. She had clearly stiffened herself to comfort Jamie and deal with the media. Dylan's hand lay on his sister's back and my heart filled with love for him. I thought how selfish suicide could be, the impact it would have on that family, on Jamie. It was a burden he would always carry and which might have reverberations down the generations. And I was a little angry for what my daughter had had to witness.

Frank was coming, in spite of my reservations. He suggested that we drive Dylan's car. He didn't like to be seen in his big flash car now. Large, ostentatious vehicles were out. It didn't look good, he said.

Now he came down the stairs, a little thinner, in his dark suit.

'It's very sad,' I said, my stomach knotting at the thought of what was to come.

Frank paused. He shook his head. 'It was only money.'

Epilogue

Frank and Ella waved me off, Frank in his dressing-gown, Ella with Crouton in her arms. They were standing on the front step in a patch of sunlight. The sun was high in the sky and it was a breezy, bright day.

Frank went to shout something but seemed to change his mind, clamping his mouth shut.

'Good luck, Mum,' Ella yelled after me. I waved at them. I was anxious to be gone, away from their chatter. Ella had blindsided me with destabilizing talk of what she was going to do after she finished her degree. She had sat down to the table, a slice of toast in one hand, saying, as if it was no big deal: 'People are being told by the Law Society to plan careers outside law. The bottom has fallen out of the profession. A lot of people are freaking about it but I'm chilled. A law degree is a good training and I can always work with Dad.'

The way her eyes had darted away and not met mine told me that in fact she was trying to raise the notion at a time when I might be too distracted to bat it back to where it belonged – outer space.

'We'd make a good team,' Frank had said, looking chuffed.

I'd wanted to leap forward, like a Springer Spaniel, and wedge myself between the two of them shouting, '*Noooooooooo!*' Instead I had swallowed a mouthful of coffee and said nothing.

I did not want my daughter to get sucked into the Frank Lawlor vortex, to apply all that keen intelligence to helping him sort through his mess. Frank was plotting and planning, back hustling. He was making fairly frequent trips to India. 'There's opportunities there, Anita girl, for the taking – if all the ducks fall into a row. And a fella could get a fresh start in a place like that.' He was also working for the bank, to develop and sell off the sites he had formerly owned. Who better to do it? It wasn't the bank's main business. 'I work for the banks. I'm a bank worker,' was his big joke.

He was not a hundred per cent on the up yet. Sometimes he still mooched around the place gloomily. It was only a matter of time, though, before he cooked up some grandiose new scheme.

I had swallowed my objections. I would not allow my family and their concerns to intrude until later when I might have to go into battle. For now the day was about me.

Dylan was long gone. He had a job at Eden in Temple Bar as a chef. He was learning to make some beautiful things. Things I could eat more securely without my female fear of excess flesh. No woman, however confident, ever wanted a fat arse. The rest of the time Dylan worked on his portfolio. He wanted to get into NCAD. That was his goal. NCAD was the Harvard of art colleges so Ella and I were trying to nudge him towards a portfolio course in case his hopes were dashed. Frank had – outwardly, at least – been very positive about the move. He tried to talk to Dylan about art although this often ended in Frank cursing the dealers who had sold him 'fucking crap', which was now 'worth feck all'. Dylan was polite if noncommittal about these overtures.

Dylan was doing well, though, tumbling up the path in the morning to go to work. He no longer shrugged himself back into the bed when you went into the coach house in the mornings. Not even at the weekends when he was up early working on his art. I liked to think that the sense of entitlement we'd bred into him was receding a little.

Maureen's Donal had recently made an offer to buy the Wexford site that had heralded the end of Frank for thirty per cent of what Frank had paid for it. The bank, Frank said, were seriously considering it. Maureen would have plenty to crow about.

Frank had a bit of money salted away. I wasn't sure where. It made me feel uneasy. He had borrowed all that money and not paid it back; although he had lost a lot too, he had essentially walked away.

'Lookit, Anita,' he'd said, with some force, when I'd tried to winkle it out of him. 'I might not be a feckin' saint but I conducted my business along ethical lines. I kept a lot of lads in jobs for as long as I could and I paid all my subcontractors more or less. Yes, hands up, one of the development companies I used went into liquidation but I paid the bulk of what I owed to the suppliers in so far as I could.'

I wasn't sure whether to believe him, but he was certainly soldiering on. He did, I had to admit, have spirit. The heart attack and near bankruptcy hadn't taken him down. Yes, I saw doubt in those eyes sometimes – the brass neck was not so brassy – but he was still bold Frank Lawlor.

So we went on together, Frank and I. There was no great rupture between us. I felt reasonably sure that he would not stray again. But I knew that, at the first opportunity, he would be wheeling and dealing. I also knew that, even if he reverted to type, I was a changed woman. I had a goal and even a sense of mission: I was repaying a debt. As ethical checks and balances went, it was far from perfect, but it was the best I could do.

I was now on College Green and the gates were well within my sight. I felt a little tired. I had tossed and turned throughout the night. I was almost at the railings and I felt a catch in my chest, a fluttering feeling of happiness and nerves.

I was about to pass through Front Gate, under the arch. I paused so that I was standing stock still under the cloudless blue sky, an island in the middle of a stream of babbling bronzed students. I would join the throng in a minute and be borne forward across the cobblestones, the august buildings on either side, my backpack – with A4 pads and pens – on my back.

Frank had wanted to come with me, to see me to the gate, but I hadn't let him. I needed to keep him at bay. Somehow allowing him come would have made today about Frank, rather than me. With his outsize personality he had a way of making things about him.

I might meet Ella for coffee. I'd promised her it wouldn't become a habit. But it was my first day and it would be nice to have that back-up. I would be called a 'crinkly', she'd said. That was what her friends called the mature students. I was very mature. In some ways I had always been a slow starter.

Later I would meet Shannon and Maeve. Ciara was away with her daughter, who was, apparently, on her way to becoming a tennis champion. We didn't really talk that much any more and I didn't miss her. Shannon was on a day off from her job as a paralegal. She hated it but it brought in some money. She had come to an arrangement with the bank about the house. They had been given a holiday from their mortgage as Jimmy was still out of work. They wouldn't be able to hang on to it, I thought, unless Jimmy started working again. Shannon had spirit, though. After the initial shock about her changed circumstances had worn off she'd gone out there and started battling. And she'd discovered that the standard of teaching in the national school her boys were attending was better than it had been at the private school. She was studying for the conversion exam that would allow her to work as a lawyer in Ireland.

Maeve was home from Portofino. She had a new little girl called Sloane, who had been deposited in the arms of a Filipina nanny almost as soon as the umbilical cord had been cut. On account of her dark skin when she was born, she told everyone that Sloane had jaundice. Pierre had gone back to France, not knowing that he left behind a little Irish baby. On her visits to Ireland, Maeve's drinking appeared to have reached the point where a visit to rehab might become inevitable. That was why we were meeting in a coffee shop, although I knew she might be a little lopsided by the time she arrived. I took the odd drink now, but I remained cautious.

I was standing at the entrance to Trinity. It had been some journey to get there but before I went in I had to make a call. A call that had been a long time coming. I had to tell Animal that I had finally walked the short distance up the road to Trinity College. I wanted to tell him he was right: it had been a galaxy away. But I – Anita Lawlor, née Butler, from the Coppinger Street flats – had finally got there.

Acknowledgements

Many thanks to Patricia Deevy at Penguin, for my first break and for her unfailing good humour. Thanks to Michael McLoughlin also, and to all at Penguin Ireland and England, for their help. And to Hazel Orme, for her excellent editing skills. Thank you to my agent, Sheila Crowley, for all her brilliant help and without whom there would be no book, Sarah Lewis, and to all at Curtis Brown. A big thank you to Alison Walsh for her much-needed encouragement. Special thanks to Paula O'Brien, for all her support and for help with some of the historical information on Dublin. Thanks to Denis A Hickie for his shrewd, if direct, counsel. Thank you to my aunt and godmother Marog O'Brien, for some of the lively turns of phrase she supplied! Thank you to Conn Harte-Bourke, for his stoicism in the face of deadlines, for his good humour and for being Conn. Lastly, thanks to my English teachers, Rosalin Ni Laoire and Marion McCarthy, and to my history teacher, Mícheál Ó Súilleabháin. And in memory of my late headmistress, Eibhlin Ni Drisceoil.